WILL BAKER

POCKET **STAR** BOOKS

New York London Toronto Sydney Tokyo Singapore

This book is a work of fiction. Names, characters, places and incidents are either products of the author's imagination or are used fictitiously. Any resemblance to actual events or locales or persons, living or dead, is entirely coincidental.

A Pocket Star Book published by
POCKET BOOKS, a division of Simon & Schuster Inc.
1230 Avenue of the Americas, New York, NY 10020

Copyright © 1993 by Will Baker
Interior illustration by Julie Johnson

ISBN 0-671-79045-5

First Pocket Books paperback printing March 1994

10 9 8 7 6 5 4 3 2 1

POCKET STAR BOOKS and colophon are registered
trademarks of Simon & Schuster Inc.

Cover art by Kam Mak

Printed in the U.S.A.

for Malinda, Cole, and Montana

ACKNOWLEDGMENTS

I would like to thank, especially, several generations of students in my fiction workshops, who persistently ignored my prejudices against the fantastical and outlandish products of the unshackled imagination, and thus tempted me into writing just such a book.

1

THE PARK WAS SO WELL LIT THEY DID NOT NEED HEAD-lamps until they were on the access road to the checkpoint, about two kilometers distant. By then they had joined other vehicles—Choctaws, Javelins, Leopards, even an old Jeep-Jumper—moving in a single lane toward the Preserve. Scanning front and rear on the monitor, his father recognized some of these vehicles, and as traffic thickened and they began the stop-and-go rhythm of the checkpoint, the radio came alive with greetings and chatter.

"Frankie," one of the voices said—a deep voice that called itself Big Red—"Hear you got your kid with you this year. You gonna give him first blood? Over."

"Hey, Red, how ya doin', grandpa? Yeah, I got little Ronnie here." His father turned from the microphone in his hand and grinned briefly at Ronald. "Green as grass, but we're gonna find 'im a kill. Over."

"Before you know it that kid will be bringin' you Gink ears."

"We'll settle for prize buck."

"Put some money behind that," another voice broke in. "What say a pool? Five thousand apiece? Half pot to the big rack and half to most weight, dressed out. An even five, Frankie Boy. You copy?"

Big Red booed in affected outrage at such a paltry sum, and other voices spoke up to argue over terms of the bet. Ronald could not tell whether the others were joking, though he was sure his father was.

"Great bunch of guys," his father said and hung up the microphone, because they were now only two vehicles away from the checkpoint.

Ronald wondered how his father knew they were great guys. He did not recognize any of the names, did not remember seeing any Big Red at their house. He had never heard anybody call his father "Frankie Boy." He decided these had to be very old friends, from before he was born. Still it seemed odd they never came to visit.

"Card," his father said, as they eased up to the guard station.

Ronald fumbled with a zipper, got the pocket open, and snatched out the little plastic card. Just in time, for they saw on the monitor the probe emerging from the cubicle beside them. A moment later it found the socket in the side panel of the Choctaw and sank home with a little *tunk*. The image of the cubicle, an aluminum frame holding walls of one-way bulletproof glass, dissolved and they saw the attendant inside, a bald man with a moustache, wearing the green shirt of the Preserve Corps with sleeves rolled up.

He could see them, too, Ronald knew. A little bubble of a fish-eye lens on the control panel would transmit the image of a thin man with close-cropped gray hair and a boy, small for his thirteen years, both dressed in identical cammie jumpsuits.

"Hiya, fellas," the attendant said, barely glancing up from the multiple screens he was watching. "Let's boot up those cards."

His father took Ronald's card and slid it and his own into a slot on the dashboard. In a moment they heard the faint, insectlike chatter of switches opening and closing, a whirr of scanners. The probe was logging them, checking his father's hunting record, programming their route for the day.

"Well well!" The attendant looked up from his screens with a startled smile. "Mr. Drager. Pleased to have you with us, sir. First time for the young fella, huh, Mr. Drager? That's nice. I see you were the same age when you nailed your first one."

"Right. Four-pointer. Iron Mountain, wasn't it?"

"A hundred twenty-eight pounds. One of the last muley crosses. Quite a string you got, Mr. Drager. Hope you make it thirty-two. And good luck to you, son. You got a great instructor there."

Ronald smiled politely at the lens. His father was a famous man, which seemed to make clerks and attendants talkative. Inside he was squirming, wanting only to get over the border into the Preserve, to the end of the road where, he hoped, they could open the hatch. He had of course been to a Museum Preserve, but he thought a Hunter might somehow look different. Like the ancient times he read about. It would be dawn soon, and surely the terrain would change. It would be different from the miles and miles of tree plantations, the conifers all in contoured rows, plastic pipes laid out on the bare gray slopes.

"Looks like you fellas drew a good sector," the attendant went on, looking again at his monitors. "Redfish Summit."

"Right. Great."

Ronald could tell his father, too, was impatient. All the parameters and conditions for their hunt were logged by now, but the attendant went on.

"We do have one little problem."

"What?" His father leaned forward, frowning. "What's up?"

"I'm afraid it's a restricted area, for beginners like your boy. In-vehicle transit only." The attendant stretched one side of his mouth and *tsked* with his tongue. "Had two attacks in that region last month. A surveyor in an old Javelin got hit pretty bad. Both cases nobody even saw the bear. The Bio boys are looking into it, but the study's not done yet."

"Goddamn," his father said. He dropped a hand on Ronald's thigh and squeezed hard. "We were really counting on it."

"For someone like you, Mr. Drager, an experienced hunter, absolutely no problem, absolutely. But. . . ." He *tsked* again and pulled at his moustache with a thumb and forefinger, indicating doubt. "Those big, uncollared rogues seem to be getting smarter every year. Teaming up with each other, and so forth. . . ."

"Man, you know how much it means, that first time. I know you do. A whiff of that air and a look at the country. Earth right under your feet." His father's hand was still squeezing, and Ronald realized he was supposed to say something, to help.

"I really wanted . . . ," he began, but stopped because his voice sounded so small and miserable. He was all at once aware of how much he expected from this day. "I studied the permit manual," he said in a stronger voice, "real good. *Real* good."

"Knows it backwards and sideways," his father cut in, jocular. "Field repair. Spotting spooks. Any emergency."

"Well. . . ." The attendant puffed up his cheeks and blew out a long sigh. Then, after a few moments' thought, he began to grin. "I bet you got a problem—just a minor glitch—in this Choc. Couple of worn cleats, maybe? Sensors tend to foul?"

His father laughed, relieved. "How'd you guess?"

"Have to check 'em every now and then."

"Absolutely."

The man reached out and with two fingers hit a keyboard. Their computer, which had been silent, now clicked and whirred briefly again.

"Okay, Mr. Drager. Random external equipment checks permitted. Half-hour limit. Have a good hunt."

"Thanks, my man," his father said. "I really mean that. Thanks a million."

They heard the *tunk* in the side panel again and the man's image was gone. When the cubicle reappeared they were already moving away from it, and Ronald could see that it was dawn, and the Feederway before them cut straight through a forest toward a horizon where rank after rank of mountains reared against a pale sky.

"Those days, they thought everything, even the stones, had a spirit. So called." His father gestured with his cup at the canyon before them, where a silver ribbon of water wound in and out of clumps of willow and aspen. "They had stories about living among animals—a woman marrying a lion and men flying around with eagles—and there were dances, with horned masks and so forth, that were supposed to call the spirits. Or appease them, I forget which."

They had not yet actually begun their hunting. His father had sensed Ronald's excitement and, with a wink, had decreed a maintenance check soon after they left the Feederway. At the top of the first high ridge they halted to have a look around and drink a cup of coffee outdoors.

His first on-the-ground view of the Preserve had shocked Ronald. The thin, cold air hurt his lungs, and the landscape was not colorful, as he anticipated from the photos in the manual. Redfish Summit was nearly twelve thousand feet,

4

and already the peaks around them protruded from a mantle of new snow like a row of black, rotting teeth. The lower slopes were covered with bleached grass and irregular patches of ragged, misshapen little trees, dull green with many dead, bone-white branches.

Ronald wondered where they had taken the photos of the straight pines and brilliant flowers for the manual. Certainly not here, in this season. But perhaps that made it a good place to hunt. Animals might avoid you by seeking out a barren habitat.

He knew from his Bio-studies how the wild animals had been changing rapidly, even mysteriously, during the last century. Cooperation, for example, between species that had consumed each other for millions of years: bears and insects; snakes and birds. Then there were those species—deer and rabbits among them—that were upsetting traditional theory. Classical Evolution was being rewritten by RAM and SHIVA.

He smiled to himself, pleased that he was remembering his lessons so well. Rapid Adaptive Mutation. Symbiotic and Holistic Interspecies Variation and Adaptation. The biologists still hadn't agreed on what to call it or how to explain it. But in less than two decades, dolphins and whales had actually developed codes to thwart human eavesdroppers. Small deer had also learned to make burrows, and birds and squirrels were communicating much more sophisticated warnings, over a much larger range.

"My grandfather," his father was saying, "who went into the woods with an old-fashioned laser and backpack battery, used to claim you could feel a buck in your bones." He glanced at the heavy ring on the middle finger of his right hand, a hunk of yellowed ivory set in silver. It was the eyetooth of an elk, handed down from his father's father. "The one superstition I allow myself." He chuckled and blew steam away from the cup before taking another sip. His cheeks were a bright pink, as if he had been slapped, and Ronald had rarely heard him talk so animatedly. His father was, he realized, completely happy.

"Did he think he could . . . talk to them?"

"Oh no. Hey, scout, you ought to know better. The Indigies were probably the last to believe that. Way *way* back. Of course there are cases of primitive communication. . . ."

Ronald looked away. He wished, at this moment, his father would stop telling him what he should know, stop criticizing or complimenting him. Their half hour was almost up and he wanted them to look out over the canyon, sizing up the sector assigned to them, watching maybe for a hawk, sipping coffee. Aware of each other but not having to say anything. Real hunters.

"Anyhow, no talk involved there, let alone spirit. Spirit is nothing but brain in high gear. Right?"

Ronald shrugged and did not turn to look at his father.

"What I feel in *my* bones is this damned wind. Let's go, scout. Get that buck with your name on it." He threw out the dregs from his cup, collapsed it, and slipped it into a pocket. Ronald did the same, and as they hooked their helmets from a fender, the timer inside set off a warning beep.

Wheels retracted, the Choctaw moved quietly now on soft rubber cleats, powered only by its batteries. A mist, an oil and water emulsion, sprayed from the rear bumper, suppressing odors. Occasionally his father scanned the ground ahead for tracks or spoor, but so far they had cut no fresh sign. They were working down a draw toward the canyon floor, and it was so steep the anchor-spike had dug in twice to keep them from sliding or rolling.

In the gyrochamber they noticed only an occasional tilt or slow rocking, and Ronald kept his attention on the front scanner screen. His task was simple enough: to spot the game and aim the launcher. When they got to the canyon floor, it had been agreed, he would practice driving the Choctaw and scanning at the same time. This was difficult duty. It was all an experienced man like his father could do, to drive at full speed through dense cover and simultaneously track and fire.

He zoomed back to extreme wide view and flipped to infrared, so as to penetrate the willows along the small river, now almost within range. For a moment the scene was static, a photographic negative done in shades of orange and violet. Heat from stones along the bank, bare to the sun, created shuddering waves of color. Then several of these stones pulsed and shifted, a hurrying together and separating of amoeboid spots.

"Dad!" he cried. "Lookit!"

"Oh *ho!*" His father flashed him a grin and swiftly flicked a series of switches. The anchor-spike drove down and then disengaged itself, secured to them by a thin cable of braided polymer fibers, and the Choctaw accelerated downslope, bounding and sliding, rappelling off the anchor.

"Tracker!" his father yelled and slapped him on the shoulder. "Come on, Ronnie!"

Ronald switched back to normal light and groped for the tracking stick, searching the screen in the same place where the hot spots had moved. He could see a band of willows, tilting crazily as the Choctaw jounced the last few yards to the canyon floor. Shadows wove swiftly behind the shuttering branches, crossing and recrossing like a school of fish.

The vehicle accelerated again with a lurch that threw him back against his seat, and the willows rushed toward him. His fingers closed around the tracking stick and instantly the little circle and cross hairs appeared in the middle of the screen. He jerked the stick right, swinging the circle after the racing shadows.

"Whoo-e-eee!" His father hunched over the wheel, cackling. "They're gonna break out! Load up and watch for the rack!"

Ronald glanced down, frantic, his free hand fumbling along the row of buttons under the monitor screen. He punched one, and when he looked up the Choctaw was bashing through the willows, over the bank and into the river. A sheet of water momentarily blurred the scene, but a wiper instantly squeegeed it away so that he could see the band of running deer, so close-packed that they looked at first like a single, huge beast, gathering and stretching itself in a rhythmic gallop.

The hunters had lumbered up over the far bank and were beginning to climb fast now, closing on the herd. The animals were dodging around every clump of brush or scatter of trees in an effort to throw off their pursuer. Ronald's heart was leaping with the deer, creating a thunder in his chest, and his father had to shout to him twice.

"The rack! Wait for the rack!"

He had managed to center the circle in the herd and now he leaned forward to scan intently for the horns of a buck. The bodies of the fleeing deer seemed to pour over one another, a waterfall streaming uphill, tan and gray hides slashed and broken by the shadows of foliage. He thought he glimpsed a curved fork of horn, but when he switched the targeting circle there the image had vanished. Then, without warning, the herd split around an outcropping of rock.

His father cursed and they swerved after the band that had turned straight uphill. Again Ronald swiveled the circle into the hurtling avalanche of tails and hooves and ears. In the mass he thought he saw again the sharp angle of a rack, then another, and another. "There!" he cried. "There!"

He steadied the circle and noted the dot of red light on the control panel. The minimissiles were loaded, and if Ronald touched the button on the top of the tracking stick, a hair-thin laser would strike from a port in the Choctaw's turret and bounce off whatever was in the little circle. This beam, reflected back to the port, carried exact data on the density and velocity of the target, and triggered the firing of the appropriate mini, an inch-long missile no thicker than heavy wire that could carry a paralytic agent, a radio tag, or enough explosive to demolish the heart and lung cavity.

The deer were only a few yards from a stand of trees too dense for the Choctaw to overwhelm. Ronald's thumb slid the cover from the firing button, and then his breath stopped, for he saw the great rack of horns, a heavy branching into space above a huge, lunging thing. "Dad," he whispered, "oh God."

"Hold it!" his father cried, reaching suddenly to the panel and hitting a button that extinguished the little red light a fraction of a second before Ronald's thumb flexed on the firing button. Nothing happened.

"Spook buck," his father said through his teeth. "Goddamn it." He powered the zoom and as the scene rushed nearer, Ronald saw the tremendous buck dissolve into a shifting pattern of flanks and necks, here and there the dark jewel of an eye. Then the herd crashed into the trees and in seconds had disappeared utterly.

They braked to a stop, and a cloud of dust drifted over the screen. Ronald let out his breath finally. He was trembling all over and his eyes were unfocused, for he was still seeing in his mind the great deer, the horns like dark lightning and the long legs reaching.

"I saw it," he said. "I saw the rack. . . ."

"Thought you saw it," his father said shortly and took a

deep breath. He struck a fist on the control panel. "The little bitches."

"How can they do that?" Ronald turned a dazed smile to the screen. Nothing moved on the hillside but the cloud of dust they had raised, drifting now into the trees.

"Habit," his father said. "The does always crowd around a buck to protect him. I guess they fell into a pattern once, way back when, as if they were hiding one, and it fooled a hunter. So they keep doing it. Sometimes there's a buck in there and sometimes it's a spook. Getting harder to tell." The smile he gave his son was quick and tight. "We almost started your record with a red tag."

"I'm sorry," Ronald said and looked down at his hands. Resting lightly on his knees, they still trembled. "Thank you."

"It's okay. The bastards seem to be getting trickier. You'd swear sometimes they could *think*." His father switched the Choctaw into reverse and they spun around. "Speaking of thinking, what does your manual say?"

"It . . . it mentions RAM and conditioning and. . . ." Ronald wrinkled his brow and closed his eyes, trying to recall the passage.

Many animals have developed elaborate systems of disguise and mimicry; selection has favored those who work as a group to "fool" predators. . . .

"Come on," his father said, sounding impatient. "I mean how do you spot a spook? Practically?"

Ronald flushed. It was a quiz, and he was still light-headed and nervous from seeing what was not really there, from almost having logged a miss on his very first shot.

"You watch very carefully," he said lamely.

"Watch what?" They had recrossed the river and his father had turned on the undercarriage scanner, looking for the anchor cable which had been jettisoned at the bottom of the slope.

"The . . . uh . . . the placement!" He exhaled a sigh of relief. "If it's always in the most crowded spot."

"And?"

"And . . . *size*. Sure! It looked so big. . . ." He turned eagerly to his father. "What would you say, Dad? That one? Two hundred fifty?"

His father laughed. "You ding-a-ling. It weighed absolutely zero. It wasn't *there.*"

"No . . . I mean if it—"

"Ifs don't count. It looked big, was all. It was just air, buddy. A bunch of shadows. A spook. Nobody's seen a buck that big for a hundred years."

"I read," Ronald said carefully, "that in olden times they could sort of . . . hypnotize people."

"Buck fever. So called." His father looked hard at him for a moment. "Baloney. Reading about old times is fine later on, for a break, but you should stick to the manuals for now. Hunting is a privilege. You have to earn it, as you ought to know."

The sensor pinged and his father stopped, backed up, and hooked the cable. When the toggle at the end had been re-threaded on the winch, he activated the release on the anchor-spike and began to reel it in. They waited, no sound in the cab but the high, faint hum from the winch.

Ronald wanted to say he was sorry again, or part of him wanted that, but he felt his throat tighten with shame and self-loathing whenever he took a breath to speak. Of course he knew access to a Hunting Preserve was a rare advantage, one reserved for those, like his father, who ranked high in Resource Management or Distribution. Only executives of the great tree plantations or utility grids or energy banks, and retired military men were eligible.

Even then competition for permits was fierce. You had to know the manual from cover to cover, maintain an all-terrain sport vehicle like the Choctaw, and be ready to take advantage of your forty-eight-hour permit on short notice. And you could lose your certification, too, by logging too many misses, or too many kilometers for the kills you did make, or by ranging outside your assigned territory.

So Ronald knew he was very lucky. He was there on the Preserve with a master outdoorsman to guide him, as the checkpoint attendant had said. He was always very lucky. Lucky to be in a wealthy family. Lucky to go to fine schools. Lucky he could someday be a manager like his father. But, inexplicably, the weight of all this good fortune sometimes left him miserable.

The anchor-spike dropped back in its chamber with a clang.

His father adusted the hydraulic pistons so as to lower their downslope drive track and keep the Choctaw roughly level as they crawled along the riverbank.

"You tracked fine," his father went on, "when you finally had everything together. The trick is to jump 'em and press hard, so they don't have time to get that spook pattern going. Didn't matter this time, because I overrode you. Barely." His father raised his eyebrows in wry, jocular reproach. A perfectionist. That's what everyone said about his father.

"How did you *know?*" Ronald asked abruptly.

"What? How to chase bucks? Hell, son, I—"

"No. I mean how did you *know* it was a spook?"

His father hesitated, shot him a glance. "Experience. You can tell."

"In your bones?"

His father laughed and glanced at him again, then bounced a fist lightly on Ronald's knee. "Experience."

"You hardly looked," Ronald said.

"You pick up a feel for it. The shrinks could explain it—subliminals, pheromones, gestalt, stuff like that. We might as well stick to the river until we get to those limestone bluffs. We'll take another equipment check there." He gestured at the screen. Ronald could see, far down the canyon, the knobs and ribs of white stone. "You had luck with infra, so try that whenever you see some thick brush. The thing is, a man has to go on automatic in those situations. Training and practice run the program, because there's no time to think. Something you gotta work on, buddy."

"I know," Ronald said.

He understood the reference to shrinks was to remind him of his last Profile at school. Counseling had been recommended, to counteract his tendency to wool-gather or dream about ancient times, when he should be monitoring some problem alertly. His marks had fallen in the last year and at the library his card had been restricted. He could have history only once a week, and no fiction at all for a quarter. His bad Profile had also been behind his father's earlier remark about sticking to manuals. He had to get serious. Had to be worthy. In only five years he would be going for Ginks. That was when—he understood—he would be given the elk-tooth ring.

"It's a sport and a lotta fun and all that. . . . Damn! We

must have bunged up the cable port popping down that draw. I'm showing no seal there." His father frowned at a point of hot, orange light in a row of cool blue ones. "We don't need to scam the maintenance checks anymore, anyway. So the point is, scout, in back of the fun and the good times, always back there is the competitive thing. We're sharpening ourselves at this, just like the wolves used to do with their young. It's the whole reason for the Preserves. This is invaluable real estate, my friend. It was a goddamned battle to convince the public that an old-fashioned sport like this was a reasonable use. A lot of people were saying the concept of wild animals was archaic and counterproductive. We went to hearing after hearing. . . ."

Ronald had discovered that he could go on his own version of automatic during his father's lectures, since he knew them so well. He kept his head up, as if alert, watching the screen from the corner of his eye, but in his mind he could be as near or far from their conversation as he liked, could think about whatever he liked. This story of the establishing of Preserves always led to the same conclusion. Men like his father persuaded Congress that hunting made keener leaders, and the retired officers argued that there was no difference, except in scale, between hunting deer and hunting Ginks.

The Ginks were nevertheless the most challenging prey. They were the primates nearest humans, though smaller, hairy and usually darker. There were fascinating legends about them, and in history he had learned how they came to inhabit the Wastelands in the Southern Hemisphere, how they had gotten their name—a coinage from two slang terms from an ancient war.

His teacher explained how humans, too, had once been brutes. They saw old photos of deformed ears and lips, filed teeth and scarred genitals. Some students, he remembered, became ill. But dominant cultures—all from the north—had gradually learned to sublimate natural aggressive impulses into productive work, paving the way for the magnificent edifice of civilization.

Before the Federation enshrined the principle of cooperative sublimation, however, southern continents tilted the world into the horror of the Last Wars. A few nations, engaged in territorial disputes or revolutions, enlisted certain ignorant and violent tribes and gave them access to highly destructive weaponry. There was an awed hush in the school-room as videos from the last century showed the grinning men in uniforms, their fists raised, the great balls of fire and tow-ering clouds, the land scourged of everything but burnt and twisted skeletons.

Then the scenes of widespread hunger and disease. The cancers and lesions, the trees only a foot high, birds with two bills and dogs with five legs. More students got ill from these images, but they were all moved to tears and a pounding heart at the story of the Great Recovery: the courage and sacrifice of the leaders who founded the Federation, the scholars who exposed the errors of relativism and so-called humanism, the sealing off of the Wastelands and the intensive cleanup and management of all remaining resources.

And finally the startling discovery of *lapsis*. A remarkable tale of the origin of a species. Apparently, in one remote highland city, the only survivors were from an international maximum-security prison, ten stories underground. These convicts escaped into a radioactive land where they encoun-tered refugees from another abandoned facility—a primate research center. The chimpanzees were of course capable of interbreeding, and the offspring of this obscene union formed the ancestry of *Homo lapsis*.

These creatures, their ranks swollen by other refugees and "the human detritus of holocaust"—he remembered the phrase because it taught him two big words—had a certain hybrid vigor. Scavengers and cannibals, they managed to sur-vive in deep caves, in territories so blasted by bombs and ravaged by flood and wind and sun that almost nothing else could live there. At the Wastelands museum he had seen mostly lizards, scorpions, vultures, bats and coyotes. These animals were grouped around a family of Ginks, similarly stuffed and posed.

The type still possessed predominantly humanoid physical features. They were not always hairy, and some specimens were hard to distinguish from a computer reconstruction of early man. Because so many of their ancestors from the South-ern Hemisphere were red- or black-skinned the Ginks tended to be darker than humans. Still, some were very near the preferred Northern standard—a light maple, like Ronald's mother—which he had not inherited—and of course many humans were born as dark as the darkest Ginks, but these aberrations were almost always corrected by chemical application.

The Ginks' degeneration was obvious, however. They dwelt in burrows and used only basic tools of wood and stone. They ran naked in summer and never cut their hair. Although *lapsis* was clearly not human, in the beginning philanthropic efforts had been made to tempt the creatures out of the Wastelands. Only thirty years ago the Federation sent expeditions bearing food, medicine, and expert behaviorists, but the Ginks attacked them all, mad and indiscriminate as a hive of angry bees.

Many said it would be a simple, straightforward matter to exterminate the Ginks. But others objected to the expense. A few in the Federation argued that they were useful in medical experiments, and could supply organs for transplant, since they were the species most closely related to humans.

Ronald's father scoffed at all these reasons and claimed that the Ginks were, plainly enough, an invaluable opportunity to train young people in combat maneuvers and in competitiveness generally. There was no substitute, he said, for the old-fashioned cunning required for Border Patrols. So even though the civilized nations of the Federation had given up conventional warfare as too costly, many countries still sent recruits into the southern regions on regular forays. You can't learn to really hunt, his father always said, until you've *been* hunted.

Of course Ronald had heard the tales veterans told. That if Ginks caught you they would roast and eat you. That they slipped over the border and murdered people with tiny poison darts that looked like ordinary thistledown. That they carried off young girls and had children by them that looked like ordinary people, and these mixeds were then sent north to spy.

He was too old to believe most of these tales, though it was a fact that once in a while mixeds were uncovered. Even in wealthy, upper-class families there were sometimes sudden, inexplicable abortions. Or—this was more common—newborn babies, hairy and large-eared, were found abandoned in the poorer sections of cities. In one controversial experiment such an infant had been raised by a famous woman scientist, in her own home, and had developed—with special training—intelligence measurably above average in some areas.

It was also true that a few recruits or sportsmen were lost every year, usually through their own carelessness. These cases made sensational news; though—Ronald's father said —they were negligible, given the kill-count for the Ginks, which ran to the hundreds of thousands. Mostly the Ginks had only darts and stones, but some of the poisons they made from plants and dried insects were exceptionally virulent, and they had occasionally built, out of native rock and timber stolen from plantations, traps and deadfalls large enough to damage a recruit vehicle.

Ronald was not himself very interested in either the experimental or military uses of these odd, small creatures. He had searched out books by early investigators who expounded on their peculiar drawings and crude caves, their language with its elaborate declensions and interminable ritual stories, their cannibalism and purported talent for taming animals—even reptiles and insects—

"Son?"

Ronald heard in his father's voice a familiar note of dangerous calm. "I was thinking about the Ginks," he said hurriedly. "About what you said about the Preserves and competition."

His father did not smile. A glance at the screen told him they were almost at the limestone cliffs; a good ten minutes must have gone by.

"We're almost there," he added weakly.

"Son, you know I brought you on this trip hoping I might break through to you? Make some kind of contact?"

"Yes, sir," Ronald whispered.

"And for the last five minutes I've been talking about your record at school, not about Ginks. I just asked you—twice —whether you liked your counselor."

"Sorry . . . I . . . I didn't mean—"

"Of course you don't mean. You don't mean *anything*. That's the whole goddamned trouble." His father's voice was still not loud, but it had gained an ugly intensity. He was snapping switches as he spoke, checking their progress on a grid map superimposed on the screen, turning on the ground sensors. "You dream along as if you had forever and the sun will always shine and mama will always be there to wipe your bottom. You think you can go on stuffing your head with that ancient junk and meanwhile let your education go to hell, your solid courses, and somehow I'll get you into Tech anyway. You keep this up, sonnyboy, and you're going to skin your nose bad. Real bad."

Ronald's face was burning. He stared straight ahead at the monitor, wishing the limestone bluffs closer with all his strength. He knew where this lecture was going to, and he dreaded it.

"You worry us sick. We're starting to wonder if you'll ever manage *anything*. Let alone kill a few Ginks, which any cretin in a decent search vehicle can do. Let alone find a job and start a family. Let alone—" The ground sensor emitted a soft beep, then another.

Instantly Ronald's father slowed the Choctaw to a crawl and edged it closer to the water. With one sharp gesture he signed Ronald to switch on the tracker board. In the first 180 scan, both of them saw the cluster of shapes moving along the bank. Without being told Ronald went back to a normal screen and zoomed in, not too tight. Through the sun-stippled trunks of aspens he saw a gray flank, a slow twinkling of legs. The deer had not seen them yet, and a moment later reached a small clearing. Ronald had activated the weapons system and now waited, one finger on the load switch.

Three does and a pair of fawns emerged first, the young animals so spindly and delicate he thought they might collapse. Then came a group of adult does moving in a hesitant, stiff-legged glide. Then another group, but this time at their center rose a rack of horns, unmistakable and stark.

Ronald touched the switch and the tiny red light went on. He had the targeting circle directly on the buck's neck, just below the jaw, and knew that this was no spook. He could see the pale fur around the throat, the black-tipped ears, and even the rough, noduled texture at the base of the dark gold horn. He had already thumbed off the cover of the firing button and now breathed very softly, keeping the cross hairs steady on the buck's throat.

The whole herd stopped as suddenly as if they had been

shot, developed, and printed, all at once, in a single photograph. He had not seen heads lift and turn, for he was concentrating on switching the circle back onto the target he had overrun, but now the deer were a ring of black, glistening orbs staring at him from the monitor. The eye in the center, the buck's, seemed to give out a cold, dark fire, and as Ronald stared at it the surrounding scene grew dimmer, more insubstantial.

"They see us," his father hissed. *"Fire."*

Ronald breathed in very slowly, his thumb poised on the button, then breathed out again. The eye blazed, darker and darker, and he could no longer see the borders of the screen.

"Goddamn it. . . ."

At the same time the buck's head jerked and Ronald closed his eyes and jammed down on the button. The mini made a dry puffing sound, no louder than the exploding of a single kernel of popcorn, and an instant later the Choctaw surged forward, accelerating.

"Stick him again! Good boy!" His father whooped, and when Ronald opened his eyes he saw that they were almost upon the buck. The animal went down on its knees, bounded ahead and to one side, and went down again. Ronald was trembling so badly that the circle wobbled on and off the great arched neck. He fired anyway and by sheer luck hit the deer. It flopped over at the impact and its legs flailed uselessly. Twice it tried to raise its head again, but now the weight of the rack was too much. The muzzle stretched along the ground, the nostrils blowing a little dust. The rib cage rose once with a long, shuddering intake, then collapsed and did not rise again. Ronald saw the eye still wide open, and turned away as if struck.

"He did good . . . got a little zoned out with game in his sights but . . . sure, a kill is a kill. Yeah, yeah . . . soon as we look around a little . . . before dinner absolutely. . . ."

His father was leaning on the grill of the Choctaw, talking to his mother on the cellphone. Ronald was perhaps thirty yards away near the mouth of a tiny side canyon that sliced through the limestone ribs of the gorge. He had asked permission to roam on his own—staying within hailing distance —and his father had agreed. The thirty minutes allotted for kill-care and another thirty to inspect the cable port gave plenty of time.

Ronald had talked to his mother first, working with all his might to keep his voice controlled and nonchalant. She had cried a little with joy, and he knew a pang of regret in his pride. He was different to her now, he realized; he was suddenly older, almost a man, because he had killed his deer. A two-shot flag, which was not that bad for a neo, and an impressive rack, now lashed to the turret of the Choctaw. Through her tears his mother had made a rueful joke, saying she would even overcome her natural distaste and have a venison barbecue.

Ronald thought of her back in their camp unit at the Rec Village, lounging in a dressing gown on the sofa. She would have gone shopping, probably, in the morning, or perhaps on a Nature Drive with some of the other hunters' wives. Then a workout and soak at the spa, perhaps a massage. She liked relaxing in the Resort Villages of the Preserves, where she could enjoy the view and the fragrant breeze from the forest. But especially, Ronald could tell, she warmed to the change in her husband, to the enthusiasm and vigor that transformed her Frank whenever he drew a permit.

They were jabbering now like pretech kids, his father's laugh echoing from the stone bluffs. Ronald was glad for them, and relieved that he had for once made them proud. But he felt a strange, unsettled emptiness as well, a feeling that first came over him when they had climbed from the Choctaw to stand over the dead buck. His father had put a hand on his shoulder and gripped hard. "Nothing like it," his father said in an odd, soft voice. "Nothing like it anywhere."

He had been dismayed, also, at the speed with which the deer was hoisted on the telescoping boom, its throat slashed, and its body cavity opened with the electric sawknife. The rack was severed from the skull, the forelegs cut off, and the carcass stuffed in the cold chamber in a matter of a few minutes. With a steam hose his father had blown away every trace of blood from the boom and rear bumper, and with the Choctaw's little retractable blade he scooped a shallow trench, pushed in the pile of guts and the forelegs, and covered them with earth. It was all over long before Ronald's heart had calmed.

He still felt a bit unsteady, but the walking seemed to help. He had never been on such uneven terrain, having to pull himself up sometimes with his hands or jump from a ledge or log to the ground. When he looked up to take in the canyon, the thin bright snake of the river, and the sharp, dead-white peaks beyond, he seemed to grow lighter, as if gravity were actually lessening. Birds must feel like this, he thought. How peculiar.

But he was already beyond his limit, for he could neither see nor hear his father now. It was, he realized, the furthest he had ever gone away from his world, and the farthest into the world as it had been in ancient times. He had read about that world a good deal, but this was quite different. The landscape seemed endless and much more disorderly than anything in a book. There were sounds, too, that puzzled or surprised him. The wind muttering and honking around the limestone buttresses and caves. The sudden raspy gabble of a squirrel. The murmur of the river, amplified by the canyon walls.

He stopped, breathing deeply, his heart thudding. The air was much thinner than he was used to. And very clear, too. It was amazing how the far canyon wall seemed to loom near. He could see minute fissures and strata, individual skeletons of bushes, a dark patch or two ringed by green moss—springs seeping through the rock. In only a few minutes all this had been revealed to him. If he kept walking he might see more and more.

Walk? He laughed aloud, startled at his own absurdity. Why should he walk? The Choctaw was there to take them wherever they wanted to go. And he had been promised a lesson in driving and stalking. He should get back. Reluctantly he turned and began to retrace his steps. The sun had dropped a few degrees and the light in the canyon had changed. It fell in great golden shafts through crevices in the rock or between stands of trees on the rim, and the trail before Ronald was now broken by long shadows.

In a few minutes he heard his father's voice faintly. He could make out no words, but from the rhythm and tone he guessed the conversation was no longer with his mother. Probably he was talking to other hunters in the sectors adjoining

Redfish Summit. Perhaps bragging about his son. His son who was now a young man. A *hunter*.

Ronald lengthened his stride. The muscles and sinews of his body felt strong and elastic, his joints loose. The lightness, too, was still there, as if he might bound into the air and not come down, but bound away still higher. He laughed aloud again, for no reason at all, and uttered a low whoop. Through a break in the rock, he could see his father, sitting now on the hood of the Choctaw, with the hand holding the cellphone propped on his knees.

The long shadows from the canyon rim had reached the man and the vehicle. Night comes fast here, Ronald thought. And what a deep black there, behind that little outcrop of stone. As soon as he noticed it, the shadow seemed to change shape. He stopped, fascinated, to watch. An illusion of some kind. What was it called? *Mirage*.

The dark blotch changed its shape again, and then again. A sort of finger extended from it toward the Choctaw, and then the rest of the shadow began to flow into that finger, to swell and to boil. . . .

Ants!

A cavern, empty and cold, appeared in Ronald's chest, and he could not seem to draw breath into it. Why didn't his father look around? He had to run, he had to scream right now, before that swarming black mass touched the vehicle. They would find any crevice, any ill-fitting gasket—the cable port!—and then millions, *millions*. . . .

He drew in air with a gasp, preparing to yell with all his strength, when two things happened simultaneously. He remembered a phrase—*symbiotic predation*—from the section on emergencies in his Neo manual, and he saw the bear.

It was not more than a dozen paces away, screened from his father's view by a great boulder sloughed from the canyon wall. The huge, immobile creature seemed an instantaneous apparition. It had not been there on his ascent, but it was now entirely, solidly, and minutely present. Ronald could see bits of leaf in the shaggy fur of its flanks, flecks of slaver on the black gums of its lower jaw, a little cloud of steam from the nostrils. The bear was watching him intently, the eyes like tiny, polished pebbles.

The air in his lungs came out in a whoosh and he took two

staggering steps as if he intended to sidle around the bear. He saw the beast's shoulder muscles tense under the loose hide, and its muzzle jabbed the air twice, as if taking aim on him. Ronald halted. He was completely emptied of feeling; he could barely breathe. Yet his mind retained a startling, mad clarity.

He saw the black finger of shadow creeping swiftly now along the side panel of the Choctaw, then to the edge of the open hatch. Another scatter of phrases from the manual went through his mind like leaves before a gale . . . *reversal of classic symbiosis . . . meat-eating ants . . . scouting and scavenging . . . only the bones. . . .*

His father, head thrown back to laugh, abruptly shook his free hand. Ronald saw him twist to glance from side to side. An instant later he rolled off the hood with a cry, a kind of gargling scream. He was beating both arms against his body and dancing up and down furiously. The phone sailed away, end over end. Ronald uttered a soft moan and took another tentative half-step.

Again the bear gathered itself, drilling at him with its tiny, opaque eyes, and he faltered, his whole body beginning to shake with sobs. He saw his father scramble up the side of the Choctaw, slipping on the black mass, grasping finally the hatch and wriggling, thrashing through it. In a moment the hatch cover sucked itself shut, but not with its customary clean *thwop*. This time the carcasses of ants dulled and softened the sound.

The engine hawked twice and then gave its throaty grumble of full power. His father had gone to the main plant, and Ronald's sobbing took on an urgency of hope. The Choctaw could cover the ground between them in a matter of seconds. His father would see the bear and load a Max 4 and they would be . . .

But the vehicle lunged backward first, striking a tree, then shot ahead at an angle as if to climb the canyon wall. It careened off a column of limestone, kicking up a spray of fragments, ran in a long oval up the canyon—away from Ronald—and back, tearing through the willows and aspen saplings. The Choctaw bucked to a stop, spun around on one track, and a straight, thin line of fire struck between the gun port on the turret and the hillside two hundred yards away, where a jet of earth and smoke spurted up with a heavy thud.

From a dense clump of willows at the riverbank another bear came at a shambling run. The tremendous body, bunching and elongating inside a coat of rough gray fur, did not seem to be moving rapidly, but even as he registered this impression, Ronald was astonished to see the bear leap onto the Choctaw's back, its weight rocking and sinking the vehicle a few inches into the soft ground.

Two more lines of fire jumped from the turret, which rotated wildly now from side to side. A branch blew off a dead snag fifty yards away. The bear, riding the turret, hooked one huge paw under the hatch and heaved. Ronald heard the squeal of metal rending. The Choctaw bolted ahead again, slammed into a low rock outcropping, and sent a piece of grillwork spinning into the air.

The vehicle canted sharply then, trying to climb the outcropping, triggering the anchor-spike, which drove against the solid rock and hoisted the whole rear end. The tracks spun futilely aloft and the Choctaw toppled over on its side, spilling the bear to the ground. The beast rolled once and bounded instantly back onto the undercarriage, between the whirling tracks. The powerful shoulders flexed and Ronald heard again the sound of titanium alloy plates ripping apart. A shower of sparks spewed around the bear and the howl of the engine began a rapid decrescendo.

From beneath the vehicle the ink-black shadow began to spread its fingers again. A moment later a lump of the same glistening, swarming black surged out the hole where the hatch cover had been torn clean away. The lump moved in a slow roll toward the river. On the bank it stopped, swelled, and writhed. For an instant it was almost erect, almost human, then collapsed again into a seething mound.

With a grunting cough the bear came down from the smoking, silent Choctaw and loped to this mound. He hooked into the heap and his claws came away red. He hooked again, experimentally, but there was no movement so he backed away, shaking gobs of ants from his paw.

Ronald began to run and scream, but the sound seemed to him very high and thin and distant. He knew the black mound was his father, knew that the bears would wait for the cleaned bones—he had read so in the manual—but most of all he knew that the first bear, now moving into his path, huge and high like a wall, would tear him into bits.

He saw the head swaying over him, yellow fangs on either side of a red flop of tongue. A heavy forelimb was upraised, exposing gray-black pads on the underside of the paw. He ducked and fell on his hands and knees. The blow caught him in the side and knocked him through a complete somersault, so he ended in the same position. He had time to draw a single, ragged gasp before he was struck again, this time on his other side. He came to rest on his face, hugging his knees under him, and felt himself losing consciousness.

He was dimly aware of a sour, powerful odor, a blast of hot air on his neck. He felt something wet slapping him about the ears, and then the collar of his jumpsuit and a fold of his skin were clamped in a vise and he was lifted off the ground. Through a blur of tears he could see they were approaching the overturned Choctaw, where the gray bear was prying at the rear compartment. The deer in the cooler, he realized, and then was amazed at himself for thinking this simple, logical thought.

Ronald was dropped in a heap a few feet away. Then the two bears together dragged the deer from the wreck and ate most of it. He nearly threw up at the smell of raw blood and the cracking of joints, but managed to keep himself quiet. More simple thoughts came to him. The hunter in the next sector would be suspicious about the phone connection abruptly broken off. A patrol of fast jetcopters might be sent. His mother would be worried, of course. His poor mother. The manual said to lie still. Flight or resistance triggered aggression.

He realized he was pursuing these thoughts, one by one, in order to keep his mind from thinking the dreadful thing it wanted to think. But it was not until much later—after the bear had turned him over with her nose and batted him again, seized his shoulder in her jaws and dragged him for a quarter of a mile—that he understood his ordeal was only beginning.

It was dusk, but by the glow in the sky he knew they were moving south and west, out of the canyon and toward the ridges covered with snow. Once, the bears halted under a shelf of rock and a few moments later Ronald heard, briefly and far off, a jetcopter passing.

His coveralls were torn and one hip was raw from being dragged over the rocks. His ribs ached from the blows the bear had dealt him, but there was blood only where her fangs had broken the skin at his collarbone. He began a stumbling crawl between the bear's legs to relieve the pressure from her jaws. She released him immediately and cuffed him ahead of her with a growl. He cringed, but she only nosed him onward, and in this fashion they worked up the slope.

He felt that he was only prolonging his misery by a few hours, and he was stupefied enough by fatigue and cold to think about simply stopping so that the bears would have to kill him and eat him on the spot. But as they neared the brow of the ridge, he saw movement, dark shapes against the banks of snow that glowed dimly in starlight. At first he thought they were smaller bears, for they were covered with fur, but they moved more nimbly and remained erect. Then he saw the long shafts they carried and heard their voices. They were speaking a strange language full of coughs and trills. They wore cloaks made from the skins of animals, and under cowls of thick fur their faces were only a patch of darkness. Ginks! They had to be.

With one exception. The largest of the pack had a face as pale as the starlight on the snow and a beard like a wedge of stone. As this company approached, the bears slunk away to one side, and it occurred to him, for the first time that afternoon, that his life might not be over after all.

2

GODDAMN HIM, ELISE WAS THINKING, ONE OF THESE TIMES I should just pull out and go home, let him fry his own damn liver for dinner. And go to bed with his precious vehicle afterward. She was curled into her recliner, pretending to watch an old holo-enhanced movie on the box, but really only fretting herself silly.

The table had been set, wine chilled, and salad tossed hours ago. Before that she had had a light workout, hot tub, and facial at the Health Center. Before that she had gone window-shopping with a couple of the other elk widows, though she declined stopping off for a drink afterward, the final time killer. Time was what elk widows killed, while their husbands were out massacring wild beasts.

She had been through this routine often enough to know that her rage was the measure of an anxiety underneath, but this time both feelings were definitely more intense because Ronnie was involved. It especially upset her that Frank apparently had no conception of how much she would worry if he ran late on this particular hunt. After making his dutiful phone call he had gone blithely off, their son in tow, forgetting her entirely, and was now broken down or caught in traffic or—more likely—drinking and bragging in one of the Feederway joints where the returning hunters congregated.

Surely it was that kind of thing. Frank was obtuse about her feelings, but he was, ultimately, a most meticulous man. He always knew what he was doing, wherever he was. She touched a button on the arm of the recliner and froze the small figures inside the box of light. The sound track went off and in the ensuing silence she noticed that a corner of the projection field had weakened, causing one character—a young man in a top hat—to disintegrate below the waist.

She pressed another button and the security video screen above the holo shuddered and then cleared to reveal the courtyard and parking lot of their building complex. A lone vehicle was just entering the lot, but it was a brand-new Leopard. She watched it cruise the first row and then find one of the few remaining spaces. Two men got out, laughing and stretching. In a moment a white electric meat van scooted up a basement ramp and wheeled down their row. A kill in the cooler, obviously.

She left the video on and got up from the chair, cinching the belt of her robe and then loosening it again. The phone ought to ring at any moment. However preoccupied Frank might get, he would never be the last one through the checkpoint. Though of course it would be terribly important to him to show Ronnie off, joke and tease a little with the other men.

The earlier phone call came back to her with a small but intense pang, several emotions colliding at once in her uneasy heart. Ronnie had been excited and proud, of course, though he made a great effort to explain in a grown-up and matter-of-fact way how he had tracked and shot. At the same time she detected tremors of shock and uncertainty in his voice. *Mom, it was looking right at me. And its eye was, like, really, really bright. And then this deer was just . . . just a sack of meat all of a sudden. It was strange.*

He was such a funny boy. Silent for long stretches and then in a flash alive and talkative and boisterous, caught up in some idea picked up God knew where. *Erratic,* one of his teachers wrote. The counselor had a more elaborate phrase: *autodisjunctive.*

Elise was in the kitchen now, putting on a pot of water for tea. She smiled at her own swollen image on the polished metal shoulder of the pot, remembering how the word had panicked her. She thought it might be a rare nerve disease, a brain lesion. No, the counselor smirked, it's worse in some ways. Your boy is very talented but he cannot discipline his thoughts. In common parlance, he lives in a dream world.

This was something she and Frank already knew, of course. Even as an infant Ronnie had a habit of crawling off to play by himself. He often ignored his bright, noisy, clever toys and stared at pictures on the wall or a fly on a windowpane. He held long, meaningless conversations with the air, and cried mightily if interrupted.

Their doctor had dismissed these quirks as a mild case of Infant Stress Syndrome, fairly common among the gifted. And Ronald was gifted. He passed the entrance exams for Pre-Prime Workshop at fourteen months, a good four months before the average, and once there he seemed to adjust well to other children. In Primary he was second among males in their district, and seventh overall, with a special flair for theoretical mathematics.

So they had both been elated. Frank talked expansively of a career in MaxCom design or even Policy Systems, if his son's social skills could be brought up to the mark. But in the first two years of Second School, serious problems began to surface. Elise had gone over that time carefully in her mind and realized now that the signs of trouble had been there all along.

They had accepted, for example, their son's recurrent, abnormal idleness. He would overwork for days in order to be alone for a few hours, apparently doing nothing. At best he would devour a stack of books or tapes. Never useful, modern works—always ancient texts, mere curiosities. In class he irritated teachers because he was inattentive, yet somehow mastered his lessons anyway. His schoolmates gave him the nickname "Little No Beep" and began to ignore him.

This year the bouts of idleness had increased markedly, and Ronnie's grades began to slip. Frank attempted firm advice and gentle correction, without result; worse, his son's failure left Frank so distracted and short-tempered that his own work suffered. For her part, Elise felt torn between them. She knew how much her husband hoped for their son's future, how he yearned to propel the boy into the last and highest circle of power; but she understood also Ronald's odd, secretive side, his weakness in controlling his daydreams and the shame he suffered over that weakness.

That was always her problem, Elise thought. The understanding woman. Talk to Elise, she *understands*. People didn't realize that you could understand too damn much. She watched her hands rend the packet of tea, spilling loose bags on the counter. Easy, she told herself. They're at some roadhouse. They're happy. Doing man stuff together. They're probably on their way out the door now. That's what this whole thing was about, after all. Bringing father and son together.

The water was not quite hot so she turned again into the living room. The two men and the meat van were gone from the lot, and she could see only three parking spots left. The rows of vehicles, painted in dull camouflage patterns, seemed eerily silent and still under the hard white light from floodlamps. Inside the units people were finishing dinner, taking a second cup of coffee, going over the exciting moments of the day's hunt. In an hour or two the Lounge would begin to fill up with couples ready to drink and dance away the last hours on their permits. It was nearing the time she had set, in her mind, as the ultimate barrier. Until then she wouldn't *really* be afraid. . . .

In the holobox the miniature personages remained frozen: a man gesturing, a woman with her mouth fixed in a dark O of surprise, the youth missing his lower body. Above this little tableau of arrested life, the rows of motionless vehicles shimmered faintly in a silence extending itself second by slow second. And then, in one great rush, Elise was terrified.

Her first thought was to get dressed. Her boots and parka. Her thermal body sock. She was already flinging clothes out of the closet when two alarms went off at once, as if synchronized. She ran into the living room, where the message panel was blinking and bonging, and hit the answer button savagely with her fist. Behind her in the kitchen the teapot was shrieking a single, high, steady note.

On the miniscreen of the panel she saw the unit manager, and behind him the two Preserve Rangers, sweating in their bulky jackets. She saw everything in their faces, their compressed mouths and averted eyes, before the manager even spoke. She heard only certain words: *emergency . . . sorry . . . please come to the desk. . . .* But she was already walking, not toward the door but toward the kitchen, to lift the shrieking little pot from the burner. All the rest of her life she would remember that journey as her first floating, underwater steps in the long return to sanity.

3

PHILLIP JAMES ("PJ") FEIFFER KNEW HE WAS ON NO ORdinary assignment when he ran into Black Jack Skiho at the elevator on the hangar deck. Skiho was North Federation, a Euroslav, flat-faced and straw-haired and built like a fireplug. His nickname, an ironic joke on the surface, was an otherwise accurate metaphor. Like PJ he worked—when he worked—on special assignments, off the record. And when he hit he hit hard, without warning.

"They can't need both of us," Skiho said in amazement that was only partly feigned. "Hey, PJ, maybe you got the wrong building."

PJ grinned. He loomed over Skiho by a quarter of a meter and outweighed him a good ten kilos, but he knew from the few times they had worked together that the short man was his match in every other way. "Maybe the aliens have landed, or we got an ice age arriving early."

"Can handle," Skiho said and cuffed PJ lightly on the shoulder of his field suit. "How you cruisin', man?"

PJ laughed aloud at the dated slang. Black Jack had done his NorthAm language studies as a cadet, and learned perfectly the idioms of twenty years ago. "Cruisin' low," he said. "Far from the public eye."

They were in the elevator now, a soft gray cubicle of light that seemed not to move at all, but they felt the sudden hollowness under the ribs that meant they were dropping in near free-fall, deep into the bowels of the Intelligence Command HQ complex. They waited quietly until the hollowness was replaced by a swift drag of gravity. In a moment the cubicle hummed and its doors retracted with the sound of a mechanical lung inhaling.

They stepped into a corridor as wide as a street. Men and women in the light blue uniform of the Internal Authority hurried along it, some pushing carts stacked with computer disks and data templates or aerial holo projectors. Both men turned to the right and strolled together, ignoring the glances and whispers of the passing clerks. They did not appear to feel out of place in baggy field suits, with helmets dangling from waist clips.

"I'm making a guess this has to do with that missing kid," PJ said. "Assuming you watch the news once in a while."

"The one the bear got last month? Naw. Why? Simple. They got fifty S and R teams they can keep on that one. Come up sooner or later with something. Hair, bone, fiber— something."

"Drager," PJ said. "Guy's name was Frank Drager. You're getting sloppy, Black Jack. He was in line for A-Sec on the Energy Council. First-class hunter. Led border patrols back in the days when you went in with six guys in a light cruiser and nothing hotter than an M-6 in the turret."

"So"—Skiho hitched one shoulder—"he made a mistake. Out of his vehicle, I think I heard."

"Lots of mistakes these days," PJ said. "Or haven't you noticed?" He delivered this line neatly during a gap in the flow of people and carts, and Skiho did not reply until a few moments later when another space appeared and he could not be overheard.

"I noticed," he said.

They were both thinking, PJ knew, of the same short list. Most people were, though depending on your job and level in the Fed the order of the items could differ. If you were in EcFac, the issue was productivity. A mysterious slide there. If you were in Agro, then it was the new viruses and blights working since the Great Climate Shift. Meanwhile the Bio and Med people were worried about tough adaptive strains of flu and cancer, and the Eneco experts were having trouble with their formulas for everything from resource recovery to information margins.

In their own division of Insec—Parks and Border Buffers —PJ and Black Jack were aware of a few similar signs of . . . trouble? Change? Curious coincidence? It was hard to put a finger on. An occasional important memo disappeared, swallowed up in the circuitry without leaving a trace. Surveillance modules malfunctioned, seemingly arbitrarily. Agents who had been for years steady and precise as molecular clocks suffered sudden attacks of nerves. Bureau chiefs fell into a profound funk, unable to work or rest or (least of all) explain what had gone wrong.

Nobody—so far—was talking sabotage. The most convincing theory PJ had heard came from the Psych engineers. They noticed that rehab and rec times were getting longer, that some tranqs—both slammers and smoothers—lost their effectiveness almost overnight. Long-wave stress patterns, their argument went, could get into phase and reinforce each other. You could wake up some morning with your head full of fire, or dense fog, or a spilled drawer of ideas that were definitely not yours.

But that theory didn't account for the new viruses or this missing boy. By itself a hunting accident wouldn't mean much, but PJ knew that there had been a rash of similar encounters. A couple of small boats upset by killer whales, no known provocation. Hives of bees going haywire. Several bear and wild dog incidents. And more than once there had been missing bodies, lingering doubts.

It might all mean something, or it might not. PJ was keeping an open mind. It wasn't unprecedented for a man to stage a tragic accident in order to escape the stigma of suicide, and he had seen peculiar runs of misbehavior in certain animals before. As one of half a dozen final clearance investigators, it was his job to keep an open mind. And to trust no one.

"Intelligence and Security," Skiho said, reading the first words on a sign at the intersection of their corridor with a smaller one. "Absolutely opposed concepts."

PJ smiled at this correspondence with his own train of thought. As they turned down the side corridor he said, "So what is it this time? We risk our tails to find out what they don't want to hear? Or we keep them from learning what everybody else knows?"

Skiho barely smiled. "Not my meaning here," he said. "I mean—" He stopped abruptly, then looked up along the low ceiling of the corridor. "Screw it. You suppose they're bugging us already?"

PJ probed the walls and ceiling with quick glances. There were only a few doors in the hallway, rectangles of steel with small peepholes of one-way glass. He shrugged. "Could be. You know Fat. He'll wire anything."

"Screw it." Skiho looked hard at PJ. His big, flat face was glum. "There's too much weirdness around, man. I'm gonna take a chance and tell you something, whether you want it or not." He had lowered his voice to a hiss, leaning close to PJ. "First thing is, a couple months ago I'm checking out a poaching report in the Gila Preserve and I run into this Bio team. The crew chief is real close-mouthed. Catty bitch, too. I have authority over her, of course, as an investigator, but she doesn't want to show me any samples, any specimens. Whips out a letter on Insec stationery. *Viability Study*, it says. *Alpha-class priority*. Got that?"

PJ widened his eyes slightly, acknowledging the import of this bit of information. Every bureaucrat in the Federation trembled at the prospect of a V-study. Such review meant an operation was in question, could be canceled.

"Second thing, I call on a friend of mine in Docs, a lady who has some serious access, and she tells me, yeah, they're doing V's on *all* the Preserves, not just the Hunts but the Pub Rec and Research too. Kiss of death. I tell you, man, somebody is after our jobs."

PJ managed to keep his stance loose, his features relaxed,

but under his ribs he felt the old queasiness. More than once certain factions in the Federation had tried to annihilate or at least shrink the Preserves. The less developed provinces argued that the notions of wildlife and hunting were remnants of ancient imperial states, and the Preserves would contribute more to the economy as marginal plantation areas or waste storage sites. The same radical elements tried every year to launch programs to terminate the Ginks and recolonize the Southern Wastelands.

"Somebody," PJ said finally, "is always after you. Rule of the Universe." Skiho snorted in disgust and PJ went on, not wanting to seem trivial. "But V-studies, that's ominous. And they didn't tell us about it, which is downright sinister." He smiled wryly at Skiho. "Of course a good investigator like yourself can always get work."

Skiho looked hard at him and PJ lost the smile. Neither spoke for a long moment, and both were all at once aware of their comradeship, their similarity. Though they had never talked of it, they knew that given the choice they would always work the Preserves and Border Zones. They had grown too fond of solitude, the heightened alertness and adrenaline rush of stalking, even the occasional hardship and discomfort of their work. And in both men, in a far and dark corner of the mind, was a fear that the world had evolved beyond them, that their way of life was doomed.

"Okay," Skiho said then, "but today we're on the job, right?"

"Right. Eyes open."

They grinned at each other, leaving unspoken the second part of the old patrolman's dictum. Assholes shut. Then they strode to one of the steel doors and inserted their security cards in the slot below the sign: *InSec 2-B Margin Lands Director, C. S. Fat Insert card.*

A holo was running in the large wall chamber and without turning to greet them Solomon Fat waved over his shoulder to indicate soft chairs flanking his desk. PJ and Black Jack sat down and began watching. They recognized the area, a tremendous canyon in the high country just over the border of the western section of the Wastelands.

A Bantam, one of the new light patrol vehicles, was tracking fast down a dry streambed. Just ahead of it a Gink female was dodging through the brush that lined the banks, dragging her young. When she tried to bolt across an open place something flickered out of the vehicle. Two steps further she went down and the youngster began to scramble up the bank. Then a set of doors on the turret sprang open and a quadrant of rockets flashed out, bracketing the little figure; a moment later it was thrashing in the tight mesh of a net that had bloomed between the rockets, and two men were running from the open hatches of the Bantam.

"Nice work," Skiho observed. "Did you save it?"

Fat touched a button on a panel recessed into his desk and the holo darkened and evaporated. Before it faded the figure in the tangled net was already curling in upon itself, as if to sleep.

"No. Not this particular one." Fat had swung around to regard them, his face fixed in the same eternal smile with which he blessed all things, living or dead. His dense, black eyes, pinched up at the corners, did not blink. "But let me show you something, gentlemen." He punched another button on the panel and spoke into it. "Tima? Come here."

Leaning back into his chair he looked at Skiho and his smile broadened slightly. Fat's people had come from the Orient many generations ago, but they preserved a deliberateness and polish that were a polar opposite to Skiho's rough, boisterous manner. "They are after my job too, my friend. The V-studies you were speaking of are going on in this bureau right now." He glanced at a stack of papers on his desk. "I intended to tell you today, but obviously you have your own dependable sources."

PJ and Skiho did not exchange a look, but each felt the other's slight shift of attitude. They had been observed and recorded, then, probably from the moment they left the hangar deck. A very sensitive assignment, indeed. And perhaps more of the indefinable weirdness Skiho had postulated.

"The Progressives have always been ready to eradicate this archaic system of privilege—as they view it." Fat uttered a soft, private chuckle. "Despite the facts. It apparently makes no difference how many great leaders acknowledge the contribution of the Preserves to their own development, or how many Psych engineers prove that this redirection of natural aggressiveness is vital to the stability of the Federation. . . ."

PJ cleared his throat with a certain ostentation, and Fat sighed. "Of course you men know my lecture. But the whole business is now complicated by this unfortunate accident. Drager was a man of great promise, a master hunter and innerloop executive, but the real problem is the missing boy. The Progs are trying to drum up a mystery, even a conspiracy, and they've been lucky. The best of our search teams, with Bio experts along, have found only a few fibers. The animals left the area very quickly and kept on the snowline. Very purposeful, one might say. Which has led us to suspect—"

A panel in the wall behind Fat slid aside and a small figure in a light blue uniform stepped into the room. Simultaneously and involuntarily PJ and Skiho took in a short, sharp breath. What they at first had assumed to be a child was in fact an immature Gink, apparently a female. She was a little lighter than most of her species, the color of seasoned wood, but had the typical hair: straight, coarse, jet black. Her nose, however, had been expertly sharpened and tilted upward in the NorthAm fashion. From the moment the creature entered the office her gaze was fixed on Fat.

In spite of himself PJ fumbled vaguely at his belt, though his sidearm had been left in the copter as regulations required. The Gink female turned instantly toward him and bowed.

"I am very sorry, sir," she said. She spoke clearly and without detectable accent, though there was a peculiar lack of any inflection in her voice. Turning back to Fat she waited, at attention like a new recruit.

"My God," Skiho said in a hushed tone. "Alive."

Fat beamed. "This is Tima, gentlemen. A full-blooded Gink, captured successfully eight years ago, which would make her approximately fifteen now. As you heard she speaks NorthAm, also Euroslav and a little PanSino, besides her own barbarian tongue. She can operate base programs up to the Delta level and, as you see, wears clothes and keeps herself clean."

PJ regarded Fat with open admiration. "How?"

"A bit of luck. We surprised her playing outside a warren and she apparently had not yet—for some reason—developed the shock syndrome. Also very unusual, the parents and siblings came out to try to rescue her. Their autopsies were ordinary, but clearly she is genetically endowed far beyond the usual range of the species. Her MP battery scores are subnormal in many categories, but she . . . ah, but why not show you? Tima, see if the gentlemen would like anything."

Tima was already moving as Fat uttered this last sentence, PJ noted. She stopped in front of Skiho and bowed low, then moved to PJ and repeated the gesture. He heard her inhale through her nostrils and he felt her presence in some odd way, as if she had created a faint current of air. He also noted that the surgeons had succeeded in making her almost handsome. "Thank you, sir," she said, then glided swiftly to a low cabinet against one wall and opened it.

"I have a reason for introducing you to Tima," Fat said, "beyond my I hope excusable pride in the first successful complete domestication of *lapsis*. Perhaps you have guessed what it is."

PJ and Skiho exchanged another glance and then Skiho nodded. "You connect the Drager kid with the Ginks somehow?"

"Not somehow. Very specifically. Look at this." Fat slid open a drawer and produced a flat metal box which he slid across the desk top toward the two men.

PJ picked up the box and flipped its lid open. Inside on a cushion of cotton fibers was what appeared to be a perfectly straight section from a very thin reed. At one end a thread, no thicker than a hair, had been wound tightly around the reed, and the other end was stoppered by a splinter of wood. PJ pursed his lips, interested. "Messenger ant cage," he said. "Coastal, I would guess. Where'd you find it?"

On the side of the room where Tima bent over the cabinet they heard the clink of glass and tableware, and now she came before them again bearing a tray. She presented it first to Skiho, who took the small glass of perfectly clear liquid that was nearest him, and then to PJ, who set down the box and lifted away a taller glass packed with ice and graced by a wedge of lime.

"You will be shocked when I tell you," Fat said. He waited for Tima to add two lumps of sugar to the cup of steaming dark coffee she had set before him. "You *did* want a vodka and a gin and tonic?"

PJ grinned. "Come on," he said. "You told her before we got here."

"Must have," Skiho added. "But . . . no ice. Sometimes I take ice, sometimes I don't." He glared at Tima. "Just luck."

"Oh, but it is more than that, I assure you. She can tell exactly what you want. Sometimes before you want it. Quite remarkable, really. What we don't know is whether other Ginks have this ability, or have it in the same measure."

"It would have to be smell," PJ said. "Or else the Clever Hans syndrome."

Fat chuckled again, his shoulders jerking silently. "We have several people working on it," he said, "and it is nothing so simple."

"Impressive," PJ said. "My compliments." He glanced again at Tima and then tilted his glass at the open box on the table. "So where?"

"Hunting Preserve Four, the Central Rockies. Near a place called Redfish Summit, at about eleven thousand feet. It turned up three weeks ago."

"Where this Drager thing happened. I know it." Skiho put down his glass on the desk. "It must be a plant. That's way too far north for Ginks."

PJ whistled a single, low note. "Up until now," he said. "There was an unconfirmed spotting in the Great Basin a few months back—four or five males all on their own—but I'd never have thought. . . ." He looked sharply at Tima, then at Fat. "Are you sure . . . ?"

"Oh yes. She is extremely well trained. Her grams and scans indicate she has almost completely repressed her early memories. We can speak freely." Fat sipped the coffee and then tapped his lips fastidiously with the napkin Tima had placed at his elbow. "I hope this affair is beginning to fall into place for you gentlemen." He glanced at Skiho to punctuate his last word with genial irony.

"If the Ginks took the kid, then I see your problem. The media will be all over the story."

PJ laughed briefly, without humor. "All over us, you mean. Perfect opportunity for the Progs. They can set up their howl for termination of the Ginks—and the Preserves too."

"I think we could maintain a remnant experimental breeding population," Fat said with an almost formal nod at Tima.

"If we can capture a few more like this one before they learn to shock themselves to death in the nets. But speaking as a lifelong Conservative, I find termination an abominable solution. It is expensive and inefficient, as well as cruel. But if it becomes widely known—it is already suspected in some quarters—that these creatures are ranging so far north, and stirring up animals to the attack, and carrying off the sons of influential people. . . . Well, gentlemen, you can imagine." Fat paused and opened both hands on the desk top, palms up, as if to reveal some vital evidence. "The Progressives will certainly seize such an opportunity. The Federation is already experiencing considerable stress, and the policy of balanced aggression and border buffering, which is the keystone of our agency. . . ." For the merest fraction of a second Fat's smile became a grimace of pain.

No one spoke for a long moment. Tima was the first to move. She glided swiftly to the cabinet and returned bearing a small platter and a tumbler of water. On the platter were three capsules filled with a grayish powder.

"No, Tima. I shouldn't." Fat spoke as if to himself, watching Tima set the platter and glass on his desk. Then he beamed again at the two men, his round yellow face like a cold sun. "So I am depending on you, boys. And we do not have much time."

Skiho tossed off the last of his vodka. "We recover the kid, if he's alive. Or if he isn't, we make sure nobody finds out what did happen to him."

Fat said nothing and his black eyes were opaque, unmoving.

"Right," PJ said softly. He had never before heard Fat refer to agents as boys, and this incongruity made him abruptly aware of the gravity of their situation. "I assume we start immediately."

Fat remained motionless and PJ got to his feet. After a moment's hesitation Skiho also pushed himself out of his chair.

"And this conversation never occurred," PJ went on. "And if we run into trouble we don't call you." He lifted one finger and touched his brow in a mock salute. "Good news or no news."

"Just us two," Skiho said, already on his way to the door. It was less a question than a musing aloud. "I'm flattered."

"Actually . . . " Fat said then, his voice barely audible. His black eyes rolled to one side, toward Tima.

"Whoa." PJ reversed himself and took a step toward the man behind the desk. "You can't be serious. As an experiment, fine, but——"

"It is a risk, I admit. A very small one, however. And consider, gentlemen, the advantages. She has retained the language and some memory of the territory of her childhood. She is a very able servant and requires little supervision—as you have seen here." Fat was smiling broadly again. "And most important, you understand, is to recover the boy alive —if by some miracle the Ginks have not eaten him—which will require great stealth or, perhaps, great subterfuge. That in turn requires great subtlety, an instinct. . . ." His eyes swerved again toward Tima, who was watching his face with the same steady intensity. "What she has, in short. I repeat, gentlemen, her abilities in this line are extraordinary."

"But for the love of Christ, Fat." Skiho looked at PJ, his face almost comically woeful. "We'll be going day and night. For weeks, maybe months. On the ground some of the time. Living on pills. How——"

"You believe she is too slight, too weak, too slow. Oh, gentlemen, you are in for a surprise." Fat began to chuckle again, but PJ and Skiho did not notice. They were watching Tima, who had inverted herself and stood now on her hands, the long, black hair hanging to the floor. Then she lifted one hand away, so that her entire weight balanced on one arm, and arched her back until her heels rested neatly on the back of her neck.

For a few long moments there was no sound but the wheeze of Fat's private laugh. Tima's arm flexed and shifted slightly, maintaining her exquisite balance, but her muscles did not tremble with strain and her breasts, swelling against the taut fabric of the uniform, rose and fell with an even, regular breathing.

"Goddamn it," PJ expostulated. "We're not entering a gymnastics contest."

Tima's head rotated slightly. She was looking at each of the men in turn, and though her expression was upside down, PJ thought he could detect a slight frown of uncertainty. Fat moved his chin almost imperceptibly, and like a spring tripping, Tima whirled back onto her feet and into her former erect, eager posture.

"How long can she hold that one-hand stand?" Skiho blurted. He looked uneasy.

"This is crazy." PJ glared at Fat and Tima in turn. "After everything we've said about how vital this deal is—the V-studies, the media poised to jump, the Progs. . . ."

"That is precisely why I think she must accompany your investigation. If I did not believe she could assist, believe me I would not risk it." Fat's smile did not alter, but PJ sensed an intensity behind the man's careful mask. "And after all, she is an experiment of great potential value to me. But I will not *order* you to take her. I simply express my strongest belief that you will maximize your chances of success by doing so."

PJ and Skiho stared at each other for a moment. PJ lifted his arms to shoulder height and then let them flap back to his sides. He opened his mouth as if to protest again, then shut it with a snap of teeth.

"She rides with you," Skiho said.

"You will not be sorry," Fat went on smoothly and lifted a hand toward PJ in an apologetic gesture. "Everything but her personal kit is already at the hangar and both copters carry extra rations. I took that liberty to avoid delay. She will meet you on deck with Major Hake, who can brief you on the search so far and provide secure codes. Good luck, gentlemen."

"Yeah," PJ said. "Thanks."

As the two men strode out the door Fat picked up all three capsules of gray powder and his smile broke open, finally, to receive them. Tima already held the tumbler of water ready.

4

FOR THE FIRST THREE NIGHTS THEY RAN. RONALD FELL often, and sometimes a muscle cramped so badly he had to drag himself on all fours. The knees had gone out of his jumpsuit, exposing his bare and bloodied skin, and one of his boots had split open at the sole.

He did not run smoothly, as he had learned to do at school on a level AeroBalance treadmill that adjusted speed automatically according to an H-L monitor. This shambling trot, over rock and root and snowpack, required constant alertness to the pitch and texture of the ground. But he was so exhausted and numbed by cold that he could not maintain concentration, so again and again he plunged off the trail or tripped.

He knew the whole company was traveling slower because of him. He did not care, because he knew the Ginks were only waiting for him to die, so the she-bear—Mata, he had heard them call her—would leave him and then they could go on at their best pace. Or maybe they would eat him first. Certainly they had wanted to kill him straightaway, when they first saw him in the freezing twilight on Redfish Summit.

There had been a hurried conference, in a language like a wind through leaves and clattering branches. He had seen heads turn toward him, threatening gestures with the lances whose tips glittered in the moonlight. Finally two of the dark shapes detached themselves and approached him, but immediately Mata moved to intercept them, rumbling a warning. They called to her, prodded at her with their lances, but she batted the shafts aside and rose on her hind legs with a roar that sent both Ginks scampering backward.

Later the same night they had stopped briefly again, Ronald a little apart with Mata and the big male bear lounging near him. The huddled Ginks rummaged in pouches slung from the shoulder and soon he could hear them chewing. Carefully and deliberately the tall, pale man approached to within a few steps, talking as he came, and though she rumbled again Mata did not otherwise menace him.

"Teeklo," the man said, "my name." He tossed a strip of dried meat onto the ground in front of Ronald. The she-bear snarled and slapped one paw over the offering, then sniffed it thoroughly before settling back on her haunches.

"You die pretty soon, I think." The man grinned. "Poor Mata loses all her cubs. So eat now, make her happy."

Ronald said nothing, but after a moment he reached out

very slowly and took the dark, twisted rope of meat. The bear watched him with tiny, bloodshot eyes, swinging her snout back and forth. He began to chew. The meat was tough and tasted of mold, but the juice from it made his stomach convulse eagerly.

The man had laughed. "A warrior must eat his mother's bones, we say." Then he had turned and walked away.

And so it had gone for the next two nights: running always except for the one brief squat over a bit of moldy meat. Running and running, on feet like blocks of ice. Staggering and falling and sliding and scrambling after the dark figures hurrying, always hurrying, over snow phosphorescent as a corpse in the moonlight.

Ronald did not understand why he was not permitted to die. He thought about death in the rare moments when he managed to rise above his pain and bewilderment. Death appeared to him as a chance to sleep, to sink into a great, dark, soft bed where he could forget the blot swarming from the overturned Choctaw, where he would not imagine his mother sitting alone in his room crying, where he could above all stop running.

Sometimes when he fell he lay still and tried to float into that darkness, but Mata always rooted him up, nipped his haunches and back until he cried out weakly and staggered erect again. Once, in a flash of hatred, he slapped her on the ear. She reared back a little and grumbled, then cuffed him swiftly, right and left, and he curled into a tight, terrified ball. He recalled instantly the claws hooking into the writhing shadow of his father, and knew he did not want to die that way.

Nor would Mata allow him to freeze. They were moving along the spine of a mountain range, in snow more often than not, sleeping during most of the day in caves and burrows. The Ginks wrapped themselves in their fur capes, but Ronald's jumpsuit, even if it had been whole, would not protect him from the bitter cold. The first morning he had been the last one allowed into the small cave, so he was most exposed to the wind and drifting snow at the entrance. The pale human had glanced at him contemptuously, grunted, and then thrown across him a small pelt, a sort of vest made by linking with thongs the front and rear paws of some animal.

For a long time he huddled in the gray light, his teeth clacking with the violence of his shivering. The hide covered only his back, and he could feel on his legs and feet the lash of wind, gritty with driven ice crystals. Gradually he was going numb, while the knife-edge of cold moved up along his ribs. He had begun to drift in and out of consciousness, to sense the great, black softness that would gather him in, when he heard low moans.

He did not realize they were his moans until he broke them off with a yelp, when Mata clamped her jaws on his ankle. She pulled him summarily out of the cave and then uphill, his body sliding easily over the snow. He struggled feebly, moaning again, wanting to go back to the velvet darkness. *Afterwards,* he thought, *you can eat me afterwards.* She dropped him beside two mounds and began to dig between them, her great paws beating out the snow in clumps and showers.

In moments she had exposed the flanks of the two boulders and dug into the frozen scree between them. She turned around and around in this space, sweeping it with her fore-limbs, leaving a shelf of snow on the uphill side to join the two boulders. Ronald, watching her work and listening to her grunts and whistling breath, thought of nothing. He was too tired and too sleepy even to feel afraid. When she moved toward him he only closed his eyes and waited for her breath, the slash of her claws, the grinding of fang against bone.

Her jaws clamped his shoulder and one paw hooked under his body, then she lifted him and carried him to the place she had cleared. This time she did not drop him to the frozen ground, but collapsed slowly herself into the hollow between the boulders, pulling him against her belly. His face was rammed into her coarse fur, and one heavy front limb fell like a log across his back. He nearly gagged at her dense, rank odor, both musky and slightly fishy. Then he felt her tongue on the back of his neck, like wet sand. He struggled feebly, managed to twist his head so that he could breathe more freely, but he could not budge his body.

And in a few moments, as pain began to move back into his lower limbs, he realized that she was warm, actually hot, the mighty pumping furnace of her heart radiating into him head to toe. Through the hide of her belly he could hear other sounds too—deep, hollow rumbles and gurgles, a muffled grinding. It reminded him of the sound track of a holo shown in his geophysics class, on the birth of volcanoes. That was the last thought he had before he sank away—not into a starless, final night, but into a throbbing, rough-walled, suffocating chamber of heat.

So it had been for three days, all of them gray and gloomy under storm clouds. They rose before the light failed, ate scraps of the dried meat, and then trekked relentlessly into the darkness. The Ginks moved with an odd, swinging stride, their toes pointing inward; and though as Ronald watched them they never seemed to be hurrying, he could barely keep up at his scrambling trot. They did not talk, and several times—acting on what signal Ronald could not determine— the Ginks broke ranks and scurried under overhanging shelves of rock or, even more mystifying, crouched on all fours under their fur capes and moved about cautiously, seemingly at random. Each time, seconds after these maneuvers, he heard the distant hissing scream of a jetcopter.

Near the end of the fourth night he was jarred out of his stupor by nearly colliding with the Gink in front of him, the smallest of the company, one barely taller than Ronald. The creature whirled on him and there was a white flash under the fur cowl. "*Dako!*" he whispered hoarsely between bared teeth.

Mata and the male bear were ranging somewhere behind Ronald and higher on the ridge, out of view. The Gink thrust his face near Ronald's and lifted his short spear. With a slicing gesture he drew the sharpened head through the air a few inches away from Ronald's throat. "*Dako,*" he repeated and then wheeled swiftly to move after the others.

Seeing the creature's face at such proximity gave Ronald a shock of surprise. The Gink seemed actually very young, perhaps not much older than himself; and so regular of countenance he looked remarkably human. Certainly he did not resemble the exhibits in the museum, whose features were coarse and misshapen.

A moment later he realized something else, even more startling. He had run into the young Gink because they were now moving down the slope at a much slower pace. It was nearly dawn, light enough to see that the snow occurred now only in patches and the trees were larger and shaggier, more like the ones illustrated in his manual. It was warmer, too. He put a hand to his cheek and was amazed to detect a light film of perspiration.

Through a break in the forest he saw that the sharp, white peaks now lay behind them, while ahead were softer heaves in the earth, sheathed in a dense, feathery green. The trees were all the same, growing on contoured terraces. From a distance the whole area looked like an immense golf course. The plantations!

Tears jumped into his eyes and the scene blurred. A memory materialized instantly in its place, vivid and achingly immediate.

He and his father had gone once to a very old plantation. His father was inspecting, because the Administration was concerned about production figures, and Ronald had tagged along, allowed out of school on a parent-sponsored field trip.

The plantation director had taken them on a tour and they had gotten out of the vehicle at the boundary of the last field, where it abutted on a Temporary Preserve. Temporaries were forests cut long ago but then left untended, on ground too poor or too steep to warrant reclaiming. The boundary itself was only a strip of gray, sterile earth twenty yards across.

It was spring, the sun bright and the air very clear except for the showers of pollen blown now and then from the trees in a gust of wind. The pollen was what the two men were talking about, the pollen and theories about genetic management, diversity versus predictable yield—all kinds of figures and statistics that Ronald did not yet fully understand, though he dutifully made entries in the little notebook he carried. He would have to write a field report to make up for missing the day's classes.

He did understand that—from the point of view of the director—the shimmering golden veils that unfurled from the Preserve were bad. They corrupted the selected stocks by spreading tough, scraggly genes. The main question now was whether it was cheaper to spray a much wider lane between the two populations or merely to abandon this whole section of the plantation and let the weeds have it.

Watching the trees bend and sigh, Ronald tried to see them as bad. Some were indeed ominously large, and several, unlike the perfect cone shapes on the plantation, had twisted or skewed tops and protruding dead stumps of limbs. But the gestures they made were not threatening. They were slow and stately, even mournful, as was the deep moaning they made in the wind. The long, undulating clouds of yellow dust seemed like offerings to their regimented fellows on the other side of the barren swath. They were joined in this effort by various low bushes and creepers that frothed at the border and, here and there, sent a slender finger into the sprayed strip.

Ronald had heard the director talking about this problem too. Regulations, regulations, the man had fumed. You find the perfect weed-remover, meets the tolerable toxicity level, and some goddamned gooseberry or morning glory begins to develop resistance. The word *morning glory* had attracted him, and he begged the men to show him one. They seemed at once pleased and embarrassed. He knew that names like *gooseberry* and *morning glory* were not the real names of the plants. They belonged to the old systems of folklore. Precise number and letter codes were now used in all scientific and government documents. "No morning glories here," his father had said with a sidelong smile, "but Bill can show you a WL-420."

"Four-twenty-two," the director said. "The bastard has speciated locally."

He led them to a place where a walkway bridged the boundary strip and they crossed into the Preserve. Then a path took them to a clearing only a few yards into the forest. There they saw a splendid, dense tapestry of flowering plants—runners and clumps, sprays of tough stalks, each with a spike of bloom, tiny bushes and matted vines adorned with individual blossoms like strings of Christmas lights. There were purple bells and splashy yellow petals and little trumpets red as fire, and sprinkled throughout, small winking stars of luminous blue-white with a violet flush at the core. These were the morning glories, Bill said. But in Ronald's mind the word had already attached itself to the whole field of riotous color.

Bill had gone on to point out dozens of the common weeds, identifying them by number and often by the old folklore names too: lupine, paintbrush, daisy, owl clover, shooting star, monkey flower, devil claw, bluebell, vetch, trillium. For nearly an hour the men seemed to forget their business and themselves. They were testing each other in quickness of recall, laughing aloud at many of the names that sprang up.

What Ronald remembered most clearly, however, was the ancient tree they had seen on the way back. He had not noticed it at first because, though very tall, it did not rear over others in the forest. The top had broken off a long time ago, leaving a dead gray-white spear on the ground. But the body was alive, and huge beyond anything he had ever seen in a book. It had been scarred on one side and a great, gnarled boil had formed there. The crevices in the mosaic of shaggy bark looked wider than his hand, and some of the stubs that were once its lower limbs were as big around as a whole plantation tree.

It leaned, and a little over halfway up the trunk a limb had rotted out, leaving what looked to Ronald like an empty eye socket. He had the peculiar feeling the tree could sense them approaching. The men had fallen silent and he noticed that they, too, were looking at the tree. "Big fella," Bill had said, and made a vaguely apologetic gesture. "Some mix-up in the inventory or a lazy cruiser missed it a long time ago. Anyway, too much rot to be good for much." His father had looked amused, but said nothing.

They walked off the trail to the base of the old tree and leaned far back to stare up the mighty column of the trunk. Ronald touched the bark with his fingers and found it coarse but surprisingly soft, overgrown with a thin layer of gray-green moss. The men went around the base with arms outstretched, fingertip to fingertip, and announced its girth at nine meters, minimum.

And then, all at once, the interlude was over. The director and his father had hurried Ronald away. They seemed gruff, even a little angry with him. And something else. He had struggled to divine what. It was something hidden, something afraid to reveal itself. It was like . . . shame. He was puzzled. Had they done something wrong? Simply walking in the Preserve, using old words, looking at the ancient tree?

The mood lasted until they were back on the plantation, where they had left their vehicle. By the time they drove away, the men were talking figures again, costs and slowdown. The director remarked that it looked to him like an absolute toss-up: spray it or give it up. Six of one. His father had agreed, as far as hard money was concerned, and then turned suddenly to Ronald. What did the future Energy expert say?

Leave it alone, he had shot back, so swiftly that both men laughed aloud. He had been thinking of the old tree, and he guessed that the men were thinking that way too. After the laughter there was a silence and then the director glanced at his father and said, "Suits me." His father had only nodded once with a slight smile, but Ronald knew that meant the tree was saved.

Grief wrenched at him then, caving in his chest and sending him to his knees. He was not crying for the old tree, but for his father, who would never go on any more inspections or walk in a glade full of blooming weeds or smile that little smile of secret kindness that made up for so much fussiness and criticism. And he was crying for himself—he grasped this in a flash—because he could never tell his father how much he loved him for saving the broken tree and never show him that he could change and stop daydreaming and become a good hunter and a manager and a soldier who went on patrol and killed Ginks. . . .

The thought went through him with a delicious, savage pang. Yes! Kill Ginks! He hated them, instantly and thoroughly. They were responsible for his father's death. The bears were only dumb brutes. He saw how the Ginks manipulated them, prodding sometimes with the handles of their spears, tossing the beasts a bit of gristle or spoiled meat. Doubtless they could train a bear to follow the ants and disembowel vehicles like their Choctaw, teach it to scavenge human flesh.

He hated them, too, for keeping him alive, torturing him with this journey, for their silent, swift pace, their shunning of him at every stopping point. He would bide his time and watch and finally escape—those plantations below were very large but all roads would lead eventually to an administration and maintenance complex—and then the alarm would be raised, and he would go out in a jetcopter with the emergency Strikeforce and they would avenge his father, they would make these creatures pay dearly. And so . . . he must *live!*

He got to his feet and rubbed the ragged sleeve of his

jumpsuit over his wet face, blinking. He felt stronger and clearer of mind. For the first time in three days and three nights he stood fully erect and stretched his arms over his head, clenching his fists.

Then, turning, he saw the two bears only a dozen yards away. They were behind him and slightly uphill. Mata was sitting on her haunches and watching him with the same drilling intensity she had shown the first time he saw her in the limestone side canyon. He was startled, for whenever he had lagged or fallen before she had always urged him onward, grumbling and pressing him with snout or claw.

"Mata?" he called softly and frowned at her, but she did not move. He took a step backward, paused, and then took another. A glance down the faint trail they had been following revealed no sign of the young Gink. He inhaled a long, shuddering breath.

The plantations were actually within sight, though he had no experience in judging how many kilometers he would have to walk, uphill and down, to traverse the yawning gulf of air between this mountain and the distant carpet of smooth green. But surely it would be easier than what he had already done. If only they would not follow him. He would run as far as he could. . . .

He had lifted his foot to take another step away when Mata rolled onto all fours with a growl and in two bounds was upon him. She came with her lips peeled back over her yellow fangs, her eyes small and red-hot. She upset him with one blow of her paw and seized him at the waist, hooking the cloth of the jumpsuit in her teeth. Then she lifted him from the ground, rising on her hind legs and plunging down again, simultaneously shaking him violently from side to side. His head whipped and his legs pedaled furiously in thin air. For the first time he felt the true power of her, knew that with the very slightest of additional effort she could snap his neck like a stalk of dry grass. He underwent a spasm of pure panic, shrieking and thrashing with all his might.

The fabric of his jumpsuit tore and he flew through the air, struck the ground on his back, and rolled. He was up and running then, mouth wide open, headed not downhill toward the plantations but along the faint trail. He had made the choice without thinking, his eyes seeking frantically ahead for

the shadowy line of Ginks. Behind him he could hear the slap
and thud of Mata's paws, a deep *whoof* from the bellows of
her lungs.

He was on and into the circle of Ginks before he saw them,
and trying to stop he tumbled and fell flat. When he lifted his
smudged face, spitting out dry needles from the duff on the
clearing floor, there was a roaring in his ears that grew louder
and louder. Stunned, he looked around the ring of dark faces
and bared white teeth. It was a long moment before the panic
ebbed away and he realized that they were laughing. Laughing
in long hoots and high, thin squeals, in barks and yips, in
caws and whistles. Here and there around the circle seated
Ginks fell over backward, legs kicking wildly in the air. He
scrambled up on all fours, holding a crouch, and before he
could stop himself he was screaming back at them, *"Shut up!
Shut up! You animals! Filthy animals!"*

They laughed even louder, slapping and jabbing each other.
Following their stares, Ronald saw that Mata had ripped out
the whole seat of the jumpsuit, so his buttocks were bare.
One severed trouser leg had dropped and gathered about his
ankle. He jerked the cloth over his knee and tried to scream
again, but choked on his rage and embarrassment.

A Gink flung his cape aside, sprang up, and ran a few steps
along the trail before turning and running back, eyes wide in
an expression of insane terror. With one hand he jerked up
his breechclout to expose his bare buttocks, and then sprawled
into a somersault and came up crouched beside Ronald. After
a second or two he looked up, mouth agape, a droll imitation
of someone stupefied by surprise.

This performance brought another chorus of hoots and
cackles and squeaks, and Ronald's face burned. But when the
creature beside him also mirrored his fierce expression and
cried out, *"Shit ep! Shit ep! Eenimools!"* even Ronald could
not suppress a twisted smile. Except for the mispronunciation,
the mimicry was remarkably exact.

"That is praise," said a voice to his left, "to call us animal."

It was the pale human. He, too, had laughed and was still
grinning as he spoke. He had loosened his cape from his
shoulders and Ronald could see now that his hair was long
and streaked with gray. Like the Ginks he seemed very thin,
a man made of rope and cording under a taut hide. Something

glinted at his breast, a bit of metal on a string. It was bent and discolored, but Ronald recognized it—a "dog tag." The old NorthAm military tradition, maintained still, though all identification was now by electronic tattoo.

The other Ginks were still hooting. Ronald was aware that the Gink crouching beside him continued to mimic his every move. On some impulse he could never explain later, when he considered how it had determined his very life, he turned and stuck out his tongue, then extended it to touch the tip of his nose. He had discovered this talent as a child, and knew that a few others could do it spontaneously, but the rest would never manage, strain and waggle as they might.

He was lucky. The Gink blinked in surprise, stretched and curled his own tongue, but could not come near the tip of his nose. He squeezed shut his eyes with effort, and the other Ginks were convulsed by hilarity. Some of them writhed on the ground as if unable to breathe. The mimic stood up with an imprecation and sauntered back toward his place in the circle, directing a gesture at Ronald that was obviously some kind of insult. Following the same malicious impulse, Ronald executed an identical gesture at the retreating back, and was rewarded by a final and tremendous roar of laughter that brought his adversary around again with a startled frown.

One of the Ginks at last raised his spear and brought the butt down hard on the ground. The laughter subsided into sighs and grunts, but many continued to look at Ronald with barely concealed friendliness. The Gink spoke sharply and gestured at the sun, which had risen far enough now to send columns of light across the clearing.

Ronald could see that this leader was older than the others of the company. His brow and cheeks were netted with fine wrinkles, though his body seemed as wiry and muscled as the much younger ones around him. When the circle had quieted he gave a short speech, gesturing several times with the spear toward Ronald and twice toward Teeklo, the pale one. He referred once also to Mata, and at the sound of her name the she-bear grumbled briefly from the shadows at the edge of the clearing. When the speech was finished the old leader nodded at Teeklo, who turned to Ronald with a small, wry smile.

"They are all surprised . . . no. . . . What is the word? I

have not spoken my native tongue so much, for years. So I forget. They are . . . astonished! Yes, that's it. That this boy is still alive. His people have no bones, we say. All fat. We thought Mata would discover you are no cub and then the cold would kill you. But Mata is . . . what do you call it? Anyway, too old. She cannot smell so good. So now we are stuck on you . . . *with* you. Goddamn it!" Teeklo laughed to himself. "Sonofabitch. Yes? At least I can still swear. Anyway it is a . . . dilemma. I remember the horns." He laughed again, tossing the long, gray hair over one shoulder. It was as if he were thinking aloud, ignoring Ronald.

"One horn is that now this boy knows how far north we go and where we walk. So we should have killed him. But Mata would not stand up for it. The other horn is that the trackers are surely looking for you. We must get back to our tunnels, but you make us slow. And if they find out we are bringing a young boy to our land, they will come and kill us all. And we never take someone against their wish. Better to kill them. Better for them, too."

He looked away from Ronald, pondering. There was a long silence. The Ginks seemed to be watching him keenly, some of them fidgeting impatiently, and Ronald realized then that they were waiting for him to speak.

"I . . . don't . . . understand," he whispered, and immediately the Ginks broke into an excited jabber. Some gesticulated with their spears, and two tried again to touch their noses with extended tongues. "I . . . why not, please, just let me go?"

"Because you will tell everything. Where we went, what we did."

Ronald opened his mouth to protest and in the split second before words came the whole company fell completely silent. Teeklo and the Ginks stared at him, at his parted lips. He hesitated, aware of tension all around him. Mata grunted again in the shadows.

He understood all at once that Teeklo was right. He would of course tell everything. He would be so relieved, so happy to see his mother and his classmates and teachers. . . . Tears filled his eyes and at once the Ginks erupted again into their excited gabble.

"Careful," Teeklo said quietly. "Mata has already explained how you try to run away."

"Explained?" Ronald stared at him wonderingly.

"I do the best I am able in this language. Rusty, don't you say? After so many years. And it is not a very good language for these things. Mata is the first of us all to know what you are thinking, even with her old nose. The Pobla next." He saw the incomprehension in Ronald's face. "The ones you call Gink. The ones you call animal." He looked hard at Ronald, unsmiling. "That is a word of praise, as I said to you. You want the highest word of insult, call them *piksi*."

"What is that?" Ronald asked, aware of another flurry of chatter around the circle.

"The word for your people. Once my people." Teeklo grimaced. "It means ghost-eater. Those who eat the spirits of others. Alive."

Conscious of the flush in his cheeks, Ronald looked away. "What is . . . *dako?*"

The young Gink he had nearly run into looked up immediately, pointed at Ronald and laughed; and the others laughed with him. *Dako! Dako!*

Teeklo leered at him. "So you have a name? So soon. It means . . . let's see . . . little and . . . not clever." He frowned, concentrating. "Ah! Runt! The weak one. The one you expect to die. Yes, runt!"

Ronald's face was aflame now. But before he could speak the old leader said something—he heard the word *dako* again—and pointed with his lance at the sun. Others around the circle struck their fists against their chests, evidently a sign of accord. Several began to dig in their pouches of soft hide or woven grass.

"Kapu says we cannot wait any longer. This is very dangerous here. The trackers will be coming." Teeklo's face had set again, and as he spoke he was folding his fur cape into a tight bundle. "Kapu says Mata, our old friend, has explained also that you are now afraid to die. Since you run so fast, with your ass hanging out." Teeklo allowed himself a thin smile.

"That is improvement. And your tongue trick shows us maybe you want to live—which is not the same thing. Even Kapu laughed, so maybe you are good for something."

The others had also made compact bundles of their fur robes, and three of the Ginks gathered up these bundles and disappeared into the bushes. The company was now either naked or garbed only in loose rags or deerskin wrapped around the crotch. From their pouches they had taken hollow sections of reed, unstoppered a wooden plug from one end, and were now spreading the contents—pastes of charcoal, moss green, a yellow-brown like the trunks of the trees—on their arms and legs and faces. There was an obvious resemblance to the camou pattern on the remaining rags of Ronald's jumpsuit, and several of the Ginks pointed and smiled.

"So you must give us your choice. Die or live with us in our land."

"I want to go home," Ronald blurted out. He could not hold back a sob.

Several of the Ginks looked up and uttered a soft coo, like the calls he had heard from pigeons in the city parks. His sobs were shocked out of him, for the sound seemed sympathetic and comforting.

Teeklo did not stop the busy work of his hands, applying the paints to his legs, but he looked at Ronald for a long moment. The distance and contempt of his habitual expression were gone, but what remained was unfathomable to Ronald.

"No," he said then. "A dilemma, I remember, has only two horns. You must choose. Your father gone, you only a boy, only a runt—we understand how you have wanted to die. A Pobla would make himself die, with his spirit alone, but you. . . . Anyway, we have a doctor along with us, and he has brought easy death, pleasant death. Our old ones use it if they have forgotten how to leave their bodies behind." He said something to a Gink across the circle, the same one who had clowned an imitation of Ronald's pratfall. The Gink rummaged in his bag and tossed out a glass vial stoppered with an elaborately carved wooden plug.

"But if you go with us, you must want to go. Not think of escape. You must be one of us. If you try to run away again Mata will strike you."

Two Ginks had come to flank him on either side. Teeklo handed the vial to the clown, who seized Ronald's wrist and held tight, while he stared into Ronald's face as if it were a fogged window. The other Gink, his pouch of color tubes ready, took Ronald's other arm.

"But she . . . she saved my life," Ronald whispered.

Teeklo smiled the tight smile again. "She believes she knows what is good for you. Hurry now, you must decide." He was on his feet, as were most of the others. The company looked like pieces of a picture puzzle, a scene of sun-dappled forest broken into man-shaped fragments.

"How can I just *want* to go," Ronald said, apparently to himself, for his voice was muffled, barely audible. "Not think about . . . everything."

"Yes," Teeklo said impatiently, "you people are no good at not thinking. But we have no time." He glanced quickly at the sky. "Tell us! Do you want to die or go?"

Ronald sat stunned. He felt the grip tighten on both his arms. The Ginks on each side of him were still staring, watching his face with the preternatural attentiveness of children before their first holo. So death was possible. Possible right *now*. The memory of his longing returned—the black, velvet night that could take him out of the cold, his fatigue, this mad dream. Did he want it? He stared at the vial clutched in the clown's hand. A few drops of that black syrup and he could be asleep, at ease, forever.

"What about you?" he said suddenly, his voice stronger, almost accusing. "Why didn't they kill you? You were"—he gestured at the metal tab dangling from the man's chest—"in the service, on patrols. . . . Why did you go with them? Your family. . . ."

Teeklo turned away and Ronald saw the muscles along the man's back jump and twitch, as if he had been struck with a lash. When he spoke his voice was low and had an edge Ronald had not heard before.

"If you stay alive for a few moons, perhaps I will tell you."

When he turned back to Ronald his face was again blank as stone. "Now *speak!*"

But Ronald neither spoke nor thought at first. He moved, wrenching his wrists free and scrambling to his feet. Then he managed to say, "I will go!" But before the words were even out of his mouth the two Ginks beside him whooped and began tearing off the tatters of his jumpsuit and smearing the greasy, resinous colors all over his naked body.

5

BACK IN HER SECTION OF THE BARRACKS TIMA SET ABOUT preparing her field kit as soon as the orderly left the room. Her hands moved like small birds foraging in a hedge, picking through the neat rows of medicines, compact clothing tubes, mess kit, rain gear, climbing ropes, direction finder, and flare gun. Every item went into her pack as neatly as a piece in the many 3-D puzzles she had assembled in tests.

Someone was, she knew, watching her during the first minute or so. She had long ago found the lens, inside the grill of the atmosphere regulator, but she did not have to be facing it, or even thinking about it, in order to feel their eyes on her. This time it was just a duty officer. She could tell if Major Hake or Fat was observing. Hake was a bothersome moth on her skin, bumbling at the nape of her neck, while Fat's look slid over her like a big snail, leaving a silver track of self-admiration. Sometimes she had to pretend her shudder of revulsion was a reaction to fatigue or chill so they would not suspect that she was aware of their spying.

When she was finished she left her pack at the foot of the bed, one pocket unzipped for last-minute additions, and turned to the monitor and control panel on her desk. Hake himself answered her second buzz.

"What is it, Tim?"

"I would like to have a last ten minutes on the roof run, sir."

She stood perfectly straight before the monitor, though Hake, when his image popped onto the screen, did not even look up from the manual in his hand.

"Right." He nodded absently. "You're all packed, right?"

"Yes, sir."

"Notify control, okay? Talk to you later. Real busy now, Tim, so . . . out."

His image shrank away into darkness and after a moment

she pushed the call button on the log. When the query flashed onto the screen she keyboarded her PI and a request for clearance to the roof run. Simultaneously the screen showed *granted RR 10 lim,* and she heard the lock release in the door behind her.

She went quickly to the only other item of furniture in the room, a large metal closet-cabinet, and threw open a drawer. From a small box under a stack of shirts she took a thin, white tube, about the size of a child's crayon, which she slipped into a pocket of her uniform. Then she was gone, pulling the door snug behind her, soundless on her light, traction-tread field boots.

Two clerks, a man and a woman, boarded the elevator with her. As always Tima kept her eyes on the floor and gathered herself into a stone. It was one of the first things she had learned as a child, how to bear any pain, any terror, without moving or crying out. How to grow into the mountain underfoot and be blind, deaf, and unfeeling as its granite heart.

Because she could feel their intense hostility. Especially the woman's. It was like a flaming brand swung near her face. The piksi women often loathed her with a ferocity she had never sensed in another living thing. At close quarters, as in this elevator, she had to work hard to quell her impulse to flee or bare her teeth in warning.

The men, on the other hand, usually wanted to consume all of her, but they, too, kept their feelings hidden. Like this man, still talking with his companion, laughing a little and skipping his eyes over Tima with each turn of his head. His murderous, unhealthy lust was as plain to her as if he stood over her with a knife or chain, his little rod quivering in anticipation. He aroused in her no urge to run—in fact the danger here was in letting go her laughter—for she knew she could, in a quick snare of arm and twist of body, break his neck.

But the effort of withdrawing into herself taxed her, at a time when she needed her resources, so she was glad when the two got out onto the observation deck. She was alone the rest of the ride, and when the doors snapped open finally to reveal the roof garden, she almost cried out in surprise and joy, for the area seemed deserted.

The trees and shrubs and flower beds were carefully tended

to look untended, growing on variously shaped mounds and swales of topsoil. She took one of the winding paths across the roof, inhaling deeply the scents of bay and evergreen and rose. Of course they were all piksi plants, but she reveled in them anyway. They—and the birds—were her salvation. She had first risen out of the coma induced by her capture when a researcher, on a whim, had pushed her gurney into a garden. Dim as they were, her doctors had soon grasped how much her performance depended on daily exposure to the outdoors, and ever since, she had enjoyed access to this area, one of only four patches of green on the whole base.

She bowed and murmured briefly before the oldest tree, a tiny, crooked pine, and then hurried across the track to the safety railing that bounded the garden. The top portion of the railing was made of clear, curved plastic, impossible to climb, and through it she could see the runways and docking ports, the office and maintenance buildings of Insec, and beyond these a flat, hazy expanse of plain. Roads cut the plain into great trapezoidal blocks, and to the east a city was staked along the horizon under a smudged sky.

An inspection craft was just taking off from the rear runway, its wide, hooked wings folded back to reduce friction in the lower atmosphere. With a soft hush it angled up sharply and began to diminish into the blue. It was the four o'clock patrol, which would investigate anomalies turned up in the last four hours of satellite surveillance. They were still looking for bears, she knew, though dozens had already been tranqued and tested with no matchup yet.

Smiling, she waited for the little thunder roll of the inspector craft to fade away. She was alternately scanning the horizon and watching the nearby video camera which swept slowly back and forth on its mount in a dwarf pear tree. For about four seconds her upper body would be concealed by a fan of leaves, leaves which she had spent weeks teasing and talking to.

Finally she glimpsed something above the distant plain, the merest point or pulse of light. She concentrated her vision and in a moment saw it again, a fleck, a glancing reflection from some turning surface. She removed the slender, white tube from her pocket, concealing it in her palm. When the video camera reached the right position she lifted it swiftly and blew hard into it, her eyes shut and her cheeks distended.

The hollow leg bone vibrated so rapidly she felt it only as a generalized sensation of energy, as if the soul of the great bird had momentarily flown back into this one small strut from its former dwelling. The sound was a thin, shrill note, gone instantly in the wind, and before the camera swept her again Tima had hidden the whistle in her hands.

She stared at a point just above the horizon. After perhaps a minute she saw the flickering, nearer now. It was late afternoon sunlight, glancing from the spread wings of a vulture. Twice the flashes came. After a short glide the bird hooked, staightened, and hooked again.

She waited for the lens to vanish once more behind the clump of leaves and then blew twice into the bone, varying the pitch. This time the vulture shifted immediately in the wind, tacking and wheeling. It could see her now, she knew, and so she pocketed the whistle again and stretched as if loosening her muscles, lifting her spread hands high. She flexed her fingers, waved and crossed her hands. Her head was thrown back and she seemed to be laughing thoughtlessly, enjoying sheer movement in the open air.

The vulture responded, sliding, banking, and occasionally stroking with his wings. Far out on the plain, almost to the dark, jagged edge of the city, another of the great birds, hanging motionless over a Thruway, saw this movement and broke away to mime it. And miles beyond that, at the base of a range of foothills, a third picked up the pattern, and in a canyon cut into the flank of the first mountains a fourth. . . .

6

BAXTER ALWAYS HELD THAT THE ONE VIRTUE OF LIVING IN a remote suburb was the time it gave him for reading on the Bulletbus. And readers, he further held, were an endangered species. He meant by that paper-readers, people who still enjoyed the rustle of pages and the smell of ink.

Most of his companions on the ride homeward peered into the fold-up screens of their lap computers or wore the new compact virtuals—bubble helmets that delivered a miniholo directly into the skull. Baxter thought the bubbles ridiculous—they made people look like giant eggs with limbs—and also unhealthy, despite the manufacturers' claims that images could be aligned three inches from the eye without risk. He preferred to glance up now and then at the real world, even if it was only to observe covertly his fellow passengers, before returning to muse over some article in *Newstime*.

The magazine was the last of the old-fashioned weekly journals, which of course had not for generations published anything new or timely. Nowadays they specialized in commentary by various authorities, philosophers, gossips, and wags. Baxter liked the quaint style of these opinionated scribblers, their tendency to fulminate and apostrophize. He styled himself as a bit of an eccentric, a true conservative, an antiquarian of sorts. Not, of course, like the fanatic fools who were agitating for a return to primitivism, to the absurd dreams of the past.

Certainly not like the young man sitting across the aisle, who had been staring at Baxter in a familiar way ever since they left the terminal. This young man affected a briefcase and wore his hair at the absolute maximum tolerable length. He also was a paper-reader and carried a cumbersome old book with a tattered cover. Baxter had little doubt the young man belonged to one of those radical organizations calling for all sorts of demonstrations and reforms. The Ecominis or Retros. Believers in having less, throwing away more, and doing nothing. Perhaps this one imagined he could recruit a new convert or wangle a contribution, simply because Baxter was by himself and a fellow reader, a small man with thick glasses who might be taken advantage of.

I'll set him straight, Baxter told himself sternly, if he says a word. There's a world of difference between actually advocating a return to chaos and indulging in a little harmless nostalgic browsing. One can appreciate a funny old myth, some scrap of superstitious nonsense, but to pretend to *believe*. . . . Sometimes Baxter wondered if censorship might not be a good idea. It took forty thousand years, after all, to escape from barbarism, but there were people now ready to rush back into it overnight.

He frowned in the direction of the young man and tried to return to *Newstime*. But here, too, he was uncomfortable. He was in the middle of an essay by a retired member of the Council, a self-styled social theorist, who was ranting on about the recent failures of the Conservative NorthAm government. This critic went to an opposite extreme, and wanted to overthrow every policy older than five minutes. The writer had taken as his text the sensational hunting accident involving the Energy official and his son, arguing that outmoded, elitist Preserve policies were responsible for the tragedy.

Baxter read:

Like their swooning sentimental ancestors who argued for the "natural" (do nothing) approach to all things, the current Con gang seems to feel little Ronald Drager's disappearance can be overlooked as a rare fluke. They would have us forget that this is not the first such incident. And that some scientists suspect a pattern in these attacks involving interspecies collaboration. And that despite several investigative patrols no trace of the bear or the boy has been found.

Meantime our long-suffering average yoyo is beginning to wonder whether "management" is Conlingo for disaster. For our leaders are still pouring money and personnel into the bankrupt policy of patrol and contain, while Ginks are still the all-time favorite sport for Conservative squires. We have even heard rumors that certain high officials have caught some and trained them as pets. At public expense, of course.

The Federation, slow as it is, is aware of the challenge. It is time, we think, for a review of the Preserve system. Progressives must take their stand. We grieve for the Drager family, but they have made our point. For starters, no more privileged Preserves. Then, sweep the border clean. If the Creatures of Night cannot be driven out, then they must go the way of the Bronto—

"Can you believe this guy? This rockenroll about Creatures of Night and the average yoyo?"

Baxter sat bolt upright, startled. Engrossed in the argument, he had not noticed the young man leaning across the aisle to spy into the pages of the magazine. Such impoliteness left him momentarily speechless. Reflexively he pulled the *Newstime* closer to his chest.

"I read it already anyway," the young man went on, grinning. "I've read everything about this case, the missing kid. Wanna know my theory?" He nodded to supply his own invitation. "Kid panicked when the bears charged. Ran off and wandered around up there in the rocks and fell down a crack. Ginks had nothing to do with it." He looked triumphantly at Baxter, who noticed now that the man's necktie was not real, but only a photograph printed on his shirtfront as a joke.

"Well," Baxter said. He compressed his mouth to signal his extreme displeasure. "I really wouldn't care to say." The man was clearly a mountebank of some sort, or perhaps deranged. Best to ignore him.

"I would," the young man said with a satisfied air. "Somebody had better. I mean, the stuff going on these days is *outrageous,* you know? The Progs are right about that at least. The Fed, oh boy, is 'aware of challenge.' Ha ha ha. The Fed, my ass."

Baxter's head jerked as if he had been slapped, and he shut the magazine. The young man waited, expectant, and in a moment Baxter found his tongue.

"Really!" he said. "That is . . . unwarranted. Unwarranted, if you will pardon me, sir. There are problems right now, everyone knows. There are always—have been always—problems. But the Federation. . . ." He stopped, gasping a little, unsure which aspect of this vast and sacred subject to broach first.

"Oh yeah, we all know." The young man put on an expression of exaggerated, earnest reverence. "The Great War breaks out. The big boom-boom, back and forth. Only down south of course, through proxies. Didn't want to blow up our *own* selves first. Then our great leaders see their mistake at the last second and pull back from the brink. We form the Fed. We outlaw big boom-booms. We seal off the battlefield wasteland. Good folk up here, bad freako mutants down there. We're the Triumph of Civilization. What a load of *crap.*"

"But that war was . . . was. . . ." Baxter controlled himself. He had decided the young man was very likely a mental patient. It would do little good to point out the obvious to him. He glanced furtively around the bus but no one was looking their way. The bubbleheads couldn't look anyway, of course. These plastic ovae loomed over the seat backs, mocking Baxter with their bright, blank surfaces.

"Horrible? Unthinkable? The Final Holocaust?" The young man laughed, doubling over red-faced in genuine mirth. "Sure, sure, worship the Fed." He extended his arms and raised his head as if to begin prostration. "Oh brilliant ones! Oh genius! Let's *not* destroy the world. We've blown off one hemisphere, let the other—ours, of course—be saved! Oh joy!" He dropped his arms and leered at Baxter. "And how did we get into this situation in the first place, ladies and gentlemen? These very same noble leaders, right? But okay, admit our ass is saved one way or the other. So now where are we? Hey? Where are we?" He leaned still further toward Baxter, his thin, sharp face full of a malicious eagerness.

"I," said Baxter with careful precision, "am on Bulletbus forty-seven." He examined his watch. "In thirteen minutes I shall be at Olive Terrace, where I shall get out. And I am grateful, most grateful, to the Federation for that privilege. I don't say things couldn't be better, but I have no intention of returning to an age of violence. Some people seem to forget how close the human race came to . . . to caves and raw meat and—"

"But wouldn't it taste good, though?" The young man's expression seemed to Baxter positively demonic. His eyes burned and his lips were drawn back over small, yellowed teeth. "Something *real*, friend. Big hunk of bloody pig leg and a nice warm fire and maybe a little Gink—"

"*No!*" Baxter held the rumpled *Newstime* tight to his chest, as if it were a shield, and pressed himself as deeply into his seat and as far away from the young man as possible. "This is . . . I beg your pardon. . . ."

"No? So back to Olive Terrace and the little wifey and maybe kiddies too? Got a little spot of yard, a little woodshop in the basement, friend? Watch a little holo before beddy-bye?" The young man glanced out the window of the bus and made a quick, inclusive gesture.

They were above ground, passing Hawthorne Hills with its contoured lanes, recessed condos, and strips of greenery surrounding the central mall. Shelter and food, order and light. The gift of PacRim culture: the maximum number in the minimum space, at average comfort (defined by a complex set of equations).

"Go to sleepy litt-ah ba-yee-bee," sang the young man hoarsely. "When you wake you patty-patty cake and your stupid litt-ah life is o-o-ver." He beamed at Baxter. "Thanks to the Fed. Or the Cons or the Progs. They're all together on this one, friend. They all think they can take care of us. Illusions, friend. All illusions." He seized the tattered old book on the seat beside him and lifted it so Baxter could read the title on the spine: *Ancient Battles*. Then he flopped the book open and held it out so Baxter could see.

A miniature videogame occupied the interior, its tiny squirts and darts of luminescence hidden by false borders made to look like pages. The young man laughed in a swift, coughing burst at the sight of Baxter's face, then shut the book with a crack. "They are not what they seem," he said mysteriously. "Listen!"

Baxter held his breath. Certainly the young man was on some kind of illegal stim, or combination of chemicals. Baxter's strategy now was to remain silent and move as little as possible, keeping his own expression calm and neutral with a minimum of eye contact. There was no sound but the rapid ticking of electronic sensors that kept the bus in its lane and properly spaced.

"Too fast," the young man said. "They have to adjust more often."

It was true. Baxter had noticed it for months—or was it a year now? Thruway traffic had gotten more erratic, and there had been some serious computer errors, bad pileups. He glanced toward the driver's compartment, saw that the woman was keyboarding.

"The paint is flaking off the idols," the young man went on. His manner was sober now, conspiratorial. "Cracks. Dust. Lies. There's so much to tell you, friend. And here's your station coming up in a couple minutes or so. This whole thing about the kid and the bears is just a diversion, another illusion they want us to believe. Control is what they want, lover, *control.*"

The young man waved a hand swiftly before Baxter's face. "Hey—I was right about the woodshop and the yard, no? Look at me, man. It's okay. No harm intended. We have the Fed, you say. But the Fed has *us*. Me too. Keeps us alive, keeps us healthy. Oh yeah. Half the people in here have got plastic joints or a baboon heart or a sheep stomach. What for? Because the Fed is so compassionate? Because it needs them?" The young man brayed in ridicule. "To show its *control,* man. That's why they hate the Ginks, lover. That's why they keep looking for this Drager kid. They got out of control, see."

Very carefully Baxter was folding his magazine and slipping it into one pocket. In a few seconds he knew he would feel the bus begin its deceleration. His hands were shaking slightly, but not with anticipation. This conversation had disturbed certain thoughts he had hidden for a long time. Shameful thoughts.

"They even control your words, the way you think. They tried to rename the plants and animals scientifically. Whereas people used to be named after animals, you know. Great idea, hey? You could be Lone Wolf or White Otter or Crazy Horse. Me, I got a bird name—and guess what, you're the first person I'm telling it to—I'm Snowy Owl. They're extinct. How's that? Ha!"

The young man rose from his seat and stretched out his arms, crooking and waving them like a bird's. He bugged his eyes and pursed his mouth tight, cocking his head at Baxter. Baxter heard the tempo of the sensors change and a moment later felt a slight lurch as the bus began to reduce speed. A man two seats away removed his holobubble and shook sweat-dampened hair as if emerging from a shower.

"There used to be expressions," the young man said, still waving his arms. The seat-belt light began to pulse over his head. "Lion-hearted. Don't give a rat's ass. For the birds." His face lit up with an insane glee. "For the birds!" he cried. "This whole system is *for the birds!*"

Others had also removed the bubbles or folded up their lap computers and now turned toward the commotion the young man was making. He was staggering in the aisle, arms spread as if to glide, croaking at the top of his lungs to drown out the auditory alarm which had gone off over his seat. The porthole to the driver's compartment opened and the uniformed woman looked out.

"Miss!" Baxter shouted and raised his hand frantically to beckon her, warn her that she was dealing with a disordered, potentially dangerous personality.

The woman looked anxious and after a moment turned back inside toward her control panel. Then Baxter heard a very loud sound, a tremendously bright, brittle sound, and there was a sparkling explosion at the front of the bus. Bits of light were spraying toward him, pattering down, tinkling on the floor of the aisle. Then came a great wind that tore papers and loose coats from the luggage rack and sent them gyrating about the interior. The bus slowed suddenly and swerved, jerking its passengers against their safety belts and hurling the young man off his feet.

When the bus finally halted in the emergency port, Baxter sat stupefied, his face drained of all color. He was not staring at the gravel-sized particles of glass on the floor or listening to the roar of traffic, coming in loud now through the shattered windshield. He was watching the bits of fluff floating down slowly along with stray scraps of paper. One rested on his knee and he saw that it was a feather, a golden shade at the base with bands of darker gray leading toward an iridescent blue-green tip.

Although all around him people were jabbering—someone was even crying, apparently hysterical—Baxter heard what the driver said when she emerged from her compartment, glittering fragments of glass on her cap and shoulders, a red line on one cheek.

"Flew right *at* me," she was saying dazedly, "the kind with the white band around its neck . . . long tail. . . . Please, people, let's be calm . . . a big bird. . . ."

On the floor then Baxter saw the bird's head. It had come off above the white band, or else the driver was mistaken. But the eye was open, bright and black as a wet seed. As he watched, the beak opened and closed in a final, soundless cry.

7

WHEN THE SHADOW FLITTED OVER THE EARTH AT THEIR feet the Ginks cringed for a moment, then a few looked up and uttered hissing cries. Ronald saw the wide-winged shape glide between rows of the plantation trees and recognized it. Only a common buzzard. Its naked knob of a head cocked, and apparently finding something of interest, it banked and returned to balance for a few moments directly above them. Then it began to slip and weave a little back and forth in the invisible current of air, the feathers at its wingtips spread like fingers.

The Ginks were excited. They formed a hurried circle and gestured at the poised bird. Ronald wondered at their simplicity, decided this was an example of the superstition which had once kept even the human race in a condition of backwardness and ignorance.

Earlier, when one of the group located a heap of odoriferous fur, the shell of a long-deceased skunk, and tied it on a length of vine, and again when two others made up a bundle of light, brittle thornbushes, he had correctly guessed that these devices were to be dragged behind them to hide their tracks and scent. These strategies showed a crude intelligence, but now the whole company was wasting valuable time and risking discovery by halting here to jabber. This, after they had painted him so carefully and warned him by gestures that they must now move rapidly, over dangerous ground, to avoid detection.

Most of the day they had crept through plantations, each identical to the last except for the change, from tract to tract, in the height of the trees. Ronald could see no landmarks in this bewildering sameness—the long, straight rows of conical trees, the sprinkler lines in every other row, an access road every fourth, and at each section corner a small utility building.

But the Ginks appeared to know where they were going, though they doubled back often or took odd, zigzag routes across certain areas, and twice they had to follow long detours to avoid harvesting crews. Ronald caught a glimpse of the huge humpbacked cutter that snipped off the trees and stripped away their branches, then stacked the logs in bundles. The bundles in turn were picked up by big tractor wagons that followed like a line of hungry children in a cloud of dust.

Ronald had seen it all before, tagging along on his father's inspections, but this time, even at a distance, the scene seemed strange and a little frightening. The grunting and roaring of the cutter, the whine of the choppers that turned branches to mulch, the rumbling of the logs into the wagons—after days of ice-bound silence such cacophonous racket made him flinch, and like the Ginks he moved at a stealthy trot to give this turmoil a wide berth. Only later did it occur to him that he had ignored his best opportunity to escape. He was surprised at how readily, how thoughtlessly, he had gone along, sprinting and then crouching where his naked, painted body would be invisible in the shadows.

Even here, now, he felt a twinge of impatience waiting for this chattering conference to end. They had to get on. But to what? And why did he care? His impatience turned into a small pang of fear. What was happening to him? Was he so stupefied with fatigue and grief that he was forgetting who he was and what had happened to him? That some of the Ginks now smiled at him and stuck out their tongues did not make up for what they had done, and his promise—was it a promise, exactly?—surely did not bind him to assist in his own abduction. . . .

Behind him Mata wheezed and shifted her position. Ronald realized he must have done something again to make her uneasy—picked at a scab on his knee or pulled at his hair. She had been restive ever since they first entered the plantation and the male had refused to follow. The two growled and feinted at each other for five minutes before the other bear set out at a lope, angling back toward the snowy peaks. Mata had appeared confused, running first one way and then another, and several times tried to nudge Ronald with her shoulder, as if directing him to retrace his steps, before finally settling down again at his side.

"Hush, Mata," he whispered. "I'm not running away. Just thinking."

He had begun talking to her during their rests, lying against her warm, thick fur and listening to the symphony of her digestion. It calmed him to hear his own voice, normal and drowsy, and allowed him to order and consider the fragmentary thoughts that came to him while they trekked through the night. The old she-bear did not seem to mind, and even appeared to listen to the syllables resonating against her ribs.

"I just wonder why everything seems to go on the same, outside you, even when things—terrible things, I mean—have happened to you. I wonder if Teeklo—"

As if he had heard his name, Teeklo turned and beckoned to Ronald urgently. The conference had reached some decision, apparently, for the Ginks were silent, their expressions determined. Ronald got up and strolled toward the group, deliberately nonchalant. If they could waste ten minutes in idle fussing over a vulture, why should he hurry?

Teeklo seized him by the shoulder as soon as he was within reach. "They are coming after you," he said with hoarse irritation. "You forget? You are with *us* now! A Pobla, even a boy—but never mind. They are coming, goddamn it son-ofabitch, and we are still six hours from our first tunnel. We must split up. You—"

"Who's coming?" Ronald stubbornly kept his eyes averted. "You were all so busy with that old bird and . . ."

Teeklo's grip tightened. Old Kapu said something behind them, sounding peevish. "You know nothing. Those birds can write in the sky and they tell us to *move*." Teeklo shoved Ronald away and indicated with a jab of his lance which way they would go, toward the sun. "All of us, *dako*, are risking life for you."

Only three others accompanied Teeklo, Ronald, and Mata. Kapu, Ap—the doctor-clown—who dragged the dead skunk, and another with the bundles of thornbush. The rest of the company went south, leaving a column of faint tracks in the gray plantation soil.

Ronald understood the main group was to act as a decoy, and he was all at once ashamed of his foot-dragging. It sobered him to think that the others were taking a mortal risk for his benefit. A moment later, he was aware of the ridiculous irony.

Here he was feeling guilty, as if it were bad manners not to crack along in one's own abduction. And yet. . . .

Every few kilometers Ap passed out a handful of broken dry leaves, and Ronald chewed his along with the others. He was barefoot and clad only in the scanty diaper made from the rags of his jumpsuit, so he felt essentially naked. His first embarrassment had given way to a secret, tentative enjoyment, a sense of lightness and freedom. The cool air on his bare skin and the warm dirt between his toes seemed to invigorate him. He felt he could keep moving for a long time, weightless as the wind, yet in sure contact with the earth.

His body felt completely alive, and he felt completely in that body. Even his cuts and bruises, the soreness of muscles, his general fatigue, were vaguely pleasant. Every sensation seemed strangely fresh and exhilarating. It occurred to him that he could not remember being outdoors with no clothes, even as an infant, and it amazed him that no one had apparently known about this simple tonic.

The tree plantations were giving way to vast blocks of orchard and cropland, and as they descended the air grew warmer and drier. Sprinklers were going in some fields, and Ronald longed to run through them, for he was sweating and very thirsty. Instead they undertook long detours to avoid the wet ground, where they might leave tracks.

They were running most of the time now, from ditch to culvert to fence corner, or whatever cover they could spy out. Ronald understood that these were the minutes of maximum danger. Mata groaned with anxiety as she humped along beside him, and Teeklo's face was still and concentrated as a mask. They saw many long, blowing trails of dust from utility and patrol vehicles, and time and again they had to race back to a hiding place they had just left. Once they had to steal around an entire five-kilometer field because the tankers were spraying, lumbering back and forth in the air overhead. Some of the white mist drifted down on them, stinging Ronald's eyes and making his throat raw.

When they neared the border the haze over the fields turned dusty rose in the last sunlight. The land now appeared a paler gray, and for the first time Ronald saw signs of neglect: in the orchards, an occasional dead tree or holes where trees had been, and in the stands of corn and cotton and hay, patches of yellow weeds. Potholes marred the access roads and some of the utility sheds had fallen in.

Beyond a field of brown, ragged cornstalks he could see the wide strip of bare earth and the white line of the wall. Every five hundred meters along the crown of this wall, he knew, there was a scanner, and every thousand, a guard tower with either a robot unit or a border squad.

Kapu led them along the edge of the cornfield, crouching and stabbing often at the ground with his lance. Ronald guessed he was looking for the entrance to the tunnel Teeklo had mentioned, though he could not imagine a passageway stretching so far, underneath the whole field and then the wide bare strip and wall.

He was too exhausted to imagine anything in particular. It had been a long time since he had sipped water from the skin bag Teeklo carried, or chewed any of the leaves—which had, he realized, both abated his hunger pangs and upheld his spirits. Now he caught himself stumbling and reeling, almost asleep as he walked.

Kapu bent suddenly to one knee and began to make an odd squeaking sound, sucking air past his pursed lips. The Gink dragging the thornbush did likewise, and Ap dropped his rag of dead skunk and joined in. This cacophony of high-pitched squealing made Mata restless and put Ronald's teeth on edge. It seemed dangerously loud, and even as this thought crossed his mind Ronald saw a glint of light from the nearest tower, a half kilometer distant.

The cornstalks beside them rustled and two narrow, whiskered snouts jabbed forth just at Kapu's bended knee. Immediately he reached in his shoulder pouch and tossed out two handfuls of small, dark kernels, and the creatures advanced into full view. For a fraction of a second Ronald thought they were dogs of some exotic breed—slick, fat, sharp-nosed beasts built close to the ground. But they were rats, the largest he had ever seen, with blotchy hides and long, thick, pink tails. They devoured the food with a steady, audible crunching of small, very sharp teeth.

Ronald looked at the tower again and saw that the tiny, intense point of light still burned. At the base of the wall before the tower was a low, heavily reinforced structure, one wall of which now folded itself smoothly aside to expose a square of darkness.

"Look out!" he cried, pointing. Teeklo turned, followed his gesture, and saw the Leopard patrol vehicle advance out of the cavern. He called out urgently in the Gink tongue.

Kapu did not move from his crouch and his concentrated scrutiny of the two rats, who sniffed now at his hands. He was still making the sucking squeal, and one of the creatures reared and answered, baring its teeth, before wheeling and wriggling away into the cornstalks, the other rat only a step behind.

Then all of them crashed into this miniature yellow forest, following Kapu, who was following the rats. Over the clattering of the dry stalks Ronald could hear the whine of the Leopard's power plant. It would be on them in fifteen seconds and could fire in less than that if the crew were not thinking capture. He was behind Mata, who battered a wide path with her great shoulders, but he was lagging, for he had no reserves of strength left.

Ahead he saw an opening where the rats dove under a loose heap of fallen stalks. Kapu and the other two Ginks reached the heap and jerked it aside; for it was, Ronald saw, woven together as a unit in order to serve as a cover for the large hole underneath. In quick succession the three dropped out of sight into the hole, feet first.

Teeklo reached the opening next and paused, his hands spread and reaching back toward Mata and Ronald as if to rake them to him. His mouth was open and Ronald knew he was yelling, urging them on; but the noise from the patrol craft now overwhelmed everything, a paralyzing deep-toned shriek that seemed as much inside his skull as without.

Ronald looked over his shoulder in a reflex of fright. Simultaneously he saw the nose of the Leopard, the turret swiveling to track him, and something struck him on the hip and spun him off his feet. Momentum carried him through two somersaults and brought him to the edge of the shaft into the earth.

He felt Teeklo's rough hands under his arms, hoisting him and dragging his feet over the lip of the opening. Once more he looked at the Leopard. He saw Mata's back as she reared before the hurtling vehicle, saw the laser's pulse of brightness and then the abrupt distortion of space made by the exiting missile. Mata's back opened, unraveled in a skein of red and white threads. She seemed to expand and yet in the same moment collapse onto the earth like an empty coat.

Then this scene was wiped away by a curtain of darkness, rising paradoxically from the bottom of his field of vision. He had dropped into the hole and was sliding down an incline on a fairly smooth surface. Above him the faint light from the opening winked and small clods cascaded around his shoulders. Teeklo, apparently, had jumped in behind him.

There was a solid thud and a brief increase in the light from above, a new rush of clods and pebbles, some of them smoking. He heard Teeklo curse. Then he collided with an earthen floor and felt hands pulling him aside. A moment later Teeklo bumped and rattled to a stop on the same floor.

Someone lit some kind of taper, a sputtering, greasy yellow flame. By its light Ronald saw they were in a chamber with three or four passages cut into its rock walls. Kapu and Ap were crouched on the floor, each feeding one of the rats directly from an open palm. After the ping of the last pebble from Teeklo's descent there was an eerie quiet, broken only by the brisk crunch of rats' teeth and quick, harsh breathing.

The biggest rat finished its portion and repeated the action of rising on its hind quarters and then turning away. This time it darted into one of the side passages and stopped, only the heavy, pink tail protruding back into the chamber. Kapu seized the tail in one hand and hissed at the rest of them over his shoulder. Teeklo spoke to Ronald as the old Gink crawled out of sight into the passageway.

"We split again," he said. "Keep hold of me." He took Ronald's hand and clapped it on his shoulder, then moved to follow Kapu.

The Gink holding the taper blew it out just before following the second rat into another of the passageways. Ronald was left to shuffle after Teeklo along a corridor just wide enough for one. He was constantly scraping and bumping against the rough walls, and cold water splashed under his bare feet.

Twice he felt a faint shock along the tunnel walls, and each time Teeklo cursed in the darkness and hurried even faster. The Leopard must have called a support vehicle with an augur and crawl missiles. Ronald was still light-headed and weak from the wave of panic that had passed over him, but he no longer felt paralyzed. The darkness resolved into whorls and seething dots of intense color, where he saw again what had happened, imagined what he had not quite seen.

"Mata," he whispered aloud. He saw her rear up, her tremendous shoulders dissolving into streamers of glistening red and white, her sudden shrinking and falling.

Teeklo's back flexed under his fingers. "Gone. And for a little piksi. You had better learn how to run now, Dako. Because none of us would do that for you."

Ronald shuffled on, saying nothing. He bit his lips and worked to keep from seeing the terrible vision again. He was glad for the darkness and the rude shock of the stone walls around him, for the pain in his bruised limbs. It seemed right, after such horrors, that he should be buried here under the earth and far from the light of day.

8

"HONEYCOMB ISN'T THE RIGHT WORD," POST CAPTAIN Quarles said, gesturing at the crater. "Honeycombs are regular. This is like a crazy maze in a carnival. A thousand entrances, a thousand exits. And ten thousand dead ends. They do it that way deliberately." He glanced swiftly at Tima, standing at attention behind PJ.

They were in a dry cornfield on the brink of a pockmark of slumped, raw earth. An odor of hot metal still hung in the air. With a pencil Skiho was idly poking at a blunt, curved little spike lying on the clipboard he held against his middle like a small table. "An old girl," he said. "Long past cubbing, I would have said."

PJ was smiling at Captain Quarles. An easy, comradely smile. "The patrols?" he suggested. "Maybe you could summarize?"

Quarles scowled at the horizon. "You wear out augurs, you wear out recruits, and you try to track the sneaky little bastards . . . I mean. . . ." He expelled a breath in a huff of disgust. "Listen, you guys have spent time on the border, right? So you know Central never understands our probs here in the field. I'm telling you, for three years I've filed reports on what's happening—the tunnel complexes and raids and kamikaze birds and last month we lost a brand-new Jav, a supertech 504 hunter-killer, just checked and cleared. *Brand-fucking-new*, guys!"

Skiho had sealed the blunt spike into a plastic bag and clipped it to his board. "Maybe a senile old sow bear got it," he said brightly.

PJ shot him a warning glance. "Ouch," he said to Quarles. "How?" He seemed all sympathy.

Quarles looked hangdog. His hands had become active, wiping themselves on his fatigues, adjusting his belt and holster. PJ could see alcohol had burned the man down to nerve and bone. Tiny purple veins gave his narrow nose a glow, and now and then his whole head twitched slightly, always to the right, toward the Post a half kilometer away. Responding, PJ assumed, to the tug of a bottle stashed somewhere in his quarters.

"How? *How?*" Quarles laughed briefly, bitterly. "Ask her." Once more his eyes struck Tima and bounced away. "I tell you they're digging them faster than we can find them. Then they'll shoot a big one straight up, couple hundred feet maybe, until it's just *under* one of their trunk lines. They lure a patrol down that line—send a few fast raiders as a decoy —and the vehicle breaks through the crust into the big shaft. They narrow it just enough at the bottom so the tracks hang up and the augur's got nothing to bite but air. A bunch of them are positioned in a side tunnel right at that point and if the crew is green—listen, free-falling two hundred feet can scare a kid shitless—and they forget to close the ports—"

"The Ginks pop the turret full of, let's see . . . tobacco spray or pigpepper or maybe even wasps?" Skiho seemed to be thinking aloud, to himself.

Quarles stared at him. "Yeah," he said. "Yeah. So you read my report?"

"No," Skiho lied. He, too, smiled. "I just practice thinking the way they think." He turned to PJ. "We can have the captain run these samples in. Get the geneprints back to-morrow. But I say this old gal is the one. Let's move."

"Shit," Quarles said. He looked again toward the white wall and beyond. "If he was the Drager kid he was sure a filthy little bugger. No clothes or shoes. I didn't know . . . I mean, the driver never said—"

"Hey, it's all right." PJ gripped the captain's thin shoulder briefly. "Tough job. I've been there, I know. You did what you could."

And damn little it was, he thought. *A whole day lost. And you could have had him. Could have called Insec and been quietly promoted, with a fat bonus. Instead of reassigned to jerkduty, which is where my report will put you. Just in time for Thanksgiving.*

He continued to beam his encouraging smile at Quarles, one frontier warrior to another. "If you could expedite these samples . . . and just not mention in your Dailies that our research group happened to find them. . . ."

Quarles gave him a sardonic, reproachful roll of the eyes. Of course he knew they were not really a Bioteam. He was stuck in a remote Ag province, overage for his rank and a little too fond of the juice, maybe, but he knew the score. A Gink in a Fed uniform with a clearance card? Anything that weird had to be top pri Insec. Anyway, everybody knew strange shit was flying these days. Even the new recruits had heard the rumors of a V-study, and he, a regular line captain, had actually filed a top secret report or two.

Samples of which he had revealed to this pair in the first hour of their interview. He thought he should establish his credentials, even though having the Gink standing around listening made him nervous. His report dealt with how before rainstorms, flickers had been chiseling the insulation off wires to the videoscanners on the wall. The bare wires shorted out when wet, and that was when the raiders crossed.

PJ had pretended to marvel, though he and Skiho had known that bit of information for some time. They had, as a matter of course, read the whole file on Quarles and his re-gion. A tiny piece in a larger and crazier pattern.

Birds had been going goofy for about three years. Whole flocks of waterfowl, their pattern so tight they looked like a great, pulsing inkblot, flew up the intake scoops of cargo craft.

And Quarles's flickers were by no means alone. Sapsuckers, yellowhammers, woodpeckers—anything with a spike to drive—had taken to drilling through plastic and light metal, shearing small wires and exposing larger ones. And some of the big fellows—raptors, herons, cranes, even the galliforms—were wheeling over Feederways and—there was no other way to express it—aiming themselves at vehicles, splattering themselves in suicide collisions that left emergency lanes clogged, traffic snarled, and drivers too rattled to go on.

"I hear what you're saying about the augurboats, Captain," PJ said, as they began to stroll toward Quarles's old 400 series, parked at the edge of the cornfield with its plant still idling. "Maybe if you could lend us a shielded hoverjob, we'll just park our copters with you on remote. If we need 'em, we'll call 'em." He did not bother to phrase the idea as a question. They all knew Quarles had no choice.

"Only have two X-4s in shape," the captain said, a little pettishly. He hadn't counted on any requisitions beyond simple resupply. "We'll be short—"

"We'll see you get a replacement. Within the week," Skiho said. PJ caught the undercurrent of cruel humor in his partner's tone. Quarles would find more than his vehicles being replaced.

"What about your . . . crew?" Quarles turned his head slightly, just enough to glimpse Tima behind them. "She sleep in a locker?"

PJ and Skiho laughed easily, politely, but said nothing. This was the kind of thing they both dreaded. They heard the smirk in the captain's voice, and they knew the story of the Gink in uniform—and a female at that—would be all up and down the border within a few days. Fat was a colossal fool to think his experiment would not stir up a typhoon of derision.

"So she's a tracker," Quarles went on, and laughed maliciously. "And runs a kitchen. Amazing. How do you guys handle it? I mean, I can't stop my finger from itching around her. Trigger finger, I mean." He winked lewdly at PJ.

"Regulations," PJ said easily.

"Sure." Quarles's grin widened. The laughable military code. "So you have to bring her back?"

It was of course the key question. Fornication with any other species was—on the books—a serious offense, entailing dishonorable discharge and a prison term. But every recruit knew that occasionally a patrol trapped a young Gink too inexperienced to put herself under and out. That could be sport for hours, even days, and safe enough as long as the men snuffed her afterward and kept their mouths shut.

"Afraid so." Skiho shrugged. He looked over his shoulder and saw that Tima had lagged, putting herself out of earshot. He looked at his clipboard and frowned.

"Too bad, guys. Big tits for a Gink, and not too greasy, either."

Quarles intended to shock, to make them remember how men on the border really talked, men on the line. His voice had grown harsher and cracked a little. He licked his lips and swaggered the last few strides to the old Javelin. He needed a drink, and he was losing patience with this creepy threesome. Some Con had sent this probe, he could tell. No guts for the job that had to be done. He had to send in their samples and give them the X-4 and not say a word, not a word about anything, but he didn't have to kiss ass, for Insec or anybody else.

"We'll walk back to our camp." PJ halted several yards shy of Quarles's vehicle, and Skiho nodded assent, his eyes already scanning the ground. "Maybe pick up another sample or two."

Quarles threw back the hatch and turned to regard them. His thin face was now a deep rose, heated with the unfamiliar exertion of self-control. "My guys have been all over this field," he said. "And the goddamn Ginks have pitfalls everywhere. I can't authorize any OV moves."

"We'll take the responsibility. Thanks for your assistance. Captain." PJ lifted two fingers in a gesture both casual and dismissive.

Quarles was raising one hand to reply in kind, but he arrested the movement and his expression suddenly changed. When PJ looked around he saw Tima standing at attention, her arm cocking the blade of her hand in a perfect, parade-ground salute. Her face was expressionless, remote: the face of an utterly devoted, fanatic volunteer. She was as trim and straight as a light field missile, cocked and tracking.

On the crown of her head, like an incongruous, frivolous ornament, sat a tiny bird with a green head and pale gold breast. In the momentary stillness the bird cheeped twice. Then Tima's arm snapped down to her side, and simultaneously, like a splinter of sunshine, the bird rose and arrowed into the sky directly over the Javelin.

"A-a-a-gh!" Quarles was striking himself on the collarbone, his teeth bared. PJ thought for a split-second that the man was having a fit. Then he saw the white streak on Quarles's shirtfront.

The captain recovered himself. He glared at Tima, at all of them. "Ah fuck it," he hissed. "Just *fuck it.*" He brushed once more at the white stain on his shirt, then twisted into the cockpit and slammed shut the hatch. The Javelin growled, swung smartly ninety degrees, and was off in a spray of shredded cornstalks.

Skiho was bent nearly double, whacking the clipboard on one thigh, and PJ found his whole frame shaken by a laugh that erupted from deep in his belly. They had been more wound up than he realized, after three days on this assignment. The presence of Tima, the strain of dealing with losers like Quarles, and the realization that the Drager boy had almost certainly gone under the wall—all these had curtailed their usual banter, the running jokes they invented to ease the pressure. Now all at once they were loose again, happy at their work, relishing the prospect of striking out tomorrow on a long probe into the Wastelands.

"Nicely executed run," Skiho said. He was looking speculatively at Tima. "Didn't know she commanded a bomber wing."

PJ grinned at his partner. "Think of what we could do with a flock of pigeons at a Prog caucus."

He, too, had been watching Tima covertly. There was no change in her earnest, devout expression. She continued to avoid looking at either of them directly. And yet—what was it? Some slight shift in posture or the way she carried the shaft of black hair between her shoulder blades. For a moment or two an easy, wordless familiarity had existed among the three of them, something like what developed among new recruits.

This last analogy brought a twinge of apprehension, and PJ twisted off the last of the smile on his lips. "Anyway," he went on briskly. "We won't get invited to the Post tonight for drinks, and we've got to check out the X-4 first thing tomorrow, so let's get back."

"Copy." Skiho glanced at his clipboard. "I'm still hoping to turn up a frag from another subject, so let's break some more rules. You guys go on and I'll snoop over this field a little more."

PJ met Skiho's glance, the intense, insolent blue eyes. Quarles would have a tag on them, probably. Their small infractions—separating on patrol, moving on foot without perms—would get back to Fat. And Fat would smile to himself and say nothing. The pleasure they knew in their line of work, PJ reflected, had a lot to do with the breaking of rules.

"All right," he said. "But don't keep us waiting for dinner."

"What's for?"

Skiho had already turned away, begun to scan the ground, when Tima finally answered. PJ noted her hesitation, and understood it. She knew she was being tested again.

"Veal parmesan, asparagus with fresh mayonnaise, wild rice, wheat roll, pear compote." Her voice was clear, neutral, precise. A bird call, PJ thought. Did she think about what she said, any more than a bird would?

"Seven?" The lilt of inquiry was machine perfect.

"Copy," Skiho said as if to himself, moving away now through the dry, rattling stalks. "Our little bombardier."

By the time they reached the old loading yard at the edge of the Post compound, PJ was tense again. They had set up their kitchen in the lee of a small hangar where the copters were docked, and unrolled their sleepsacks in the crew quarters of the same structure. Ostensibly all this was to keep up the pretense of being just another routine research team, bivouacking at the pleasure of the Post commander. In fact PJ preferred the privacy and simplicity of field quarters, the little routines of camp life.

The trouble was, with Tima along he had nothing to do. Setting up and breaking, cooking, logging the route and base stats—she was handling it all. Doing it perfectly, he had to admit. His only job, as the line official in charge of this Program Four Experimental Extension—Insec jabber for taking a Gink, alive and unrestrained, on patrol—was to log her performance daily into the onboard Capcomp, their locked and coded link to headquarters. So far he had marked a monotonous series of 100s.

Just now he was sitting in a folding chair with his back against the warm metal of the warehouse wall, the mini keyboard on his lap, watching her out of the corner of his eye. As usual she gave no sign of awareness that she was being observed. She was unfolding the foil corners of the foodpaks before sliding them into the wave oven. Lithe, quick, never a wasted motion. More like a mechanic than a cook, he thought. Or a surgeon.

But the bird crapping on Quarles. He should log that, he knew. Under *discipline*. Tima must have done it, of course. Fed the creature a few grains of some seed or provoked it somehow. Anyone with border experience knew the Ginks had such skills. But how had she done it? A half-dozen steps behind them, only a few seconds after he had glanced her way and seen nothing? It took two or three reinforcements to teach even the cleverest lab pigeon a simple new pattern.

Any administrator with code clearance would laugh at him, reading such a report. *Bird (see desc.) ob. on head of SE, took flight and released droppings (i.e., excreta) on Cpt. Richard Quarles, PC. Dlb. infrac. sug.* Such a note could also weaken his recommendation for Quarles's transfer. He would sound nasty and picky, as if acting on a personal grudge. PJ sighed and punched a key to open the last window: *Personal*. The Insec category for nagging hunches, intramural politics, confessions, whistle-blowing.

Here maybe he could say something more general, try to get down the bothersome feeling he had about Tima. She almost never looked directly at either of them, kept always to some task. On the trip in she ran a trainee flight simulation, practicing 45-degree hovers, or monitored the topo infra. Completely absorbed, PJ would have said, except that. . . . He expelled a breath audibly.

She had now finished setting up the portable table and positioning the magnetized dinnerware on its surface. She did not look at him, but paused momentarily over her open pack, before fishing out a towel and small toilet bag. It was maddening. PJ was sure—without knowing how he knew—that she read his exasperation perfectly in that single breath.

Tima moved away toward the solar shower stall at the rear

of the hangar shed. She was outlined against the flat, bare runway that rippled in its own heat waves, and beyond that, an expanse of hazy plain sectioned into tremendous blocks by utility roads. As she approached the corner of the building she shook her head. Her thick, black hair lashed once across her shoulders and then settled on her back like a live thing. At the same time her hand tugged at the zipper below her chin.

PJ had looked away from the keyboard in his lap. He heard the zipper start with a tiny, rasping exclamation, but then it seemed to hang up and her gait changed. He was reminded of an animal trying to free itself from some entanglement, shrugging off a net or leaping from a bog. The posture he had seen as precise and guarded was dissolving; or rather emerging out of it, almost snakelike, was an undulating, prehensile form. A form at once graceful, poised, and lazy.

At one level he knew these changes were insignificant. Tima had shaken her head and slowed her step, preoccupied by the balky zipper. She had exposed scarcely a handsbreadth of tan, smooth skin, just beginning to swell. Yet her movements were subtly different, so different he was at once startled and fascinated. He remembered all at once an odd bulge he had seen in one of her thigh pockets the morning after their departure from HQ, and he realized with a disorienting shock what it was. Her underwear. She rolled it tight into the pocket and wore nothing under her jumpsuit. Nothing at all.

The zipper began again; and for a half second PJ had the remarkable and exhilarating sensation that he was drawing it down effortlessly with an invisible power in his own eyes. He saw the swell clearly, a profile of one breast through the widening V of the suit. Time slowed to an infinitesimal crawl, yet she went on—she was almost to the corner of the building, soon to disappear—moving with the leisurely ooze of a big cat, her whole body apparent to him now beneath the tents and billows of fabric, as if the camouflage pattern of the cloth were indeed only leaves and shadows.

What he saw was, he realized only moments later, confused with what he imagined. She did not actually walk out of her uniform, as a deer steps out of a forest. She was not actually turning toward him, looking directly at him, finally, like a hungry animal. He did not actually feel her breath on his face, warm and spicy as the air from a zoological garden. But those images had already begun to blossom in his mind; and it seemed to him that Tima was slowing still more, lifting her head to look his way, as if she were a delayed holo following the pattern of his fantasy, when the alarm went off at the back of his mind.

Instantaneously, simultaneously, Tima shrank and ducked around the corner, the fluttering tail of her towel the last thing he saw of her. PJ had lunged forward, tilting his chair back on four legs with a bang. He was staring at the shimmering, dry seabed of the runway, the tiny green light on the wave oven, the table neatly set for three. In his chest there was a little thrum of panic. He opened his mouth to bark a command to Tima, summon her back for interrogation, but shut it again with an irritable snap.

For a second he had suspected a high-frequency bug. Some sublim mindbender, planted by a Prog mole to screw up the expedition. Or a crazy superexperiment Fat hadn't told them about. But that was surely paranoia. Bugs had a very short range and were limited—so far as he knew—to negative head stuff: insomnia, anxiety, bad dreams, and obsessive behavior.

What he had just felt had started out exciting, pleasurable, like some of the new quasi-hallucinogenic euphorstims. He shook his head and blinked. He needed a woman, that was all. He had taken this assignment right on the heels of a high-level suicide case, no time out at the beach for a couple of months, and it was getting to him. For a fleeting few seconds he tried to think about Jasho, the PacRim beauty he had been seeing for almost a year, but in his mind's eye she seemed at a great distance and strangely inanimate, like a doll seen through a reversed telescope.

And drowsing in the sun against the warm metal skin of the building. That had made him vulnerable. He became aware of the flashing monitor on his keyboard; apparently he had inadvertently struck some keys in righting it as he pushed away from the wall. The Personal window was still open, but the pulsing message now read:

INVALID SIGNAL
Encrypt/Cancel/Reenter?

He grimaced and his hands poised over the keys. Now what? His mind was blank, and then, gradually, he knew a growing sense of . . . the preposterous. He had nothing to report after all but birdshit and bawdy fantasies. Two days of restiveness, tension, unfounded hunches about a half-grown Gink bitch—it amounted to zero. The important thing was they had picked up the Drager kid's trail, were moving out tomorrow morning into the Wastelands. Things were on course. He smiled to himself.

The shower had gone on some minutes ago. All at once PJ heard a low huffing sound and abruptly the rush of water ceased. There was a moment of stillness, then a clattering and the sound of bootsteps approaching.

"Woo! Taken by surprise, man." Skiho came around the corner grinning, fanning his clipboard as if to put out a blaze. "Thought it was you in there so I popped the curtain back to tell you what I ran across. Spooked our little bombardier."

Black Jack looked nothing like his name. Fair and ruddy, his eyes the pale, hot blue of an alcohol flame, he seemed oddly to have grown a little larger and louder in the last hour. His cocky, abrasive cheer jarred PJ, who nevertheless made an effort to smile.

"Put together *very* well, if you like the compact type, which I do." Skiho flourished the clipboard dramatically and beamed at PJ. "But forget the beautiful behinds to be found in *lapsis*. I got some news, pal."

PJ kept the smile screwed to his face. "Yes?"

Skiho finally registered the tension in his companion. He cocked his head, quizzical and sympathetic. "You okay?"

"Yeah," PJ said, aware that his voice was too carefully natural. "Just wrestling with the log." He poked a couple of keys with one finger, exiting the Personal file.

"Well, you can add somebody else to the old she-bear and the Drager kid." Skiho's gaze was a steady, unwavering flame. "An old friend of yours was along. Mr. Most Promising Cadet. Mr. Freethinker. Mr. Funnybone."

Skiho held out one fist, opened it to reveal a little tab of soiled, twisted metal. PJ picked up the tab and squinted to make out the stamped letters and numbers.

Then he tossed the tab in the air and grabbed it in a fist of his own. "Mr. Tickles," he said softly.

9

HE WAS STILL STUMBLING ALONG BEHIND TEEKLO, CLASP-
ing the man's arm above the elbow, when they reached the
first shaft where a pale gray light edged back the gloom. He
was dimly aware of stone walls honeycombed with openings,
of scurrying figures all around them, and confused voices, like
a turbulent wind.

But he cared only for the light. His sobs were an upwelling
of relief, even joy, at the simple gratification of seeing. His
own hand, a luminous pink crab on the solid branch of Teeklo's arm, was a miracle. So was Kapu's silhouetted head and
so was the thin silvery slash of water that ran in a neatly cut
stone channel near his feet.

There was also a low platform or altar of stone, directly
under the shaft that admitted the gray, diffuse illumination.
And from this slab rose a twisted fork of tree, a haze of palest
green at the tips of twigs that clawed upward like arthritic
hands. Here and there Ronald could see small yellow fruits,
no larger than eggs.

Kapu and Teeklo knelt before this tree, and Ronald followed suit, seeing through the blur of his tears that they, too,
were moved. Kapu began to chant, and a moment later voices
behind and to the side of them joined in. Ronald understood
nothing except the powerful current of thankfulness and a
lilting note of ecstatic recognition. Many of the voices were
high and thin, and a few unraveled into giggles.

With his eyes he ate and drank the skinny tree, the glittering
runnel of clear water beneath it. The little fruits—apples, he
guessed—glowed like opals. For how many hours had they
stumbled and crawled in darkness, the only sounds their own
breathing and the chittering of the rats? Ronald had nearly
screamed more than once, at the shock of jagged rocks protruding from the tunnel walls, or at the images that sprang at

him from the abyss of utter darkness—creations of his own feverish imagination.

Finally he had come to apprehend the turns and dips of the tunnel through the shifting muscles in Teeklo's arm. They became almost one organism, creeping and wriggling through passageways that continually intersected and branched, at many angles. The air was sometimes cold and fresh, sometimes warm and fetid as the gut of some great beast. More than once they had splashed through streams or pools, the water sometimes up to Ronald's armpits.

Now and then, as if sensing his rising panic, Teeklo had spoken to him, told him a little about the Pobla and their ways. The rats led them because these creatures alone could unerringly follow the intricate network of tunnels. Even with a map and the characters chiseled rudely at intersections, Teeklo told him, a Pobla could become disoriented and lose his way. But as long as they were fed at the beginning and ending of each leg of a journey, the rats never made a mistake and never abandoned their charges.

The creatures were still with them, he saw when the chant was at last over. They scampered here and there underfoot while a crowd of young Ginks pressed in, clamoring with excitement. Around Ronald, however, the ring of dark, inquisitive faces kept an arm's length away. *Dako*, he heard them whispering, *piksi dako!* At another remove he saw the faces of adults, and some of these seemed to glare at him, suspicious and hostile.

Ronald avoided these stares as best he could, while Teeklo and Kapu talked briefly to a group of Ginks that had arrived together out of the depths of the cavern, some of them carrying lances with strips of hide or cloth tied to the haft. He looked instead at what he could see of the village, and as he did so amazement lifted him a little out of his weariness.

The walls were a series of shelves and ladders that rose all the way to the stone roof of the tremendous chamber. Low doorways and windows cut into the rock indicated that there were living quarters at every level. Rivulets of water dropped in a series of sheer waterfalls at several points, and on some of the shelves Ginks squatted over basins apparently filled from these sources. Others seemed to be working at heaps of grass stalks or pounding and scraping with stone hammers.

He saw that the young played on some of the very highest shelves, fenced in with panels of interwoven sticks.

The floor of the cavern stretched away in a long, irregular valley. Other shafts were spaced every hundred meters or so to admit the gray light of an eternal dawn or dusk, and he noticed now that there were also unlit openings, from which came currents of cool, damp air. Down the middle of this valley ran two canals, also cut directly into the rock. One carried the flow from the rivulets cascading out of the walls, and the other, he saw at a glance, was murky with waste.

On both sides of these canals were structures, some quite large. They were made of stone blocks and, occasionally, pillars apparently cut from the trunks of trees. The two most imposing buildings rested on extensive raised courtyards. Layers of dark and pale stone alternated in a pattern, and Ronald was reminded of a picture he had seen in an old book. A temple from some ancient barbaric kingdom, but he could not remember where. Probably from this same region, where the human ancestors of the Ginks had once lived.

The size of the structures and the smooth, close-fitting blocks were a wonder. He had seen nothing like them represented in the museum. The Ginks were supposed to inhabit caves and crude burrows a few feet below the surface of the earth. Except for scrapers, hand-axes, and the chipped points of their lances, they were reputed to have no durable tools. How had they created this . . . *city* . . . and then kept it secret?

With a shock it occurred to him that perhaps there were other centers like this one. Perhaps there were even more Ginks than the Bioteams knew about. He thought he remembered a figure of a million and a half, based on the Border Patrol's annual kill rates and the projected effect of long-term lethal mutations. But it would not take many hives like this one to exceed that figure.

The experts had certainly been wrong about other things. Though he saw here and there a grotesque face, a slack jaw or idiot leer, the young were apparently able to scamper everywhere with great agility, and none of them looked as brutish and evil-tempered as the exhibits in the museum. A few had decidedly apelike noses or ears, a few were exceptionally bandy-legged or hairy, but aside from these characteristics they did not look much different from himself, filthy and naked as he was. And the Ginks had also moved with perfect ease in the Preserves—which, according to studies, were supposed to be far beyond their range.

And of course they had not eaten him yet. They had in fact laughed at a joke he made, and then taken risks to make sure he arrived here unharmed. Even if the Ginks were a degenerate species, even if they lived comfortably among rats and vultures, they were surely much more astonishing animals than people realized. They had avoided the jetcopters and the harvest crews, and escaped the Border Patrol even after they were spotted.

Ronald felt the first stirrings of a secret excitement of discovery, an odd elation that existed side by side with his anguish. He knew that very, very few humans had ever seen what he was seeing, and of those none had apparently returned to describe the vision. In the crowd around Teeklo and Kapu he saw two or three pale and long-headed creatures, and several others with reddish hair. Surely these were mixeds, which meant that the stories he had heard were not mere rumor. People—*his* people—had slunk away to live with the Ginks, adopting their primitive ways and even interbreeding.

How could this be so? In his reading of old books Ronald had encountered reports of interspecies contact. Fugitives from justice, madmen, and runaway youths had occasionally been traced to the border, then never seen again. He had also heard rumors about "throwbacks" in the NorthAm populace, the infants of certain wealthy, respectable families who required secret cosmetic surgery. There was even a handful of people who, over the last century, claimed to have lived with the Ginks and escaped to tell the tale. Almost all of these were thought to be fakes or deranged, though one woman had impressed investigators with her ability to train insects to do remarkable things.

Mostly Ronald wondered about Teeklo, who seemed to be not only accepted but treated as an equal or even as a sort of adviser. Certainly he did not appear unbalanced or slow-witted, and he spoke with a bearing of natural authority. Teeklo knew NorthAm well enough, despite his occasional clumsiness with words, to prove he must have come to the

Ginks as a young man. He was probably once a soldier, once had a name and number—though Ronald noticed the dog tag was missing after their journey through the tunnels, so he could not check.

Why would such a person have abandoned his whole world? Surely there was some shameful crime involved, or a deep and terrible wound. Yet except for the moment when Teeklo had turned away sharply from his question, Ronald had seen no sign of any hidden regret. If he survived a few moons, the answer had come, he might learn more. Moons—what a strange expression for creatures who lived underground!

The ring of whispering young Ginks broke apart now and Ronald saw Teeklo and four others coming toward him. Their faces were all purposeful, unsmiling, and the four bore their decorated lances aloft as in some kind of formal display. Ronald felt his heart squeezing harder, the blood making a rushing sound in his inner ear.

"I know you are tired," Teeklo said. "So am I. But we must bring you for a little time to be seen by Adza. Then you can eat and sleep. Come." He reached out to take Ronald's arm and guide him.

"Who?" Ronald was already moving, hurrying a little to keep up with his guards. Behind them came the crowd of young Ginks, scurrying about like leaves caught in an eddy of wind.

But Teeklo did not answer. They marched directly to one of the large, imposing buildings, across the checkerboard of light and dark stones in its courtyard, then through a huge portal made by a single oblong of stone balanced on two supporting columns. Just inside the portal a very old Gink accosted them. He was winking and smiling and mumbling, apparently to the half-dozen rats that hung at his heels, and lowered a lance as if to block their progress.

The old Gink's arms were hardly thicker than the shaft of the lance, and Ronald could not imagine such an ancient creature, in a dirty breechclout, actually defending anything or anybody. Yet all of the guards and Teeklo stopped and even bowed deferentially. Automatically, Ronald bowed too. One of the guards spoke at some length, though the old Gink seemed not to pay attention, but at intervals whispered and grimaced at his rats.

Finally this gatekeeper lifted the lance and gestured with it, directing them down a short corridor which ended in another and smaller portal. Teeklo nudged him on the shoulder, and together with two of the guards, they proceeded through this second opening into an inner chamber. Here, too, soft gray light came from shafts cut into the ceiling.

Though his eyes had adjusted to this continual twilight, Ronald did not at first notice anything extraordinary in the room. The walls were mostly plain, smooth stone, with here and there a carving in relief. He saw a coyote, a large bird of some kind, and a huge beetle. Several Ginks squatted beside these carvings, lances at their sides, and another group had gathered around a sort of platform in a far corner of the chamber.

Teeklo and the others moved toward this platform and then, a few strides away from it, they dropped to their knees. Ronald was pulled down unceremoniously with the rest. The Gink guards drew away slightly, and Ronald saw that the platform was covered with rugs on one side while on the other, incongruous on the bare stone, was an object he recognized instantly. It was as familiar to him as his own arm, yet in this new context it looked utterly alien. It was a little solar-powered radio, the ordinary cheap model that poor people took to the beach or on picnics in a park. It was connected to a wire dangling from the airshaft, and apparently worked, for he could hear a faint hiss of static and what might have been confused voices.

Hardly had he registered this startling vision when he saw movement at the other end of the platform. Someone was sitting on the rugs, and wrapped in them too, someone as small as he was. When Kapu began what sounded like another chant, and the others all around joined in, a face emerged from a fold of the rug-wrap. Ronald had never seen a face so wrinkled. All its features seemed to have clenched together, the nose and chin and brow as seamed and cracked as the knuckles of a claw.

He could not tell if the creature was male or female, only that it was a Gink and extremely old. There were only black cracks where the eyes should be, but it seemed to him he was observed. The small head was poised, trembling slightly, on a scrawny neck, and Ronald was reminded of some monkeys he had seen at the zoo—the whiskered, wizened kind that watch humans as closely as humans watch them.

Beside him the chanting went on until a hand, like a dried and curled leaf, floated from the heap of rugs and twiddled a knob on the radio. The rush of static became a distant and rapid stream of voices overlaid by bursts of music. Ronald was startled to hear a few bars of one of the popular songs going around the schoolyard—"Give My All to Everyone," by Mad Machine. The chanting ceased abruptly then and the ancient creature began speaking, impatiently it seemed to Ronald. The voice sounded like a woman's, he thought, though it was so cracked and thinned by age that he could not be certain.

Kapu got to his feet and replied at length, and Ronald guessed that the story of their flight was being told. He heard Mata's name again and saw Kapu make a gesture suggesting the trapping or catching of something frantic, and again he experienced a wave of dizziness, his mind cowering under the shadow of the horror he had seen. He tried to concentrate on the intonation of Kapu's voice, on nuances of feeling hidden in the meaningless torrent of syllables. He saw Kapu flap his arms, an imitation, surely, of the omen of the buzzard, and heard a note of urgency and alarm.

All the while he was conscious of the old woman watching him. In the maze of her wrinkles, the occasional glint of her eyes in their deep slits, one might read many expressions. Yet despite the surroundings—the imposing stone animals peering out of the gloom, the chanting of the kneeling figures—Ronald had the odd impression that the old woman was laughing silently to herself.

The stone was hard under Ronald's bare knees, so he was glad when Adza made a gesture signaling them to rise. An informal and heated discussion broke out then. More than once the Ginks looked his way, some scowling and others with a speculative air. He looked at Teeklo, who ignored him and remained perfectly impassive.

Finally the old woman lifted her dried leaf of a hand and beckoned to Ronald. He approached tentatively, glancing again at Teeklo and receiving an almost imperceptible nod. When he was close enough she reached out and ran her fingertips along his forearm. When she reached his hand she gripped it with surprising strength, lifted it, and pressed his palm over her face, inhaling deeply. Then she dropped his hand and sat still for a moment, head tilted back, her eye-slits vacant, as if asleep.

The others had fallen silent, so there was no sound in the room but the distant and metallic voice from the radio, garbled by static. *ConCom Units for young . . . stressout factor . . . good until November . . . and now the News at. . . .* The words blurred in a burst of music, a hard-driving, staccato beat. The sound was bizarre enough, but Ronald felt strange, too, realizing that he had no idea what hour—or even what day—the voice had been on the point of announcing.

Then Adza began to speak—or chant, for there was a crooning rhythm in her phrases. She went on for some minutes, during which Ronald heard only the words *Mata* and *Dako* once more. There was, he thought, something mournful about this rhythm. When she fell silent, she opened her eyes and leaned toward Ronald.

Behind him Teeklo spoke very quietly, his tone colorless. "She says Mata was her best friend, and Mata was an old fool to take you for her cub. Now she has gone to wonakubi before her friends could eat her, so we are all poorer, and here you come begging. We can't eat you either, she says. Because we gave you the choice to die, and you didn't."

Ronald looked down, away from the old woman. He wanted very badly to see Teeklo's face, catch some hint of what he should say, but was afraid to turn around. So it was true, the Ginks were cannibals.

. . . demonstrations in several NorthAm. . . . The Progressive spokesman vowed. The future of the Federation. . . . Broken strings of words were still floating on the tides of static coming through the radio *. . . reclaim Wastelands, oust Gink-coddlers and so-called. . . .*

Ronald looked up again, saw the old woman was still inclined toward him, her eyes glittering into his. Abruptly she opened her mouth wide. Her gums were dark, almost purple, and from them jutted at various angles three or four yellowed stubs of teeth. Involuntarily he jerked back, and behind him the Ginks laughed. Adza was hissing at him too, and now clicked her pitiful fangs in a rapid gnawing motion. She said

91

something, her voice cracking in what Ronald presumed was laughter.

"She wants to know if Adza doesn't eat such a skinny pup, what do you do for Adza. The men told her about your tongue. She wants to see."

Ronald swallowed, then extended his tongue and curled it upward to touch the tip of his nose.

. . . calling a miracle. Despite severe shock, loss of. . . . Our correspondent . . . for the first time. . . .

Adza opened her mouth again with a loud wheeze and batted her crabbed little hands together. "*Kish! Kish!*" she croaked. Ronald was reminded of the yawning grimaces of a monkey. She swayed toward him again and this time he steeled himself and did not recoil. "Boo," she hissed at him. "Boo rockroll?"

Ronald stared back at her. Could she mean . . . ?

"She wants to know if you can sing. The old tunes, before the war."

Ronald's heart thumped and startled a grin onto his face. He had heard rightly. Rockenroll was one of his passions. Before his library privileges were restricted, he had listened to hours of this primitive music, the chants of wild prophets in the last, violent age before the founding of the Federation. And he knew from his reading that many of these prophets had come from among the human ancestors of the Ginks, before their degenerative mutations. Perhaps this Adza was so old she remembered fragments of these melodies!

"I know some . . . but she wants me to *sing?*"

"Boo shing!" the old woman exclaimed, her body swaying now from side to side. "Shing rockroll!"

. . . exclusive now, at the bedside. . . . Only hours ago . . . second transplant. . . .

Ronald took a deep breath. In the privacy of his room he had risked humming a few of the chants. It was of course forbidden to play them over public media, since research had long ago shown that these ancient rhythms could indiscriminately stimulate powerful, irrational, and erotic currents. He had no idea, beyond what could be gleaned from footnotes, what tempo or intonation was appropriate. Nor was he very good at the specialized mathematics of modern music—almost all of which was generated by elegant programs working through a battery of synthesizers.

"Try," Teeklo said softly. "Sing."

He licked his lips and cleared his throat. For all he knew he might be skewered and roasted, served up in bits to this old hag, if he botched his little song. Which should he choose? Words broke and fluttered out of his mind in startled flocks. In the huge, cold chamber there was no sound and everyone was staring at him, waiting.

"*Sing!*" Teeklo hissed.

All at once he began, his voice a high whine in his own ears, like the howling of some small animal.

> *I cannot get any . . . sa-a-a-tisfa-a-a-ction . . .*
> *Though I try, and I try, and I try,*
> *I. . . .*

Adza nodded her little knob of a head at him and began to sway from side to side. Encouraged, he took a deeper breath and sang louder, trying to match the beat to the old woman's movement. Then he heard a few of the Ginks begin to hum, and on the next verse Teeklo joined in too.

By the middle of the song Ronald knew he had pleased the old woman and most of the company, for they had filled the great room with resonant sound, the butts of lances thudding on the floor and hands clapping together. Adza was gaping in evident delight, crooning her own ungrammatical, barely recognizable version of the tune. A corruption, Ronald guessed, of her ancestors' original. Tactfully, he worked to imitate this new dialect.

Kaint ginno-o-o sadisfa-a-a-shun. . . .

When the last note echoed up the stone light shafts, Ronald expected a chorus of grunts and hoots, the noises he had come to recognize as approval. He was himself smiling broadly, triumphant and relieved, so the ensuing quiet confused him. But all except Adza had become instantly sober again, faces blank and eyes downcast. She alone continued to rock from side to side, mumbling now in her own tongue.

Hastily Ronald looked down at his feet and composed a serious expression. Again, underneath the old woman's thin, dry voice, he was aware of the wash of static and garbled voices from the radio. A moment later Adza ceased speaking, her eyes and mouth shut tight, her face a blind, intricate maze of seams and wrinkles, like an aerial photograph of an ancient desert. There was a moment of unnatural stillness.

Then Ronald heard his father's voice. The words emerged abruptly, flotsam bobbing past in the hiss and crackle from the radio, and only later was he able to recall a few of them: . . . *cannot rest . . . hope . . . our son. . . .* But he knew that voice, its timbre and accent and edge; knew it through the cheap little mechanical speaker, through all the warps and interference of landscape and electrical field, through all the circuits and filters and equalizers of recorders and transmitters; knew even an unfamiliar quality in that voice, a faint but somehow terrible hunger. His father, his own father, had spoken from somewhere, somehow! *Alive!*

He uttered a sound and groped at the radio. Another voice, not his father's, said something about an inquiry and a denial from a director of something and then the staccato music surged in to drown everything out and he heard a roaring white noise inside his own skull even as he went down again into the black tunnel through which he and Teeklo had stumbled for so many hours and which now expanded in a long, smooth rush until there was nothing left but an utter, empty darkness and a kind of rustling or whispering, very very far away.

10

HALF THE ROOMS IN THE HOSPITAL WERE FULL OF flowers—roses, mums, orchids, carnations, and pungent, blossoming herbs. All of them Elise had quietly shunted away from Frank's private suite. Not only had he been nauseated by the odor, he reacted even more violently to the sight when his bandages were being changed. Now that the first skin grafts had apparently taken, he was allowed to sit up with his one good eye uncovered for a few hours in subdued light.

Elise understood that he wanted nothing in the room that suggested vegetation, nothing that would remind him of things that crawled. She considered it a miracle that he managed to hold on to his sanity, an even greater miracle that he was already talking to people—not only herself and the surgeons and nurses, but investigators and dignitaries as well.

But his talk troubled her, too. Not only what he said, but the intensity of it—an undercurrent of fanatic desire. He had to speak carefully and softly through his swollen tissues, but the urgency of his hatred came through, like heat from coals under the ashes of his seared body.

"Holos," he was saying just now to the woman leaning near and listening with an avidity Elise found unpleasant. "My wife will give you holos of him, just born and as a little guy." He raised his head slightly from the pillow and swiveled his look toward Elise. "Anything."

"It will help," the woman breathed, "immeasurably. The people must know—must *feel*—what this means."

"I want . . . I want every last one. . . ." Frank groaned and his whole body surged to the limit his padded restraints allowed.

"I know, I know. We will do it, Frank. Do it for you and . . . for your son."

And for yourself, Elise thought. *For the People.* Danielle Konrad did everything for the People—as the Progressives defined that sacred entity. The People were good, the People were true, the People were infallible, visionary, sensible, strong, loyal, just, courageous, and on and on. They were merely misinformed and manipulated. And only temporarily, of course. Until the Progressive Party could return and guide them back to the right path.

"I'll look," Elise said, referring to the family holo file. She made no attempt to disguise her dry disdain, and the other woman granted her a quick, false, professional smile that told Elise clearly enough how little her opinions mattered in any case.

"Such an ordeal for both of you," Danielle went on in a husky contralto. "But the whole world is going to know your contribution, Frank. The whole world. And very soon you will speak in your own . . ."

Elise stopped listening. The irony was numbing, like some

raw, strong drink. Frank had spent his entire career working to defeat the policies Danielle Konrad personally articulated. Konrad was the chief ideologue for what Frank used to call the Poops—the Party of Outraged Pinheads—and he had more than once mercilessly ridiculed her busty swagger and inflamed rhetoric, her deliberately unstylish dress and avoidance of cosmetics.

And now he was using his first tiny store of strength, after an incredible physical and mental ordeal, to collaborate in what Elise could see would be a publicity campaign unmatched for bad taste: a garish, histrionic exploitation of their personal tragedy to forward the Progressive agenda. Already, on all the major networks, there were images of little Ronnie, shots of the Emergency Rescue team cleaning away clots of blood and dead ants from Frank's horribly disfigured face, clips of dignitaries hurrying to ally themselves with the new martyr. Already on her desk were unanswered faxcalls from agents and studios wanting to buy rights to her "story."

She understood the game that was being played. Frank's position in Resource Management was only one rank below Cabinet, which would make him the highest-placed member of a Conservative Administration ever to defect to an opposition party while in office. At the moment Konrad and her gang refrained from trumpeting this conversion—Elise grudgingly acknowledged the word now—only because the public might suspect the claim. A man recently and horribly wounded, his only son eaten by wild beasts or in the hands of brutal savages, might make any sort of rash decision.

On the other hand, Frank's former colleagues were of no help at all. They had in fact botched the situation utterly. After the Medvac copter had discovered Frank, unbelievably, alive—clotted blood from his slash wound had mired the ants and distracted them from stinging—the dispatcher took almost an hour to send out an alert on Ronnie. He was apparently busy trying to help a checkpoint guard cover up an authorization of extravehicle movement. Then the Preserve bureaucrats stiffly refused help from a nearby military base —until it became clear that their own rescue teams had failed miserably and they needed someone to share the blame.

Meanwhile high Con Administration officials had sent the vanloads of flowers and rushed to Elise's side to comfort her—and be holoed in postures of alternate compassion and heroic determination. But the whole incident was looking more and more like a very costly embarrassment. There was already evidence indicating a Gink presence beyond normal ranges, and bizarre rumors had surfaced—new levels of collaboration between Ginks and noxious wild animals, then an even more sinister suggestion that Con researchers were secretly training captive Ginks as part of some covert border operation.

On top of all that came Frank's abrupt change of attitude. The party had doubtless hoped his first words would be a confession of gratitude, a reaffirmation of his faith in the Administration's goodwill. Or at the very least a discreet silence, encouraged by a large disability settlement. Instead they now had a renegade on their hands, and a simmering scandal that could endanger their hold on the government. Elise got the distinct impression they would have heartily preferred a dead hero.

There was perhaps one exception. The smooth, round little PacRim named Fat, who had been charged with the preliminary investigation because the incident had occurred in a Preserve. His opaque smile, his polite and yet intense questioning, his final assurance ("A recovery? Oh yes. Oh yes. Why not? Such an unusual case.") had told her that he accepted nothing yet as inevitable. In particular—and it was this that struck Elise most deeply, for no one else went so far—he appeared to share her intuition that her son might, somehow, be alive.

On the other hand she did not trust him, or anyone else just now. Including herself. In a matter of days she had known the great, swinging hammers of grief and terror, then the sudden and dizzy lift of hope. Now came a renewed dread at the realization that her life was being swept along by inscrutable, monstrous forces she could not understand. And she doubted, for the first time, that anybody understood them.

The man she once depended on for clarity, for his shrewd good sense and grasp of essentials, was now one great scar inside and out. He lay before this woman he had once dismissed as a bad joke, the two of them panting and cooing their hymn of hatred. She could see in his little feverish lunges how this talk of mobilization, of sanitized frontiers, of ultimate

solutions, was exciting him, energizing him almost in the way
she had once been able to do. And the smile on Danielle's
broad, pale face—Elise was suddenly giddy with a new sickness. It was a moment before she recognized it as jealousy,
and then she pulled herself erect, hot with shame.

"I think that's enough," she said. "He's had enough for
this morning." She rose, all at once light and tense.

Danielle touched Frank on one bandaged hand and said
something too quick and low for Elise to catch. Then she
came away from the bed, radiating her brisk, forthright
charm. "He has such incredible guts, and such a *heart*. But
of course you know that. You're his wife." Danielle's smile
was frank, respectful, disarming. Elise thought briefly of picking up the pitcher of ice and water on the nightstand and
pouring it over the woman.

"Just a couple of minutes," Danielle said matter-of-factly
as she went past Elise and opened the door. A man in a dark
suit, carrying a notetaker, stepped quickly inside, followed
by Dr. Fitz. "The networks just can't be put off forever with
substitutes. You know how they are. So we compromised.
This is George Olin, from InterNews?"

The man was bowing deferentially before Elise and somehow at the same time stepping toward Frank. There was a
pale spot on the crown of his head and she thought, irritably,
that the man was too young to be losing his hair. Frank had
all his, though of course they had shaved it off.

"What is this? My husband needs to rest—" She stared at
the doctor as he glided toward her, took her elbow.

"They agreed to draw lots, Mrs. Drager. No holos, only
one representative for five minutes, just a few words. Your
husband"—he glanced at the mummy on the bed as at a
religious icon—"insisted. And Ms. Konrad agreed to cut her
visit short to slip this in."

"He's—"

"I really think," Dr. Fitz said earnestly, "that we would do
more harm trying to keep him strictly isolated. He *needs*
contact. A certain kind. And speaking of rest, Mrs. Drager
—" He looked tremendously arch and reproachful and tugged
at her arm.

She twisted away to look back to the bed. The young man
had pulled up a chair and seated himself at Frank's side.

Already he had the little keyboard and recorder open on his lap, his face flushed with privilege and responsibility.

"Let's do the biggie first," Elise heard him say. His voice was soft, nasal, confidential. "After all you've been through, sir, the tragedy and the horror—what keeps you going? What *can* you look forward to? News of your son?" The clicking of keys halted and the man looked up, his smile agape with anticipation.

Frank's head flopped back and forth on the pillow to signify negation.

"He's *tired.* Can't you see he doesn't want—" Elise stopped, shocked at the plaintive wobble in her voice.

The head flopped again, more vigorously.

"Just life itself, sir? What? What do you most want to see?" The man leaned forward and his fingers flexed over the keys.

Frank smiled and in the hush that followed they all heard and understood his dry, firm whisper.

"Extermination," he said, and then smiled so broadly that one of his new lips split and a bright drop of blood welled out.

11

AT FIRST THEY HAD PUT HIM IN A SHALLOW CAVE BY himself. He woke up lying on a woven grass mat, a pelt thrown over him for warmth, a pot of clean water beside him. In his stupor he heard a startling, agonized howling, and dragged himself to the mouth of the cave. Through the eternal, gray gloom from the light shafts he could see a ring of young Ginks squatted a few yards away. Some played with the big rats beside them, while covertly watching Ronald or chattering among themselves. Beyond this ring, in a neighboring cave, a group of females had gathered. Their dark faces shone in a flickering glare from four torches, as they bent over something on the ground.

Finally he glimpsed a form, huddled on a mat strewn with

bunches of some dried fiber. The howls came from this creature, though the females nearby provided a chorus of sympathetic moans. The strangeness of the scene and the piercing
cries repelled him, so he retreated to his pallet and sat facing
the darkness. He pulled the fur around his shoulders and
sipped a little of the water, which was cool and tasted faintly
of stone.

Over and over he heard the voice from the radio—a few
words, thin and raspy—coming through the steady cataract
of static, as transient as the glimpse of a running deer through
broken shadows. Yet he was certain it was his father's voice.
Hope . . . our son . . . we cannot rest. . . . Weaker, a little
unsteady to be sure, but hadn't the broadcaster mentioned
shock and loss of blood? Somehow, unbelievable as it seemed,
the jetcopter they had heard flying over the snowy mountain
must have discovered the horrible, writhing black heap and
turned it back into a living father.

Hope! Surely that meant the search had not been abandoned! His father not only lived, but knew, or guessed that
his son also miraculously survived, and so patrols would continue until they were reunited. For a time Ronald shed tears
of gratitude and relief. He knew a spasm, too, of intense
yearning, an impulse—so strong it frightened and disoriented
him—to claw through the earth over his head toward the light.
And yet. . . .

He shrank a little inside the pelt he clutched. An unease
went through him. It was a nameless feeling, a tightening in
the middle of his back and an urge to look over his shoulder.
Yet connected to his father. Or to what he thought were the
last memories of his father. A certain frowning look aside
from the wheel of the Choctaw, the pressure of a large hand
on his shoulder as they stood over the dead deer with its dark,
unblinking eye turned up at them, a tone of voice. . . . *You're
going to skin your nose bad, real bad. . . .*

An odd thought came to him. He saw himself again, naked
and dirty, running away from the patrol vehicle in the cornfield. But the hatch on the Javelin was thrown back and a
head suddenly emerged. His father's head, smiling fiercely.
He slowed and waved, began to smile back. But the vehicle
continued to rush toward him, expanding, looming higher,
his father's face larger and larger like a great, grinning moon.

"*Ya mahanakun.*" The watcher smiled and showed her open hand. "*Leema delo ya kish.*"

"*Na.*" Kapu nodded and slipped his sack from his shoulder, then swung it to a place beside the pot of coals.

Teeklo was already watching the scampering young, trying to guess their game. "What little has he learned?"

"He can guess the marked one without his eyes, sometimes. If he has not dreamed for a few days. And he has two new *tohanakun.*"

Teeklo nodded and stepped nearer. The young were dancing about a fat male with huge, cupped ears thrusting through his coarse hair. Now and then the fat one, his eyes squeezed shut, lunged after a toddler. Then the whole group squealed and bounded back, charged with a delighted terror.

The *dako* saw the newcomers and stopped, head raised alertly. Teeklo searched and found in the boy's expression no trace of the horror that had been there at first, but no trace either of Ronald—that soft-featured, wistful, curious soul. This creature had only just learned to recognize the others by touch, to nibble their lice, and to hum a simple duet.

Kapu had come nearer, watching too. "*Ya tchatsinaku,*" he called softly. "*Tchi-tchi . . . tchi-tchi. . . .*"

The boy crouched warily, moved sidewise. Some of the other young were attracted and clustered around him, pinching and sniffing. "*Pi'si dako! Pi'si dako!*" they squeaked. The fat one lumbered up, beaming, but before he could grasp anyone the watcher pounced on him, seized one of the great ears and tugged him away, laughing and scolding affectionately. The others followed, except the *dako,* who still crouched and stared at them without blinking.

"He lives," Kapu said. "He is coming."

"Slowly." Teeklo frowned. He did not trust entirely this new being, whose presence had begun to flicker through the dense clouds in the boy's skull.

"Another thing," the watcher called to them. She had come back now leading the smallest, who had a leg so bent that he could hobble erect only with support. As was the case with the others, his deformity had been invisible or overlooked at birth, and he had been allowed to draw breath; and once the *kubi* was inside them, all Pobla were honored alike.

She set the little cripple directly in front of the *dako,* who had squatted now on his heels. "You will see the new one here, if we are lucky."

She rose and began to clap her hands and chant softly. After a moment Kapu and Teeklo joined in. It was the backward-breathing game—common in this season of new winter, when the Pobla rested mostly below ground—a beginner's exercise in finding and holding one's shadow. The exercise always made Teeklo uncomfortable, because he could never go beyond the mingling at the very surface.

The others gathered, excited, to watch or clap along. The rhythm slowed and steadied. The two subjects seemed to be drowsing, lulled by the soft chant. Each breathed the other's breath, then gave it back. Teeklo felt the moment when *naku* appeared; as if a mighty bellows were blowing them all into one flame. Except him. Teeklo held himself away, watched covertly, and saw the *dako*'s face had gone blank.

But his partner, the tiny stumbler, was shuddering, inhaling long and deep. The little body sat so lightly it appeared to be lifting away from the stone floor. The watcher picked up the cripple then and set him on his feet, and they watched the little one take a step and then another without faltering. The *dako* had not moved a muscle. "*Ya!*" the watcher said, breaking off her chant. "See? He is hungry to come out. He pulls the others, and steadies them."

"*Ya delo tohanaku,*" Kapu crooned. "Little playmate, one who has no name. Who is, who has no name? The One with No Shadow, the Terrible One, *ya!*"

Still the boy did not move, but Teeklo saw the words strike him. He seemed to have grown paler and smaller in the dim light from the airshaft, which was only a crack in the stone vault overhead.

"*Vasan kubin, vasan kubin,*" Kapu went on, keeping the rhythm of the backward-breathing chant, "the shadows come to breathe you, breathe you. . . ." He gestured to the watcher, who began to shoo her group toward the entrance. "Breathe into your shadow, take your shadow's name. Who is it has no shadow, who is it has no name?"

Teeklo did not see the *dako*'s lips move, and did not recognize the voice that came from him: "*Ya!*"

Kapu turned his head slightly, without looking at Teeklo, and sang, "Bring her now, bring her with the pearl of light."

So they were going to take the first step toward the naming. This had not been planned, specifically, for today. Teeklo was apprehensive, even though they had talked with the whole Council about this unusual approach. Backward-breathing was, after all, only an exercise for the very young.

"You think he is ready?" he whispered, and moved to lift the pot from the shelf. He took away the lid, revealing the dull red eye of the coals, and set the pot beside the boy. Then he went back to remove a handful of withered leaves from the shoulder bag. The watcher had lost her smile and was now poised alertly, waiting.

Teeklo nodded and signed her to go. "You were right. He is here. We have decided to try. You know Jati, the mother . . . she must bring us the shadow hole now. Quickly."

The watcher hissed at and prodded the reluctant, made the older ones hold the hands of the littlest stumblers, and hurried the whole bewildered group away. Kapu had gone on with his chant, and now held out his open hand. Teeklo gave him half the bunch of leaves. When these were scattered into the pot, a cloud of white smoke, thick and pungent, boiled out. Kapu waved the smoke toward the boy, still singing.

> "Round-belly, earth, mother,
> spit and make this clay-ball,
> sing to him, make him spin,
> weave your shadow, in and out!"

They were repeating the last phase of a birth ceremony, discovering and conferring the proper name, as if the boy had just been taken from the womb. What worried Teeklo was the close connection to the incident that had finally unbalanced Ronnie. Bad enough to have seen his own father's face eaten away—but then, only a few days later, to witness the braining of a wet newborn!

Several times already the boy had fallen back into this vision, huddled into it for hours, whimpering and biting his tongue bloody. These attacks had come without warning, triggered by trivial things—the sight of a group of females around a fire or a sleeping infant. The Council had come up with a diagnosis: amazingly, the piksi boy must have realized he, too, had no ghost. To keep breathing, in the face of such knowledge, was the most horrible mistake imaginable to the Pobla. But piksis of course did not know how to die, so they went into their madness, a living death.

Yet, after his first delirium, this boy had regained some semblance of awareness and balance, and each relapse seemed a little shorter than the last. It was surmised he had somehow glimpsed the new *kubi* whom the mothers had driven away. So Adza had decreed that the name of that new shadow, still unhoused and still near, would be divined and given to the *dako;* and the mother—who had no wish to take in a piksi —would immediately give him away to Teeklo.

> "Little snake, little egg, we call you,
> mother swarming, mother weaving,
> Shadow of the Shadows, we call you!
> Swallow light and bear us the dark!"

Teeklo heard the mother come in, but he did not turn. He was watching the boy's blank, still face for any sign of the madness that had haunted him. Wreaths of the smoke drifted between them, and it seemed to Teeklo they had all become ever so slightly translucent, while Kapu's voice resonated more and more solidly, making them vibrate like reflections in a pool of water.

At the periphery of his vision he saw Jati arrive beside Kapu. In her hand she held the thin, twisted stalk of dried cord, the wrinkled shadow-hole once joined to her own flesh. She had cut herself already on the thigh and now smeared the cord there, so it came away glistening bright red.

Teeklo had brought the stone knife from Kapu's bag and given it to him, and the old Pobla reached out now and slid the blade lightly down the boy's bare chest. When the red line appeared and thickened into a rivulet, he took the twist of cord and held it over the smoke.

> *"Mother, earth-house, open!*
> *Give this shadow home!"*

The mother swayed; Teeklo saw her breast heave. Then her voice came, tremulous, barely audible. . . .

"*I am open, he is home!*
Now comes his shadow!"

She cried out, and began to pant. Kapu reached out and clapped the shadow-hole over the red streak on the boy's chest. Teeklo saw the shock go through them both, and then the boy began to shake, so pale he seemed to be burning with a cold incandescence. *Oh Christ*, Teeklo thought, *it was too soon, he wasn't ready, we'll lose him now. . . .*

A sound came from the *dako,* a grunt as if he had fallen a long way and struck hard. Because of some trick of the smoke he seemed to disappear and then materialize again on his feet. His expression was now, indeed, full of madness, but it was not the horror Teeklo expected. This was a madness that showed its teeth in savage, awakened desire.

The sound the boy uttered was a deeper version of an infant's first, raw bellow of need, but it shaped itself into syllables they recognized:

"*Na . . . na . . . ku. . . .*"

Kapu had breathed the last of his song, and the mother had dropped to her knees beside him, her panting slowed to long sobs. Teeklo, too, felt a wave of exhaustion. He was immensely relieved that the *dako,* erect and bawling, did not seem to have slipped back into the nightmare. Perhaps this shadow was agile and strong, stronger than most, and could live in this strange piksi body.

"You will give him away," Kapu whispered.

Between sobs, Jati replied, "I give him away. Burn the shadow-hole." She rose and spoke to Teeklo for the first time. "You are mother now. You must name him." She turned and left them, bent slightly and shuffling her feet, as if movement pained her. The boy was looking fiercely, swiftly, from one to the other of them. The shape of his face seemed to have changed, become narrower and more mobile, and his color was warmer, darker.

Kapu looked up, smiling a little. "You will not find mothering this one easy, *mahanaku.* Old Mata should be here to do that work." He threw the bit of bloody cord and the rest of the leaves onto the coals in the pot, making again his soft *tchi-tchi . . . tchi-tchi . . .* , and in a moment the boy squatted again on his heels.

"We will go into the smoke again, *delo kubi, tchatsinaku.* We will find your name. Then we must teach you."

Teach you everything. Everything. But especially to keep forgetting who you were. Teeklo was contemplating the blank, fierce face. So far Kapu had been right, the ceremony was going well. Still, Teeklo was uneasy. This strong shadow was restless, and what once was Ronald Drager would eventually return. They had a limited time in which to bring the boy and his shadow into harmony. If they failed. . . . *Sudden death. Or a truly mad thing, a monster.*

As far as he knew, no piksi had ever been *born* as a Pobla, even in this symbolic way. Dangerous, surely—and exciting. Teeklo knew abruptly a pang of feeling he did not at first recognize—something wistful, but a little sour. He breathed in a little of the smoke and closed his eyes. *My boy the monster. Forgets himself. As I can't. Ronnie is gone somewhere, but I have always been Tickles. Yes, sir, Cadet Tickles.* He sighed and grimaced, as Kapu began the naming chants. Envy. That was it. Mother was envious.

12

"AND WHEN THEY STRIPPED OFF THE WALLBOARDS . . . OUR *home,* our own *living room,* where I picked out all the patterns and had drapes made. . . ." The woman sobbed, poked at one eye with a little, folded tissue, and then managed to go on, though her voice wobbled up and down over a good octave. "There were jillions of them, just *jillions,* crawling and swarming out of these holes, like little caves, everywhere in the insulation and everything. And we had to move. Had to leave our *home,* because it had gone too far. Earwigs. I mean, *earwigs!* I don't understand how they could . . . I mean, our government. . . ."

The sobs overtook her again and she sat down abruptly. Her husband encircled her with a protective arm and looked almost accusingly at the young man standing behind the podium-complex at the head of the room. There was a chorus of sympathetic murmurs from the crowd and a man called out, "Us too. They ate the place up, from the inside."

Baxter did not join this chorus, though he shifted his feet in discomfort. All through the evening's presentation, the charts and holos and the young man's smooth commentary, he had been increasingly uneasy. For some time he had known things were not going properly in the world at large, but he had always been able to count on himself at least, on his own standard of excellence and performance.

Now there were these interior . . . disturbances. Random thoughts that upset him. A vague but ghastly little mood. This mood had invaded him even before he met the lunatic on the Bulletbus, before the bizarre collision with the pheasant, though those incidents had precipitated his decision to pursue some answers. So he had come to this meeting as a concerned citizen, wanting a credible account of what was going so wrong with everything. Instead people were stirring up unhealthy ideas with their silly tales of earwigs and ants.

It was a neighborhood meeting at the Olive Terrace Community Center, sponsored by the campaign committee of the Progressive Party. The young man, in a sport suit with no tie, had presented the party's views on the big issues, as outlined in an hour-long holo. Baxter watched colorful electronic models of new strains of virus as they learned to enslave the antibodies hurled against them, saw crops seared by blight that originated in untended Preserves, heard alarming statistics on the increase in border violations by small bands of Ginks.

They had even been witness to some poignant clips of the now famous Drager tragedy: the overturned wreck of the sport vehicle, the swollen and disfigured face on the stretcher, even the boy who had been lost, smiling from his motortrike on the patio of a luxury home. They heard Danielle Konrad, a voice like a brass bell, calling for justice and truth and an investigation into the attempted Conservative cover-up of this incident. Then came what was purportedly the voice of the victim himself, bitterly denouncing his own party and its policies of accommodation.

During the question period after the holo, however, Baxter's neighbors seemed inspired only by the ants who had caused such terrible wounds. Story followed story about the ravages of algae, termites, flies, and moths. The most modern exterminators and sterilizers seemed to work for six months or a year and then signs of diabolical insect presence turned up again.

"It's an epidemic," the young Prog spokesman said knowingly. "Nobody knows how big." He explained swiftly how termite populations had taken to building superfluous queen chambers even in soft plastic, and other species—earwigs and roaches most particularly—had quickly occupied these spaces. He hinted that the problem was another version of the flawed Con policy of laissez-faire, the idiocy of cultivating "unplanned diversity." An attempt, Baxter could see, to segue back to the main subject—helping the Party of Tomorrow launch its massive Gink eradication and Wasteland recovery program.

But the good citizens of Olive Terrace were stuck on bugs. One sharp-witted old woman in the audience chastised the young man by reminding him that these infestations had begun during a Prog administration, and the current government was spending more than ever on household sanitation. "You might try your hand at a few stink beetles," she suggested tartly, "before you start planning to kill off all the poor Ginks."

Her intonation, rather than those last words, brought a few gasps and here and there an approving grunt. Baxter felt his discomfort increase. He knew that among the very old, one sometimes encountered this tolerant attitude toward the degenerate species. Usually the offspring of those radicals who had, in the last century, sent humanitarian expeditions to the border. Expeditions often massacred outright, and successful, ironically, only in bringing death to any *lapsis* they managed to corner.

"An excellent point," the young man said with a disarming smile at the old woman, who was watching him as alertly as a hawk. "And one we must address, by all means. Progressives don't believe in avoiding hard choices." He moved back toward the podium, a little booth with control knobs for the holo and various chart stands and light-beam pointers. "Let's take a look at the record."

Glancing about the room, feeling furtive, Baxter became

aware all at once of a barely perceptible change in the level of available light. His own eyesight was not good, yet he preferred old-fashioned rimless spectacles over contacts or implants. He believed the beveled thick glass transmitted and amplified peripheral light. He was thus, he felt, more sensitive than most to subtle alterations in ambient illumination.

Automatically he looked at the indirect light wells in the ceiling and saw that one of them had gone out. He blinked at this small inlet of shadow, then blinked again. A few motes of dust were now visible against this bit of darkness, caught in the rays from adjoining lights. One of these motes did not swirl and float like the others. A bit larger, it swayed in a long arc and then all at once dropped a few inches.

Baxter looked away abruptly and sat up straighter in his chair, trying to concentrate on what the speaker was saying. Instead he thought once more of his wife's dog, Lancelot. A sprawling heap of fine, pale hair with two sad and rheumy eyes. Scrumptious Toodlums to his wife, but something far more sinister to Baxter. His discontent veered suddenly in the direction of dread.

For the third (fourth? fifth?) time in the last week an awful thought surfaced: perhaps he should seek medical help. He'd already gone so far as to look up the name of what his problem could be. *Saprophagy.* His mind recoiled from the word and he shook himself. In the chair next to him a woman turned with a modest, encouraging smile.

"I know how you feel," she said. "It makes my flesh creep too."

Baxter stared at her in alarm. Had he spoken aloud? Was she reading his mind? But no, it was the young man still droning on, showing them now on a chart how certain ribosomes could be reprogrammed to spread intraspecies aggressiveness. Teach self-destruction at the cellular level, that was the Progressive solution. Those jillions and jillions swarming over each other, mandibles and barbed claws clacking, slashing, and chewing, eating each other alive.

Baxter thought he was going to be sick. He forced his attention away from the easy, voluble sing-song of the man's narration and from the chart, where headless little snakes of molecules were squirming into knots of rudimentary, vicious intelligence. Only a few years back he had himself done a paper on the parallels between these molecular exchanges and the information flow patterns in large corporate and government agencies. Normally Baxter adored parallel and pattern. Charts and diagrams, in four dimensions, were his specialty; and to enter their endless intricacy and perfect predictability was for him the most exquisite joy life had to offer.

Normally. And Baxter had always considered himself paradigmatically, absolutely, inarguably normal. So when one day Phyllis had murmured as she often did that Lancelot was so sweet she could gobble him up, Baxter ought not to have even heard her. Or noticed how she took one of the silken ears between her teeth or buried her nose in the cloud of golden hair to root and make smacking noises with her lips.

But he did notice. And more than notice. It had occurred to him. . . . Baxter lurched on his chair, his mouth dry. As soon as the young man entertained another question he must use the interlude to flee. He could not take much more. He glanced again at the ceiling and immediately saw the tiny speck drop again. It decelerated smoothly and halted perhaps three feet above the young man's head. For an instant a broken thread of brightness appeared in the air between the speck and the light well in the ceiling. Spider.

The young man was laboring through his explanation of how the whole notion of "wildlife" was misguided and perilous, of how there was only life, period, and life was simply the complex coding and configuration of proteins. The noblest of human aims was to understand and control this coding, in order to enhance the welfare of society. And what most inhibited this aim was the wrongheaded philosophy of allowing unmonitored or debased populations to scatter deadly genetic material.

The residents of Olive Terrace looked variously desolate, angry, and bored. And beneath his ingratiating smoothness, the young man was on the verge of boiling over. The effort of maintaining his pose of casual confidence was exhausting, and the absorbent agents protecting his suit from dampness were wearing off.

The spider had disappeared into the young man's hair, though Baxter still glimpsed a sliver of light from the strand leading to the ceiling. Watching the insect's final, jerking descent, he had completely forgotten his vow to escape from the meeting. The young man was urging the Olive Terrace residents to some kind of petition. It was taking shape as a sweeping plea to do something about repulsive weed growths, high interest on remodeling loans, and inferior surgical rejuvenations. But only the hawk-faced old woman claimed the neighborhood and its inhabitants were both looking worse precisely because of their cosmetic efforts. This old woman, Baxter knew, was the specific object of the weed provision; for years she had refused to mow her own lawn, despite repeated citations, so whenever her grass reached an intolerable rankness a maintenance crew had to spray in the middle of the night.

Neither watching the spider nor half-hearing these arguments had succeeded in clearing Baxter's troubled mind. In fact the dangle and sway of the tiny speck in the middle of the room somehow paralyzed him in his chair and pried open the lid over the horrible dark abysm at the bottom of his being; while the voices in the room lost themselves in echoes and became a meaningless buzz and rumble that drove every single thought from his head, leaving only disconnected images, more and more disturbing images.

Scrumptious Toodlums lost his hair, became an obscene, naked gray worm. Then his wife's face shriveled, though her body ballooned suddenly, popping buttons. Her skin underneath was also gray, before it ruptured to reveal an amazing jewel-cask of colors. Fascinated, he watched these blues and greens and dark satin reds slide over one another, contract, distend, and then rupture in turn, releasing something opalescent and bubbling and aromatic.

He swallowed a mouthful of saliva, and heard the woman next to him whisper anxiously, "Are you all right?" He didn't answer. Couldn't answer. The glancing thread of light seemed to billow toward him, and his eyes crossed slightly. He saw double, then triple, then quadruple. He thought of the two huge cockroaches and experienced a dreadful relief.

He knew that all evening long he had been trying to avoid them. They were always what he most wanted not to think about. They lived in his basement, where he kept his woodworking tools and paints and other household chemicals. He had told nobody about them, because nobody would have believed what they did, how they watched him from a shelf or the corner of the room or the ceiling, waving their antennae alertly, two dark hands cupped slightly as if to conceal something underneath themselves. How they watched and watched and then rocked their big bodies in approval or disgust.

He could not even explain the practical things, how creatures so huge squeezed into the tiny openings around electrical conduits or at sink outlets, or what they ate to make themselves so monstrous. Truly almost as large as his own hands, with delicate but powerful limbs, they scurried over the wallboard faster than Baxter could lunge after them.

For of course—at first—he had tried to kill them. With poisons, traps, a swatter, and finally a small hand-weapon. But they were always too swift, and seemed to know about the weapon even as he reached for it. He got the distinct impression they were mocking him, provoking him. After he blew a hole in the window and had to spend an afternoon replacing it, he found a small pile of droppings directly on the open pages of a manual at his workbench.

At some point he realized that the roaches were connected with the ghastly mood, the visions that had begun to haunt him. They appeared on those days, and finally it happened that even as he recalled a ripe smell or an ooze of something rotten he heard the rapid, excited click of their claws on the floor, so that he could not tell which came first. And when he wheeled to stare at them in horror they rocked and bounced in a furious glee.

He had hurried into the library, searching for some material on what he feared was a mental disorder, had run across a number of ancient legends and stories. Once some of the protohominids had worshiped beetles, while others held the devil was a fly. There was an old tale about a man who awakened after a nightmare to find himself . . . He writhed on his chair, for the memory of this tale was insupportable. It was driving him mad. *They* were driving him mad.

The woman's hand was on his sleeve, gripping him with surprising strength. The images of other faces turned toward him in sets of four, as if he were looking through a kaleidoscope. The voices in the room had ceased, except for the woman's low hiss. "I said are you all right? Are you having an *attack* or something?"

The glint of light was directly over his head now. He thought he felt an infinitesimal touch in his hair, a brush as light as that of an imaginary wing, but his whole body was suddenly galvanized with a powerful, strange current. His very frame was humming, a million million tiny voices were speaking to each cell in his being, speaking the high, thin squirrel language of fastforward. He was connected to an unimaginably vast system of beings whose whole purpose was the gathering and synthesis of information. Light, temperature, moisture, acidity, location, caloric value—these were only the crudest and most obvious assessments. Their aggregate, correlated in neuron and nucleus, soon reached an intricacy and subtlety beyond the scope of any instruments of measurement. In the abdomen of the tiny spider, for example, were parasites already digesting microscopic mites from the skin over Baxter's skull, and so assimilating the fearful odor of all he had thought or dreamed these last two hours.

Thus the phantom roaches inside his thrumming skull were transmitting along the gossamer strand to their fellows crouched in the light well, and these in turn could gnaw a complex tracery on the wall of the basement trash compactor, a pattern that flies could read and around which slime molds could shape their commentary, so that spreading out as scattered egg cells, new colonies, the word of these two would go forth—the triumphant prophecy of careful, insidious conquest—a text amplified by every energy-release of organic decay, moving south fifteen hundred miles in the stored food reserves of monarch butterflies, or much faster under the fingernails of careless flight attendants, or still faster yet as an itch that interrupts a holo transmission by satellite (a pause or dropped word as the anchorperson thinks fleetingly, uncontrollably, of scratching), a message absorbed and interpolated with countless other messages collected and flashed from cell to cell toward the great centers—the termite mounds of the desert Wastelands, the cliff-hives of Himalayan bees, the tremendous ant colonies beneath the ruined jungles.

Baxter knew none of this in the way that he might normally know what he thought he knew. But his body understood. It was on the floor, paddling on hands and knees toward the exit. His clenched teeth did not keep back a froth of drool. Even after the connecting thread had snapped, this new force propelled him smartly along the carpet. It was a terrible, exhilarating urge toward earth. Dark, damp, rich earth. The excrement of worms, a microbial glut, the fungal swarm—everything rotting, rooting, writhing, reeking, reaching to clutch and devour.

But there were claws reaching for him, too. A surrounding cluster of eight-armed and eight-legged creatures. They bellowed a meaningless song of fear and revulsion and anger. They wanted to keep him from the earth, from the sweet, rank darkness, from his connection to this terrifying excitement. They wanted him back in the light, in the room, in his mind. He struggled, his spectacles flashing, but they carried him, bound, to a smaller room where a man came finally and held a little bright metal tube to his forearm and then the darkness came to him, suddenly and overwhelmingly, but he knew that in the heart of it the two dark hands were waiting and he would join them, a third hand, just the same, flexing and rocking, brushing and touching, vibrating delicately in that tremendous current of intelligent energy.

13

THIS SEEMED TO BE HIS FIRST CLEAR MEMORY, THIS moment, now, sitting up bare-chested and sweating, while Teeklo and Kapu sat opposite him and talked. It was a strange place—a kind of room square-hewn out of stone, with woven cloths and wooden utensils hanging from the walls. They were much nearer the surface, for a spear of actual sunlight fell from the ceiling and struck the floor with a glittery brilliance.

Ronald was fascinated by this luminous column, though it made his eyes ache. The vividness and solidity of everything around him was almost unbearable, and made him feel peculiarly empty and insubstantial. As if the smoke from the small clay pot at his side were drifting right through his ribs, or into his brain. These fumes, it seemed, had been in his mind for some time, veiling things or drawing aside to reveal startling images.

He blinked and said, "Yes."

For some reason he knew that Teeklo had asked him again if he understood the danger of going outside, how after being in the burrows all winter one would want to linger and dip a hand into the water or sand but how one must always keep moving. For he was going outside again, for a longer time. Somehow he knew that too. Adza had commanded it. He was going with Ap and . . . what was his name? He looked at the creature lying at his feet. Its head was cocked to stare up at him, gold eyes above long, pale whiskers, small ears laid back.

"You called him Yellow," Teeklo said. "It will do, until you learn our language better." He smiled at Ronald tentatively. "You are here now, I see. It has been a long time and you must be tired after such a . . . journey. But we must still go over a few things. The hard things."

For a moment the veil of smoke shifted and swirled inside Ronald. He glimpsed the stone hammer rising, the dirty little hand holding out. . . . He shook himself, staring hard at the pool of hard, bright light on the floor. The talk—the talk had gone on a long time about this. He had learned a little, he understood now. How for many years the Ginks had starved and their young were so often deformed. The darkness and the contamination and hatred of piksis and of themselves too, until finally someone laughed as she ate—a little girl but she had become the first great priestess. And so the ceremony, the Feast of the Dead. . . .

"Kapu was just giving you the novice teaching for . . . for . . . what is that word?" Teeklo grimaced and pulled at his beard. He, too, was naked to the waist, and damp, dark curls of hair crawled over his pale chest and shoulders. "When a child is playing tricks? Not nice?"

"Naughty?" Ronald suggested. "A bad boy?"

"No. The word for what the bad boy *does*."

"Mischief?"

"Yes! Mischief-teaching. It is what you need for the easiest raids, the lowest risk. But now you are here and seem a little stronger, I want to go back and be sure of some things. Now that you have your ghost back." Teeklo smiled at him slyly, eyes widening comically, like a child's stuffed toy.

"Ghost?" He glanced again at the slow swirl of smoke and

knew instantly that they had already talked of the strange other being that spoke with his voice, had even given it a name. "*Pahane,*" he blurted. Snaketongue. The cat at his feet yawned and stretched slightly, laying its muzzle over his instep.

Teeklo laughed. "Very good. You remember. But don't let him in just yet. Snaketongue is like a cub. He will chew you and throw you around, and you have been thrown around enough the last few months."

Months? That could not be. He looked at his hand, at his crossed legs. They were dark, except for the scars. Old, white scars, that had been raw and red when last he looked. On his feet were sandals of woven grass, and already they were ragged, half worn-out. "Ghost," he repeated stupidly.

"In the Pobla tongue the word is *kubi,* shadow-maker. You see, for us everything is just backwards from your piksi world. As if you—the you here right now I mean—could change places with that patch of dark that follows you around, growing tall or short as the day goes, imitating whatever you do." Teeklo turned and spoke swiftly to Kapu. The old man rose and stepped on his bare feet to the center of the room. Thrusting out his hands he waved them in the shaft of sunlight, creating a play of shuttling, blurred forms across the floor.

"Then *you* are the dark, empty one, and it is the master. You have no thought, no desire, no will, no anything. It has all the color and depth and power. You follow—no, not even that, for there is no time—you just *move* and *do*. You have no weight, no force of your own."

Ronald was staring, fascinated, at the darting shape on the floor. Kapu had joined his hands to make beating wings and the cat was up now in a crouch, head slung low and alert. "Of my own," he whispered, his mouth dry. He was remembering his panic in the black tunnels.

"Oh yes, it is . . . terrifying. To be so helpless. But then think—imagine—a great bird, an eagle or crane, and he is soaring near the sun, so that his shadow is huge and swift on the ground, swifter than he is himself, leaping across canyons and mountains and yet close on the earth, actually touching the leaves and stones and startling even the mighty bear, irresistible—that is now *you!* Free! Effortless! Untouchable!"

The shape on the floor floated, sliced, hung fluttering. Yellow pounced, his paws hooking on the bare stone. His unblinking eyes swiveled frantically from side to side as the dark wings slid now over his back and pulsed there mockingly for a moment before gliding on.

"But," the boy breathed, "but *you*. . . ."

Kneeling, Kapu brought his hands low and the shape grew darker, sharper, the separate fingers visible. Yellow spread his big paws, ears flattening.

"Ah yes," Teeklo said softly, "helpless still, but the other, what took *your* place—the ghost—is not. The ghost can come down, come closer. . . ."

Kapu brought his hands gently, slowly toward the floor. To the boy it seemed that the black prints beneath were rising right out of the stone. The cat's haunches rocked from side to side and from his throat came a low, querulous growl.

"Until it comes right into you, and you into it. Together, you see, but not the same." Teeklo's smile broadened, and Kapu, too, was grinning as he squatted with both hands pressed flat on the sunny floor. Yellow held the crouch for another long moment, and then his growl deepened and softened and he nudged Kapu's hand with his nose, at first experimentally and then as a playful caress.

"This is not easy, I know. We are cramming too much, but we are afraid of losing you otherwise." Teeklo looked somber and a touch stern again, his familiar manner. "And time is growing short for us. We know there is a volcano rumbling in the piksi world. They are growing hungrier and hungrier. You went a little mad, seeing that we eat the flesh of our dead, but for us what the piksis do is so much more horrible. They would suck out our spirits and let the body live on, make a work-thing out of it. In fact they cannot live without feeding on ghosts. And you cannot fill them up, ever."

Teeklo stared into the wisp of smoke from the clay pot, and he seemed to be talking to himself. "They make you into one of them, forever hungry, the living dead, the arrogant creatures who think they are gods and must recreate everything in their own image. Until you cannot leave any wild thing alone. Until you must keep hunting the others, trapping them, eating their ghosts so you can make the bodies do as you like. Until you—" He stopped and a clench of pain passed swiftly over his features. "You? It was *I* once. Oh yes, the hunter!" He laughed, a sound at once soft and sharp. The cat, once more curled at the boy's feet, raised its head and growled; and Kapu dropped a hand lightly but firmly on Teeklo's shoulder.

Teeklo shook his head and smiled grimly. "Sorry. You see, how subtle and far-reaching? I am not free of it yet! But anyway, this hunger for ghosts is what is driving their Border Patrols. It is also why they keep talking about reclaiming these 'Wastelands.' They pretend they want minerals or land or security. But it is only the wish to capture souls, make them into mirrors for self-admiration, or if that fails, then to destroy them."

With an effort, Teeklo looked at the boy again. "*Pahane*," he said. "You know the truth of this. The school you went to. The life you were given to lead. You were only a shadow then, one of those little dolls with strings. But you were not so good a doll, eh? Your ghost was still alive inside somewhere, and Mata smelled it and made you her cub. That is why you are here, why you chose to live with us. Why you ate of Pobla flesh, the flesh of that boy you saw born, and why when your father—"

His mind was not in the smoke now but crouched on the floor like the cat, the shadows playing under its spread claws. Attracted, baffled, frightened—frozen amid a scatter and shift of startling possibilities.

"Oh yes, we know. I heard it broadcast again before the battery failed. He is alive. Kept going by the desire for destruction—or so Adza guesses, and she is almost never wrong about that kind of thing. And of course you love him. Especially after he—in a way—rose from the dead. You want to go back—*Ronald* wants to go back—as a shadow yearns to fly back to its creator. But Pahane casts his own shadow. And it was Pahane who told you to eat of your brother's body. His body."

Like the cat the boy lifted his eyes, unblinking, pupils shrunk to pinholes. He breathed, in and out. The stone under him was hot, cold, then hot again.

"Yes. His flesh is now yours. So many that come are twisted, without arms or legs or heads. Spirits caught in miserable, ruined caves. You have given him a home and a life. He, too, is Pahane. Pahane is Pobla."

He breathed in and out again. "I ate," he whispered. Another of the great waves seemed to lift and drop the room.

"Yes," Teeklo said gently. "Yes. Listen to me now. For generations and generations the piksis sacrificed themselves and this world to make weapons that could kill not only themselves but almost everything alive. They used these death machines to lie and bluff and extort until the game became too expensive. But they didn't want to 'waste' their investment, so they— But why repeat all that? It upsets even to remember."

Indeed, the cat was on its feet again, prowling furtively, and Kapu was frowning. "But you see why the Pobla grew familiar with hate—hate still is haunting many of us—and had to learn not to detest themselves? By consuming their own deformed flesh, honoring the ghost of another by taking it into oneself? Why we never waste any part of being, body or spirit? In the hardest times, you know, the old and weak among us give themselves immediately to the children. *Weave a basket with my hair*, goes one of our songs, *and carry these bones to the feast*. And in our great celebrations that is exactly what is done. A Pobla ghost is powerful, and can leave the body it lives in anytime. But listen, Pahane, that is enough for now. You will break like a stick holding yourself that way. We do not expect you to change overnight. You will eat lizard and beetle and perhaps a little fish for this trip. Like Yellow."

Kapu said something to him then in the Pobla tongue. *Kish* meant "good," he had known already, and to his surprise he recognized several other words as well. "*Kish!*" he repeated. "*Pahane vasi tondu!*" Pahane goes outside!

Already getting to his feet, Kapu laughed delightedly and gave a ringing whoop of approval. Though he maintained his serious face, Teeklo, too, managed to look pleased. "With Ap and Yellow you will get plenty of practice," he said. "They don't know any piksi."

The odd feeling of emptiness, of being made out of smoke, persisted as they climbed the ladder of tough, twisted grass that hung inside the stone shaft. He did not mind the height, the swaying of the ladder, the dazzling sunlight. He was Pahane. He was going outside. *Outside!*

For weeks he must have seen only stone walls, or felt their cold, dank breath on his face. The hellish red glare of the torches and hearth fires had been no help; they always seemed to invite rather than repel the shadows. When he clambered from the top of the shaft, the brilliant sun and brisk wind staggered him. His heart was pounding and his vision blurred. There was laughter in his ears and he felt hands on either side, holding him erect, back to the wind.

"Pahane leemat kubi, pakish dako."

It was Ap, speaking right into his ear, grinning wide. The young Pobla carried a spear and bore a coil of grass rope over one shoulder, while from the other was slung his bag stuffed with leaves and medicines. On his other flank, Kapu and Teeklo had also picked up spears at the entrance to the shaft and stood now gazing away, silent, at the immense crack in the earth at their feet.

He blinked until the tears ran down his cheeks and his sight was clear again. He had seen a holo once at school, an educational feature on the canyon regions. The narrator had listed all the statistics on radiation and rapid erosion, the great depths and constant shearing; and his father had once explained how the Wastelands were unreclaimable because temperature extremes, high winds, and deluges kept ravaging and reshaping the landscape. *Treacherous,* had been his father's word.

But nothing had prepared him for this tremendous crack in the earth, forking and forking again into lesser cracks, some of them intersecting to cut out great precarious slabs and spires, exposing layers of pink sandstone or dark lava or mineral green shale. These crevices plunged down and down into a deepening gloom, where fractured cliffs and columns took on strange shapes in the retreating light. He thought he saw a great bird brooding over the abyss, a man's hooknosed profile, a colossal hunchback. Everything seemed to float, finally, on a bottomless darkness.

There was no sound but what he took to be the wind funneling through this immense stone maze: a distant, hollow, fluting roar. He could see a haze of green in some crevices, and smell a hint of rot in the air. It was already spring. Here and there a long veil of dust peeled away from the canyon wall and undulated along the chasm. At other places the bare stone shivered a little in the heat from the sun. Otherwise nothing moved. Though the men around him kept silent, he was aware of a change of mood, the presence of a common emotion of very high voltage. He thought suddenly of leaping, falling from the edge forever.

At his feet he heard the cat growl again, and a moment later the animal trotted off toward the canyon rim. It moved in a kind of swift shamble, loose inside its tawny coat, the big paws flopping carelessly in the dust.

"He's right. We should not linger here," Teeklo said. "Take radiation only when you have to, on the move." He placed the spear in the boy's hand. "The Pobla do not make a great show of parting—bad luck, we believe—so we will simply go now. Ap and Yellow are going to teach you scavenge and mischief. For a moon or two, or perhaps more. *Leemat kubi, Pahane.* Learn like a shadow."

The strong and nameless emotion was still with them. It surrounded him like a wall, keeping out a host of thoughts, of memories. "*Pakish dako,*" he said abruptly.

Teeklo and Kapu had turned, were moving away, but he heard one of them chuckle. Tugging at his hand, Ap laughed too. No good being a runt. He was Snaketongue, following the young Pobla, who was following the cat, already gone over the canyon rim. Under his sandals the fine dust splashed like water and then scurried away in the wind.

Behind him he felt the crowd of shadows hurrying, the memories and uncertainties and fears. He did not look around. They would lurk after, he knew. They would come for him at night, or whenever he had to go back into the burrows, but now his ghost would be with him. He would need this ghost, this Pahane, to deal with the colossal, ruined land before him.

14

WONDERWORLD WAS CERTAINLY THE FITTING BACKDROP for a clandestine chat. Danielle had worn black fatigues, a slop coat and her old droog glasses, but it was a wasted disguise. She could have been in a bathrobe, or an evening gown, and nobody would have noticed. Many of those waiting for a studio were already in their paraphernalia; though underneath the garb of soldiers or mental patients or butchers one could recognize techschoolers, young office workers, regular burb couples. A scattering of furtive, middle-aged men carried their gear in light stuff bags and kept their eyes to themselves.

She lounged near a row of boutiques off the main lobby. A desultory trade there, except in the snack shops. For the masses, traditionally, fantasy and sugar went together. She had herself always preferred the carbon rings with a more spiritual jolt. Even when she was a schoolgirl, and these emporia had been a favorite hangout.

Occasionally she got a curious glance from one of the youngsters. She could have been his mother, but in this game that could be an advantage. Anyway she would be watched for a time, she assumed, and so had laid down a couple of tranqs to keep herself easy. The contact would presumably be in the deep dark: the most unlikely might be the most likely, so she ruled out nothing that came into the lobby.

Yes, the perfect place—if you liked irony. The palace of illusions, where she was going to get in touch with the ultimate reality. Big Mister D. She took in a long, luxuriant breath and let it out in a rush. She would handle it. It was a stage you went through, boosting into a new level of power: a blast and burn you eventually jettisoned. The people she was working with now had known she could do it, had seen it in her before she knew herself.

A slender kid in a dark blazer, a school uniform, had angled suddenly in her direction, though he kept his face averted. Fifteen, at the most—long lashes, a haze of silken down on his upper lip, and a single, angry pimple. Cuddly little thing. Talk about unlikely. Danielle pushed away from the storefront she had slouched against and gave the boy an inquiring, encouraging smile.

"Hi." He managed to look into her blue, opaque droogs, his face heating up. "I . . . I wondered if you were waiting for . . . someone. You look like a . . . a teacher." He grimaced as if in agony. "Oh God, you are. I don't know why I'm doing this. I'm sorry, I'm really sorry.".

Danielle tilted her head, smiling now in plain amusement.

Not this one. She waited another beat, then laughed. "How sorry?"

He had lowered his head so he could look up at her through the long lashes with a glimmer of distant, desperate hope. "I would do . . . oh! I'm so ashamed I would . . . oh God!"

He was good, really. Very, very good. He was actually blinking back tears, cringing just perceptibly, promising an orgasm of shame.

"You're a cunning little beggar," Danielle said, "but I am, actually, waiting for someone."

"You could do anything," the boy said rapidly. "Go with a fifteen-minute ticket." He extended a hand and she saw a little fuse box full of white capsules. "New Blue Razors, slice 'n dice. Then whatever you want, all the way. I'll take anything—"

"Forget it." She wrinkled her nose and settled back against the storefront.

"Fuck you, grandma." He ducked his head, still with his gaping, embarrassed grin, and turned away.

"My pleasure."

So. WonderWorld to underworld. A little creep for every occasion. She didn't remember, in her own school days, that these places had been quite so tawdry. Interactive Virtuals had always been part of growing up, and most people got their real sex education in neighborhood parlors like this one. At thirteen she had herself belonged to a club. But the place they'd gone was safe, homey even, run by a couple of sweet old gayboys who winked and waved them through with no ID check.

It was all clumsy and crude. Kid stuff. And ultimately boring, except to the types who were pathologically vicarious to begin with. It was only your hologhost, after all, who sucked or got sucked, who whipped or cowered. You could make your likeness laugh or cry or come or lose its head, but you could never actually take its place. So you outgrew the Virtuals, because you couldn't forget anymore, entirely, that what you were—really, *really*—was just another lump of meat wired to a projector.

How *would* she know the right one, when he—or she—appeared? Well, she just would. The way everything else, so far, had fallen into place. Or almost everything. All she needed now was insurance. It would be expensive, but these free-lancers were professionals, the top of the line. She knew from the way they had first contacted her. Just a mailer from WonderWorld with a big X on the front and a date and time. It would only be necessary, she was confident, to allude to the name.

Every wizard in her business had one perfect opportunity —one occasion when all the planets were aligned, all the omens promising, and one's personal mojo irresistible. So ran the legend, anyway, and like others in her trade Danielle had playfully encouraged that sort of puffery. Divination, sorcery, telepathy, cryptomancy—these were useful, humorous metaphors for the indefinable savvy, the unerring, elusive hunches, that guided the greatest talents in Pub and Promo.

Still, she had never before been mystical about her gift. When they called her a media witch, she only laughed. Then she found herself at the center of a fairy tale. Then her own little hunch led her right into the very heart of power. She had seen enough now to know that this was it, this was her shot, the big one. She had a chance to choose the future. Not just her future. *The* future.

And then came the little hitch, bump, tremor, chill—she smiled to herself, a thin smile. She supposed you could expect that, in any line of sorcery. No one could micromanage the forces of darkness, so powerful and swift and secret. The smile faded and Danielle moved on, as if window-shopping. One in a million, she told herself. An incredible fluke if that boy were to be still alive, a kind of disastrous miracle, like getting struck by a meteor. Yet it was at least possible. Fat had sent his best agents to check, she knew from her own sources, with his little Gink lab rat as guide.

There was also the disturbing report from the Border Officer, disgruntled at his transfer. An alcoholic, but with no motive to invent such a tale—a boy, a human, running with Gink raiders, and a bear carcass whose geneprints Insec had "misplaced." The story seemed to her incredible, after so many weeks. The weather and altitude and distance, the mauling by a mad bear. . . . How could there be any real hope? A few hours, maybe a few days, at the most. Some elaborate deception of Fat's? But surely . . . by this time. . . .

Alive. Like a hiss, a jeer, the word invaded her, shocked

her out of her bemused tranquility. She glanced around, impatient, but saw no one approaching. The boy in the blazer had disappeared, and the lines at the ticket booth were shorter now.

She frowned into the dark glass of a shop already closed, one selling cheap animal costumes, tigerskins and ram heads. She hated being evasive with herself. She had already admitted the possibility, however farfetched. She was here, precisely, to arrange for any such eventuality. It was just that she had never done this particular kind of contract before. And it was redundant, of course. Insurance they would surely never need.

From the studios she could hear a faint, muffled cacophony of sound tracks. Swelling symphonies, screams of pleasure or suffering, thunder and rain. Only in fantasy did the one-in-a-million become commonplace. The perfect body, the ultimate domination, the extreme violation—they were consumed and refabricated every fifteen minutes. Only in that way would little Ronnie Drager ever exist again. A horror fantasy, but one nobody would ever forget. One of history's hinges.

She remembered the day, not a month ago, when she had glimpsed that promise. She had already found the harmonic range in the Drager item, the human-interest spin that was becoming a gyro for the whole NorthAm mood, lasting and lasting on into spring. Then there was the bonus rush she got from the father, that incredible hot blade of a madman with no face. She had seen that she could make something positively Greek out of this family, the child martyr and the father twisted to vengeance. Archetypal, yet modern—a hybrid of holosoap and myth.

And just then, it seemed, she had merely looked up and there was the chauffeur from the limovan handing her the bouquet of signed cards. She had read the names and immediately called her secretary to cancel the next two days' appointments. Then she picked up her handbag and stepped into the limo, which took her to the shuttle port, where she boarded a leased express—she was the only passenger—to an artificial island, one privately owned for generations.

They dressed in beachwear, chatted over drinks on a shaded lanai, kept things amiable. She had met a few of them before, but never such a concentration of wealth and influence. These were the most powerful information dealers in NorthAm society, a cross section from industry, finance, and government. Party affiliations, she understood instantly, were meaningless here.

Danielle had been amazed at their youth and vitality. Hard to tell, of course, how many transplants or grafts were behind appearances, but one and all they posessed the lean, bright, headlong manner of ambitious new billionaires. Their bodies bore no trace of superfluity, and a certain cold, diamondlike purpose burned in their glances.

In that first session she learned enough to be dizzy with anticipation, and profoundly moved. As if—she understood in a flash—she had been told she was carrying a child. What was at stake here, however, was the fate of *billions* of children yet unborn: nothing less than the future of the human species. For these people had the courage to articulate openly the nightmare that lurked nowadays in every workplace, every living room, every chamber of government.

Civilization, in the traditional sense, appeared to be disintegrating. Nothing dramatic and overwhelming, just a steady, subtle erosion. Everyone knew the hard evidence, the numbers; but only a few visionaries grasped—this was their common ground, what brought them together—a primary insight: that the whole structure was, after all, no more than a set of assumptions, certain habits of mind, an alloy of lusts and fears malleable as a dream. Culture was, had always been, an airy thing, a creation of genius. An artifice of the few, to entertain and inspire the many. The world ends—as one of her hosts remarked—not with a bang but with a dull story. Which meant that only a bigger, slicker dream could save it.

Her new friends were charmingly immodest on this point. Wealth and education had given them a certain, large perspective; and vice-versa—they had made fortunes, after all, by amassing and controlling information. Yet the key thing was not simply to be rich and exercise power. In the end one had to take responsibility for . . . well, for everything, really.

She remembered how the NumberCrunch woman had put it, with a lighthearted laugh, over their second giant Tropical Fizz. "All power is a bother, and absolute power is an *absolute* pain in the ass, dear. Believe me, *we* know how God feels."

They called themselves the Network. They had links to

similar organizations in the PacRim and EuroSlav capitals. "Black Widows," the head of Investment at the Federation Bank told her with a mock-sinister waggle of fingers. "If you don't mind the gender imbalance. We're spinning away here in the shadows." A GeneCo man frowned and shook his head. "Plasmids, episomes, phages . . ." he said. "Infecting the whole biosphere with new protein info. Hey, we move at *viral* velocity."

The NumberCrunch woman reacted with a touch of heat to these antiquated and inhuman metaphors. "My God, what are you saying? Remember, *we* are running the show. Have been for five thousand years. And now we're going to do it *right.*" She had then turned a brilliant smile on Danielle. "With Danny's help, we're going to rescue Northern Civilization from all its bugs, literal and figurative."

They praised Danielle extravagantly for her handling of the Drager affair. She had, they said, taught them to see its tremendous implications. But as she listened to the discussion, her thrill of pride was transformed into amazement. They saw much, much further than she had dared. They took for granted that her publicity blitz would propel the Progressives to power, and with sufficient momentum to begin radical revisions in public policy. That was, however, only a beginning.

The Federation had become a shell. It had always existed in order to mediate and compromise, to balance and integrate the economies of the Three Worlds. It was designed to calibrate and correct, but it had no ability to initiate, no *imagination.* And in the great struggle that was about to take place, a lack of imagination would be fatal.

The plan was basic and simple. They were in contact with a number of free-lance operators, small darkside units both in and out of government. They were already putting people into the demoralized Con party, agents who would purge the last remnants of its extreme right wing—the traditionalists with their absurd, romantic, and dangerous beliefs—and rebuild a constituency.

Then, on the surface, they could maintain the tradition of campaigns and elections, debate and controversy. But only as drama, sheer spectacle, an ongoing series. Informal and invisible, the Network would script and produce every aspect of NorthAm political and economic life. They would tap into the deep phobias already coalescing—thanks to Danielle—around the Ginks, the Wastelands, and every dangerous and noxious species. They would muster the energy of a crusade behind pursuit of the final goal of history: to manage, consciously and absolutely, all earthly forms of life, for the enhancement of the highest of those forms.

And when the time was right. . . . The Fed banker stopped and merely smiled, and the others smiled with him and they all looked at Danielle, who smiled back her perfect understanding. The Federation would wither away and be replaced, or they would inhabit its shell. It made absolutely no difference.

All the world's a stage. A line she'd heard a thousand times without realizing its scope. That a play must have an author and director, even an angel. Her new friends laughed at this flattering reference, and they all knew a powerful, communal joy. They were going to put on—and it was, this time, no hype but plain truth—the Greatest Show of All Time.

Well, the conflict so necessary to great drama had come soon enough. At their third meeting—this one in the less glamorous context of a hotel suite—she had had to tell them about the border incident, the misplaced geneprints, and Insec reconnaissance probe. She would never forget the quiet in the soundproofed room. Oh dear, someone had said then. Oh dear oh dear.

"Evidence?" the banker had asked, and Danielle would always admire him for his matter-of-fact tone.

"No tissue," she had answered, with a smile that sliced through every face around the table. "Yet. We presume."

She had been up most of the night formulating strategy, and so went straight on into her plan of sending infoteams into the burbs and backroads to develop petition drives and to stir up public outrage generally. The Cons had nothing to counter with, at this point, but wild rumor. The Insec probe was probably only an effort to find and destroy evidence, a sign of desperation. The chance of young Drager's having survived was so remote. . . .

The banker had sighed, lifted one hand at the wrist. He did not have to say what they were all thinking. There was no place, in their new dream, for chance. He observed, instead, that the Cons could not be allowed to tamper with evidence. A federal grand jury would have to be empowered to supersede Insec. Surely the facts would come to light. One fact would be enough, someone else added. Tissue, the banker repeated with a half smile.

They were all looking at Danielle. We can help, of course, the banker went on. Consultants, assistants, whatever you might need. . . . He cleared his throat, and Danielle saw, finally. For just a moment she felt giddy, out of breath, and then she sliced them again with her smile. They were offering her the starring role, the radiant center of all risk, all glory. They were gambling that her will to create was like their own, implacable and without scruple. With all their ease and charm, they were careful with nuance, and Black Widow was not so wrong an image after all.

"Put me in touch, I'll take care of it," she said, knowing the conversation was over, forever.

Four days later she opened the envelope containing the WonderWorld brochure.

"Mama, come listen to me."

Danielle started, hearing the high voice and feeling simultaneously a tug at the hem of her coat. A street urchin, a boy of nine or ten, she thought at first. He was wearing tucked trousers, pump shoes, and a red sweatshirt with a logo. In one hand he swung a voombox, the wires running to goggles around his neck.

She blinked and yawned in her nervousness. She hadn't seen him approach, had drifted off. . . . The boy was grinning at her, something arrogant in his slouch.

"Hey," he said, "big girl. I like it. How about we get an ice cream?"

She had taken a breath to laugh, to dismiss and ridicule, when she saw that the face was not a boy's. The features were cut too deeply, the skin pitted. It was a man, a—

"You never seen a pit dwarf? What you been missin'. Good things come in small packages." He swung the voombox, tilted his head suggestively. "What say, mama? An ice cream, and I'll let you watch my stuff. Got a little tape here just for you. You the witch, right?"

She nodded, collected herself, and walked without a word toward the nearest brightly lit refreshment booth, the Scoop

Shop. She felt foolish, a little disoriented, and angry at her inattentiveness. "Fatal Fudge," he called after her. "Two scoops."

When she came back, balancing the absurdly stacked cone, he took it from her and handed her the box and goggles. "Plug in, mama, and just listen." He raised his eyebrows and extruded a tongue, pointed lasciviously, to touch the dark crown of chocolate.

She saw then the holo unit was a fake. It was a two-way radio, with mike and earphones built into the goggle frames. She took off her droogs and hooked the goggles over her ears, but propped on her forehead so she could still see. She heard a channel switch open to light static.

"Can you hear me?" The voice was female, neutral, a receptionist's tone.

"Yes."

"Good. Keep strolling. Your little friend will take care of himself, you don't need to worry. It's better if you don't know our organization by name, if we operate entirely on trust. We recommend simple yes or no answers. We understand there is a slight chance of a possible problem?"

"That's right. Yes."

"We understand you want a zero-margin confirmation, on a single party?"

Danielle was gazing across the foyer, where several studios had disgorged a small, milling crowd. Some were gape-mouthed, apparently laughing, others blank, as if stunned. They looked like animated dolls, entirely mimetic, for she could hear nothing but the faint static in the earphones. A single party. They were all single parties. She was conscious of making a great effort to believe. Life reduced to such an ordinary, pathetic phrase. She swallowed. "Yes."

"We already have some idea of this. We understand your hesitation. Let us explain that we will not, tonight, make any final determination or agreement. At this point we need only a preliminary indication of the area of concern, identification of the party. For example—listen carefully—would further research and development be necessary?"

"What?" She replied before she thought, forgetting the admonition for yes or no answers. What were they talking about?

"Research and development." The flat voice took on the faintest shade of impatience.

Danielle glanced at the dwarf, who was twirling the cone into his tongue, paying no attention to her. What did that mean, "area of concern"? A code phrase, perhaps. But how was she to recognize it? Why would an R and D team. . . .

"WonderWorld is a facility for young people," the voice went on, now with a definite edge. "A child's game. And for you, developing knowledge. Dangerous knowledge."

All at once her face flamed and she exhaled between clenched teeth. *Shit.* "Yes, yes all right." Or deadly knack. Straight acronym. How idiotically simple, Danielle Konrad. R and D, our boy exactly.

"So we would pursue research and development." The voice was again impersonal, so colorless the effect was one of parody.

"Yes. You have it. Child's play."

There was the briefest of pauses. "That's enough. Very good. There will be a ten-day waiting period before we reach you again, for finalization. We remind you contracts are not revokable. We—"

"Wait," Danielle said. "What—"

"Others are negotiating terms. Your interests seem to be in good hands. This concludes the introductory process, unless you have questions."

After another second or two of static, Danielle said no and the channel switched off.

Her little friend was well into his second scoop, a dark smear at one corner of his mouth. He had been leading her by a few steps, keeping them away from the press of customers in front of the studio gates, but now he lagged beside her.

"All through, mama?"

She removed the goggles and hooked them on the voombox, handing the unit over to him. "Through. Thanks for the equipment."

"I got all kinds of equipment." He made a movement of his shoulders and hips, obscene and insolent. "You ever been climbed by a midget, mama?" The tongue darted again into the ravaged dome of chocolate. "A monster midget?"

Danielle did not bother to answer. She was still thinking

of the bizarre conversation over the radio. Its swift, empty efficiency gave her an odd shiver.

"But we don't get to do clientele. Just a lowly messenger. Too bad. You're absolutely my plate, mama. Big tough girl. Oh, I do like." His eyes went the length of her, and returned, in the same way he worked over the ice cream.

"How sweet." Danielle had to smile at his jaunty lewdness. This organization at least had a sense of humor, to send her a full-grown lecher in the body of a child. A clever hint, too, that they already knew the name. Father and son together. That made her, she supposed, a holy ghost.

"Anyway, I can't hang around, mama. So long and thanks for the treat."

He popped the tip of the hollow cone into his mouth, winked, and broke away from her. She watched him swinging the voombox, exactly like a carefree boy, until he vanished through the exit. In a moment she moved to follow.

Riding the belt to the parking lot, she did not see the lighted store windows, the passersby. She felt a little ungainly, yet strangely light. A balloon. Yes—she remembered all at once watching as a child—a birthday, surely—as a red balloon escaped and lofted higher and higher, and she yearned to follow, yearned so hard she felt the earth falling away beneath her. She felt that way now. Cut free and rising. And this time—she caught her breath—she would not come back until the world had changed.

15

WATER AND SUN DETERMINED THEIR LIVES. IN MANY OF the deep, narrow canyons there was neither, and he and Ap had to hide from the scouring wind in caves or behind ledges of sandstone. Yellow had only to shutter his eyes, fold back his tufted ears, and curl up until he was indistinguishable from the stones. Sometimes the gale was hot enough to make them gasp, and other times it cut like ice, but these changes seemed unrelated to the weather above them. This weather they saw as a band of light high on the canyon walls and a crack of sky overhead, variously deep blue or some shade of gray.

They traveled most often in the dry streambeds at the bottom, where the sun might reach for a scant two or three hours at midday—unless the air was full of dust. Now and then a trail took them along a sheer cliff face and once they actually reached the rim, from whence the boy got a glimpse of a kind of rotting plain, seamed and split and gouged, where nothing moved but distant billows of dust or lightning flickering out of low clouds on the horizon.

But they did not tarry there. He knew they were moving deep in the canyons and sleeping in caves both to evade satellite surveillance and to minimize exposure to the radiation. They also had to avoid much of the water they encountered, however seductively it bubbled up in clear pools or dripped from rock walls, ringed by the fresh green of reeds and moss. *Pakish!* Ap would say, shaking his head at Pahane and seizing Yellow by the scruff of the neck to keep him back. *Loobool pakish.* Then he would see that the greenery sprang up through a litter of small skeletons.

Loobool was water. Ap had sung him a song about it that emphasized how the word sounded like a fat drop falling into a deep well. He sang the song to himself over and over, and had dreams in which he became a river and traveled over the ground, effortless and fluent, for miles and miles and then hurled in a long endless arc over a cliff, his hair blowing back white.

He had such dreams because each day their goal was water. For food they took only strips of dried meat and pinches of some mummified leaf from Ap's shoulder bag (except once when Ap had dug fat, white worms in a deep cave and eaten them by the handful), but it was thirst that drove them, haunted them every moment.

The air was dry as the inside of a furnace, and even the sand underfoot seemed to pull moisture out of their bodies. He imagined he heard tiny rivulets whispering, the brush of ferns over a clear surface, a tinkling under rocks. The memory of the canals around Adza's temple made him run his tongue over the fine grit on his lips and swallow hard.

But until they had encountered this ice-river, Ap had allowed only handfuls from rare springs at the back of the deepest caves. Even these were sniffed and tasted carefully first, and twice they had survived on the few bitter drops chewed out of a pale, fleshy plant that grew in a patch of damp sand. So when Ap began to dance and gesture that morning—shouting *Loobool, Pahane! Loobool dina kish!*— he had not understood that the deep mutter he heard at the mouth of a side canyon was not wind but a great, heavy rope of water diving out of a cave into a basin scooped out of the stone.

And cold! So cold it drove all the breath from his body when he stepped into it. Ap had laughed like a lunatic at his chattering teeth, yet both of them lunged, gasping and blowing, again and again into the big pool. After so many days of thirst and the incessant dry wind, the shock of breaking into the brilliant pool was exhilarating. His mind became as clear and empty as the water.

By means of gestures and a diagram drawn in the wet earth, Ap seemed to indicate that the river came from the melting snow in the mountains in the Preserve where Mata had first seized him. He shook his head in disbelief, but Ap only laughed and went off to gather bunches of a long, tough grass that grew along the bank. For an hour or two they worked to braid these strands and then weave them into crude blankets with a hole in the middle for their heads. These garments felt awkward and crackled with every movement, but they kept out the chill.

Then the Pobla man searched out a scraggly shrub growing from a crevice in the rock just above the stream. With his spearpoint he sawed out a forked branch, and with a few fibers split from the longest blades of grass he lashed this fork to the haft of the spear, making a crude hook. In reply to Pahane's inquiring frown he made a sinuous movement with the flat of his hand and pointed at the column of water jutting from the cave.

Next Ap overturned stones at the edge of the basin and picked a handful of hard-shelled, segmented creatures from their undersides. These crawlers he stuffed in his shoulder bag, grinning at Pahane's impatience and puzzlement. He indicated with a jerk of his head that they were to enter the cave, and uttered a half growl at Yellow, who had been watching them—disdainfully, the boy thought—from atop a large boulder well above the water.

The animal rose and stretched, its claws grating on the stone, and shook dust from its tawny hide. Its jaws sprang open, revealing the broad red tongue and curved fangs, then chopped shut. With a bound it was down and past them to the brink of the rushing water.

He took his spear and followed Ap, who was picking his way along a ledge leading to the cave mouth. They followed the ledge inside and then along the rough inner wall, where it was immediately twilight. He was surprised to find a rim of ice crystals on the rock under his hand, and his breath appeared before him in puffs of frost. The river ran swift but untroubled, like heavy, dark glass. The sound of its passage was a vast, echoing whisper.

As the light failed, Ap hooked one hand in Yellow's back. When the cat turned occasionally to look at them, its eyes glowed like gold-green lanterns, a spike of darkness across the center of each. They moved more slowly now, and without being told he grasped the hem of Ap's grass garment. A few steps further and the passageway bent sharply, leaving them in utter blackness. He followed Ap's footholds by touch alone, as exactly as he could. Just the thought of plunging into the rushing cold water made his skin shrink over his bones.

The cavern expanded then, the sound of the river changing to a deeper and more restless tone. He felt Ap's hands over his own, guiding them, and understood that this was to be a silent form of instruction. The man stretched out to touch the surface of the water, and by the slight pressure of the flow the boy realized they were at the edge of an eddy, while upstream the tongue of the current raced faster. With fingertips he followed as Ap took a fistful of the crawlers from his bag and thrust them deep into the slow whorl of water, the reversed spear with lashed-on hook in his other hand.

They were now sprawled flat on the stone bank. Yellow was so near that he felt stiff whiskers brush his cheek, and the cat's low, rasping purr was louder than the muttering of the river. The thrum and echo of these sounds and the grip of the icy water on his arm seemed to occupy his whole existence; in the darkness the rest of his body and mind had been annihilated.

He could feel the small hard-shelled creatures as they wriggled to free themselves from Ap's fist. Halfway out, they squirmed furiously from side to side. Then something slid along his forearm, a long shape, at once silky and solid. Something else bumped into his knuckles. He felt Ap's fist yield to a tugging, just before the hand bearing the spear hook drove into the water and jerked back hard.

He was thrown aside in the recoil of Ap's shoulders. There was a great commotion, a thrashing and slapping. He heard Ap yelp in delight, then a snarl and a loud, wet crunch. After another slap or two, the crunching began again and went on steadily. He knew Yellow was eating, cracking bones, and he recognized the thick, cloying odor of blood.

Ap began to chant. An odd, dissonant melody, it seemed to match itself to the mutter and hoarse whisper of the river. Notes darted in and out of hearing, syllables blending sometimes perfectly with a ripple or sigh from the stream. Without ceasing the chant, Ap drew him back to the bank and they began again: the handful of wriggling creatures thrust down into the current, the hook lifted and ready.

This time the fish came immediately and he felt several sharp nips at his submerged hand. Yellow was again beside them, his breath hot and rank, and when Ap heaved back the cat struck with its paw and dragged another thrashing shape onto the rocks. Ap moved swiftly away from him; he heard a sharp thump; then the fish was thrust in his arms.

He could feel the hard, slick body shivering, its skin like metal somehow thrilled into life. When there was a sudden convulsion he held fast, startled at its power. The shivering ceased, and then the long body went heavy and still. Ap stopped his chant and for a moment they were quiet and motionless in the dark. Then a coil of twisted fiber was produced from the shoulder bag, and Ap guided him through the motions of threading the fish on a length of his twine.

In the next attempt Ap missed with the hook, which the boy guessed was used to catch the fish under its gill plate when it came after the crawlers. Then for a time there was nothing, until their hands were too numb to feel anything in the freezing water. They moved a few feet further along the eddy and there caught two more in quick succession.

After these were threaded on their string Ap pressed a lump

of crawlers in one of his hands and put the hook in the other.

"*Pahane shima,*" the man breathed into his ear. "*Ayom-pari.*"

Almost the moment he broke the surface the fish were plucking at his fist, but when he squeezed reflexively they shied away. Ap had reached down with him, and now pried gently between his knuckles, showing him how to let the crawlers protrude. A fish seized one immediately and began to worry it.

"*Kish! Kish! Gopa!*"

He lashed down with the hook, but was too late and too clumsy and Ap laughed. He took the boy's spear hand and demonstrated a quick, stroking motion. Beside them Yellow growled impatiently. But once more the fish had vanished and they had to draw back, their arms dead from the cold and the crawlers escaping between fingers too numb to feel.

They moved again, this time to a point near the head of the eddy where the faster current entered. Here the problem was too many fish, most of them small. Each time he lowered his handful of bait they swarmed after it, pecking furiously. He tried several times to hook something, and then all at once the pecking ceased. An instant later he felt a solid tug, a crawler ripped in half.

He stroked swiftly with the hook and a sudden drag nearly pulled the spear haft from his grasp. He heaved but the weight on the spear was now alive and resistant, a wild jerking he could not control. Ap grunted and seized his forearm, and their combined effort drew the hook to the surface. There was an explosion of spray, drenching his face and chest, and he felt Yellow lunge beside him.

The twisting body that hurled itself at them was strong enough to slap his arms aside. He felt Yellow's back bucking against him, as if the cat were riding a thick branch whipped by a high wind. Ap fell across both of them, yelping his high laughter. The slapping and growling and exclaiming went on for a good while, until several sharp thuds brought the sound of a long shiver of death against wet stone.

Pahane, too, was shaking, from excitement and the cold dash of water. Ap took his hands and laid them on the still form of the fish. It was longer than his arm, and as thick as his leg.

"*Pahane leema kish,*" Ap said, and through the darkness the boy heard the warmth and pride in the man's voice. He had learned well; this was *shima tak,* the biggest of their catch.

"*Vasan tondu,*" he said, and clacked his teeth for emphasis.

"*Ya!*" Ap laughed and began swiftly to fashion another twine string for the new fish, for it weighed nearly as much as the other three together. Then he slung the whole catch from the middle of his spear, and with this burden between them they began slowly and painstakingly to retrace their steps toward the light, Yellow again leading the way.

In the sunlight the fish were silver with a band of iridescent colors on their broad sides, pink flame with a halo of pale blue and green. *Redfish,* the boy thought in wonder, the very region from which the river was supposed to flow. Could it be? Hundreds of miles, underground? He remembered some mention of a fish—the name would not come to him—that once migrated annually to the sea, but they were long extinct.

Ap pointed out various peculiarities as he stripped out the guts and threw them to Yellow to pick over. The eyes were shrunken and milky—Ap covered his own with one hand to show they were blind. Their snouts were sheathed in tough, cartilaginous plates, some scarred and dented from fractures; their tails and ventral fins fanned out nearly half a meter, feathery and semitransparent. The Pobla's gestures indicated that these features helped the *cheen* navigate through rock-bound rapids.

Ap split the fish in half and draped the sections over a flat, sun-heated rock. The raw flesh was a deeper shade of flame, and they peeled away strips of it to eat. A day earlier they had gone into a cave from whose sides warm water dripped, and there Ap had broken off white crystals of salt. Pahane found that he could dip the thinnest strips of flesh in this salt, and after only a brief while in the sun they became crisp and tasty.

They ate, dozed, and ate again. The wind was luckily balmy and light, finally driving the chill of the ice-river out of their limbs. Yellow lay fully extended on his rock, his hide tight now over a swollen belly. He did not move other than to yawn periodically or flex a paw in some dream pursuit.

Pahane was still eating, though chewing very slowly. He

had never experienced so rich and dark a flavor, had never felt food move into his body with such force. Looking at his bare body—he had shed the grass blanket and now lay on it—he could see, under the dust and dried blood, that he was all bone and tendon, like the Pobla. Yet he felt strong. Hunger and thirst and fatigue had gone away completely; he could not even remember them. It was as if the powerful, silver fish were gliding through his own blood, ready to leap or thrash at any moment.

His shadow was also with him, in him. A daytime shadow, he had noticed, for the most part. At night, in the deep caves they slept in, huddled against Ap and Yellow for warmth, he often felt himself completely Ronald again. Sometimes he thought he heard his father's voice breaking through the static of the wind hissing over sandstone, or he saw a vision of his mother doing some ordinary thing—raking in the yard or bending over a dish in the kitchen.

These visions still brought waves of grief and yearning, squeezing tears out of him, but they seemed now to pass like dreams. In the morning he ate heartily, smiled at Ap's clowning, and even felt refreshed. Now and then he knew a pang of guilt, usually connected to his schoolwork, but he soon recognized that this guilt actually grew out of a secret relief at escaping from his studies.

Pahane, on the other hand, seemed to have learned many things effortlessly, during the long troubled sleep of his convalescence. Dozing again now, full of an easy, lazy strength, he understood clearly that Ap's songs about *loobool* and *cheen* had been songs of gratitude and respect. He found he could sing the songs silently to himself, from memory, and when he finished he felt a blissful contentment, followed a moment later by a quickened beating of his heart and then a vision of a cataract where the fire-bright fish plunged and reared, twisting up and over the seething torrent. It was as if the swift, cold water and the silver beings that lived there were also ghosts and could gesture to him.

The plunging and rearing were frantic, the frothing river implacable. In his bloodstream a feeling he could not name rolled and lifted. This was not his ghost; this was an element vaster than the dream river, vaster than the great plain he had glimpsed, vast beyond comprehension. Yet it bore him lightly as a bit of seed-down, bore all things alive, even as they soared and swam and leaped and hurled themselves toward or away from one another. The river and the arrowing, plunging fire-fish were full of light now, the light of rainbows and shattering diamonds, until he was no longer conscious of their forms, only of a radiant fountain in his mind, a sun at first small but growing, intensifying. . . .

His eyes were not quite closed, and he sensed a flicker of shadow outside his skull. He blinked and lifted his head in time to see the dark blade scything past, so near he heard the whistle of wind through feathers. He saw also the talons extend and spread, then clutch and lift away a whole half of the big *cheen*.

He and Ap sat upright at the same time and both cried out. They watched the methodical beat of the great wings, rising steadily down the long, crooked canyon. They stared then at each other, at Yellow still snoring on his rock, and in a moment erupted in wild laughter. They were aware of mirroring each other's reaction, passing from dumb amazement to outrage to a helpless gape.

They laughed until their bellies ached, Ap hopping up and down like a toad beside the remaining fish halves. Yellow was awake now and grumbling, pacing back and forth with a scrape and click of claws. Pahane was certain the cat was offended by such antics, for he avoided looking directly at them and snarled irritably into the air. And this, for some reason, made them whoop even louder.

But all at once Ap grew serious, pointing at the fish and at the crack of sky overhead, then at the band of light receding up the canyon wall. When he spoke, with more gestures, Pahane heard words that had become familiar. *Zelag tak,* great distance; *loobool delo ya pakish,* bad water and not much of it; *sulo nitamo,* new weather. And a new word: *mahn.* It was, he gathered, a big canyon, a round canyon. Ap shook his head. *Piksi mahn!*

He grinned and slapped Ap on the knee. Of course. A mine! He knew they existed—the only outposts in the Wastelands, besides the border stations, where his people lived all year round. He struggled to remember scenes from the educational holo. Molybdenum, he thought, or manganese. The huge scoops and trucks with their lead-plate shields, the workers in cumbersome suits with helmets and air filter packs. New crews every few weeks. High salaries for hazardous duty.

So this was where Pahane would learn what Teeklo claimed was something like mischief. Part of a young Pobla's training. What was the word?

"*Tchat?*" he ventured.

Ap looked up from the map he was scratching out in the dust and grinned back at him.

"*Tak tchat!*"

16

PERSONAL
Insec/RA/Cdfx   759921876-PS   SeCom   2/23/2132

How can I know? Maybe it's me. But something is definitely up. Fat said zero about this kind of weird. When I think about that 1st time, his office, I think she also had fix on him but he didn't know it. She watches all the time, watches both of us, doesn't even have to use her eyes—which I can't prove of course. And that causes or is connected to the hallucinations, I'm sure, though ditto no proof. Now today for 1st time these hlcns not only sexual. This time thot I saw inside her womb and there was an animal of some kind, raccoon or weasel or mongoose, etc., but with Skiho's face. A shock of course to find out he was rutting on her in the shower. Couple months out, guy's pecker can rebel, but still. Thot this was a sensitive op, class op.

Took 2 caps Rzr-mix and felt OK for 1 hour only, effects wearing off quicker.

Right now we are sweeping Area 23 NE Quad D-11, watching a storm develop just south in 24. Black Jack in his sleepsack, I'm doing this obviously, T across cabin supering ystd's takes for anoms yet I am dead sure she knows this is about her. Fifteen mnts ago asked me to review possible. Like leaning over a pit full of alligators and flowers.

Thinking just maybe I shld pop a slider, go ahead and do her too. Watch for sudden moves. That way if she is up to something I'll be ready. Bitch is strong, no question, but I can rig a nail shot, a hammer just in case. Research, we can call it.

PJ hit three keys to encrypt the file and cerberus it, then exited in two stages to protect his access code, and yawned convincingly. The onboard was keeping their X-4 in a long oblong pattern, the big hovercopter lifting and dropping with the contours of the terrain. The rad shields were in place, leaving the navigation room suffused by a greenish, submarine glow from instrument panels and their small desk lamps.

When he stood up Tima gave no sign of acknowledgment. She remained poised over the horizontal table-screen, her light-pencil ready, seemingly concentrated on the supers shuttling past. PJ experienced a flash of rage. His fingers twitched at the thought of digging themselves into the straight, heavy hank of black hair. Jerk her erect, make her look directly into his eyes and admit what she was doing.

With an effort he made himself turn aside and approach the water cooler. The tension was getting to him. He rested his forehead against the cool metal skin of the tank and with unnecessary deliberation removed a plastic cup from the rack. What *was* she doing? Possibly nothing, which meant then that he was a headcase, or that the Insec quacks had misdiagnosed his stress level and set wrong dosages.

After the first hallucinations he had refiled his medstats and taken the tranqs recommended, but without appreciable impact on the problem. The problem. Christ, what was the problem? This was supposed to be what he liked to do, his career. Cruising the Preserves and the Wastelands, monitoring the game and Gink populations, working with other professionals, the best.

But this one was driving him crazy. Bats, the old expression. Punching the button and rotating the cup idly as the water trickled in, he had a vision of an undulating black cloud, a cacophonous whispering of wings. Why bats? Silent screaming, maybe. An incessant chitter-chatter just beyond the range of hearing, a scratching directly on the surface of the brain. That's what it felt like.

He sipped the ice water, moved two steps to the side, and punched the med cabinet. He ran a finger along the rows of bottles and ampules, the small drawers for tabs, injectors, bandages. He could feel her taking note of this action, too, though there was no fluctuation in the hum of shuttling supers.

Oh, she was good all right. Fat's smugness was justified there, if you were talking pure job performance. Twice already she had picked up possibles and they had gone in, but no luck. A couple of coyotes starving to death in a dry lake bed, and a flake of debris from some old satellite burnout. Uncanny on the ground. Saw everything and never seemed to tire. Part of the problem.

What, he had asked himself twenty times already, was the point of this experiment? Of course it was possible—theoretically at least—to domesticate them, make servants out of the young ones, even a kind of worker class. But at what expense? What was Fat's budget on just this one case? It had all been tried anyway, by the goody-goody reformers of the last century; but except for a few border units that had trained captured infants as trackers, he knew of not one viable example.

PJ had located the box of tiny injectors and pinched out one of them with tweezers. He had left the cabinet door wide, so as to block Tima's view, but found himself hurrying as if she might guess what he was doing. Filling the injector capillary from a small bottle, he cursed under his breath. She warped everything. The whole idea was badly warped. They fought like demons to *be* animals, wallow in filth, eat their own young, live in burrows. Would rather commit suicide than enter a vehicle. Half ape anyway, some of them. So why . . . ?

He was trembling a little, and it took three tries to insert the injector under the nail of his left index finger. The drug was a KO and paralytic. A hammer, as they said, driven by a nail. A hard squeeze of an arm, shoulder, or buttock would send it home through a couple layers of cloth. Stop her cold. Only in case. He expelled a breath, smiled. Better.

He selected another bottle and shook out two capsules, hesitated, then made it three. He held them in his palm, deliberating, the cup of water balanced again in his other hand. Maybe he should crosscut these sliders with a couple of razors, a sure though not recommended way of reaching maximum alertness in his detachment.

His breath wheezed out in a silent laugh. Detachment. Problem and solution together. Parts of his mind kept detaching, uncoupling, breaking off. He had to get some distance on that. Detach himself wholly. He threw down the three caps and took a swallow of the water, warmer now. The fine line between getting outside yourself and flying apart.

One of the parts now was Tickles, whom he hadn't thought of for years. Ted Keelough, his best buddy and most formidable rival. The two of them the hottest trainees Insec ever had, natural hunters; and between them always the question: who was toughest, smartest, fastest? Both of them loving patrol, living for it, earning—for their very first assignment —the job of raiding villages for signs of mixeds. The ideal duty—swashbuckling research—to launch a brilliant career.

So where was it now, all this high promise? PJ had located and opened the razors, small, dark red tablets. Two maximum, his readouts said. Fuck the readouts. He shook out four. He would be superkeen when it came time. Came time to come. Meanwhile review the concept of career. Top agent gets to the bottom of things. He made a crude funnel with his hand and poured the four tabs into his mouth, then swallowed them with what remained of the water.

Tickles went crazy. If you could go bats in the old days, you could go Gink now. The agency listed him as missing and scrubbed the record, but everyone in Special Op knew. In retrospect PJ had seen the signs clearly enough. The man had become obsessed with live specimens, collected far more than the program needed. Truckloads of extras had to be eliminated, which only provoked Tickles into gathering more.

Before long he was in trouble for ranging too far from a vehicle, staying out too many days. He got moody and quiet, turned down his rec breaks and furloughs until HQ finally forced him to take them. PJ had tried to talk to him, best-buddy style. Mostly it was like lecturing a stone. "Maybe we've got it backwards," Tickles had said to him finally. "Maybe we're the fallen ones."

At the time PJ had been flabbergasted. That oldlady sen-

timental crap. Noble beasts, primal innocence, big mama
Nature—the absurdities and errors of two centuries ago. No
serious person could believe such nonsense. Yet Tickles had
entered a long letter in the vehicle onboard when he deserted,
a letter full of such archaic notions. He had also disassembled
his weapons and neatly folded his uniform according to specs.
Schizo, surely from a tumor, PJ had believed then. Now he
would not make so confident a diagnosis. A mark of his own
brilliant career as agent.

He had let the cabinet door swing wide to expose the polished metal mirror on the inside. He watched the face there
flick out a small, mocking smile. The lean and capable master.
Gray temples but sinewy shoulders, excellent vision. A fine,
sharp instrument. *Agent*. An all-purpose gent. Able to track,
chase, kill, or capture. Always dependable. Your humble
servant is at hand. One exception.

The sliders had kicked in, so when the memory emerged,
swift and clear, there was very little shock and he let it come.
Two years after Tickles disappeared, he had descended from
his vehicle to take some geneprints from the scorched ruin of
a Gink encampment. He was in a narrow canyon whose walls
were pitted with caves, and when the pebbles came skittering
down from one of them, he knew a family of Ginks was in
there digging for its life.

The vehicle had a lift ladder so he was on them in seconds,
his weapon drawing down on the cowering group. He saw
young so he had hesitated, considered switching to stun, when
he realized one face had a beard, was a human face under a
layer of dust and dried blood. Was in fact Keelough's face.
They had stared at each other, making not a sound, while the
others went back to clawing madly at the rear of the cave. A
moment later they had broken through into one of the
honeycomb of tunnels that represented the Ginks' emergency
escape system, and a moment after that they had all scrambled
out of sight, except Keelough. He had backed slowly through
the opening, never taking his eyes from PJ's face, and PJ had
not moved a muscle.

Later it had occurred to him that he had passed up an
opportunity for promotion. He might have stunned Keelough
and taken him alive, perhaps saved him. But he had known
somehow that Tickles had gone somewhere irrevocable, was

in a place from which he would not, probably could not ever return. So he had taken his samples, said nothing to the rest of the crew, and logged the patrol with no mention of any survivors. Under *Followup* he had entered *neg rec*.

Now he was no longer sure that the place Tickles had gone was the filthy horror chamber of insanity. Though of course there had been an upswing in headcases over the last few years. Part of a greater upswing in, as Skiho put it, general weirdness. The cracks in the Fed, the infighting between Progs and Cons, the V-studies and Fat's experiments, this over-blown Drager case—the image in the mirror flared its nostrils and eased him into a calmer, leveler place.

His training came back to him. Priority analysis. These hallucinations and the hunch that Tima was responsible. That was what he was investigating. He closed the cabinet door, his reflection narrowing, then disappearing in a slice of light.

He was back, far back, and still climbing, feeling cool and refreshed. Sliders had been developed in part to protect agents from the more sophisticated interrogation methods. They had a marvelous ability to allow the body to respond naturally to the most powerful signals—pain or pleasure—while at the same time they kept the brain free and acute. One could experience the most intense storms of sensation with an imperturbable clarity, as if body and mind were at last completely separate.

He was getting a little boost now from the razors too. They were rocketfuel, working primarily on the faculty of reason, but with the interesting side effect of cutting in sensory inputs with diamond precision. Hallucinations, if they came, would have a maximum clarity and intensity. But he would be evaluating them, at top speed, from the vast blue distance established by the sliders.

Moving toward Tima, still huddled over the table, he felt like liquid ether—weightless, capable of flowing around or vaulting over any obstacle, poised to become pure fire in an instant. His mind was now swifter than thought: he saw his checklist of alternatives and actions. He was a headcase; she had planted a beetle on him; a new metapsych syndrome had hold of them both. The experiment would be to probe, stir, evoke, observe, enhance whatever seemed to be developing.

And along the way, of course, he intended to have some fun.

17

THE DROPPINGS WERE FRESH UNDER A DARK CRUST, AND lay in the middle of a trail winding along the brow of a ridge. Yellow showed his teeth at the sight of them, while Ap picked up one lump and mashed it between his fingers. He peered intently at the smear and then inhaled it deeply. He smiled, but there was no delight in the expression. "*Tak piksi dawag*," he said and gestured at the boy with his soiled hand. "*Nali.*"

A big piksi something. He wrinkled his nose and frowned, but leaned close enough to get a whiff. It had become routine, this study of excrement. Ap made him sniff even the oldest, driest scat—bits of duff from cave floors undisturbed perhaps for years—and each time delivered a lecture, of which Ronald understood very little.

Yellow found most of these repulsive exhibits, and Ap always observed the cat's reactions very closely. Often the two of them exchanged speculative growls after poking and sniffing. Even he could see the hard seeds, bristles of hair, fragments of bone, but these merely indicated diet. From Ap's crude gestures he gathered sex and age were also generally obvious, and a great deal more to be inferred. Everything, apparently, stank meaningfully.

Now, for the first time, he caught a nuance of odor that was familiar. Instead of the musky rankness he expected there was a blander, sweetish scent. The smear on Ap's fingers also appeared uniform, smoother. He remembered then the little box for Duke, the puppy he had been given three years ago. Duke had chewed through a cord and electrocuted himself, and Ronald had been so upset his parents had decided against getting another pet.

"Why, it's a dog," he said and laughed aloud in disbelief. A big dog, too, by the size of its stool.

"*Dawag.*" Ap nodded but his expression remained serious.

149

"Piksi pakish dawag." He indicated that they would continue, but cautiously, with Yellow in advance.

The actual mine was very different from the holo Ronald had seen in his Resources class. The class version briefly showed new power shovels operated by workers in clean white full-protection suits, followed by scenes of grassy slopes and tree-lined ponds—the filled and restored site. The reality—which he now glimpsed only at a distance, for Ap seemed increasingly apprehensive—was a tremendous, irregular gorge from which came long plumes of dust and smoke, and along the walls of which crawled huge machine-insects.

He assumed this mine, like most, functioned also as a toxic disposal site. After ore was excavated by one colony of the insects, another would move in to dump waste into the ravine. A few smoldering mounds at one end of the main gorge held aloft clusters of what appeared to be dead sticks, and metal pipes burrowed into the surface of these mounds. He supposed the sticks represented trees, and now remembered that such pipes drew off hot interior gases to generate electricity, an efficiency measure praised at length in the class holo.

At the moment they squatted behind an outcropping on a ridge, overlooking the main transport road into the mine, as they nibbled at pieces of a big lizard Yellow had caught. The dried redfish were all gone now, and the fetid, oily taste of the reptile made Ronald gag. The heat and dust were also worse here, and the water had taken on a metallic taste.

Nor could he see the point of their privation. His limited vocabulary was insufficient to follow Ap's explanations, and they seemed to be only skulking about the perimeter of the mine. Though they moved very carefully, and Ap was continually glancing skyward, they had seen nothing but the long convoys of ore wagons and once, at the very edge of the horizon, a jetcopter skimming over the canyons.

His discontent was not all physical. It also unnerved him that both his companions played with the lizards before eating them. Anytime the three of them sat in shade to rest, the reptiles would cluster around or even on them; Ap would stroke their bellies and Yellow trapped flies, then allowed the lizards to snap them from his paw.

SHADOW HUNTER

Ap had managed to communicate that the lizards tasted better if they were taken in a good mood, and that eating them was an emergency measure but reasonable besides, since if they all died from the sun or bad water there would be whole clouds of insects on their corpses, a tremendous feast for the lizards. After that Ronald could not get used to the small, heavy bodies wriggling across his skin, and he detested the way they did push-ups on their forelimbs, and stared at him with their eyes like tiny, glittering seeds.

As Snaketongue, he had thought very little, mostly to acquire more Pobla words. Snaketongue was a kind of alertness, an immediate knowledge or feeling about things, and above all an intense pleasure in sensations—a stone surface under his feet, the wind cuffing him, or the scent in a water-cave. But Snaketongue seemed to be withdrawing, so that his old memories surged back.

The very surroundings that had exhilarated him now appeared harsh and strange. Twinges of horror and aversion at what he had done stirred up once more his desperate, interior conversations with himself. What was he doing, running about nearly naked, smelling offal, eating things foul and raw? *Who* was doing these things? He had to admit he was now, even in daytime, mostly Ronald. Going along with things, but secretly growing more and more apart, alone and desperate.

The earth vibrated slightly under him, and a moment later another convoy came into view from the lip of the main excavation. The wagons were huge, so covered with dust they appeared to be broken blocks of the landscape rumbling off on their own. Each tractor engine pulled six of the wagons on giant balloon tires, and this convoy, like the last, consisted of nine engines spaced perhaps three wagon-lengths apart.

They were traveling very fast, though the gravel road was uneven and serpentine. The last wagon on each unit emitted a bright fan of water that diminished, though it did not eliminate, the fog of dust thrown up by the great wheels. The wagons were tightly covered and the engine cabs shielded with metal plates, except for the monitor and intake slits. He remembered, then, hearing his father talk once angrily about excessive hazard pay for miners, about the problem of rapid transport from mines to smelters, to diminish contamination. The convoy rumbled and lurched toward the horizon, the wagons swaying dangerously on curves. Through the veil of dust left behind they saw then a smaller vehicle, a long-snouted carrier of some kind, also shielded, following in their wake. Ap hissed something unintelligible and shrank behind the rock outcropping, motioning Ronald to do the same.

The cruiser veered off the road and halted. As dust settled around it, a side hatch sprang open and out came one, then two, then three figures. It was a moment before he recognized them as dogs, for they were a breed very different from little Duke. Rangy, heavy-shouldered, flop-eared, they fanned out at a swift trot away from the road, noses to the ground. Around the neck of each hung a collar with a small transmitter pack attached, and even as they watched, one of the dogs changed direction abruptly in response to some signal.

He knew from Ap's manner that these patrol dogs were dangerous. Obviously they were meant to supplement the cruiser's tracking system, give it greater range. They were sleek and active, weaving back and forth along low ridges or between gully walls, pausing to investigate closely certain boulders and spiny bushes scattered over the desert. On their side of the road a mottled dun and black hound angled nearer, moving toward a long draw which led directly to the out-cropping where they squatted.

Ap hissed again and laid a hand briefly on Yellow's shoulder. Then he jabbed his spear down the slope behind them and Ronald understood they were to run. He had learned already to step from stone to stone, so he set off in a kind of skipping dance, aiming for a dry wash at the bottom of the ridge. He heard a growl and a peculiar spitting at his heels but did not turn to see.

When he slid into the wash only Ap came after him. They crouched and peered over the rim. Yellow was running in tight circles just below the outcropping, her wide paws sending up explosions of dust. Then she gave an astonishing series of bounds to one side and disappeared behind a second out-cropping, this one a collection of splintered columns of rock.

Almost simultaneously the hound appeared on the ridge-line, ran along it a short way, then picked up the fresh scent. They were close enough to hear the excited whine, the rapid in-out sniffing as the animal began to spin around in Yellow's trail. For some moments the circling became more and more frantic, before the hound struck out in a loose spiral. On the other side of the ridge the cruiser's engine cleared its throat with a hoarse roar.

They saw the dog stop and hold one paw aloft, saw muscles ripple along a shoulder. The muzzle lifted and swung to point toward the broken rock columns. Yodeling, the animal lunged forward, paused again once to nose the ground, then reached the base of the outcropping in a state of barely controlled delirium.

Afterward he never remembered seeing Yellow leap. The cat was simply there like a monstrous, tawny growth, claws hooked into the hound's flanks, jaws clamped into the back of its neck. There was a tremendous brief commotion, a flashing and rolling within a spray of dust, and then Yellow was gone. The forelegs of the dog were also trying to run, but only succeeded in dragging the inert hindquarters a few feet. The yodeling had become something higher, agonized, final, and the transmitter had erupted into a piercing whistle. As the cruiser surged over the ridgeline, the dog's head swung drunkenly as if still searching for spoor, and then fell to one side as the body began to stretch and tremble.

The cruiser flowed swiftly as a snake, barely pausing to shovel the dying animal into its hold. The sensors had locked on to Yellow's trail and the craft soon accelerated, leaving behind a haze of dust. As soon as it had disappeared over the next ridge they ran. There was no attempt to hide their trail in rocks or keep to the shelter of overhanging banks. Speed alone mattered now. They followed the wash for half an hour and then broke out across a rolling plain until they picked up a small ravine cluttered with waste.

Apparently the fill had been hurried and imperfect, and erosion was working to reestablish a canyon. They moved through a jumble of rusty skeletons and twisted plastic frames, around metal drums whose warning labels were weathered away, over ragged, moldy bales of compressed fiber. Ap was pointing constantly with his spear, calling "*Yat! Yat!*" and indicating to Ronald he must avoid this or that place. The smell was unpleasant, at once chemical and rotten, and several times they passed the heaped bones of animals.

He was soon feeling dizzy and gasping for breath, whether from exhaustion or the foul air he could not say. His legs felt like rubber and he had cut his right foot on some projection from the mess beneath them. A dreadful, squeezing pressure had developed inside him, as if his mind had run out of room. When they climbed out of the ravine he dropped his spear, staggered, and fell to the ground, his stomach convulsing and heaving up a few scraps of dark lizard and a thin, bitter liquid.

Ap squatted beside him, fear and excitement in his expression. He was jabbering something, but between retchings Ronald heard only *tchat, mahn trook, loobool,* and one new word, *jutsa.* He raised his head, which felt heavy and dense as a large stone. Ap was pointing, first at the sky, then away. When he managed to follow the line of the spear haft he saw the road again and joining it now a long line of transmission towers. The angular steel workmen, thirty meters tall, marched endlessly over the hills, arms akimbo, bearing swooping cables charged with the millions of volts the mine consumed.

He still did not understand what they were doing, why they had sacrificed Yellow, where they were going. Did not understand why they slunk along this corridor, why they should be excited by every little cloud on the horizon. All this danger and hardship was supposed to be for his instruction, part of his decision not to die, rather to live with these creatures, according to the whim of a senile old woman. But what sort of living was this? Stinking . . . vomiting . . . sobbing. . . .

For the tiniest sliver of time he saw again a scene from the instructional holo. The company lounge, with old headlamps and drills and picks on the walls, the managers reclining on divans sipping ice-crusted drinks. . . . He yearned to be there with them, clean fabric on his skin, tasting the cold, sweet drink. He would tell of his adventures and they would listen appreciatively. Among men of experience. Powerful men, like his father. . . . He cried out.

And then the vision was annihilated, because the ghost bounded into him, stronger and wickeder than it had ever been. It was as if a being with Yellow's agility and power had leaped and clenched him from within. Something broke as swiftly as the patrol dog's back, and began to jerk in its death throes.

"*Pahane!*" Ap crooned. "*Pahane takishya Pobla!*" He

picked up the dropped spear and struck the boy across the back, grinning wildly. *"Tonpa Pahane!"*

And he was up and running again toward the distant ribbon of road and the line of silent, rigid men bearing their hoses of power. Pahane was singing one of the water songs, about being a river. His bones were full of a weightless dark; he was only shadow, pouring over the ground.

It seemed no time until they were at the last small rise overlooking the road and the phalanx of towers. Pahane knew, in that inexplicable way he had, that they would have company, so the ground squirrels were no surprise. When he sat among their burrows he felt his exhaustion as a pleasant lightness of frame, as if he were a bare tree the breeze was blowing through. Ap was already preoccupied, chirping and chirruping at the squirrels. A few sat up some distance away, like a scatter of pegs driven in the ground, and answered back.

He caught something of alarm and urgency in this exchange. When through his backside he felt the rumble of another convoy he thought that this might be the reason, but even after the wagons—*trooks* Ap called them—had gone, the chirping went on even more insistently. Ap was on his hands and knees, miming a frantic digging. Snouts were poking now from burrows only a step or two away, and when he looked down, Pahane caught one squirrel actually sniffing at his heel. The ghost in him laughed through his fatigue and the squirrel whirred at him sharply. He hunkered down and pretended to dig too, but Ap shook his head and got to his feet.

From his shoulder bag the man took the last handfuls of dried leaves, the medicine that could make hunger and weariness retreat. He gave Pahane a quantity, stuffed some more into his own cheek, and began to scatter the rest as he moved along the rise. Behind them came a horde of the squirrels, nibbling greedily at the fallen leaves.

Pahane packed his jaw and hurried along beside his teacher, curious and amused. He noticed for the first time that Ap had taken a strip of some heavy wire from the waste dump and wrapped it like a snake around his spear. The metal was a dull, dark red and crusted with white flakes of corrosion. When he caught Ap's eye he touched the spear and said, *"Na?"*

Ap smiled swiftly. He lifted the spear and touched the wire against his other forearm, jerking away as if burned. *"Jutsa,"* he said. Then he pointed to the southern horizon. *"Da loobool."*

Pahane looked and saw that the scatter of little clouds had come together in a darker bank, now ranged over the hills at the edge of the world. *Da loobool.* Thunder water. A storm of some kind, and probably rain. In the next moment he breathed the truth of it, felt the difference on his skin. The land was giving off an odd, antic energy, as if exhaling its last, concentrated aridity. The fur on the squirrels seemed to glow when he looked at it, and the hair on his own forearms and neck prickled.

They had entered a gully, which he saw became a dry riverbed further down the slope. Just after the road curved around the base of this slope, a bridge carried it over the streambed, and beyond this bridge the road dipped, then struck straight over the plain toward the border.

Using the spear, its weight increased by the coils of heavy wire, Ap was digging furiously into the downhill bank of the gully. He had already thrown the last dried leaves over that bank, and Pahane saw the squirrels were digging there, some of them apparently beginning burrows almost at the edge of the road. Their bottlebrush tails waggled vigorously and he was astonished at how rapidly they wormed out of sight.

The ghost continued to laugh at all this absurd exertion. How hilarious. To come so far and endure so much, to be so tired and dirty and then to dig madly in the dry earth! Ap looked up, his flat brown face streaked with sweat, and grinned. *"Tchat!"* he shouted. *"Tonpa, Pahane!"*

So they must hurry. Why not? Since none of it made sense anyway. He laughed aloud and set his feet and drove with his spear at the gully wall. It became a contest. He struck and struck, then dropped the spear, crouched and clawed away the loose dirt and rocks with his bare hands, a parody of the squirrels. Ap was working the trench at an angle slightly steeper than the grade of the gully, leaving a stable spur of earth between them. They did not speak, though Ap gave a whoop whenever he forged ahead and Pahane continued to laugh at intervals for no apparent reason.

Twice more convoys passed. Each time they stopped work

and Ap crept out of the trench to observe. Pahane supposed he feared another patrol vehicle, but there were only the trucks and wagons. The second convoy was longer, however, and seemed to be traveling at a higher speed, shaking the earth enough to collapse a small section of the trench.

It was late afternoon before they ran into the first squirrel burrow. Ap crowed and did a hopping dance, shaking the spear, before he plunged an arm into the hole and they heard the squirrel's surprised chirp. A moment later Pahane broke into a second burrow and Ap fell backward in glee, kicking arms and legs at the sky.

They were both glistening all over with sweat, and now Pahane felt a definite chill in the wind. A glance upward startled him, for the cloud bank covered a third of the southern sky and racks torn from it already raced directly overhead. As he watched, a bright crack appeared on the horizon, then another, but he heard nothing. The ghost in him began to expand and exult, rearing into the heavens to inhale the swift, forerunner clouds.

Ap had sprung to the crown of the gully, from whence he was whistling and chirruping. Down the slope the squirrels answered. When Pahane climbed up to see, the *tchat* strategy finally became clear to him. At the point where they dug the trench, the gully was in a shallow draw between two hills. One of the hills ended at the curve, just before the bridge over the dry wash, and the other became a ridge that dropped more steeply until the road sank and bit through it. The piles of fresh earth marking the squirrel burrows made a rough, irregular line down this steep ridge, leading to the cutbank above the road.

If it rained, water flowing down the gully would fork into the trench, and the trench was connected now to two of the burrows, so a path would be created down the steep ridge. The other burrows would conduct some of this flow underground near the road, or even beneath it. A sudden new channel, then, and softened ground at the bottom of the ridge where the water would strike at maximum force. But surely the amount of rain would not be sufficient to do much damage. In this desert waste. . . .

He looked doubtfully over the landscape. The sun was almost on the horizon, shining beneath the advancing mass of cloud and casting immensely long shadows. Funnels of dust were still gyrating slowly here and there on the plain, and the bleak hills and mesas still bore the colors of a slag heap, rust and soot and ash, though the most distant had taken on tints of purple and indigo. A land burnt and scourged and parched for generations.

He thought of the last weeks, the incessant hunt for the merest trickle or drip to sustain life, the treacherous pools bordered by rank green springing from whitened rib cages. All the water they had seen, including the big, cold river, would scarcely be enough to slice down this ridge and over the road. A textbook recollection came to him: rainfall in the Wastelands averaged less than four inches a year, with extremes of seven or eight in the wettest seasons since the Great Shift.

Yet the wind in his face felt fresh and cool now, almost like mist. The bright, crooked cracks of lightning appeared more often where the cloud bank rolled up from the horizon; and at last they heard a far-off cannonade of thunder. The squirrels had all disappeared, scampering back up the gully, and Ap seemed to be doing nothing now. He stared at his feet, as if idly dreaming, grinning idiotically.

Then Pahane realized the Pobla's lips were moving. He was chanting, and Pahane understood finally why these creatures were always singing. It was their way of counting time. What was the ceremony here? He leaned forward to listen and Ap nodded and began to sing aloud. It was a short song about *da loobool,* the storm, and turning his idiot grin on Pahane, Ap indicated by tweaking his fingers that he was on his third repetition.

Why was time important here? His frown was taken as a question and Ap grinned wider, pointing at the road without breaking the perfect monotony of his song. The convoys, Pahane understood. They passed at regular intervals and the Pobla wanted to anticipate the next one.

Before there was time to consider a reason why, Ap conveyed by further gestures he wanted Pahane to learn the song, take over the count. On the third round Pahane had it. Like Ronald he was good at memory work, though unlike the schoolboy he seemed to relish the challenge of perfect mimicry for its own sake, even when he could not always follow the sense. Satisfied, Ap turned and trotted off the way they had come, back toward the mine.

The sun had gone behind the western hills, leaving a lurid red stain on the sky and one edge of the thunderclouds. The gray mass overhead was now visibly rolling and curling like smoke. The wind had stiffened, and his hair whipped like a pennant behind the lean staff of his spine. The Pobla words took on meaning. He was asking the wind to bring the clouds, and the clouds to speak, and the thunder to hurl down a river.

At his seventh cycle through the song he heard a faint sound under the moaning wind, like soft, rapid footfalls. Then he felt the first huge drops hit his brow and chest. They burst in a spray, leaving wet stars on his dusty hide. The chant lifted out of his lungs, taking his ghost with it, and together they ran with the storm. He was in the clouds, and in a bright bolt his glance found Ap running in the ravine, an antlike figure bearing some bit of metal. Then he was higher still, in a swift maelstrom, and in the shattering illumination he saw the mine, the long convoy rolling from the pit, and beyond that another presence, a silhouette moving, running toward them. Long hair, slight build, a woman. . . .

He came awake with a start, still singing, Ap already beside him with the curved metal panel taken from some wrecked vehicle. His fingers and two gouges of his heel in the earth told him he had been through the chant twenty-three times. Both of them were wet now, though the great drops came in irregular gusts. They sang together as Ap carried the panel to the end of the trench and laid it over the openings to the two burrows, then tied to it a length of the twine from his bag, which he doubled and then doubled again into a light rope.

A dark veil had fallen, blotting out the red sky in the west, and as they began the thirtieth round this veil swept over them. The rain hissed like a great descending lash and struck the land so hard they felt the earth vibrate like a drum under their feet, while above them the thunder bellowed in triumph.

Ap sang at the top of his lungs, eyes closed and head tilted up into the downpour. Pahane imitated him, and felt immediately the wild, living force slapping him full in the face, filling his mouth with cold sweetness. He managed to drink between a gasp for breath and the next chorus, and it was water whose like he had never known. His ghost grew a root into his body, then became a tree flowering greedily upward into the rolling clouds.

At his feet he heard a low, brutal chuckling. Down the gully wriggled a sluggish, muddy snake, a thatch of dead twigs and a dented plastic bottle balanced on its snout. It careened past them, then divided at the trench. The smaller branch ran as far as the bank and the panel, where it coiled and writhed restively. The light was failing and through the wavering columns of rain they could barely see the stream pour down the gully and become broader and slower as it entered the old riverbed and rolled under the bridge.

At their feet the brown snake thickened steadily, and under a skim of debris it became swifter, more avid. The chuckle deepened into a sullen muttering and near where they stood a whole section of the gully bank was swallowed with only a sigh of protest. The trench was seething too; a finger of water ran over the bank and vanished into the broad sheets of runoff, their surface pocked and riddled by the drops pelting down.

In the roar of downpour and the chant resounding in his skull Pahane did not hear the convoy approaching. He saw the long cones of light fan briefly through the darkness some kilometers away. He was sure Ap saw them too, but there was no interruption in the chanting. Of course the timing had to be exact, he saw that now. The lead truck had to round the curve and cross the bridge just before the torrent from the diversion hit the road. The panel, jerked free like a bathtub stopper, was to release that torrent.

They were finishing the forty-ninth cycle, and Ap tugged experimentally on the length of rope. A stroke of lightning suddenly exposed them, a halo of spray about their glittering bodies, the gully at their feet full of a foaming, gouging dragon. The rivulet overrunning their trench had begun to eat a two-foot path into the ridge. They saw also that the first truck was approaching the curve at the base of the hill. In the flash of stark light the convoy did not seem to be moving at all; it was fixed like a high-contrast photograph, a miniature set in a gallery corridor of vast darkness.

"Tonpa mahn trooken! Pasonki!" Ap screamed, breaking off his chant. Pahane thought he heard the whine of engines through the guttural roar of water, and more trucks were

visible now as silhouettes in a chain of headlights. Ap heaved on the twisted twine rope, cried out in frustration. Pahane sprang to help him and felt how the line vibrated tautly in the current. But with both of them hauling, the panel began to slide, a little at first and then more easily.

They heard a gurgling, a drawn-out sucking sound, and the rope yielded all at once. Ap fished the panel out and quickly untied it, stuffing the twine back in his bag. He seized Pahane by the shoulder and hurried him uphill, away from the trench.

They were just in time. Even as he scrambled and slipped from the muddy bank, Pahane felt it giving way beneath him. There was a new tone in the water's voice, as soon as it had undermined and split the trench bank through what had been the first two squirrel tunnels. Hurtling down the steeper ridge, the first tongue into the new channel had sounded harsher and more insistent, but as the main body of the river-serpent shifted to follow the plunge, they heard a booming and clashing, as of great drums and cymbals. Boulders were being uprooted and rolled like dice as the stream knifed a new pathway from burrow to burrow.

Safely on higher ground, they turned to watch. The first set of headlights strobed along behind the bridge superstructure, then slowed. They heard the squealing of metal on metal and all at once the light cones tilted up and rotated to one side, into the empty black night. There was a dull thud, a shock rather than a sound, and behind the tilting lights a spray of orange sparks.

The second and third pairs of headlamps now shuttered through the bridge. This time they heard the twin crashes distinctly and both sets of lights went out almost together. The lightning came again, and in its stuttering brilliance they saw the ore wagons strewn like battered toys, the lead tractor rolling over in the fountain it created against the current, and the fourth truck rounding the curve and beginning a long, yawing skid into the bridge.

Pahane found himself jumping up and down beside Ap in the cold rain, possessed by a glee so powerful it brought tears and shrieks. The ghost was out of his breast again, down the hill and into the cabs of the tractors as the bits of glass sprayed over the fumbling, howling drivers, as shields and frames buckled and the cold, dark fist of the water punched in everywhere. He was the shadow the thundercloud had cast over the wild river and he felt the might of them both above and beneath him, inexorable and uncontained, mad and bad beyond anything he could ever be himself.

Then Ap pulled urgently at his shoulder and they were running again, in a long zigzag toward the road ahead of the ruined convoy. He ran in total darkness, by the blueprint the lightning had burned into his brain, and knew when Ap halted that they were almost underneath one of the towers. He thought he could sense the humming of the cables swaying above them.

Ap grunted at some task, and a moment before the Pobla shoved the bare spear into his hands Pahane knew what it was and what was going to happen. When Ap pushed him he was already moving away from the tower, and the thunder showed him the man climbing, the heavy wire looped over his back.

Ap climbed swiftly through the struts, not straight up but in a complicated back and forth pattern, stopping and starting at certain intervals. Pahane knew this was to avoid detection by the security monitor, though the storm and darkness would likely foil the device anyway.

He was still dancing in place, galvanized by his glee and an anticipation of spectacle. But he held his breath when Ap crept across the shoulders of the tower and balanced above the cables. He winced when the uncoiling wire dangled free. Then he shouted with excitement and relief as Ap dropped his crude conducting bridge into place. The section of wire turned white-hot instantly, then melted away in an incandescent shower, but not before one of the cables parted with a sharp report and curled away as if in slow motion, spewing sparks.

One end slithered over an adjoining cable, which also exploded in a tremendous pop, and then others blew in geysers of bright, burning metal that revealed the slashes of rain still coming down. On the ground the collapsed cables continued to buck and nozzle sparks wildly for a time, but finally lay flat, their glowing ends only twitching a little and sending up acrid smoke.

Ap had swarmed down the tower and now sprang over the loose cables like a grasshopper. When lightning flickered again, Pahane could see his own glee reflected and intensified in his brother's grin and jittering, crazy gait.

"*Tchat! Kishya Pobla tchat!*" Ap embraced him and they whirled around and around in the rain, staggering and falling finally in the mud, where they lay for a while and laughed and cried. But fire had broken out and was consuming one of the trucks on the bridge. The huge, slowly undulating sheet of flame would be a beacon, and it seemed to Pahane that the rain had lessened slightly. On the other hand, the mine would have to run on its emergency backup systems, which would slow any response. Also the wrecked convoy blocked the road and the cloud cover hampered any air search. It had been a perfect deed so far, one which left no tracks. Squirrels and an untimely deluge had done it all.

Still, before morning. . . . He sat up and groaned. Ap laughed but then uttered his own grunt of weariness and reluctance. There was no time to gloat. They must move back into the canyons before the rain became too light to wash away their footprints, before the investigative teams showed up, before the sun came to dry up what pools might collect in stony places.

They got to their feet slowly. Ap found a scrap or two of woody plant stock in his bag and they shared it before setting off at a trot through the steady rain. They would be moving all night, Pahane knew. But he had no doubt anymore about his strength. He would remain light and indestructible as a shadow. Pahane could see things hidden from Ronald's eyes, knew things that Ronald could never learn from holos. He laughed aloud. That, for example, a whole year's rain could fall in one night.

18

SHE FELT WHAT WAS IN HIM BEFORE SHE SMELLED IT. FEAR and lust driven way up the scale by pills. All his little moves around the medicine cabinet. Trying to hide something, like a little dog. Pathetic. For piksis everything depended on seeing. "A darkside op," they said. "No eyewitnesses." "Good looking."

A very few, like Skiho, simply lacked all sensitivity. To them a nameless fear was an abstraction, a mystery, irrelevant as an old arcane myth. Skiho dealt with the strange by dismissing it. He had no personal insecurities. He made her laugh with his boisterous grunting and insistent pounding, like an infant greedy for the teat, while she lay beneath him and thought of how easily, at that moment, she could kill him.

This one, gliding toward her now, incandescent with new chemicals, would require more care. He had some ability to read the language of the world, the signs continually made by the earth's children to one another. Though only, in his case, those everyday signs concerned with predator and prey.

She brushed a button unobtrusively and the tape she had already prepared, a careful splice of supers from the last three days, was substituted for the realtime scan of the sector directly below. In his current condition, she guessed, PJ would never notice.

He was leaning over her. His hand dropped to her shoulder like a great white leech.

"What've we got, Bomber Bird?"

Since the incident with Captain Quarles, that was their name for her. She did not look up, but let her body relax a little, sending a message through the white leech, up the arm, and into his neural column.

"Another possible, sir. Three or four subjects may be moving across our area. Overall bearing approximately six degrees, south by southwest." She stopped the tape and switched to composite cumulative model function.

"Really?" He hooked a swing stool with one foot and sat beside her, so near his breath stirred her hair. "Show me what's down there."

She understood. She was a deep swamp to him. A zoological expedition to a place of perpetual shadows, a land of giant reptiles and grotesque, fetid blossoms. He was full of hard light now, a concealed luminous power that he thought would expose her, penetrate her.

From the files she had already carefully assembled she was putting together the model that would show the path of the little raiding party. A miniature landscape appeared, the deep crevasses magically illuminated and cross-sectioned periodically, so one could see both contour and depth. A bright zigzag began to crawl from branch to main canyon.

The party existed, she already knew. A warrior and either a child or a cripple, and a desert *chaka* or perhaps *sooti*, as guide. She knew not from the supered holos and digital recombs, but from the flight patterns of the scavenger birds and a coyote who had obviously picked up a trail. The route began not far from the border station where the boy had allegedly crossed, and was meandering toward a mine, tungsten and antimony according to the map, which meant it was probably a *tchat* expedition.

PJ had barely glanced at the landscape sunken into the tabletop, and did not notice the absence of realtime input. She felt his eyes on her cheek, her throat, felt the shaft of hard, brilliant light striking into her.

"Scout pattern," she said. "Rather than foraging. If they are Gink." She leaned away from him very slightly.

"Gink," he said. "Your kind. Feel a little funny, tracking them? Or saying the word?" His hand, still on her shoulder, increased its pressure slightly.

"Should we verify?" She pointed at the crooked track of light. "Captain Skiho is asleep."

"Sedated to the eyeballs. Also sated. Forget him. You didn't answer my question."

Still she did not look at him. "Program Four subordinates," she began, "on probation—"

"—are subject to professional review only. No personal profiles or queries except under special circumstances. What have you got up there for a brain, Tima? A training manual? I'm cocommander of this fucking goofball expedition, and I decree special circs, okay? I'm asking how *you* feel about Ginks."

She allowed herself to meet his eyes. His beam of dazzling light she met with darkness, her immense and total darkness. He voyaged further and further into her, unblinking, while she waited, as still and silent as space. "*Homo lapsis,*" she breathed softly, "is a degenerated species of higher primate. Its genetic stock may contain isolated strains of—"

"So you're part monkey bitch, part scum. We all know

that, luvkins. But that's not all you are, is it, Bomber Girl?" He scooted the swing stool still nearer, his face only centimeters from her own. "Most Ginks can't stand to *look* at a machine. Can't bear the touch of fabric. They die first. But not you, Bomber Girl. You've got some neat little tricks, head tricks." He lifted his other hand and tangled it slowly into the hair at the nape of her neck, pulling her so close that the tips of their noses were almost touching. "Don't you?"

She waited in her endless darkness. She was coiled there, undulating around his racing shaft of light, yielding and absorbing effortlessly. It excited him, she knew. The green glow from the table cut their faces into stone masks, blocked with high-contrast shadows.

"Do I, sir?" She heard him inhale her breath, and saw his eyes change subtly. With her right hand she brushed one more button, and her prepared program began to run in the table's holo chamber.

"Don't you, Tima?" His voice was at once mocking and hypnotic.

She let him ride into her a second longer and then abruptly tipped her head to one side and glanced down.

"Oh, sir," she said, "I think we have a hot possible. Look at this compcume." For the first time she showed him frank emotion, what seemed a girlish grin. But their faces were so near he was surprised for a moment, distracted by the size and whiteness of her teeth. He looked down and saw the three rudimentary figures, two round blurs and a smaller, elongated creature, moving along the floor of a narrowing canyon.

"Ah so," he said.

She could feel, for one moment, the effort of his shift away from her. But then he was as before. His hands left her and he swung away, easy, remote, workmanlike. The drugs obviously included a distancer. She must be careful.

"You're something, Bomber. And you're right, we should verify. I'll take her in and"—he picked a light-pencil from a clip on the table and stroked its beam along the canyon floor behind the three figures—"we'll set down about here, three or four klicks back. You feed me the coordinates until we pull the shields and go visual."

He got up from the table and moved toward the adjoining

cockpit. Just before he lowered himself into the padded chair he looked over his shoulder and grinned back at her. "Get out the rad suits and we'll take a stroll, maybe continue our little chat. And tell you what, Bomber Bird. Part of a Pro Four's training is leadership practice, so I'm making you top poop on this. I'll take a standard field pack and you go light. Then you can show me some more little Gink tricks."

PJ settled the big copter on a broad ledge that appeared unexpectedly, halfway down the canyon wall on the shady side. His body was still made of a clear, electric ether, every move instantaneous and sure. The conversation had shown he could go from fire to ice in the space of a heartbeat. In Tima's eyes he had seen that she understood him perfectly, knew he was onto her headgame. This was going to be interesting. He felt, finally, the elixir of adventure that made his work worth his life. And once again he had gotten there by bending the rules. That's how you did it. Stay out too long, overburn your fuel, jack up too high. In a certain way Tickles had been right.

For the same reasons he wasn't going to wake up Skiho, as regulations required. He'd leave their projected route and time frame on the screen, along with a note. Anyway, they'd be back well before the watch changed. He was eager to observe Tima on the ground again, just the two of them. He wanted to monitor her, hook into the erotic hallucinations she seemed to generate, then track her trips to their source. Play her out into the open where she would have to make her move.

When they slipped into their rad suits he laughed at her through the tinted glass of his faceplate. She clearly felt awkward in the billowy, heavy coveralls, the little air-conditioning unit clamped to the back. There was barely room for the two of them and PJ's pack in the little ScooterScout they had run down the ramp from the copter's cargo gut.

They had fuel for at least four hours, and figured to run an hour or so along the east wall, keeping in the shade. If nothing turned up by midday, they could switch to the opposite side and keep out of the sun on their return as well. PJ planned to stop and exit the Scooter often, probe a few caves, and locate the right spot to trigger the mindbomb that was already ticking between them.

He had not really built into his program the possibility of actually jumping a couple of Ginks. The evidence from the compcume model was only moderately promising. Most possibles turned out to be nothing, or one of the weird species interactions that were happening nowadays. A couple of antelope and a coyote or small cat moving together. Such combos trekked differently from homogenous groups. The strongest evidence for a Gink trail was the constant speed at which the threesome was moving, and their steady bearing southward.

But they would see. He was ready for anything. Keen as a laser tracking beam. Cocked to fire. Everything in his fingertips. They had belayed down the canyon wall, rewound the cable, and were cruising fast on the wide pneumatics designed for desert stone and sand. On the monitor he could see that the sunlit canyon wall opposite was pocked with black fissures and holes, from a few of which dribbled a ribbon of water. Very little green, though. Rare patches of thorny scrub on the canyon floor, here and there a little moss.

Still, this scorched crack in the earth was supporting a surprising population of burrowers. So far the sensors had picked up scat from coyote, vulture, digger deer, lizard, and mouse. Also a pellet that might be owl, which would be a minor find. His quick check through the copter's onboard database listed *Strigidae* as extinct in this region, as of fifteen years ago.

Tima had relayed this information to him with absolute impassivity. He wondered how much she knew about this longterm trend in the Wastelands. Species after species reemerging in a new habitat, usually underground. *Lapsis,* of course, chief among them. But Ginks had no databases, no ability to correlate even elementary stats, no known records at all beyond the crude and misshapen tales that attempted to glorify their descent into bestiality. He had read translations of a few and found them ridiculous, when they weren't incomprehensible.

Did Tima remember some of these yarns? That was the kind of thing he wanted to find out. The Drager business was straight power politics, no mystery there. The kid was either dead or alive. If dead, they would simply eliminate all evidence of Gink involvement. If alive, they had only to keep him that way until he was back in mommy's arms.

But this Birdgirl Monkeybitch Pro Four experiment—now she was something unique, a true conundrum. Those creepy, bottomless eyes. Perfect for this age of ultimate weird, when everything seemed to be coming down at once. The razors in his system were at full thrust now. He was in touch with the Scooter's systems—noting that the rad level was surprisingly low here—even as he was running a quick review of the viper's nest of intrigue surrounding Wasteland policies and also keeping a channel open on Tima, his emotional radar scanning her for the first sign of those rank, magnetic images of desire.

But the first blip came from the sensors on the Scooter snout. An orange light stung the quiet blue tone of the dash. Gink, for sure. He braked to a halt, spun around, and located the track. He split the monitor screen, zoomed in on the ground, and got a close-up of a footprint, broad and splay-toed. Moving over he picked up a second set, smaller and made by badly worn grass sandals. Next to these were paw-prints, a lynx well beyond its usual habitat.

Tima remained still until the prints were processed and the profiles came up on her screen.

"First subject male *lapsis* between seventeen and twenty-five, approximately 1.7 meters, either overweight or carrying eight kilos," she said, and then went on in a slower and softer tone. "Second subject male child twelve to fifteen, *lapsis* or *sapiens*, 1.5 meters, underweight three kilos. Third subject—"

"Forget the fucking third subject," PJ hissed. He unsnapped his helmet and raked it from his shoulders, then reached over to do the same with hers, spilling out the thick snake of black hair. He grinned like a madman who sees the door of his cell ajar. "Or *sapiens!* Foot's too narrow for a Gink—and why sandals? Any Gink that old would have feet like lizard hide. Great gobs of gooseshit, lover. Maybe you've found the little lost lamb."

She smiled very slightly at him. "Sometimes," she said, "a boy on his first long raid will get sore feet. So they—"

"Sometimes. Oh yes, sometimes." He was eating at her with his clear, mad eyes. "But not this time. You knew that to start with, didn't you? You knew this was a very hot positive. You are one clever bitch, Bomber Bird."

Her smile widened, the endless black space opening out for him. "Thank you, sir," she said.

After a long moment he blinked and glanced again at the monitor. He had been disoriented. Hadn't expected it. The first of her images.

She had opened her mouth and a vine slithered out between her teeth, leaves pale green with a purplish edge, and clusters of small, fiery berries. Quick as a capture net the vine surrounded him, held him, forced a tough tendril down his throat where the berries burst in a warm flame of tart sweetness. A sensation he hadn't prepared himself for—a flavor, and one so exquisite it made him ravenous. And so sudden he had instinctively shaken it off, despite his intended program of exploration.

"Time," he muttered, and then recovered his energy and poise. "What's the frame on those tracks?"

Tima consulted her screen. "Two to four hours."

He frowned. "Come again? I thought we were. . . ." The aftertaste of the image intruded momentarily, a complex tang like a jungle reduced to a mouthful. He divided his mind, yielding to the sensation even as he darted down a checklist of possibilities. There were two parties, moving a day apart. Or one party that had made little progress since yesterday. Or. . . . He had just begun to open his mouth to ask when Tima spoke.

"You saw the updated supers, sir. The probability of two parties is very, very low."

PJ smacked his lips. "Then they are here. Close. Rad count is low, Bomber Bird, so let's fly this coop. You're in charge now."

He pressed a button and the hatch slid back, suffusing them in a dusty, golden light. Over the low hum of the Scooter they heard the wind crooning. He let her get out first, and for one fraction of a second, as she became a silhouette against the hot blue sky, he thought of a huge bird beating its wings over his head.

They lost the tracks, of course, in the stone of the cliff face. Even the most careless of raiders would move on hard, wind-scoured surfaces every hour or so, often feinting down a side canyon and doubling back. PJ followed Tima like a shadow, the antenna of the scent scanner flicking back and forth. Except for the wind and a faint whirr from their air-conditioning units, there was no sound.

Tima had stepped onto the earth as one steps onto a high-voltage grid. Power flowed into her, like a mighty river into a desert after eight long years of drought. She had to restrain herself from leaping along the trails, despite the cumbersome rad suit.

She drank the power and used it to transform herself, make herself into a mirror that reflected and intensified the man's desire. She knew she had grown silky fur for him, then feathers, and now scales glittering and opalescent. The drugs in him made her work easy. Also his piksi nature, which wanted everything at once. Now that he felt near his goal he craved her even more, a gluttony for simultaneous triumph and symbol and sensation.

His mistake had been not noticing her original, simple splice out of realtime, and never checking the log thereafter. That was her insurance, to give herself time to consider what to do. A lucky thing. For she had been as shocked as he was at the tracks. The child in sandals could be a mixed or a sore-footed neophyte. But it could also be the Drager boy. And what would she do then?

Tima had entertained no idea beyond escape. *Idea* was of course the wrong word. An idea they might detect. She had undergone enough theta sedation and deep interrogation to know the danger of trying to hide her thoughts. She kept alert to chance, rather. Brushing a leaf or weed stalk with her bare fingertips, spotting a tiny ant trail or a bird in flight, she simply absorbed the contours and possibilities of a place. Waiting, without active hope.

Now an opportunity was perhaps going to become immediate. But what about this youngster? She had picked up enough from Fat to know that a tremendous gathering surge of piksi anxiety—and potential destruction—had fastened on this incident, the abduction of one miserable boy. If that anxiety fed upon itself and became violent, as piksi worries usually did, little Drager's fate might determine also the fate of many Pobla and their land.

She did not understand why the raiders had not immediately eaten the boy and pulverized and buried the bones. Apparently the Pobla, too, had changed in the eight years of her absence. The mixeds and renegades, as she pieced it out, must have insinuated themselves into the Old One's court. The Old One might be too old now, scattered and unsure. How else could her people have abandoned, after centuries, a policy of hiding and watching, of avoiding everything—absolutely everything—piksi?

If her people had been mad enough to steal the boy, then perhaps she should help these agents recover him. Because if the enemy ever came in full force and discovered all the underground temples. . . .

The wind had died down, so they could hear the faint click of the scanner and their own breathing. Now and then in the distance a rock cracked in the sun or a veil of sand sighed over a ledge. She projected her power now in two directions, into the black mirror of her hair, where she felt the man's eyes, and ahead toward the three ghosts. Whatever she decided, she needed to locate them, pick up confirming sign. Find the cave where they spent last night. Mouse tracks would give it away. Or. . . .

She lifted her head, nostrils flaring.

"Yeah?" The man's voice was abstracted, almost mechanical. He was very far into his fantasies. But she also heard again the flicker of fear in him. Things were taking too long, doubtless. Anticipation had grown painful. The flashing spur became a dull shackle. He needed new promise. They always needed that.

She knew where to find this promise now. A bird knifed across her path, circled and came back to flutter and shriek importantly. A waxeater! When it darted away, she angled to follow its path. In a few minutes she caught the first acrid fragrance, faint yet potent. At their feet and across the hillside now were yellow-orange stars; they bloomed from fleshy, thorny discs rooted in ledge and crevasse. The bird was there too, of course, wild with anticipation.

"Pretty," the man said, and now there was a hint of color and alertness in his tone. "Something here?"

She strode swiftly on, her fingers already on the emergency cord of the rad suit. Listening to the scanner, still sunk into the luxurious mire of his hallucinations, her captain had registered nothing and came after her like a somnambulist. Soon she saw the first bullets of light, coordinated their trajectories, and looked beyond the swath of blooms to the large cave where they were funneling in and out. Under the bird's frantic cries she heard a high, steady humming.

She jerked the cord and the suit billowed away from her, the helmet bouncing off a rock in the trail. She bent, unlocked her boots, and floated out of them. Her hands foraged among the yellow-orange blooms, then passed over her body into her hair, leaving a golden dust on her dark skin.

"Hey!" He had awakened. "What the fuck! Tima, what—" She heard the pack hit the ground, pockets being ripped open. At thirty paces from the cave mouth she halted and turned. He was on his knees, cursing and fumbling at a roll of sealer tape, a pressure tank of spray under one arm. The visor of his helmet was up so that he could scream at her.

"Tigers! Get back! For Christ's sake. . . ." He batted suddenly at the side of his helmet.

"Yes," she called to him. "They will come in just a few seconds now. Strip off your suit—all your clothing, all of it —and dust yourself with the pollen. Don't scratch yourself on the thorns. They hate the smell of piksi. I'll delay them as long as I can. Hurry! You cannot keep them out."

She laughed and turned back to the cave to begin her approach. She glided very slowly, her body erect and flexible. When the first scouts came in their tight, angry spirals she stopped and waited for them to test her. She concentrated all of herself into a wordless wave of intense, luminous being, a wave of the fine, sweet energies of fecundity and sacrifice.

She had practiced, of course, in her cell during the last eight years, had occasionally been more or less responsible for infestations of the base kitchen and disposal areas, but she had not even seen any of the desert nectar-gatherers during that time. And even the most expert *tagak* among her people approached tiger bees with ceremony. Tigers were among those rare creatures, once enslaved by piksis, who crossed with fierce wild strains to form a hybrid cleverer and more deadly than either ancestor. Despite massive chemical and genetic assaults, they survived in the Wastelands and still picked off the occasional Border Patrol or road crew.

For generations the Pobla had maintained careful relations with tigers, had mastered the rudiments of their language. Still, Tima knew that to overcome the stink of those eight years would require harmony in every cell of her body, and extraordinary secretions. She entered the state in which she felt her skin open like a blossom and release the subtle and complex pheromones of submission and accord. Dimly she was aware of sounds behind her. The man's cursing had ceased and she heard the unsnapping and unzipping of clothing, a rustling and patting. At least he had seen the futility of trying to attack a hive at full strength with only light field gear.

The scouts remained puzzled. They circled again and again, the bright amber and stark black of their bodies flicking the air in glances of darkness and light. Finally one flew into her belly, a hard little slap. She did not flinch, and after a moment looked down through lowered eyelids. The tiger was crawling in a rapid circle, her abdomen cocked high, ready to drive venom deep at the first signal of deception or uncertainty. She clambered into the dark pubic hair and began a querulous buzzing. A second scout landed on Tima's forearm, more gently, and began to comb there for pollen, and then a third crashed into the hair over her eyes, floundering and buzzing before dropping onto her upper lip.

Very gingerly Tima began to tap on the skin of her own belly with one fingernail, near the first scout who now poised at the hairline, humming steadily and waggling her raised abdomen. When the tapping and waggling matched rhythm, the tiger began her circular dance, beginning with the simplest most ancient exchanges.

What are you?

I bring you sweetness.

Where is it?

All around. Near.

There were two dozen or so tigers on her belly now, and she felt innumerable others brushing into her, settling and taking off again. Some stayed and began to sweep up the pollen. Others were dancing messages to each other, and Tima knew from these that one of the scouts at least had already returned to the cave. So for now they were accepted.

She tapped the best known of the hymns to the sun, repeating it three times to honor the hive, and received in return

permission to advance nearer. Even so, the tigers were tentative. When she was within ten paces of the cave she met a
squadron of angry guards. Several butted her hard and feinted
with their spikes. The tempo and pitch of their song changed
to something deeper, more insistent. The effort of concentrating herself, sublimating herself into the right odors, was
exhausting—yet exhilarating. She knew the tigers were smelling her ghost, still her most essential life, and only this overrode the reek of the rad suit and the chemical residues in her
body. Deliberately she had signaled the location of the man
behind her and as messages of alarm came in, identified him
as a harmless drone-creature. As long as he did not move
closer or sweat too much in the sun, he had a chance.

They were on her now by the thousands, a shimmering,
pulsating shroud whose vibrations went through her and set
her ghost to resonating sympathetically. She became a field
of light, a confusion of humming brightness. They were at
her everywhere, arms and crotch and ears and nostrils. She
opened her lips and they swarmed in to drink her spittle. All
over her body there were dances, an envelope of information
so dense and rapid she could understand only fragments.
Something in her excited them, made them curious. She
guessed it was the unleashing of her power, held back for so
many years; and though she knew she was too clumsy and
inexperienced to try to enter the hive proper and speak to
the queen, she had been accepted as communicant and they
were writing everything, hymns and oracles and directions,
onto her skin.

She caught finally the message about others of her race,
three in number, and the place where they had spent some
hours. A cave not far away where there was too much water
and not enough protection from waxeaters. She tapped out
her gratitude and her farewell hymns, but they were loath
to quit her, still investigating. Even the guards were making
only ritual warning runs.

Turning back to the man, she was a figure of crepitating
gold and black, a vessel in human shape but sheathed with a
dark fire that crackled and hissed incessantly. As she approached she could glimpse him through the fluttering wings
on her eyelids. He, too, was surrounded by a whirling cloud,
but only where he had smeared pollen were the tigers landing.

His eyes were staring wide at her, and she could see into him. He had broken into all the pieces of himself there were, and these were all in flight. In the hole that was left she sensed a presence, an ecstatic refraction of his terror and desire, still capable of meeting her. She smiled. She would go into him now, and take him.

He had handled all her transformations except this last one. Before the bees he had been at his keenest, delighted at the clever sequence of her projections—down the evolutionary ladder past some protoreptilian writhing to exquisitely artic-ulated membranes, convulsing into diamondlike matrices.

But then her stripping away her clothes had thrown him off, jarred him back to realtime too abruptly. Her sleek, brown body, the taut curves and subtle play of muscle, had delayed his reaction just long enough. When he saw the tiger bees it was already too late, and he overreacted at first.

The razors at least helped him see quickly enough that his only hope was to gamble on Tima's trick with the fresh pollen. To run for the Scooter would have been a swift death. First the bees would have clogged his air-conditioner and covered the helmet visor, much faster than he could kill them with his puny bottle of spray. Eventually, staggering and crawling blind, he would have ripped a weak seam in the rad suit, and by the time Skiho found him, there would have been nothing but a sack of swollen meat.

So now, in a kind of mincing shuffle, he followed her to the second cave. The insects had abandoned him completely and he felt odd in his nakedness, as if they were somehow ridiculing him. The hallucinations had also evaporated, sup-planted by her gliding form, still composed of this sounding, busy maelstrom of bits of sun and shade.

The beautiful, balanced frenzy he had achieved with the sliders and razors had also veered out from under him, as if this stark image before his eyes had overpowered all other visions. He could not think anymore now. The thought he tried to form—something about his nakedness, the distance to the Scooter, and the lengthening shadows—collapsed and disintegrated. He had no detachment either. He had simply become what he was seeing, and only that.

And he was seeing this thing in a burning sheath turning

toward him just over the threshold of the cave, and he moved into it. The limbs that slid around him were suddenly smooth, as the singing, crawling cloud yielded and then flowed over him too. She was climbing him, raising him at the same time, and then settling on him with a swift, prehensile contraction that took his breath out of his lungs.

Then she was twisting and shuddering in an irregular staccato rhythm. There was in it a ravening force, an unspeakable greed that momentarily paralyzed him and then generated a deep pulse of rage. Simultaneously he was stung on the lip and behind one knee, then at the small of his back.

He roared and tried to drive into her, split her in two, but her legs flexed on either side of him and she braced her feet against his buttocks, catching and absorbing the full force of his thrust. Knees bent and toes digging into the soft earth, he drove at her again and again, but each time she bounded back, torquing onto him tighter and tighter. Her teeth fastened in his neck and then he was stung again on the back of his legs. He dropped to his knees and lunged to cover her, but she held him aloft with her scissored legs and using his own momentum flipped him on his back and beneath her.

He arched and gathered himself, but she had captured his wrists and now pinned both arms behind his back so he could only buck upward into her. The rage in him had exploded into madness. He wanted to throttle her, break her neck, batter her apart. But expertly she rode every spasm, every attempted blow, and with the same ruthless greed converted his lunges into further pleasure.

He was thrashing now like one decapitated, a spinal column galvanized randomly, but even this she worked into her rhythm. She was in and over and through him, sucking his whole being into her with an implacable voracity. The beestings became like drops of ice water on the tongue of one dying of thirst. He yearned for their shock, for a last desperate proof of his selfhood. Then the whole mountain seemed to lift. She contracted hard around him, a ring of pearl, and the surge crashed back. Tears spurted from his eyes and something broke in him.

Then for the first time, instantaneously, she was still, only a faint flutter as soft as the humming wings still around them, and he came into this delicate tremor, came with a volcanic force that tore him loose at the root. He gripped convulsively what was nearest his trapped hands, his own buttocks, and the hammer he had prepared added its sting to the others and hurled him, like the cinder of a dead planet, into a black and endless space.

19

SHE LEFT PJ NAKED AND UNCONSCIOUS IN THE CAVE, taking with her a half dozen of the tigers in a little basket she had woven swiftly in her hair. When she had recovered her rad suit and helmet, she retreated to the Scooter and checked its onboard for messages. Skiho had left one, grumpy and short, saying he would be in the lab for the morning and to call in ASAP.

The storm they had been tracking for two days had moved faster than expected. They would be brushed only by its trailing edge, but already a little rain blew down the canyon, rattling on the rocks like a handful of gravel. Tima could see by the long, leaden clouds on the horizon that it was becoming a big storm, very big, and she cried out in a hawk's screech of exultation. Communications would be hampered; the delay in their daily log would have an excuse; she would be hard to track.

She slipped into her suit with a grimace at its odor, then picked a few strands out of the little hair basket. The first bee out she coaxed onto her cheek. There she pinched it between thumb and forefinger, surprised and goaded it into stinging. Then she smeared the scent over her whole face, so when the remaining five emerged they reacted and stung her too.

The pain felt good to her, like a tonic that invigorated and purified at once. As the bee venom began to fatten and tighten her face she felt her *kubi* becoming stronger yet. Setting foot on her homeland had roused it. Taking the man had given it zest. Now her ghost was fully alert and alive.

The fitful rain had plastered her hair over her brow and

shoulders, but she did not don her helmet. She moved a little way beyond the Scooter to a spur of rock running out of the canyon wall. She put both hands on the wet and glistening stone and looked up for a moment into the sky, letting the drops strike her swollen, heated face. They had made her into their likeness, given her this pointed and ugly little button between her eyes. Now was her chance to become Pobla again on the outside too.

She brought her head down smartly against the stone, gasped and then struck again. She waited for the blood to well out, a rivulet of bright red that unraveled swiftly into pink threads as it diluted itself in the rain puddles at her feet. She fingered the broken cartilage experimentally, moved it back to the center with a soft grinding. That would do. When it healed the nose would be flat at least, though still far too small, and she would have recovered a measure of her former beauty. Right now the blood would serve admirably to advertise an emergency and put Black Jack off his guard.

The instant Skiho looked up from the particle microscope, a good half second before he began swearing and moving, she knew she had him too. He dispensed with the code requirement for notifying backup, and in less than two minutes the hovercopter was skimming over the desert. As they flew he threw questions at her and she gave halting, fumbling responses, pretended to be woozy and frightened.

"The tigers," she kept whispering. "The tigers . . . so many. . . ." She was vague about what had happened, let him draw the conclusion that some inattentiveness had left them vulnerable. She had been nearest the Scooter when the attack came, thought she saw PJ retreat into a cave, firing spray from a field pack. The tigers had begun to penetrate the vehicle, block the monitor, clot the air intake; she had to make a run for it.

When the copter set down in the canyon he stopped the questions and became like a machine, swiftly checking out his own gear and hers as well. He sealed the copter behind both rad shields and airlock gaskets, then they exited through the decontamination chamber. He carried a full field pack and gave her the emergency medical kit.

She wandered briefly, appearing confused, until he showed

signs of grim impatience. Then she brought him close to their trail and he picked it up on his sensor antenna. The scent was fresh, of course. He broke into a shambling run, the pack swaying over his rump. They were only a couple of hundred yards from the cave mouth, and Skiho plunged into it without a pause.

Tima came right behind him, but she had been jogging lightly, feeling with her feet and keeping her eyes slitted. Her pupils were thus already adjusted to the darkness inside the cave when she pulled off her helmet. She had no trouble locating the smooth, heavy stone she had placed just inside the entrance, or following Skiho as he staggered and groped along.

He had also removed his helmet, but it was a long time before he saw the body huddled on the floor. Even when he shrugged away the pack and knelt beside PJ, fumbling for a pulse, he did not register the oddity of finding his friend nude. Neither did he recognize the slow but strong heartbeat as symptomatic of powerful sedatives. Like most piksis, she thought, he can only operate in one gear at a time.

He was muttering commands to her, instructions for preparing a syringe and poultices, when she hit him behind the ear with the stone. He gave a single, soft grunt and toppled over his cocaptain. One arm jerked and then he was still. In the silence that ensued she heard a single scout bee zing by the cave mouth.

She meditated, holding the stone loosely in her hand. She had not known until the instant after delivering the blow that she did not plan to kill him, and that surprised her. It had to be the effect of her habit of not thinking consciously, of hiding even from *wonakubi* so that a psychcheck—even with potent drugs and hypnosis—could not reveal her intentions.

Plans of escape had occupied her mind as soon as PJ had been put away, but these did not dictate clearly what to do with the two agents. It might be better to destroy the copter in a faked crash, but if only two bodies were recovered, Fat and his trusted aides, at least, would know she was loose. Or she might destroy only the hardware and strip and drug both men for forty-eight hours. Trained in Wasteland survival, they might find their way to a mine or monitoring station in a week or so. She assumed they would concoct some disaster yarn, perhaps involving the storm, to avoid confessing how a fifteen-year-old Gink bitch had—literally, figuratively, and utterly —fucked them.

Then there was the unresolved matter of their search. It still seemed to her possible that the sandal prints they had picked up belonged to the Drager boy. If so, it worried her deeply that her people held him. The Pobla code in these situations was clear and invariable. Once he or she became a *kubi* in the community, a renegade piksi could never leave. Too many secrets were at stake.

She had been hoping they would locate the youngster, and she would see a way to recover him without great loss of life. She would do the job she had been trained for, and then an opportunity would present itself and she would simply slip away. She was, after all, only a whimsical experiment by Insec's oddball director.

Instead she had now to figure out, and swiftly, why she had not killed these two men and what she intended to do next. She was waiting for *wonakubi* to move, to take a direction. She felt a moment's contact with the great hive. There was a swarming in her mind, then an intense, collapsing point and in the next moment she had it. Outside the bee zinged by again.

It would be quite simple. She would take both of them with her and continue the search. Even if Fat's tracking team suspected something, they could not afford to put out an alert. The mission was a top-level covop and to reveal it would ruin Fat and possibly bring down the Con government. In a matter so sensitive and crucial to his own survival, the director would end by simply going along, praying for their success on any terms.

Now Skiho and PJ would be the experiment. She knew the right drugs to give them to keep them physically restrained, but capable of docile attention. They would see the value of her approach—and would have no choice anyway. Track down the boy, keeping a normal log; move him and the agents to a point near the border; put all three under with a two-day tablet; fly to an unobtrusive branch burrow a few hundred klicks away, program the copter to destruct and then disappear.

She would rejoin her people, having escaped from the land

of the cannibals, the soul-eaters. After eight years! She looked down on the two men, one too large and the other misshapen. A tiny uneasiness stirred in her mind, like a dust mote. She had let them live, two of the race of ghouls that sought to exterminate her people. The beings she had been taught as a child to fear above all. It would be the second time she betrayed that teaching. In a way, she was making the same mistake the Pobla made with the Drager boy. To forsake oneself again. . . .

She shook herself like a muskrat emerging from a swamp. She had grown so used to deception, to piksi ways of thinking. Yet it was mastering their corruption that allowed her to escape. Now she had to trick herself once more—back into the little Pobla innocent she had once been. Would the people recognize her? Forgive her? From scanning agents' field reports she knew that the Pobla were different now too, moving in dangerous new directions. Presumably the most respected *tagakin* had divined that the Great One of the Swarmers willed it so, in her infinite understanding.

Skiho moved his lips and the arm twitched again. She felt his pulse at the temple with her fingertips. From the medical kit she took a small white tab and split it with a thumbnail. Holding each man's mouth slightly ajar, she slipped the halves under the tongue. The dose would give her two hours at least, though she would have to work now in failing light and a steady, drumming rain. In the distance she heard a shock of thunder, then another. *Da loobool,* she thought, and laughed as she had not laughed for years, as a child laughs. A twenty-year storm. If those three were truly *tchat* raiders, what luck they had found!

She rigged a block from the cave mouth and winched the two inert bodies out and over the ledge, then lowered them to the canyon floor. With the power hand truck she moved them both at once into the copter, where she put them in the holding cage for large mammals and gave them their first injection. She managed to get Skiho out of his rad suit and PJ into a pair of trousers, then rolled them onto pillows and paper sleep pads.

After changing to cabin shoes and a light jumpsuit she taped a protective pad over her swollen nose and wolfed down a couple of calorie bars. Then she turned to the delicate job of filing their delinquent day log. From the outset she had concentrated on breaking the codes above Program Four. She relied mostly on her ear for minute differences in the sound and rhythm of the keyboard, though she caught an occasional glimpse of a screen. It was much like listening for the nuances in a chorus of cicadas, so that one could pick out the individual messages on temperature, moisture content, or terrain.

She was fairly confident of her ability to access properly, but had not put together a finished profile of the captains' respective idioms. Coming on line, she opted to repeat verbatim PJ's last notification of a possible and then add a storm report that concluded: *field disturbance, int. comsys failure. no damage. bum master monitor switch. proves the rule. wet out there. chk cont.*

She hoped this captured PJ's offhand, discursive manner. The internal system failure, in the midst of probing a possible, would explain their delay, and also the sealing off of the copter until a full performance check was convenient. Storm damage to antennae or a mag field surge could have caused the switch to malfunction. The hard part would be tomorrow's report on the possible. She would have to decide how much to reveal before then.

She moved to the cockpit, retracted the shields and gaskets, and took the craft swiftly up to the canyon rim, where she hovered for a moment, considering. The tigers had told her enough to warrant a prediction that the raiding party—if that is what it was—had struck out for the mine, therefore toward the storm. Her radar profiles indicated that it was indeed a titan of a storm, powerful enough to confuse and obscure the Border Authority's best security systems, and also too much for the copter to buck.

She would have to lurk on the edge of it, assuming that the party would strike back across the Wastelands toward their point of origin. They had probably come from the city around the temple of Sopan, where the old *tagak* delivered her oracles. What was her name? Asa? Daza? She could not remember, though as a very young child she attended an audience with the tiny, old woman who sang to herself. Her parents had been excited afterward, had told her she might someday become one of the *tagakin* also.

She had to resist—it had become a reflex—the memory of

what had happened to her parents on the day of her capture. Instead she concentrated on the routines of surveillance, while her *wonakubi* went out to the raiders like a ray of sunlight. She programed the copter to pace and scan along the western perimeter of the storm, donning a headset to track also any communications that might filter through the static.

She detected urgency and alarm in the voices before she heard details of the power outage and wrecked convoy. The joy that bounded through her had a certain poignancy, for she envied the raiders their triumph. More than two dozen heavy ore wagons had gone into a washout, and a fire generated out of the collisions had torched four tractors. One of the units had also been a string of waste containers full of cyanide sludge, now spreading with the runoff. The downed power cables were on the wrong side of the wrecks, so ground repair units could not reach them and the weather was too foul for a service copter. Several backup generators also failed; mice had apparently chewed through insulation on wires since the last inspection. A beautiful piece of work.

The piksis, she thought, could not bear darkness. All their lives were spent illuminating things. Electricity had thus taken the place of their souls, and all their immense power could be extinguished in an instant. The teeth of a tiny rodent could reduce them to a pack of gibbering, frightened children.

Yet, oddly, they were fascinated by the dark they fled. Skiho and PJ, for example. She flipped on the monitor to their cage and saw them still snoring on their pallets, though PJ had tossed about in some bad dream. They would need constant sedation henceforth, to ward off their anger and shame. They would feel they had betrayed the grand piksi enterprise.

Tima allowed herself a swift, bitter smile. Understand and control. The bringers of light and order. They had no notion of life without conquest; they did not see how for them all joy, all meaning, all selfhood thus depended on a dark enemy—how they were in fact in love with that enemy, but would only know it when they destroyed her.

Or perhaps PJ suspected that much. He had come into her a mad emissary of all the luminous force of reason, and fallen from her a thwarted destroyer, helpless as an infant. Would he see that she had been victorious through submission? She had opened herself to the piksis and their world, learned their language, their rules, their hearts. She had been the perfect student, perfect servant. She, too, had fallen in love with the enemy, but deliberately, in order to capture him.

For a Pobla, love did not involve conquest. It had often occurred to Tima that her native tongue contained no words for these ideas, as the piksis conceived them. The Pobla aimed only to keep the world alive and fertile, in order to play in it. *Tohanaku,* the closest word to "lover," meant playmate. And the verb *naku* might involve sex and mating, like the piksi idea of love, but it meant above all sensing and cele-brating a connection to all Pobla, and to the whole living earth, even the stones. *Connection* could not convey the power, of course—though a piksi could come close, meta-phorically, by thinking of completing a tremendous electrical circuit.

The real problem was the root syllable *ku.* "Shadow" was a poor substitute. One had to imagine that space between a shape and its dark image, the emptiness establishing their unity, as a field—again a reference to magnetism was help-ful—of forces uniting visible and invisible, finite and infinite. Behind each being was a mystery as deep as the universe, a mystery constantly articulating itself into knowable life. To "love," for the Pobla, meant simply entering this shadow space, a ghost seeing all other ghosts, their ordinary being dissolved.

Then came the ghost of ghosts, shadow of shadows, the Hive Being. She shook her head and sighed. Once or twice she had tried to discuss such matters, obliquely, with Fat. He had glanced at the data files and suppressed a yawn. All these things had been gone into, he told her, in the early stages of piksi culture, many millenia ago. Doubtless many vestiges of primitive superstition—Platonism, Animism, and so on—had been preserved by Ginks as part of their human inheritance, but they had been distorted into systems of fanatic ignorance, part of her species' unfortunate regression.

Sensitive as he was, the director could not apprehend the meaning of *ku* because he only thought about it, only "knew" it. Another dangerous piksi word. They *knew* so much about her people! The Pobla, on the other hand, *knew* nothing—their expression was *to be alive with a thing* or *to live in it.*

"Instanding" was what she called Pobla knowledge, to distinguish it from the piksis' understanding.

On the other hand, she was appreciating the advantages of the hovercraft's surveillance gear in bad weather. Machines had their uses, despite what her people preached. The infrascope and sonar topo just now were showing a lot of movement away from the storm. Scavenger birds—her usual informants—were flying fast and low. Deer, rabbits, and squirrels had forsaken their flooded burrows. She noted an occasional bigger mammal—bear or a dwarf horse from the canyons. The images were not good enough to be certain, but she thought the raiders would risk a direct route to Sopan and would therefore be recognizable.

Tima was now sure it was a *tchat* party. The coincidence of the storm, the convoys, the ruptured cables, and the mice could not be sheer accident. But the raid was purely defensive, and designed to go undetected. That was the Pobla way. Not conquest, but evasion. The raiders would of course enjoy the destruction as a huge joke—especially on the investigators, who would never even guess what had happened. Many fires, collapsed walls, short circuits, and collisions were the inspired work of Pobla youth or their animal allies; but security officers continued to classify them as freakish bad luck.

A lack of instanding, Tima thought. Only Fat's secret research teams had an inkling of how much the Pobla were capable of. They had tracked a few of the obvious channels, sight and scent messages between species; and they were beginning to get a sense of the intricacy of what was being communicated. She saw certain reports, heard scraps of rumor, that indicated a few researchers were developing a troubling line of speculation. They were bothered that another primate could talk to a beetle, whereas they had nothing to say to either.

These radical piksis bore watching. If they ever guessed the nature of the Great Hives. . . . She decided on the spot to use the hovercraft's access and comb through Insec files for hints about the direction of the most current research projects. A query to the weather people on bio effects of the cloudburst might be a plausible beginning. She opened a file and punched in a no-rush request.

The copter was on full auto, programmed to stitch along

the edge of the weakening storm in search of unusual linear movement on the ground. Insec HQ would find nothing odd about that: it was standard Search and Retrieve procedure to pick over carefully any region subjected to an unusual climate. She checked the men in the cage once more and found no change. The injections would be good for six hours, minimum. Tima could therefore tilt back and extend her seat, turn down the light, and doze. She stretched once and yawned, thinking with a smile that before long she would be able to lie, bare and supple, on a warm stone and gaze into a fire, listening to the old songs.

Wonakubi left her body then in one step. Weightless and alert, listening to the darkness, it would attend her while she slept. The heavy drag of exhaustion swung into her, settled, and pulled her over the edge and into free fall.

20

SINCE TAKING CONTROL OF THE NORTHAM BRANCH OF Insec, Fat had met with the Chief Executive no more than a half-dozen times. And only once at the Retreat, one-on-one. That session was immediately after his confirmation hearings, and lasted less than twenty minutes. Most of their communication had been in the form of very carefully worded (and coded) memoranda, or brief holophone exchanges in the same mandarin idiom.

Such distance was normal between their offices; it was a means of preserving the mythology of balanced powers. Though Insec directors were technically Federation personnel, they were always chosen from the same party as the President and served at his pleasure. They did—again according to mythology—only objective investigation, primarily surveillance. Presidents had their own darkside agencies capable of planning domestic infoscams, covops, and stings.

Consequently, when he was summoned abruptly to the Retreat, Fat knew he had, in the slang of his trade, failed to insulate the office. He half expected the Attorney General and a squad of aides to confront him. But the CE stood alone at a window, the garden and fountain outside forming a backdrop for his long, trim form. He wore fisherman's pants, sneakers, and an open-throat workshirt, and his perfectly trimmed gray hair was tousled a little, as if by a wayward breeze. He could have been any small businessman or mid-level executive on a weekend vacation, except for the expression on his face.

"Good to see you, Charlie," Stockwell said. "Take a seat. Have some black coffee?"

Fat did not sit down and made no move toward the low table, a rectangle of marble with dragon legs, where a silver pitcher steamed over empty eggshell-thin cups. "Thank you, Mr. President," he said. "It's always a pleasure to be here."

"Easy lift out of the Swamp?" Stockwell moved now to his desk and picked up a remote. "Or was it the usual mess?"

Fat chuckled with more volume than usual. His round, blank face twitched once, an instantaneous, wincing smile. He was simply not good at this. "A touch of traffic, sir," he said, "but nothing serious."

Black coffee meant the whole interview would be in code. The newsy slang meant every word might go public. He understood in a flash that he was here, alive, and still the director of Insec, simply because the Administration had waited too long to get rid of him conveniently. His various adventures —which his enemies of course blamed for the crisis—now gave him a certain margin of power.

"Glad to hear that," the Chief Executive said genially. He waved the remote and three of the four holo chambers set into the side wall went dark. The fourth channel was the hotbox, bearing at the moment only an image of the NorthAm seal over a satscope of the hemisphere, with the anthem playing very softly in the background. "Can't really chat in the middle of all this info, Charlie, so let's get comfortable. Need to get your input on a couple of things."

Fat couldn't help but be impressed. Stockwell's voice was warm, rich, and offhand. It accorded perfectly with his appearance. The Chief Executive's features had been carefully styled—lean, weathered, clear-eyed—to convey both authority and compassion, a resilient toughness with a shrewd, humorous edge. But the person behind this mask was glaring at Fat with a cold ferocity.

Only the voice counted, of course. Every elected official above a certain rank could forgo holo surveillance in at least one inner office, but an accurate sound recording had to be kept, by law, at all times. Although Insec was exempt from such regs, Fat did not mind working with a security holo running, since his own best camouflage was the perfect, benign placidity of his face. On a sound track he was likely to come off as neutral and unconvincing.

"Of course I know this ongoing search thing has the agency popping," Stockwell went on with an audible sympathetic sigh. "What with our Progressive friends rushing in to help out with publicity. And what with the natural human concern we all have, confronted by such a tragedy. Any word so far on that brave little lad?"

Fat hesitated before the CE's silent snarl. Then he nodded very slightly. "No, Mr. President. I'm afraid not. I'm afraid we have to conclude, at this point, that . . . you know. . . ." He nodded again.

"Oh dear. Yes. I know. Our poor family—and we still think of Frank as our family, no matter what—but keep trying, Charlie. Keep trying *all the way*." Stockwell's baritone throbbed with a fervent sadness, a hope-against-hope determination. Meantime he was removing two sheafs of paper from an open drawer and reversing them on his desk so Fat could read.

"I will, Mr. President. Every top agent in my office is dedicated to this investigation. We're going all out. All out." He stepped to the desk and bent over the papers.

"But I am disturbed, Charlie, at some of these very troubling rumors. I don't want to point any fingers, this is absolutely not a political matter for me, but some of our Progressive friends are being pretty irresponsible, don't you think?"

"Yes, Mr. President," Fat said dutifully, after an imperceptible pause. He recognized the first document instantly. It was a copy of an innerloop memorandum from his office, a request for daily reports on lead subject Duskyrose, Project Metamorphosis. It contained language unusual for Charles Solomon Fat, an indiscretion whose proportions he only now grasped. *Pandora's back in the box,* he had written to the team, *Eve ate the serpent. Let's put our lovely little monster out in the field at P-4.*

"Well now, I respect many Progressives a great deal. A great party, not so long ago. Great *persons.* But there's this really unfortunate obsession they have. Everything that goes wrong is the fault of the little underground critters. I mean —so I understand from all your reports—there isn't the *slightest* shred of evidence, after months of inquiry, to connect any Gink business with this boy, am I right?"

The Chief Executive's lips were again peeled back from his teeth, in an expression of almost insane rage, though the mellow, bubbling intimacy of his voice did not waver.

"Oh, Mr. President." Fat forced out another chuckle and closing his eyes, nodded again, sharply this time. "That's absurd."

"Yes, yes. . . ." The Chief Executive coughed, seemed to develop and then clear an impediment in his throat. "No shred of evidence. But this rumor about the raiding party . . . that's been checked out? This Captain Quarles had problems, I gather? Groundless, I understand?"

"Very unfortunate," Fat said. He was reading through the second paper, which was his letter of resignation appended to an unqualified admission of lying to his superiors, falsifying documents, conducting unauthorized experiments, and misappropriating public funds. "A disgruntled officer who felt he was passed over for promotions. Also with a serious alcohol problem."

"So he just wanted to get even?"

Fat did not even attempt to meet Stockwell's murderous glare.

"And maybe a little publicity?"

"That's our analysis, sir."

"Ah. Now we know who's good at publicity, eh, Charlie?" The President delivered his shrewd, tolerant little laugh. "That's why I want you to take a close look at a couple of papers here. We may try to keep politics and publicity out of the picture sometimes—when the most vital institutions of our nation are at issue—but I tell you, Charlie, realistically we can't. Now this document"—Stockwell speared a finger at the memo on Duskyrose—"is a tentative policy statement based on the new V-studies coming in from your Preserves and Border Zones. You'll note it reaffirms our commitment to moderation and balance in these sensitive areas. But at the same time public *perception*—it is all a matter of perception, Charlie boy—has to be considered. People want these rumors checked out. Just so there is no doubt. Absolutely no doubt. You read me, Charlie?"

"Oh yes, Mr. President." Fat bowed slightly toward his superior. He was being told that if his swift, rogue covop failed, all the machinery was in place for a massive, showy expedition against the Ginks. Citing the V-studies, the CE could argue this policy change had nothing to do with any suspected Gink complicity in the Drager incident. But the public would read the killing as punitive anyway—which might defuse rumor and outcry.

Other matters were also becoming clearer. The Duskyrose memo meant some of his investigators were traitors. Stockwell therefore knew all about Tima, perhaps even that she was on the hunt for the boy. A potentially explosive fact, to be circumvented gingerly. Again Fat saw that his recklessness had secured him a precarious foothold.

"So you see here we request authorization for some new and pretty extensive border sweeps. Not biodata things, but sanitizing expeditions. Even if there is absolutely no evidence of Ginks being involved here, you've got to admit they've been more aggressive than usual this winter. We *do* need some stiffer control measures. I believe the Fed will respect that. But of course nothing like the kind of all-out stuff the Progressives talk about. We stand for caution and balance in these things. Life is a complicated system, Charlie. We change it with care."

Fat thought he heard, even through the layers of affability and charm in Stockwell's voice, a rapier-hiss of irony.

"Which reminds me of another rumor we need to squelch. Particularly nasty one. You know what I'm thinking of, I'm sure. The allegations about that, uh, training thing."

Fat recalled with sudden clarity how Stockwell's aides had reacted to the first indirect proposal for that, uh, training thing. Fantastic. Brilliant. *If* a line of tractable, dependable . . . roboginks, one aide joked . . . could be developed. But that was idle speculation of course. Ridiculous really. The

Administration could never approve. Even with cover in the form of some bioscam, behavior mod experiments, et cetera. Even deep darkside. Forget it. Wink.

"Very unfortunate distortions, sir," Fat said with his best effort at severity. "After all, for a century now the Federation has been conducting experiments on *lapsis* subjects. They are a fascinating species, from a scientific viewpoint. But live specimens are, as I'm sure you know, extremely difficult to obtain."

He paused and the President cleared his throat again, a sound vaguely encouraging, yet with reservations.

"But we have succeeded in catching a few young and raising them to near maturity. Yes, one or two of our tests on these subjects are conducted in the field, but to speak of secret cadres of 'recruits' . . . well, sir, that is simply ridiculous. We have what amounts to a lab animal, able to keep itself clean and follow simple directions."

"I trust you on that, Charlie. But it's the perception thing again. It was really unfortunate that this Captain Quarles apparently ran into a team doing such a test. Of course it was coincidence, and had nothing to do with the Drager affair, but people *will* draw unconscious connections, Charlie. They just will. We have to be aware of that. So for now—for the foreseeable future—I want your lab animals to stay in the lab. Any tests still going on out there in the field, I want them called in immediately. Can that be done?"

"It's been done already, sir. As soon as I heard the rumor." Lying, Fat managed to inject a little more color and force into his tone.

"Good. Now we have this second policy outline." Stockwell used his long finger to shoot an invisible hole in Fat's resignation and confession. "If the border sweeps and a shake-up of your Preserve Ranger Corps and calling off these field tests will take care of the problem, well and good. But if the public demands it, we are prepared to initiate a new phase of inquiry and revision." Stockwell chuckled in the manner of one musing over the frailty of humankind. "Of course the Progressives will squawk that we are stealing their ideas, but that's because they've never understood us. For us, Charlie, careful analysis and caution never precluded the bold step, the unexpected move." The Chief Executive paused and examined Fat with a certain leisurely relish. "More coffee? Better take another cup, my friend, before you look over this deal. This is a big one."

"Thank you, sir. I believe I will. Excellent brew." Fat glided to the marble-topped table and poured himself a half cup, then sat down. Outside, the manicured garden seemed unnaturally still, and the fountain seemed to be playing in slow motion, more like syrup than water. They would speak henceforth in the simplest and most secret code. Yes and no. Yes, I accept your conditions and we survive or fail together. No, I am a free agent and may betray you to protect myself.

"Well, Charlie, it hasn't been an easy year, as I guess you know, eh?" Stockwell lounged into the chair behind his desk, spun himself ninety degrees on it, then back again. "The Economy—sluggish all winter, even with retro adjustments as per the new LEIs, and here it's already March and still no sign of rebound. Agriculture—food and fiber both down, and a bad pest resurgence to boot. Mining—production up but the cost factor has gone haywire. Things like what happened in that storm a couple days ago—I suppose you heard—and that's become typical. As for Energy and the Infrastructure —hell, Charlie, I don't even know where to start. We've got good people, dedicated public servants—both parties—going all out every day, the best minds in the country, and we . . . things are . . . well, you know. Everybody knows."

The Chief Executive had forgotten him, Fat saw. Had even forgotten the record, for the moment. He was probably in touch with his deepest level of frustration and pain, where he was constantly rewriting in his mind an imaginary chapter, featuring himself, in future world history. On the side wall one of the holos went on automatically, and Fat saw in one glance that it presented a market update. Five-point decline.

Stockwell did not bother to look, and merely touched the remote to wipe the box blank again. "The thing is, you see the same sag in the whole Fed. From Tokyo to Budapest. R and D teams, forecasting firms, the universities and think-tanks—a thousand theories, Charlie. But the fact is, *nobody knows for sure why*. Nobody. It shouldn't be, even. The Fed has kept the peace, and the world Economy has been a pretty well-regulated motor for a century. Conservatives—our proudest hour, Charlie—have made sure waste and welfare

are kept to a minimum, and resources fully utilized. Medical science and pure research—tremendous strides there. It ought to add up. But I can tell you, sitting here where all the reports and studies and expert opinions finally come to roost, that two and two aren't making four these days."

The two men looked at each other for a long moment. The rage had vanished from behind the Presidential mask; the famous voice had gradually lost its avuncular charm and turned weary, a little dejected. Fat had a peculiar, mad notion that they were sitting in a boat on a horizonless and bottomless sea, gently rocking. Then he blinked and set down his cup, and Stockwell went on, sounding brisker.

"And we're running out of time. The people of this country—hell, of the whole world—want some answers, some changes. A steady paycheck isn't enough. A new heart or liver or stomach isn't enough. None of it's enough if bugs are eating out your upholstery and your apple doesn't taste like an apple and your kid could still—in this age, right now— get eaten by a bear. We can say these are all crazy chance, one in a million, nothing to worry about, but I remind you of the perception factor, Charlie. People perceive that things are not going right, *fundamentally,* and we're the party in power, so it's up to us to fish or cut bait.

"Now as I said, we're willing to wait a little longer to see if these current reforms are going to take hold. Your last report mentioned some promising assets at work on the problem, and I'll keep that in mind. But if I have to I'll prescribe stronger medicine. A lot stronger." Stockwell glanced again at the letter of resignation. "Let me save some time and give it to you straight, Charlie. Let's talk about something personal." He pressed his two hands together, fingertips at his lips in an impish parody of worship. "You . . . and our friend Danielle Konrad."

Fat was deeply shocked, and credited himself with a new degree of self-mastery in maintaining his imperturbable manner. He spoke with what he hoped was a sufficient inflection of warning. "Sir?"

The Chief Executive was watching him with open amusement. Not a week earlier Fat had filed a detailed maximum security memo on the relation between Danielle Konrad and Frank Drager. They were sleeping together and Drager's wife probably knew about it. The publicity team on the case had worked desperately to figure out whether pumping this rumor would advance or derail the Progs' attack, and had made little progress. The whole matter was so sensitive Fat had assumed Stockwell would never, under any circumstances, handle it directly.

"What would you say to the idea . . ." The long fingers flexed, were touched by the pursed, smiling lips. Fat quelled a powerful pang of hatred. ". . . of working *with* her?"

"Sir?" Fat repeated numbly. It was, he realized, the stupidest thing he had said since entering the room.

Stockwell laughed. A hearty, solid laugh. There was a re-alignment of force in the room that pleased him very much. "No, Charlie, I'm not crazy. And I haven't lost track of the facts. You know I disagree profoundly with the lady on many ideological points, and I know we've been on the other side of the fence, you and I, for our whole careers. But damn it, I'm the President of *all* the NorthAm peoples, Prog and Con alike, and this is no time for partisan rancor. It's time for all of us to rethink our positions."

Fat's brain had locked into gear again with a jolt and now began to accelerate wildly, even as the President's voice droned on about a new joint task force and the spirit of cooperation in a time of trial. Obviously the Cons were terrified. Overnight, as if by magic, Konrad had made the Drager case into a spearhead for all the forces of frustration and discontent on the continent. And the woman had resources. Fat already knew significant money and talent had materialized behind her campaign to blame everything on the Conservatives—the doctrines of unplanned diversity and the fertile Other, the laissez-faire philosophy of natural balance and random change.

Her power was sufficient, Fat saw now, to turn an adulterous affair with a disfigured turncoat into a national holosoap. It would be that rare trump, the positive scandal. And Drager's wife would be no match for them. Already she had ignored Fat's advice, issued garbled statements that seemed to condemn everybody, including the Administration. And her implacable insistence that her son was alive had the ring of a denial psychosis. Thus, in the entire cast of this little drama, the Conservatives had not a single supporter.

So Stockwell was trying to staunch a torrent of defections, many of them big players in Ag and Industry. He was ready to sell out his own principles and bargain with the devil. Fat registered the new phrases as the Chief Executive went back to talking strictly for the record. *Bounded diversity. Creative change. Symmetric management.* The best of both worlds. Fear and greed, Fat thought.

Of course there had to be a fig leaf. That was part of the reason the President had not simply dumped him. Fat understood the choice he was being offered. He could sign his resignation-confession in exchange for a short grace period —in case his gamble to locate the Drager boy paid off. If PJ and Skiho managed a miracle, the paper would be torn up and Stockwell would take credit for allowing the covop.

If they didn't score, Fat would have to form the new task force and give it an appearance of "balance," the imprimatur of the Federation. Perhaps he would also act as a slight check on the Progressives' gathering momentum, a potential mole for an Administration move to recoup influence. In any event Stockwell would have Fat in his pocket. He could activate the signed resignation at any time, and instantly discredit the Insec director as a hypocrite and criminal.

The slightest impropriety, any reluctance to respond to the new deviations in party policy, even a flicker of his old autonomy, and Fat would become a sacrificial offering. Perhaps he would anyway. Certainly his experiments would cease. In a matter of days he would have to rein in PJ and Skiho. Security dictated they should eliminate Tima before they returned.

Security and Intelligence. Skiho's remark had lodged in his memory. Fundamentally opposed concepts. All intelligence entailed risk. The smarter you are, the more in trouble you will be. Certainly that was happening to him. A question occurred to him then, bringing a fine sheen of perspiration to his jowls.

Why did he care what happened to the Preserves, to the Ginks, to Project Metamorphosis? How had he gotten so deeply engaged in what began as amusing little experiments? He had always told himself that he simply liked to observe intelligent life. The springs and cogs and counterweights of the mind fascinated him. But he understood now that he had gone further, had been seduced by mystery. And Tima was at the heart of that mystery. A genetic freak he thought he had transformed into a perfect, pretty robot.

Something in Stockwell's tone signaled him that their interview was drawing to a close. The CE was talking now about the necessity of entertaining all options, being wide open to really novel ideas.

"A more aggressive interface with the natural, Charlie, that's the ticket. Creative responses to challenge. We've been the dominant species for so long we forget how we got there—the control, the intuitive mastery—our heritage. But use it or lose it, you know?

"Let's admit—I'm speaking genetically now, Charlie— there are hostile codes out there. The viral thing, and this info trading among species. Let's imagine we've underestimated the Ginks, maybe they have a glimmer of an understanding of how to exploit these hybrids. Maybe that combination *is* responsible for some of this chronic sag. Just maybe—this is only a metaphor here, a manner of speaking, so open your mind, Charlie—they've turned the natural world against us? Cut loose some very dangerous forces? Forces that endanger our environment—our plantations and energy banks and climate control stations?"

The Chief Executive had injected the fire of prophecy into his tone, and a certain reverberation of stern judgment had returned. Fat winced out another smile. Only he appreciated the irony of Stockwell's speculation. Some of the youngsters in his research unit had shown him evidence of "forces" far more startling and sinister than any the Chief Executive envisioned. There was speculation, for example, that the two oldest, deadliest enemies on earth—ants and termites—were now communicating, actually warning each other away from poisoned bait.

"What's our move then, Charlie? Well, there's a time for research and careful review, and then there's the time for action. If we Conservatives have a fault, it's caution. And tolerance, of course. So one of the things this task force would do is consider moving aggressively into the Preserves and at least the northern tier of Wastelands in order to seal them off. Put *all* species under some form of close supervision, with reductions as necessary. Get the Ginks down to a manageable max. Eh?"

Fat tilted his head to one side, an ambiguous gesture. Every policy, he was thinking, I have spent my career trying to defeat. The collapse of the Conservative cause.

"Because I won't preside, Charlie, over the collapse of my own party. We have to move and change with the times. Stay open and creative. As I have already said. Now, why don't you take a few days—say a week—off? Think this whole thing over. Decide if you want to come aboard a brand-new ship. Meantime have your staff review your field assets, see if there's any interesting new data. Say—you do any golfing?"

Fat looked long and carefully out the window behind the President. It was finally down to yes or no. He sighed and took a pen from the pocket inside his coat. Stockwell scooted the resignation letter nearer with a fingernail. "Very, very rarely," Fat said. He signed in a swift, continuous motion and clipped the pen back in its pocket. "But I do."

"I thought so," the President said, with another of his shrewd, affectionate chuckles. "Why don't we make a date next week—I'll have Stan call you—and shoot nine. You can tell me the fruits of your deliberations."

"Very kind of you, sir."

"Bye, Charlie. Wonderful to talk."

"Good-bye, Mr. President."

They waited a beat, to allow for the time it would have taken them to shake hands. Then Fat turned as if on oiled bearings and glided out of the room.

21

EARS AND SNUFFER SAT ON OPPOSITE SIDES OF THE YOUNG biochemist, pretending to be deeply impressed by his brilliant jabber. They were having drinks in the Employee Lounge of the big downtown Namco building, following a talk and visuals on this new, privately funded project.

So far everything—invitations, tickets, accommodations—had been first-class. The makeup of the group was also intriguing. Several political heavyweights from both parties, lots of very bright young scientists, some seasoned administrative staffers, a smattering of free-lance consultants and thinktankers. Spotting each other early on, Ears and Snuffer had known immediately that the deal had a max darkside, and involved big money.

"People don't realize," the young man was saying, "how sensitive an animal is to odor."

"Really," Ears said in a tone of thoughtful interest. She was a trim, plain woman in her mid-thirties. Nice legs, men often said about her, and a very intelligent face.

"I mean," the young man went on, his hands making a gesture of compressing something into a little ball, "a *single* molecule can fire a neuron in some insects. Take Bombykol."

Snuffer laughed. "What's this? We talking explosives here?"

The young man shot him a pained glance. Slender, with lank hair falling sometimes into large and expressive brown eyes, the youngster was uncomfortable around men like this Dylan Bradshaw. Large men whose thick bodies and bald heads conveyed a coarse virility, a knowingness about the so-called ways of the world. It didn't help that the man identified himself as a pathologist. Theorists had always to suffer professional fools.

"Female sex attractant of the silkworm," he said brusquely. "Effective at more than a mile, in concentrations of mere billionths of a gram per cubic centimeter."

"No wonder women are so terrific in silk," Snuffer said, and grinned at Ears. They had fucked once before, eight or ten years ago, working on a water scam in the Arctic. Though Ears was not that interested in sex. Her blast was the power of knowing things about people, just as his was removing people who knew either too much or not enough. Part of their initial attraction was a realization that he often executed, so to speak, the contracts she devised.

"I've heard," Ears said with a slight, cool smile, "that among insects males are of practically no account."

"Absolutely right, Ms. Smith, if we are speaking in metaphors." The young man glanced around the lounge, where other invitees to the conference were talking and gesturing with enthusiasm. "And even among us advanced primates, look how many tables they've pushed together around Danielle Konrad. A queen-type, for sure. If you were what used to be called a praying mantis, Mr. Bradshaw—"

"Oh, I know," Snuffer said and leered at Ears again. "Dorothy here could nibble my head off. Well, if I got the choice, I'd rather go that way."

Ears turned slightly but pointedly toward the young man. "This is fascinating. But I thought these pheromones only transmit simple messages. Alarm, food, sex—very *primitive*." She glanced at Snuffer.

The young man's cheeks bore a flush now. He had planted his elbows on the table, giving him a conspiratorial hunch toward the woman. She was prettier than he had first thought.

"Oh, Ms. Smith—or may I—"

"Please," Ears smiled warmly, "call me Dorothy."

"—Dorothy—well, again, people just don't *realize* what's been done in the last few years. Though the potential was always there. I mean, consider: with a simple molecule, say only three carbon members, you could only make five geometric isomers. Okay, that's enough for basics: alarm, food, sex, maybe assembly or nesting. But suppose we go to twenty carbons—assuming a homologous series here—what do you think we could do?"

"Open a bank account?" Snuffer asked. "Write the silkworm *Hamlet?*" He laughed in solid grunts, but the other two ignored him.

"I had that so long ago," Ears said with an affected little sigh, a mournful look. "It's a lot, isn't it?"

"Three hundred sixty-six thousand, three hundred and nineteen." The young man finally looked at Snuffer, a long, straight look. The pause was extended enough for the older man to excuse himself and rise, but he made no move to do so. "And if we go to fifty members, the number of variants is for all practical purposes infinite. Equivalent to all the sentences we could make from all the words in all the human languages we know of."

"That is truly amazing." Ears raised a small fist from the table and rested her chin on it. "So there could be a language of smell?"

"Exactly. There *is* a language of smell." The young man laughed in pure delight. He was suddenly aware of Dorothy's scent—a clean, herbal fragrance. "And we may be on the verge of understanding it—the elements, I mean."

"Hey," Snuffer said, and shifted to a pronounced accent, "we don' need no steenking languages."

It was an old game. Ears was playing the kid into a fit, batting her eyelashes and crossing her legs now, ever more desirable, while he did the obnoxious bozo routine. Between them they would squeeze this jellybean for every last bit of useful info. They already knew he had a research post with Insec, and Snuffer was curious to learn what weird new projects his old agency had going.

Ears probably already knew, since she knew almost everything, but she wouldn't tell him right away. Part of her market value depended on timed release, partial disclosures. Maintaining his silly grin, Snuffer watched with admiration as she moved the kid effortlessly from semiotic theory to office politics. There were developments, she hinted, that couldn't be discussed *here*—a grimace in Snuffer's direction—but which could explain why this new Foundation contained so many Conservatives and why the people behind it—an informal network—remained anonymous. Even why it included both economists and entomologists.

Snuffer leaned across the table and interrupted the young man's chatter. "Let me put a bug in your bonnet," he said in a hoarse, mock whisper, "before I go and let you and Dorothy have your little tit-a-tit. Way I see it, we're all like your silkworms. We all have to get *something* up our nose before we move. And like you say, Queen Konrad there has that special sweet stink these days. So what is it, fella? What did *you* get a whiff of, hey?"

He enjoyed seeing the kid recoil, shrink under the meaty hand laid on his shoulder. For the merest fraction of a second Ears lifted her mask and let him see the amusement beneath it.

"I'm a scientist," the young man said, with all the ice he could muster. "I'm interested in *pure* research."

"Oh, right!" Snuffer honked out another laugh, aware that people at nearby tables were watching them now. "Sure. Just like dangerous Danielle, the Dragonette. Think about it some more, kid. Think about how Namco turns over its offices to her, and Amair kicks in free first-class tickets. These people are interested in fucking *worms?*" Snuffer got up, laughing continuously now. "Pleasure to meet you, sweetheart. You can nibble off my head anytime you get tired of lectures. So long, fella. Just follow your nose."

He sauntered away to bellow greetings to other new acquaintances, slap backs, buy drinks, make a distinct impression as a blowhard, someone everybody would remember later. Bradshaw—the big bald guy, heavyset, voice like a foghorn. That way, if he did have to wipe a party and anything went awry or he made a mistake—a very rare occurrence, but still possible—he could disappear all the more easily. A full head of hair and a moustache would sprout, dyed a new color; he would slough off forty pounds and acquire a stoop, spectacles, and a soft, plaintive whine. Ears would supply him overnight with a new name and file, a complete social and employment history. She kept hundreds of such identities in various databanks, ready for incarnation.

Moving into a new group Snuffer felt the exhilarating freedom of his current personality. He liked being obnoxious, telling bad jokes and insulting his hosts. Definitely more lively than his wallflower and milquetoast roles. And part of the thrill was the fact that except for Ears and his contact, no one here knew that Dylan Bradshaw was a computer ghost, that he was in fact the famous Snuffer. Even Danielle Konrad, though she was probably aware of his hiring, didn't know which one he was, had made it a point *not* to know.

He shouldered past a paunchy operations officer, already drunk and crying, to reach the edge of one of the tables drawn up around Konrad. She was crisp and tough and knowledgeable, answering questions from a ring of breathy college types. Three or four of the listeners, Snuffer guessed, were her plants, feeding her prepared topics. At the moment the discussion centered on the Federation's dithering over the Gink and Wasteland questions.

"We need a serious, deep, sustained information probe," Konrad was saying. "By a brand-new team. With some new thinking. Their figures are years behind, and the very fact that a family on an authorized outing, in a National Preserve, could suffer such a tragedy—that's proof enough that Insec hasn't done its job."

Heads nodded eagerly all around the circle. Snuffer nodded too, and winked at the girl to his right. "What a woman," he crooned in a low voice. "What a handful." He kept his cheerful, boozy grin, happy to be a fictional person telling the truth. He did like brass and steel in a woman, and he appreciated the performance Konrad was giving.

She was performing for him as much as anyone. For he had told the contact it was a little too early to commit, just yet. The Snuffer made commitments with great deliberation, and he never went back on them. Of course now and then he did a wipe on his own—for practice or just the perverse pleasure of it—but when he took money for a job he had two rules. One was he didn't work for losers. The other was he neither made nor accepted cancellations.

"We want an independent commission," Konrad was saying now. She looked about her and Snuffer was pleased at how easily her eyes skipped over him. A harmless team player. "But with grand jury powers. A task force of an entirely different order of magnitude."

Also enforcement power, Snuffer thought, and he uttered a half-smothered giggle. He was aware of the girl to his right edging her chair away from him. It pleased him immensely that he could, if he chose, pluck what appeared to be a loose thread from his sleeve, brush her hair in turning to walk away, and be across the room when she hit the floor jerking with convulsions. A seizure. One of his favorite words. It contained the sound of tentacles locking on, of flesh unmercifully compacted, of foam and spittle. He had two dozen ways of inducing seizure. It was actually harder to waft a body gently out of this world—though he had ways of doing that too.

He glanced over his shoulder and saw that Dorothy had gone, taking the puppy with her, probably back to her room where she would get the rest of whatever it was she wanted out of him. Possibly it would be only a phone number, but in a matter of days Ears would work that number into complete access to the young man's research at Insec. Which would of course be only one small piece in an endlessly complex mosaic.

Ears worked at upper-level office jobs, always in administration and always near the computer command complex of the organization. But her main business was private, never mentioned on her tax form. She was a master thief. The best, possibly, who ever existed. She sold and traded information which she stole brilliantly, elegantly, from systems especially programmed to thwart such larceny.

Like Snuffer she was a legend, yet very few people knew her actual identity. Those who did know protected their knowledge as a valuable asset. They were both, Snuffer thought, unsung geniuses, and for both of them this anonymity was a necessary component in the pleasure they took in their work. For one thing, they were thus free to create a market for their services. They and others like them, a growing number. The Hindmost. Max Factor. Blueballs. Shiva. Plus many nameless amateurs—all dedicated in some manner to the grand principle, José's Law. Jerking Off the System Endlessly.

For problems created task forces and task forces created new policies and new policies created new money. And we, Snuffer thought, create the problems. The prime movers. Arbitrary as gods. That was why he occasionally hit the odd target—healthy athlete, pregnant celebrity, smalltown saint. Ears did the same kind of thing, picking at random a company or politician to ruin. They had much more to do with the formation of this new Network than Konrad or her backers realized. The mysterious malaise, the ubiquitous glitches, the erratic statistics that had the Con administration running scared and kept the commentators busy cranking out guesses—Snuffer and Ears and their comrades in chaos could take most of the credit for all that.

Still, the business might not have jelled if it hadn't been for the Ginks. Konrad was sketching out her policy toward them at the moment, and hearing its cold, scientific fury, Snuffer was surprised. The woman didn't realize how much she owed the little warts. The rumor of their involvement in the Drager case had given her the opportunity to pump the whole Progressive agenda. From one loony bear to the Ginks, from the Ginks to the whole Wasteland situation—a progression that had now taken root in the public conscience.

Danielle Konrad had amplified that progression brilliantly, anyone could see that. Here she was surrounded by the best and brightest, with whom she traded clever allusions. Many among her audience were familiar with the whispers of gossip that linked this Valkyrie of publicity with Frank Drager, the new Phantom of the Opera. And some surely guessed that she had established this link deliberately.

The heroic couple. Snuffer giggled to himself again. Passion, revenge, martyrdom—she was creating a national saga, starring herself. He had seen their images together in some tabloid. Strong stuff. He supposed that Drager's bizarre vow—never to complete his restorative surgery, to keep the single eye and half-eaten face as a symbol of the evil and treachery of Conservatism—was probably another brilliant stroke of Konradian strategy. Certainly she had made everybody in the world aware of that ravaged face. Aware, too, of the cute little boy on his WhopperWheels. Little Ronnie Drager, the tragic tyke.

Snuffer shrugged and frowned momentarily. His main hesitation about signing on involved this boy. He had a strong suspicion, though the contact gave him nothing definite, that the kid was the wipe. Despite all the public mourning, insiders believed the boy might be alive. He knew from Ears that Insec had some kind of evidence, and a probe in the field. If little Ronnie turned up he would blow apart this developing Network, cancel the first serious challenge to the Federation's doctrine of equilibrium. The kid would have to be dead, and in the right way.

Not that the idea made him queasy. Though he could not remember popping anyone that young, he had long ago settled the scruples thing for good. He considered himself a kind of Buddhist, liberating souls from the wheel of karmic suffering. You could make an argument for the sooner the better. And anyway, little Ronnie had turned thirteen. A Gink that old would be considered almost mature.

The problem was the extreme public attention, and the necessity therefore of acting swiftly. He understood that was why he was a pathologist. They would make him chief medical officer on the first crack investigative team into the field. Hopefully he would have a couple of assistants. With grand jury powers, they would be able to intercept the Insec covop team and examine its findings.

If they had located remains, it would be up to him to fabricate signs of abuse or murder traceable to the Ginks. If by some fluke they caught little Ronnie alive, he would have to figure out a way to wipe not only the boy, but the Inseč ops and anyone else on his own team who might be a witness. Quickly and credibly, before any reports were filed.

A very risky operation. He had a good idea which agents Fat would put on this case. Feiffer or Black Jack Skiho, surely, and they were no pushovers. And then if only the pathologist and his assistants survived, they would be subjected to a lot of scrutiny. Debriefings, interrogations, interviews—too much publicity, by far. With time to study his image on holonews, some viewer might notice a vague similarity between this Bradshaw and the man who chauffeured the Prog candidate for vice president five years ago on his fateful motorcade, or the fellow who stood near the PacRim ambassador just before his heart attack.

"What about Stockwell's press conference yesterday? Sounded like he was hinting the same kind of thing. Border sweeps, a possible bipartisan task force. . . ." The woman asking the question was unkempt and nearsighted. A professor of some weird sort, Snuffer guessed.

"They're not stupid. They know their policies are a disaster. So they're trying to steal ours." Danielle Konrad gave the woman the quick blade of her smile. "The rats offer to investigate the granary, or the wolf wants to guard the henhouse. We have to stop that, and we can if we act fast. We've got to reclaim this planet in the name of legitimate, intelligent life. We've got to refute—*actively*—the malignancies and perversions that Conservatism has fostered in the name of socalled 'balance' and 'diversity.' All of you who belong to unions, professional agencies, company clubs—"

Snuffer lost track of what she was saying. He had heard it all before, this endless wrangling over degrees of control, the game of the power addicts. Cons and Progs, Progs and Cons. Round after round, the Federation trying to referee and keep the contest lively. In decades past the struggle had been over weapons, population density, gene manipulation, climate—the biggies. He yearned for those old times. War, Famine, and Disease put things in perspective, and also generated plenty of opportunities to gamble and win in a major way.

Now it all came down to a few raggedyass species and their habitat, the Preserves and Wastelands, which were not even important as territory. It was a matter of symbols, Snuffer supposed, though he could not quite grasp what was being symbolized. People simply had to compete for *something*.

He was sympathetic, actually, to the Cons' position of letting a few bears and sharks and Ginks run free. Hunting did sharpen a person. It was his own trade, in a manner of speaking. A sort of homage to the primitive ancestors.

On the other hand, he was very fond of the Progs' new plans to speed reclamation of the Wastelands. Total development, total management, that was the goal of this Network operation. Nothing less than civilization itself, as they saw it. He barely managed to keep from hooting, as Konrad swung the big brass bell of her voice in final, visionary prophecies. He looked forward to the scrambling and surging, the massive commitments of personnel and supplies, the contracts—so many opportunities for himself and Ears and Shiva and Hindmost and all the rest.

If these people could keep their holosoap going. Which depended on what had happened, or would happen, to the boy. Which depended on him. Snuffer beamed with an idiot benevolence, as Konrad wound up her little speech to oohs and ahs and scattered applause. He lifted his glass to her, honking out his laughter.

He would be able to demand a truly astronomical sum. They would think it was worth it, of course. Host organisms were usually obtuse that way. This one had a good deal of fanatic energy, the zeal of the righteous. He would be able to nurse it along, bleed it deeply, for a long, long time. Until the next swing of the pendulum. To him and Ears and the rest, it was all one.

He raised his glass again, a private toast. *All power to the parasites!*

22

TWO DAYS AFTER THE STORM A HOT WIND FROM THE NORTH had sucked much of the land dry again. Water ran only in the larger river courses, and the pools that glared from a few natural stone basins were steaming away quickly. Whole cliffs had slid away in some canyons and the runoff had gouged tremendous gullies into others, but already the dust was blowing, softening, and rounding the new landscape.

Ap had altered the pace and rhythm of their trek accordingly. They kept away from remaining patches of damp earth, to avoid leaving tracks, and ran most of the night to dodge the merciless sun. During daytime they lay far back in caves, panting and heaping themselves with sand that contained some whisper of coolness. Sometimes they had to share these caverns with snakes, bats, tortoises, an occasional coyote, but all these refugees ignored each other, dozed, and waited for sundown.

Pahane understood now why the Wastelands were considered unreclaimable. The heat was overwhelming, maddening. He often felt trapped by it, like a wingless insect on a griddle. And once they had been caught in a dust storm, which plastered their sweating bodies with mud until they crackled when they moved.

He was also feeling the effects of the radiation. He woke up one evening, lethargic and nauseated, and after lurching behind Ap for a few kilometers he began to vomit uncontrollably. They rested for the remainder of that night and through the next day, Ap feeding him shreds of some acrid, dried root taken from his shoulder bag.

He recovered and they went on, but at a slower pace. Ap looked worried and often turned to scan the horizon anxiously. Pahane knew that the Pobla was watching not only for pursuers, but for Yellow. By some unspoken agreement they did not mention the cat at all. In fact they talked very little, though Ap sang often as he ran.

The songs were comforting, and filled Pahane's mind completely for their duration. Otherwise he had no thoughts, only sharp physical sensations and the wisps of dreams, which seemed to arise from nowhere and contain nothing familiar. In these dreams he became a tree, or a fish, or the wind. His ghost was quiet, empty of the fierce joy that followed their *tchat*. Nor did Ronald intrude, except now and then to perform the humdrum clerk's job of recording a new Pobla word. All energy and spirit were concentrated on the simple task of keeping his frail, wasted body erect and moving.

It was just before dawn, and they had climbed to a canyon rim to look over the terrain while the light was still tolerable. Below them a thin ribbon of dirty water crawled through a wide, sandy wash, and to the north, on the horizon, Pahane saw for the first time a few small, dark humps—the mountains at the border. He cried out in mingled relief and apprehension. They were within sight of a familiar landmark, yet he was conscious of the hundreds of kilometers of tortuous canyons and dust-shrouded plains, the rocky corridors and jagged upthrusts, that lay between them and their destination.

Ap did not respond. He was staring down the canyon which wound west and south below them. Pahane followed his gaze, but saw nothing. Planes of rock and sand seemed to give off their own dark glow in the stillness, and the advancing light had not yet begun to sculpt color and outline. The wind, still cool, stirred a few leaves on skeletal bushes beside the little stream or snatched a scarf of dust from a ledge.

Pahane squinted and blinked, glanced again at the distant line of mountains. They should decide on a route and take shelter soon. He yawned and stretched his legs out before him, scratched the scab over the cut on his foot. He grunted at Ap, a wordless question. Again there was no answer, and all at once he felt it, like a sudden intensification of silence, a pulse against the surface of his skin.

He blinked again, and there was . . . was there? A movement? Perhaps only a swirl in the fluid on the surface of his eye. He looked away, then back. Yes! No more than a shift of the tiniest mote at the extreme edge of the retreating darkness, but he could see now it had direction, was coming down the canyon toward them. Ap was on his feet, straining forward as if he could pull the speck nearer with the magnetism of his gaze. Pahane, too, sprang up and held his breath. He detected a rhythm in the advance, the swing of a four-footed creature, but there was not sufficient light to determine color.

A moment later and there was a second flicker of movement, another speck moving after the first, along its path. *"Yawow!"* Ap cried. *"Eektah yawow tonpa!"* He began to run, leaping down the steep, rough trail into the canyon, jabbing with his spear to fend himself away from boulders or to vault ravines. Pahane came after, uttering a single, sharp cry. Yellow! Could it be? Could he have followed them somehow, despite the deluge of the storm?

Two-thirds of the way down he caught sight of the cat, moving at a labored trot over a slope of broken shale fallen from the canyon wall. Another few steps and he saw that the pursuer was the other patrol hound. Its hide was caked with mud and speckled with burrs, and the twisted and battered radio unit now dangled by a single clip on its collar. Both animals were lame and slouching from fatigue, but once beyond the patch of shale the rangy hound began to gain rapidly.

Then he heard, far off, the hoarse whine of an engine. Ap and he halted simultaneously, kept perfectly immobile. Yellow caught sight of them now and tried to run faster, but the result was a drunken stagger; all his power and elasticity were gone. The hound was still closing, and Pahane could see the slaver stringing from its jaws.

Ap glanced over his shoulder and Pahane saw fear, rage, and uncertainty in his companion's face. They should flee immediately, he knew, before they were spotted. Their spears would be useless against even the smallest sidearm. Yet he wanted to hurl himself the last few steps to the canyon floor, take Yellow into his arms, dodge away somehow. A moan of frustration wrenched out of him.

Then there was a deep rushing sound, as of a great wind or fall of water, directly above them. He gaped at the sky and saw the hovercraft edge over the canyon rim and then hang steady. It was a big, heavily armed military model, camouflaged and unlit except for the first red light of the sun. He could see its scanners raking back and forth from belly ports, and as he watched, the forward battery halted, spun, and locked on to the two of them.

Ap moved then, grabbed him by the arm and jerked him under a narrow overhang of rock. There was no room to hide in this shallow depression. Pahane could still see part of the distended gut of the hovercraft; it was lowering itself, deploying the landing struts. There was no doubt it had seen them and was positioning itself for action. They were trapped, utterly.

Ap began to sing and his hands darted into his shoulder bag. Pahane had never heard this song, nor had he ever heard a Pobla voice rise to such a keening, falsetto note. *Yano* was coming. Coming, coming faster. *Yano* good, *yano* finds all Pobla, *yano* coming, coming, almost here!

Ap had found what he was looking for; he pushed the small vial into Pahane's hand, then sat down and wrapped his arms around his knees. His eyes were white blanks, the pupils rolled up into his head, and the song had become a crooning mumble. Pahane recognized the dark fluid in the vial as the poison he had been offered on the trail. It was for the old who had forgotten or the young whose *kubin* were not strong enough yet. *Yano* was death, he understood then.

Pahane stood dumbly, unable to move, as the hovercraft descended swiftly into the canyon's shadow and landed with a buoyant flexing of struts. The main plant shut down, and Pahane heard Ap's song now as only a whisper. He still could not seem to move. Ap meant him to drink the potion, he knew. Oblivion. Nothing. Or would there be . . . What was *yano* to the Pobla? Ap grew silent except for his slow, shallow breathing, and then fell over to one side.

Fear struck through the boy like one of the lightning bolts from the storm. He crammed the vial back in the bag and seized Ap by the shoulder and tried to right him, but the man's body was fluid, boneless.

"Ap!" he cried. "*Pakish! Vasi tondu! Pakish yano!* Get up! We've got to—"

It was Ronald's voice speaking now, shrill and cracking, the voice of someone frightened out of a long, deep sleep. Pahane had withdrawn, leaving him alone in this tremendous emptiness. They had all left him—Mata, Teeklo, Yellow, and now Ap. . . .

The side bay on the hovercraft had yawned open, printing a trapezoid of white light on the desert floor. Someone leaped onto the strut step and then to the ground. He fumbled after his spear, gripped it and then flung it away with an agonized sob. It would all be lost. Everything would have to begin over again. They would make him forget. He held Ap close with both arms and tried to drag him deeper into the hollow, through the solid stone.

But the figure clambering up the slope looked wrong. Too small and no weapon in sight. . . . With a shock he saw the mass of black hair blowing, realized the face was that of a woman—a Pobla woman!—and in Federation blues! She came quick as a squirrel and in a moment had wrested Ap away from him. She lay beside the huddled figure and began to croon a song. With her foot she kicked at the spear the boy had flung aside, and her eyes slid over him and away again toward the open canyon.

He was aware then of the caterwauling and snarling in that direction. He scooped up the spear and ran, zigzagging down the last slope toward the racket. Just above the canyon floor Yellow crouched on a narrow ledge and the dog was leaping and feinting, trying to dislodge him. The cat's flanks were streaked with blood, and one of the dog's eyes was no more than a red hole. The radio had finally come loose from its collar and lay smashed on the stones.

As he approached, the dog whirled, fangs bared, and gathered its lean haunches as if to spring. The head was huge, the drooling jaws wide enough to clamp around a bicep or thigh. The boy drew back the spear and his breath came in simultaneously, sudden and deep. But the animal hesitated. The rumbling in its chest diminished, the muzzle lifted, and its one good eye blinked, inquiring.

Even as he put his shoulder into motion, driving the slender shaft with all his strength, he saw the dog's tail twitch tentatively. The point of the spear flashed once and slid effortlessly into the breast cavity just below the neck. The animal hunched in surprise and alarm, emitted a gagging yelp that sent a spray of bloody froth over the boy's feet. It tried to leap away, but sprawled to one side when the spear haft dug into the ground.

Yellow dropped from the ledge with a low scream and

flattened on the ground. The boy went to his knees beside the dog and took the wobbling head in his hands. At the touch of the rough fur, a peculiar feeling struck through him. The one good eye, still tilted up, was a cloudy gray. The dog's tail thumped heavily a time or two on the ground and then its legs began to convulse and stiffen. The feeling became almost physical, as if a heavy, silvery liquid had poured into his center, holding him still over the dying animal.

When the shuddering had stopped he got up and ran, stumbling, back to the strip of shelter where he had left Ap and the strange Pobla woman. She had propped the inert body up against the concave wall of stone, which the first rays of sun had turned pink. She had also taken off her clothes and now straddled Ap—singing, laughing, and slapping his face. The shoulder bag had been upended beside her; and as the boy squatted a few steps away he saw her take a pinch of some substance and thumb it into Ap's nostrils.

He was shocked—not by the woman's nakedness—he hardly thought of that—but by her gay, almost childish laughter. He saw that she was younger than he had thought, a girl really, and that her face was badly bruised and swollen. The whole scene was macabre, for he could not tell whether his friend was still breathing or this stranger was in the grip of a lunatic grief.

Finally he caught a few words of her song. *Yano pakish tohanaku.* . . . A bad playmate, death. So she was trying to revive Ap, call him back from the long voyage already begun. The boy remembered, then, his crossing of the mountains with Mata, the bleak stone and bitter cold, his own yearning for the soft, calm, boundless dark. If one were Pobla, one simply willed oneself into shadow and traveled there.

The woman ignored him, so he edged nearer, saw a tiny prismatic bubble of phlegm bloom from Ap's nostril. He was breathing! In his joy he reached out and seized his friend's hand. The flesh was chill, but warming, like the stone beneath them. The woman's song rose in pitch, undulated wildly, and then stopped short as she leaned forward and took Ap's head in her two hands. She covered his mouth with her own and blew.

At his center the boy felt the peculiar feeling tremble like a mirror of mercury, then begin to flow, more and more swiftly, along his arm and through his hand, pouring into his friend and joining them like a magnet. The sunlight was all around now, red and gold, and with it the first, mighty pulse of heat. The woman sucked in breath and blew again into the man under her, and the boy felt a minute thrill in his friend's palm, a faint fluctuation.

He and the woman cried out together, the syllable *na* drawn out until the harmony of it resonated from the canyon wall. A few feet away, lying flat in the dust, Yellow uttered a throaty moan. The silence that ensued was broken only by the faint ticking of the stones as they expanded in the heat. And then Ap gave a sneeze, a sneeze so delicate and small, like a kitten's, that the boy and the woman looked at each other and burst into laughter.

The calorie bar tasted marvelous. An explosion of flavors in his mouth: nuts, dried fruits, sweet grains in a creamy nectar. After so many days of living on dried leaves and raw lizard, his stomach spasmed in surfeit and he was half dizzy with the shock of so much rich food.

By midmorning he was nibbling his third Takeoff! and watching last night's tape of holonews. Again he felt almost Ronald, but this time the experience was more luxurious than disturbing. To hear his own language, taste familiar food, bask in the cool, filtered atmosphere inside the hovercopter —all this was exhilarating, yet somehow insubstantial, like a dream or hallucination.

It was strange, too, speaking NorthAm to this Pobla girl with the broken nose as she worked over the keyboard, posting and filing messages so swiftly he got only glimpses of them. Without the slightest trace of embarrassment she had donned her jumpsuit again as soon as Ap was able to walk, and seemed now perfectly at home in the control room. Ap, on the other hand, had been nearly paralyzed with fear until they led him to a cave around a bend in the canyon, out of sight of the big copter. He had agreed to wait there with Yellow until they came for him, but he looked more anxious and disconsolate than Ronald had ever seen him.

He had asked the girl about that, why the Pobla were so terrified of machines, why they would rather commit suicide than be taken near them.

"You were not frightened, when you went into the burrows?" she had replied with a smile. "Or when the bear dragged you off?"

He flushed. "I . . . well yeah, of course. But it was the *bear*—and the ants. My father. . . ." His voice fell away in a whisper, the memories intruding again.

She had only looked at him, but he knew that she understood all that he had been fumbling to say. That was another disconcerting thing. Her eyes were like a night sky, at once containing and hiding everything. Ginks were not supposed to be capable of such knowledge. Of course he knew better than that now, but even so he had not been prepared for someone like this.

She called herself Tima and him Ronald, and seemed to know all about what had happened. Even about how he had survived among her people. When she asked if he wanted to go home and he shook his head—with an instantaneous vehemence that surprised him too—she had only looked thoughtful for a few moments, glancing at his cut foot, his stark ribs.

"My *kubi* is Pobla. Pahane. From the smoke. I have eaten," he said. He did not know why he spoke in this way; the words themselves came from the smoke, from those days when Teeklo and Kapu had taught him in his sleep. But she seemed to understand.

She said only, "Snaketongue. You must be both careful and curious. Yes, very curious."

They talked then about many things. She wanted to know about his trek from the Redfish country, about Adza and Teeklo. She seemed surprised that he had been allowed into the great temple. Perhaps, she said, he was *tagak*. Very unusual for a boy. He described the daydreams and visions he had had. The feeling of oneness with the fish and then with a tremendous presence of light. This was contact with *won-akubi*, she said. The ghost of all ghosts, a difficult concept.

His premonition of her arrival, the storm-vision of a woman running toward him, was not so remarkable. Pobla could catch fragments like this at any sudden change in the weather, she said. She had picked up traces of their *tchat* party in the same way. Electromagnetic, she supposed.

He quizzed her on her childhood, apologized when he saw

that the memories were painful. She was more comfortable with the story of her training, and they laughed over the similarities between his school and the secret military base where she had been programmed. He liked her laugh, as unpremeditated as a birdsong.

Then she asked him if he wanted to see how famous he had become, and when he looked blank she punched up the previous day's holonews.

The President was talking. Decisive action had to be taken, a fresh look at the facts was called for. Events in the last two months showed that a new Border Effort might be necessary. The face was familiar—the President always looked like your uncle or the school principal—as if nothing had changed and everything was in place. But then Ronald was startled to see, in rapid succession, their old Choctaw upended and eviscerated, a horribly scarred man, and a shot of himself on a motortrike. Then came scenes of troops boarding transport hovercopters, schematic maps showing arrows striking across the Wastelands, and somber men in suits sitting around a huge conference table.

He heard the phrase *Drager affair*, and finally realized that the half-destroyed face, a mask ripped and badly sewn back together, belonged to his father. He felt numb. The leering image, the word *Drager*—they seemed alien to him. But what Tima said was clearly true. What had happened to him had become notorious, had shocked the whole nation. But why?

The speed of the broadcast disoriented him. Already the scene had changed again. A scientist wearing rubber gloves and breathing through a filter unit was pinching up a small, dead bird with forceps; a line of people, mostly elderly, was marching around some building carrying signs: BUG OFF! . . . MY RICHESSE IS NO ROACHES . . . UGH! A smooth, deep voice was speaking of economic downtrend, a promising new molecule, a mine disaster.

At this last phrase, accompanied by a shot of the smoldering wreckage of the convoy, he felt a return of excitement. Pahane was there inside him, beaming like a sun popped from behind a cloud. He saw Tima turn from her screens to grin at him. She knew. Of course she knew. Again they laughed together.

"*Kishta tchat,*" he said. "*Na!*"

"*Na!*" She got up from the control console and stretched.

"A very good piece of work, especially for your first time."
She was still smiling at him, but her look was pensive again.
"In a way."

He poked the last crumb of the Takeoff! bar into his mouth,
chewed, and swallowed. "What do you mean?"

She moved to a locker, opened it, and took out a leather
pouch on a shoulder sling, which she began to fill swiftly with
small items.

"You were thinking of your father, just now."

He frowned over his smile, puzzled. "Sure. Kind of amazing, his being alive." He waited but she seemed to expect him
to say more. "And I bet they can fix his—"

"Your father is dead."

He was too startled to reply. Had she not understood the
broadcast?

"No, you . . . weren't you watching?"

"He is dead."

He laughed sharply. Perhaps she was a lunatic after all.
"You just saw—"

"You are dead too, as far as he is concerned. Anyway that
man you saw is not your father."

"I heard his voice, already. On a radio Adza had, for the
music. I know his voice."

"A bad *kubi* lives in him now and uses his body." She saw
in the boy's face that he did not believe her. She smiled again,
sadly this time. "You know what a martyr is, *na?* A living
kind and a dead kind? The piksis must have both, in order
to do some terrible thing they want to do. That man is the
living kind, his soul has been eaten. They want you to be the
other kind, the dead one."

He stared at her. "But they are looking for me. *You* were
looking for me. . . ."

"We are Insec. A secret op. Things have already changed
now. You see? All those troops on the news?"

"They . . . that's for *me?*" He felt shrunken, frailer, hardly
able to lift his hand to touch his face.

She did not answer, but snapped shut the pouch and slung
it over her shoulder. He was aware that the hum of ventilators
and the clicking of circuitry had ceased. With dismay he realized they were going to leave the hovercraft. He wanted to
see more broadcasts, talk to this girl or the rest of the crew,

try to understand. His mouth watered, too, at the thought of more meals from the galley. When Tima had opened the storage locker he had seen the frozen trays, stacks of them.

"I ask again if you want to go home."

Her tone was matter-of-fact and he could not read her expression. "I chose to live," he said, and swallowed. "And Teeklo said after I had eaten I could not leave."

She nodded. "That is true. I wish it weren't, but it is. You understand why, *na?*"

It was suddenly clear. He was too stunned to answer, though he knew she read it in his face.

"I myself thought of taking you back, turning you over to . . . my crew." She smiled again swiftly. "But I did not know your *kubi* was awake, and I cannot break our law either. But when the covop fails, the regular Border Force will come after you."

"But they would. . . ." He began in a whisper and could not finish.

"Kill. Oh yes. Kill and kill and kill. The earth will be full of shadows."

"No! That isn't fair!" He glared at her, and then began to tremble. "I didn't do anything!" His voice broke.

She came quickly across the cabin and took him by both wrists. The night sky of her look held him suspended.

"Listen, piksi boy," she said, "you are to blame too, but no more than the rest. You have not caused this particular thing. Understand? And Pahane has nothing to do with it, nothing at all. But Snaketongue is not sure of you, yet. He comes and goes, *na?*"

The boy said nothing. He was still trembling all over.

"Also I have sent a message about you in the deepest code. One man only can read it, and he will think that you are on this ship, a hostage. My crew will keep that story alive as long as possible, I think. You must tell me some things about yourself—things only your mother or father could know— and they can file these as proof. That will give us a little time."

"Crew?" He looked vaguely around the cabin.

"Yes. Come, I'll introduce you." She pulled him to his feet, still holding him by the wrists. He was startled by the strength in her body; it was like a hydraulic force from outside, operating through her light, compact frame.

They went through a hatch into the hold and along a narrow corridor to a gasket-sealed door. When the door swung open he saw two men in a room equipped with sleeping pads and bathroom facilities. One man was watching cartoons on a tiny holobox, the other was sitting on his cot staring at nothing. Tima had to speak sharply before, with an effort, they turned to look at her.

The stocky man with red-blond hair smiled and nodded. Then he waved at Ronald, as if from a great distance. "Hey," he said. "Good program."

The taller man squinted, then frowned. "Boy," he said. "The boy." He planted his hands on the frame of his cot and made as if to stand up.

"No problem, PJ. Take it easy. Slide, man, slide on through." Tima spoke soothingly. "We've got him. We're in good shape."

"Got him," the man repeated. "Little Ronnie." He sank back in the cot and shook his head. "Let's go."

"Don't worry." Tima patted the man on the head. "You and Jack have to stay here for a little while. Tomorrow you can come out and everything will be fine. New instructions and everything."

"Instructions?" The tall man frowned again.

"Messages tomorrow. Fat wants to talk to you. He's so glad, everybody's so glad."

"Hey," the stocky man said, and laughed.

"What's the matter with them?" Ronald pointed at the IV needles taped to the men's arms. "They're not—"

"Not exactly." Tima giggled.

He stared at her, and began a tentative, wondering grin. "You *took*—"

"Sh-h-h-h! It upsets him." She leaned over to kiss the tall man on the forehead. "Good boys. You have lots to do tomorrow. New games, so you have to sleep tight and get a nice breakfast."

"Instructions?" The tall man was still frowning. He pawed at Tima's wrist. "Little Ronnie. They want him. Got to get back." His eyes moved with great effort to the boy's face. "Careful."

"Oh, we'll be very careful, sir. Don't you worry." Tima disengaged his hand gently and motioned to Ronald with her head to withdraw. "You'll see. Don't forget to check the board for your instructions."

The red-haired man waved again and winked in an exaggerated, suggestive way. "O-o-oh girl," he crooned and laughed delightedly.

Tima waved once more and then stepped quickly back into the corridor and closed the door. "They'll be all right," she said, "if they stay alert and don't do anything silly. And they'll give us time to reach Sopan."

"We're just . . . going?" They had arrived at the main entrance bay, and Ronald looked around disconsolately. His mouth watered again at the thought of the food trays and energy rations in the galley locker and his whole being shrank from the memory of the sun's lash outside. He was taking nothing with him but his spear, propped beside the airlock. "But—"

"We have to move fast. In a few hours the transmissions and storages will begin. You will be officially a hostage—at least as far as Insec is concerned. We're taking the Scooter for the first two hundred klicks or so, on a tangent, so it won't be too bad. A decoy for your friends." She was keying a remote in one hand as she talked, and a panel had shunted aside to reveal the Scooter, its nose already trained on the exit ramp. "They won't like it, of course. The cat especially."

The airlock hissed and the main door began to rumble aside. Ronald turned from the blast of hot air that swept in and saw that Tima had put aside her leather pouch and was again unzipping her jumpsuit. She saw his face and stopped, one shoulder already bare. "Ah. You want me to wear this?"

He could not speak and looked away, his face all at once on fire. He seized his spear and pretended to examine some imperfection in its point. She laughed, a long trill. "Too hot," she said. With a snakelike twist she shed the garment to her ankles, kicked nimbly out of it, and slung the pouch once more across her brown back. "Pahane will get used to me. We are Pobla now. Going *home*."

23

"WE HAVE THE BASTARDS ON THE RUN," DANIELLE SAID, stepping out of her panties and draping them over her other clothes on the office chair. Here on the top floor of the Institute they could open the shutters and let in the fragrant breeze from the extensive gardens, modeled on the primeval tropics, while the business of the conference—the panels and workshops and lectures on "Purely Progressive"—went on invisibly in the complex below.

She stretched quickly, luxuriously, before moving to the little cabinet opposite the couch. She was conscious of her full, swaying breasts, of the man watching her move in and out of the light. She knew his body too now, without looking: a body that was one long, hardened scar, a white blade across the hide cover of the couch. They had learned each other quickly—in corporate offices, on the floors of committee rooms, in hotel rooms rented by subordinates.

"They are appointing that idiot as cochair, of course, but he has nothing left. He'll slide in whatever direction Stockwell pushes. You want something?" She had shaken out a tablet in her palm and poured herself a glass half full of water. He did not answer right away so she lifted the cupped hand to her mouth, arching her back.

"Fat is no fool," the man muttered. It was not easy to say if he was drowsy or contemplative, pleased or melancholic. The parts of his face that had not been eaten away were pinched together by crude seams and ridges of tissue, gathered around one dead, unblinking eye and another fiercely alert, which gave his expression a peculiar ambiguity. "No. Nothing."

She took a swallow of the water and then turned to raise the glass in an informal toast. "You are amazing, Frank. You've been up twenty hours already." She moved across the room and stood over him, smiling. "And still dauntless."

He did not answer, and after a moment, seeing that his eyes did not linger, she shifted out of her provocative posture. "A colossal fool. Stupendous. He's smashed his career for a silly, dangerous experiment and probably ruined the Con party for good. They've done everything wrong—abdicated, really—and all we have to do. . . ." She laughed, excited beyond words.

"There's still plenty to do," Frank said shortly and raised himself up on one elbow. He was looking out the window now, and far below, through occasional burbles of birdcall, they heard voices. "Besides talk."

She watched him for a moment and then sat quickly on the floor, resting her head on the lip of the couch near his bare thigh. "My baby," she said, "what's the matter?" When he still made no answer she added, matter-of-factly, "Elise. Elise and Ronnie."

He laughed, a single sharp noise that filled the room. "My tragedy," he said, "my family."

"Every movement needs symbols," she went on in the same noncommittal tone, "and I never forget that. I know it's hard but you've got to stay with her, that's part of the poignancy for the public. And we've got to keep driving, make Stockwell launch the probe. We have the momentum now."

"She won't let up." Frank spoke between his teeth. "Fat has fed her so full of shit. She lives for that now."

"I know." Danielle brushed his ribs with her fingers. "Your wife is not the realist in the family."

"Somehow they got hold of a little info—things we did with Ronnie together, jokes and so forth—enough for her to keep her fucking crazy fantasies." The patched face underwent a contortion, like the yawning or snarling of an animal.

"Darling, they're desperate. They'll do anything to perpetuate the rumor. They have nothing else now. You know that." She moved her hand to his shoulder, kneading it lightly. Her voice was at once softer and more intense. "You know the odds. A thirteen-year-old boy dragged into the Wastelands. We can imagine. . . ."

He turned to the wall as if she had slapped him. "I *do* imagine. I imagine all the time."

She lowered her head and remained silent. The voices were in the courtyard below now, louder and more relaxed, an occasional laugh. A recess. They had another half hour, at most. In the trees outside the window there was a flurry of wings, a sudden cacophony from the birds.

"My kid was going to be something special. MaxCom material. Because he had the brains, more brains than I did. But he couldn't seem to locate himself, there was a crucial part missing, or screwed up. . . . So daddy takes his boy a-hunting." Again the sharp, single bark of laughter. "Introduce him to the old-fashioned wilderness experience. Goddamned fucking fool."

"Frank. . . ." She slid up from the floor to sit beside him, her hip touching his.

"A fool among fools, fools everywhere. Coasting along with our eyes closed. A *sport*. Hunting was a *sport!*" He turned back to the woman, yawning wider. "To improve our managerial skills. Challenge and sublimation."

"I would tell you," Danielle breathed, "to stop blaming yourself. But I know you can't."

The man went on as if he had not heard. "The Ginks, now, they knew better. They knew. They've always known. Killing is the business of life." He jerked his head toward the window. "Your friends don't understand it either, all that goddamned babble over planning and reclaiming, a new government, paradise out of the desert—this conference, *conference* by God!"

"We need them too," Danielle said quickly. "And they're my allies, not my friends." The pill had begun to work. She was flushed and short of breath; she shivered slightly, her nipples erect and pink.

"We need killers. Call a conference of killers. Can we do that, sweetheart?" There was something thick and loaded in the man's voice now, an urgency and desire. "Can we have the Ronald Drager Memorial Brigade? The slimy little bastards have been busy for a hundred years, preparing for this. Their banquet. Raw like Jesus, I wonder, or basted like a turkey."

"Ah, baby," she said and then her hands were touching his face, tracing the twisted ridges and seams.

"But Elise . . . *Elise*. . . ." He ground his teeth. "She *knows* he's alive. Not because of what that patrol captain saw, or thinks he saw, or because of Fat's coaching. Don't trouble her with facts, she's a mother, so she just *knows*. And sometimes—" He twisted on the couch, as if at an electric shock.

"Frank!" She threw a leg across him, straddled him, her hands gripping his rigid head. Her hair was loose down her back and there was a film of sweat over the bright color in her cheeks. "We talked this through, again and again, every angle, and we know what they would do to him sooner or later; we know what they did to you, what they want to do always. They thrive on filth." She bent and kissed him hard, their teeth clicking together. "They say there is no evil anymore, no boogeyman or satan or bad spirit, but the words don't matter. . . ."

He arched under her as she ran her tongue over the gnarled tissues around the socket of the dead eye. He uttered a deep, drawn-out groan like that from the hold of a ship in heavy weather.

"Oh, baby, I know I know but you know what we said what you have to say about beings so foul and so full of malice—not human not *human*, Frank—and they took him. . . . He would be better off . . . better off—"

He cried out and drove into her, the wave of force traveling up her spine and snapping her head back, her eyes open to the ceiling but not seeing it, seeing far, far beyond this narrow room. She felt him losing control again over the flame inside, the searing rage that kept him working twenty or more hours every day, interviewing or speaking at fund-raisers or lobbying—the rage that, she knew, wanted more than anything to ride in a scout vehicle at the head of a great avenging force across the border but that would instead hammer into her and fuel the power of her own vision, her desire to be a mother on a scale not even imaginable to other women, mother of a whole nation, yes, the whole world. And she had the world watching, following their story, as out of the fires of hatred and passion they began to forge a new order, a more advanced civilization—like the old gods and goddesses.

They rolled off the couch, she sucking on the scar where his cheek had been. She was a big woman, but he began to pound her inch by inch across the thick rug. He was rhythmic and rapid as the firing of a gun, and she began to melt into incandescence. In a vision she foresaw herself, radiant with the heat of this encounter, at the press conference later in the afternoon. Everyone would see it or feel it, the irresistible power of their union. The creator and the destroyer.

Yet she was waiting still, one mote of uncertainty and unease held her floating above a bright sea of pleasure. In the last few hours, for the first time, she had withheld something from him. Her new team had shown her an intercept that meant Fat was working on more than a rumor now. Something unexpected, a loose cannon, a new word. *Hostage.* A looming cliff of possibility, against which she could pose only another word. A word given her casually over the phone. Snuffer. Only a word, a breath. Yet dense as iron. He was waiting now, waiting for confirmation. She had only to stroll once more to WonderWorld, speak one phrase, and then there could be no going back.

"Better off," she panted. Cupping her jouncing breasts in her own hands she pressed them into his face, felt the rough features stretch and contort. "Better off . . ."

He cried out, the word muffled against her skin, but she heard it and began a series of small, soft screams of unrestrained ecstasy. There was no need to withhold now.

"Dead!" he repeated, and then again and again, matching the rhythm of his cocking and firing hips, as if each word were a stubby, heavy missile. "Dead . . . dead . . . dead . . . !"

24

DR. KLEPPER HAD EXPLAINED THAT THEIR NEW GOAL WAS simply to render his psychosis governable, and to that end they were going to allow him periodic dietary supplements that might satisfy his fixation in a more or less acceptable way. As an experiment only, the doctor cautioned. Ultimately a disorder so profound could be contained only by severe and unremitting self-discipline, a personal commitment to find the road back to sanity.

This meant he got the occasional smear of ripe camembert, a bit of steak aged to the limit, or a truffle. Tasty, though not spectacular, and he pretended to improve. He spent less time flat on the cell floor inhaling whatever escaped the hospital's filtering system, stopped mumbling aloud to flies that buzzed by in the exercise yard, and began to use the toilet again. He did not, however, abandon his trick of storing bits of foodstuff and lint and dried skin under his fingernails and between his toes, and then transferring them in a complicated series of moves, like a base coach's signals, to his tongue.

Baxter required the occasional nip of such nectar, as he needed his daily inner communion with the creatures that lived in and on his body, just as others—or so he had read —craved narcotics or spiritual transcendence. To preserve his space in this colony, his new network of information, he understood very soon that he would have to become expert at feigning recovery and relapse. So by turns he appeared almost normal, anxious to return to Phyllis, to their Olive Terrace home, to whatever could be salvaged of his career; and then, with the smoothness and rapidity of a chameleon, he went slyly, creatively, fascinatingly mad.

At the moment he sat comfortably in the patient's easy chair, smiled on demand, and spoke convincingly. He was aware that he intrigued the doctor enormously. Klepper had been preparing a monograph on the notorious "Bug Ward," and Baxter, as a statistician with an advanced degree and no previous history of abnormality, was to be a featured case history. He presented a special challenge, Klepper had confided, unlike the other patients—who typically had worked as pest exterminators, garbage collectors, or even entomologists.

"Try to explain more fully what you mean," the doctor said gently, "about this sense of dissociation, this feeling of otherness. How does it come on?" He was watching Baxter's foot covertly.

Baxter had noticed in their very first session that the doctor believed in toes as the barometers of stress. Inside the hospital slippers he wiggled and stretched his, sensing luxuriously the spit-softened toast crumbs that he had glued between them after breakfast.

"I would look around me sometimes and notice how people avoided each other," he said. "And I kept my distance too. Even in a crowded place, you know, like a terminal or a theater—you've noticed how they shrink from any touching? Each in his seat trying to keep from rubbing elbows?"

"Private space." The doctor nodded wisely. "Extremely important." A tall, narrow man with big ears, he had cultivated a constant expression of sober sympathy.

"But look at a colony of ants," Baxter went on. "Touching, touching all the time. Passing on information, verifying a common purpose. . . ."

Dr. Klepper lifted a hand in warning. "Now, Albert. You must remember. We're *speaking* here, right now. *Language.* The human instrument of intimacy—far richer and more flexible—"

"I know," Baxter said and failed to disguise his impatience. "Words words words. We talk instead of touching. But so much of what we say is . . ." He paused and seemed to get hold of himself. Behind the thick glass of his spectacles his enlarged eyes were steady, unblinking. "I know we bugs only have the illusion of closeness and understanding. Still, it's a popular illusion, isn't it, Dr. Klepper?" He smiled eagerly, inquiringly. The good student.

"Unhappily, yes." The doctor sighed. "A couple of new patients this week. Not unlike yourself. Urban professionals who see themselves . . ." He tapped a finger on his lips, searching for the right phrase.

"Sapros?" Baxter suggested. He lifted a hand to his face and scratched his nose, thus reviving the spoor of these newcomers. It had been passed to him by the woman in the last cell on their block at lunch. He already knew much more about these just-arrived patients than the good doctor did. In a sense. "Synanthropic orders?"

"Yes, as a matter of fact." Klepper looked amused. "One is a common housefly and the other a bedbug."

"Remarkable. And two in one week. An infestation of sorts, Doctor?"

Klepper laughed outright. "Not yet. Though we are getting very short of space. Also, I was at a conference a week ago and . . ." He shook his head at the memory. "A good deal of unexpected interest in the subject. The general topics were purely scientific and political, but I spoke with a couple of entomologists—one of them knew poor Trudeau, you know, the old professor on this floor—and they made some startling claims about new collaborations among what they called psychic insects. Even ants and termites for example. Or the subtropic cockroach—but what am I thinking, we were discussing your feeling of alienation." Dr. Klepper slapped himself lightly on the temple. "Forgive me."

Baxter made a gleeful sound deep in his thorax. He was perfectly aware of the doctor's slight discomfort at having digressed so easily from routine. Baxter could catch now and then the faintly acidic odor of secretions that might precede a transformation. Probably the entomologists had infected Klepper. Like most of the personnel at the hospital, the doctor was vulnerable because he never asked himself the simplest question. Never wondered why the study of this particular delusion thrilled him like nothing else. But now was not the time to press too hard. Baxter had learned that he could best scavenge news in small scraps, working obliquely.

So he began to invent plausible answers to the questions, being careful to jig his foot now and then to keep the doctor alert. For this task he needed only an antechamber of his mind; thus he was free to speculate and dream in a vast new dimension—a wordless universe, apprehended in tiny sensations of smell, taste, and touch. Yet these savorings were unbelievably dense with information; they resembled nuclear explosions—a microscopic bit of matter released tremendous quantities of organized and articulated energy.

And billions and billions of other organisms shared in this illumination, reflected and amplified and altered it, until it was focused finally on certain centers. Of this he was already sure, though his perceptions were too crude to allow him to detect more than their southerly direction. He was also fairly certain that bees, ants, and termites figured prominently in the structure of these centers. He was himself lower than an aphid, a mere gatherer of material for digestion and transformation, but he had the advantage of his training in systems analysis and had always been good at glimpsing macroscale patterns.

In the first days after his vision at the neighborhood meeting, when the two great roaches had temporarily possessed him, he had been nearly insane with terror. But they had kept stroking, soothing, feeding him the very smallest bits whenever exhaustion overcame him. He grasped finally how to empty his brain and let the tremendous cellular events occur. He became *aware* for the first time—it was like an electrocution—of the dialogue between his stomach and the bacteria it contained; he heard the life teeming on the continent of his scalp; he read for hours, hypnotized, in the vast library of his own excrement.

He had never felt so alive, so surrounded and sustained by kindred beings. Within a few days the other inmates introduced him to their elaborate underground communication system, based on Professor Trudeau's code. Trudeau, Baxter learned, was the first modern human to realize the extent of insect intelligence. Alone one night in his laboratory, the famous myrmecologist noticed—a split second before beginning a dissection—that a queen carpenter ant was signaling him with her abdomen; he went into a kind of trance in which the incredible intricacy and order of her motion was revealed to him. Before he lost his research post and was committed, he managed to acquire the rudiments of several languages—including Old High Termite.

Using the T-code, inmates could exchange the simple, ancient truths concerning decay and regeneration, while appearing to chat about the weather, their therapy, or cafeteria food. Baxter had studied these truths intensively during his observation and screening period—though "study" was not quite an accurate word, given the amount of tasting and smelling involved. Such tasting was not work, however, but ecstasy.

Then, in a short informal ceremony which the hospital orderlies thought was a birthday party, he received a half-dozen contraband lice, with instructions for their care and nurture. He succeeded in making friends with his teachers, hid them in his mouth during the hospital's inspection and cleaning procedures, attended their every move, and was rewarded when they multiplied and gave him a positive recommendation. He thus became, in record time, a link in the community.

The human function was simply to provide habitat. Baxter thought of himself now as a sort of meat planet with strata of rich offal that supported a varied population. His eyebrows, for example, were sustaining forests for *demodex,* the microscopic nocturnal grease-eater. And his lower intestine was a seething Africa of bacteria, one-celled animals, worms. This whole population was engaged in important research and development, incessantly busy absorbing information of astounding complexity. His own skin and gut, for example, were even now recording this talk with Klepper, its implications for the future.

"Of course we all know there is a certain malaise right now," Klepper was saying, in response to Baxter's sly attempt to blame his psychosis once again on a social context. "A certain turmoil *generally*. Much talked about at that conference I mentioned. But, Albert, you've lived through other crises. We all have." He frowned wistfully at Baxter. "Adversity can enrich us."

"I couldn't agree more. But didn't you just say this is a little different? Psychic insects?" Baxter asked innocently.

"Well. . . ." Klepper shifted in his chair.

"Say, that kind of sounds like a cricket. Psychic insect psychic insect." Baxter goggled at the doctor, grinning.

"Uh? Ah, yes. Yes, it does, doesn't it? Psychic insect."

"Psychic insect."

"Ah . . . ha ha! Yes, anyway. . . ." Klepper was subtly agitated now. Baxter was preternaturally still, waiting for the good doctor to resort to his own unconscious display of stress. True to form, Klepper shifted again and simultaneously rubbed his nose—or thought he did, though in fact his forefinger probed swiftly into one nostril.

Baxter saw the guilty hand, on its way back to Klepper's desk, brush against the arm of the chair. He breathed deeply in happy anticipation. When the doctor stood to dismiss him he would plunge around the desk to shake his hand and simultaneously pinch up that tiny pearl. One lip-smack and he would ingest the range and quality of Klepper's anxieties, and within a few hours his teachers would collect them too, from his blood.

"But, ah, what was I saying? Oh yes. A very challenging situation, indeed, but not *qualitatively* different, I believe. It's just that this Drager affair seems to have precipitated a lot of long-standing grievances—brilliant political work, what that woman has done—and our Conservative administration has perhaps been clinging to some outworn ideas."

"Nature," Baxter volunteered. "The wild."

Dr. Klepper nodded vigorously. "To be sure. Of course as children we're all attracted to that sort of romantic fiction, but we can't avoid the responsibility of controlling our environment. We owe it to ourselves. Our big, brave hunters and their Preserves, with untagged animals running about and so forth—they're childish fantasies, really. Anachronisms. Diseased and unproductive species"—he shot Baxter a keen, speculative glance—"are costing us too much. Indirectly—symbolically—*you* are, ah, a sort of victim of their perversity and adaptability, just as that poor Drager family was. So, Albert, a lot may be riding—again, I mean symbolically—on your pulling out of this thing."

"Oh, Doctor," Baxter moaned, "I know."

"I even wonder if in some sense you may not be reacting to a *fear* of these new ideas," Klepper went on, his expression conveying a maximum of somber concern. "Alleviating your anxiety by, so to speak, joining the enemy. Retreating, as it were, into the ultimate mindless routine, the obsessiveness of the hive-dweller."

Baxter nearly gagged on his urge to laugh. He had indeed been afraid all his life. He had been taught to scour and fumigate and polish and flush, to loathe blot and stain, to uphold a fanatic standard of personal hygiene. Fear filth—that was the lesson of his childhood. So he grew up clean: a timid, fussy, suspicious man, preoccupied with sterile equations. He worshipped order and efficiency, dedicated himself fervently to the very values Klepper was trumpeting—complete management and predictability. The troubling malfunctions of society, in this view, were the result of sloth and weak morals, coddled by preposterous old myths from a barbaric past.

Baxter underwent a small paroxysm of suppressed hilarity. Until the two giant roaches had crept into his brain, he had never truly understood the notions of "order" and "efficiency." Had never realized the falsity and imbalance of his world, its preoccupation with pale abstractions and its assumptions about the primacy of the human. Now he realized that he had yearned, for years, to revel in putrefaction. He wanted dark, warm recesses where rank life accumulated. He dreamed of engorging himself on rich waste. Absorption, he saw, must precede abstraction. The infinitely splendid weave of rot and rebirth was revealed to him, not as concept, but as process. The roaches, of course, did not "speak" to him; they ate his brains.

Hive-dweller? Oh yes, yes, yes! As the most primitive form of life in this web, Baxter could not hope to grasp the nature of the aggregate; but already he suspected that at the center of all there was a still calm, an infinite, shadowless field of light. The tremendous sum of knowledge was just that, every mote consumed in the whole. Enlightenment and annihilation. Two perfect mirrors. The idea of "management" or "control," he finally saw, was a ludicrous cult of imperfection.

"I'm always straying off the point with you, Baxter," Dr. Klepper chided, and allowed himself a rare chuckle. "But however exhilarating our speculations, we must come back to the hard work. Getting you on the right track. Finding out the origin of this fear of the new." He glanced at the clock on his desk.

"I see it," Baxter replied, "more as a respect for the old. I'm a bit of a conservative, there. And even you—" He gestured at the exhibits on the office wall. Klepper, he knew, thought of them as humorous diversions from the labor of his monograph. They were museum prints, ancient representations of the beetle, fly, and worm. In one picture, crude and stylized, a humanlike figure was apparently being extruded from the gut of a huge grub; and in another a giant scarab was covering and presumably inseminating a bejeweled woman.

"Come come." Klepper waggled a finger at his patient. "Avoidance. These are harmless jokes. As much to show the folly of the past. Remember, back on the track."

The human past, Baxter was thinking, was hardly past. The Most Holy Ones were 300 million years old before the first primate appeared. Digesting all life layer by layer and ring by ring, compiling the archives. The first vertebrates consumed these libraries, were eaten themselves; and finally the predators died and rotted back into the earth from whence the plants assimilated the whole story again—with all its emendations and revisions—before the Most Holy came to nibble into a new cycle, and by their infinite understanding justified it all. On the track, indeed.

"It only makes sense." The doctor was speaking with an effort, and a thin film of perspiration had coated his face.

"Mankind was at a primitive social stage, perhaps not so far removed from that of ants."

"Makes sense," Baxter echoed. "Leaf-cutters, honeydew."

"You're thinking of slavery and agriculture." The doctor managed to look both reproachful and pleased with himself. "Workers weeding the fungus beds and tending aphid colonies, et cetera. Yes, impressive in its way. And early human societies may have, well, not modeled themselves but . . ."

"Sweet honeydew, manna, excreta . . . ," Baxter crooned. He grinned and goggled at the doctor.

"That's enough," Klepper said sharply. He looked at the clock, looked again, alarmed. An office intercom buzzed and a clipped, female voice said something rapidly. "You must get a grip on these urges. Just a moment, Rhonda. Stop thinking of . . . of what you are thinking about. These old cults" —he waved rather wildly at the scenes on the wall—"often involved unbelievable barbarities. Mutilation, decapitation, what have you. Foundations of mad religions. Heaps and heaps of corpses. Worm fodder. Tribes organized in—"

"In sects devoted to human sacrifice," Baxter interrupted, his head moving back and forth in small jerks, light flashing from the lenses of his spectacles. He jabbed a finger at the picture of the beetle copulating with the princess. "I spied her when I came in. *Drink the milk of Paradise!*"

Klepper's lower jaw had unsprung and his eyes rolled away from the picture. "What . . . what are you . . . what sects?"

"We might say in sect attacks. But time flies, tick tick tick! So be it. Ever more intricate too." Baxter was speaking faster, his tone a sing-song.

"Enough!" the doctor croaked. He reeled to his feet as the intercom again delivered a long, staticky message. "Back on the track, Mr. Baxter! Back on the—"

"Intricate psychic insect attack!" Baxter was up too and around the desk. He plucked up the doctor's limp hand and pressed it to his face, inhaling, while with his free hand he felt along the chair arm and found Klepper's tiny pearl of wisdom. "Intricate psychic insect attack intricate psychic insect attack intricate—"

"Sect up!" Dr. Klepper managed to snatch his hand away, though the effort made him stagger. His face was white and his mouth remained loosely open. "A very bug—uh, bad—

233

example! Your condition . . . must say . . . cricketal. I mean cricktick—" He shook his head and then struck it with his hands. "Rhonda!" he bleated, and stared in fascinated horror at his patient.

Baxter, who had dropped full-length on the floor and was again goggling at him, kept up his chattering song. He swayed a little on his elbows, joyful, still smacking his lips even as he kept up his incessant intricate psychic insect attack. It would only be a matter of time, he knew, before Dr. Klepper would be on the floor beside him, taking up the chorus.

25

AN ENRAGED BEAR WAS CHASING HIM UP A STEEP, DARK hill; he could hear her snuffling and bellowing just behind him as he clawed his way along a narrow pathway through undergrowth. He was panting and sweating profusely; his legs shook with exhaustion, and he was terrified.

It was not Mata he feared, but some nameless, terrible thing he had done. The old bear was in fact trying to help, drive him to some act of atonement. He knew he should turn, let go, give himself to her. But then a faint light appeared at the end of the pathway, what had to be the top of the hill. He strained toward this light in a staggering run, bent from the waist, his knuckles digging into the earth.

Dry leaves were crunching under his flailing limbs, but then they were not dry, they were sticking to him. He brought one hand close to his face as he ran and saw in the growing light that it was covered with the empty, smeared wrappers of calorie bars. Then Mata's hot, rank breath was on him; he felt her jaws close over his shoulder just as he stumbled out into the harsh light, gasping and squinting.

The light came from a torch thrust close to his eyes. He had been pulled up from the floor of the housecave by rough hands, and in the flickering, racing shadows he could see the room was full of Pobla men. They were silent, with no sign of greeting or even recognition in their faces. Yet he saw the boy who had traveled with the party from Redfish Summit, the one who had called him *dako*.

He looked for Tima, and saw that she, too, was awake, standing in the only open space in the room. A circle had been formed, whose inner rim was made up of poised lance blades. Her eyes were closed and she swayed, very slightly, to and fro. *"Na?"* he burst out. *"Pahane tak zelag tondila—"*

All the men in the room hissed, a sound like a wind rising and then cut off, as if a door had been slammed shut. A word he did not catch. Then a single voice uttered a sharp command, and Tima opened her eyes and began to move. The space around her flowed along too, the lance points turning always toward her, yet keeping their distance. He was prodded into position just behind her and they moved into a wide tunnel mouth, a main thoroughfare.

Ahead he heard the squealing of rats and whispers. A route was being talked over. He had tried to say that they had come a great distance, would have gone on to explain about the *tchat,* meeting Tima, sending Yellow and Ap back another way. But the hissing had been ominous and final. The feeling of dread from his dream had become confused now with the shock of waking in the midst of this menacing, silent company, and he could not quiet the pounding of his heart.

Why had they turned their spears on Tima? What had she done? A column was being formed now, with he and Tima linked in tandem on a woven grass rope. The torch went out and a jerk and a shove sent them down a branch tunnel into utter darkness. He winced and crouched, remembering the trip with Teeklo, the endless crawling and sloshing through a maddening blackness. Tima touched his face once and then floated a step ahead of him, tugging lightly on the rope to indicate turns and obstacles.

Pahane was in a cage inside him, angry and pacing. They had taken away his spear, and in frustration his hand kept clenching into a fist. But he knew that he had to concentrate, to use his imagination against the darkness. He went over carefully what had happened the day before.

They spent an hour cleaning the Scooter of all prints and skin flakes. Then they hid the vehicle in a tiny, crooked canyon and screened it over with a crosshatch of dead branches. The first burrows they located and entered, however, were deserted. The firecoals in one settlement were still warm, but every tool and scrap of food had been cleaned out of the dwellings.

"They are watching," Tima said. "So we will wait."

She went outside and blew again on her bone whistle, signaling to the great black birds that wheeled overhead. Then she came back in with a handful of twigs which she dropped on the coals and fanned into a wisp of fire. They had been moving north, gaining altitude, and it was distinctly cooler now even in daytime.

Since leaving the Scooter Tima had been thoughtful, even preoccupied. He could not entice her into continuing their conversation on *wonakubi* and how the skilled *tagak* apprehended and harmonized with it. He supposed she was disappointed. After eight years of longing to be reunited with her people, after breaking her nose and stripping away all her piksi garb, she found herself apparently shunned.

He was himself, he had to admit, apprehensive of her. During the six hours of their tortuous drive, continually hugging walls or overhanging banks, she had handled the Scooter with great skill. Almost as good as his father, Ronald decided. She also checked the onboard continually, saving bits and pieces of various files even as she navigated treacherous terrain. Yet periodically they stopped and left the vehicle, so Tima could watch the sky or examine a scuff in the earth or dried droppings. Like Ap, she smelled everything carefully. Occasionally one of the black birds seemed to tilt and slide away in response to her movements.

Who was she, then? As dust and sweat appeared on her brown body and her loose hair grew matted she looked more and more like the Pobla he had seen in the temple city. That made the practiced way she read the instruments and handled the wheel all the more incongruous. Though he missed the air-conditioning and the occasional joy of covering almost two klicks a minute, he had felt oddly relieved when they finally abandoned the vehicle. Still he wondered whether he should have split away from Ap and Yellow to take this roundabout route—and with a stranger besides.

It was clear when they separated that both of his companions—and especially the cat—could not bear to be within sight of the Scooter. Neither would look at him directly, and immediately after Ap's whispered monosyllable of agreement they had fled. At the time he found himself impatient and a little disappointed, wondering what had happened to all the daring manifested in their *tchat* at the mine. Now he saw that Ap's frozen manner was a clear enough sign of impending trouble.

He had pestered Tima to tell him why the Pobla reacted so strangely to vehicles. Her own familiarity with them proved that the aversion was not inbred. Yet he had been told—and having seen Ap's reaction he now believed it—that a Pobla would die at the near approach of a patrol cruiser.

Finally she told him. "We have this from our ancestors, the tree people. Think how the piksis killed off so many generations, and then captured the last young ones, and they always came in these machines."

But still, he argued, not all probes were hunter-killers, and nowadays most animal populations were carefully monitored and controlled. Quick adapters were increasing their numbers. Some expeditions only captured specimens—

"Worse." Tima made a face and shivered. "That is the special piksi need, to devour souls. Look what the white ghosts in the north did to all the rest. We Pobla are not afraid of *yano*, Pahane. Many times the old people yearn for it and sometimes they just go, into the shadows where it is cool and they can rest and talk. But our tree ancestors saw long, long ago what the piksis were after, what they did to other animals and to each other. How they ate beings from within and kept alive only the bodies. Ugh!" She shivered in revulsion.

He stared at her and she understood him perfectly. "But it doesn't always work. You hid and stayed alive, *na?* Pahane woke up here among us, and is getting stronger. And I kept them from my *kubi,* for eight years. So we are alike, we two." She smiled at him and he looked down, embarrassed. She laughed, giggled almost, mischievous and teasing. "Outcasts, *na?* We are like the tiger bees and bears—wild for the second time."

He heard her yawn and saw her shadow stretch and curve, unsteady in the firelight on the stone wall. "It's all right to look at me," she said.

His face was burning up. It was true that her nakedness had made him uncomfortable from the beginning, even though for weeks he had been among Pobla who wore nothing or at best a scrap of hide or woven grass. And he knew—though he could not think straight about it—why he was uncomfortable. His darting eye would catch on her smooth, muscular leg or the taut skin over her breast and could not struggle free; his glance was like a fly stuck in a dish of syrup. Some lightness would develop then inside his rib cage, the same feeling he got from walking near the edge of a sheer drop. And more than once she had seen him looking, before he could manage to turn away.

"Time for bed," he said, more loudly than he meant to. He frowned fiercely at the wall. "I'm not . . . I mean. . . ."

She giggled again. "I know. Not yet. Snaketongue is still more careful than curious. *Lidatsa kish, tohanaku.*"

He had turned his back, pretending to arrange the crude bed he had made from tufts of dry grass carried in from outside. Though he heard the rustle of her settling in, he still did not risk a glance across the dying fire. "*Lidatsa kishta,*" he grumbled and lay down with deliberate carelessness. Dream well yourself. He could not add *tohanaku.* The word had made his heart jump. Or perhaps it was the easy, drowsy affection in her tone, a quality as physical as if a ray of sunshine had heated his skin. It was a long time before he cooled into sleep.

But he had dreamt monstrosities and awakened to find the nightmare around him. Now it seemed Tima, too, was guilty of some nameless crime, and the silence and grim urgency of their guards hinted at an impending punishment. Were the Pobla afraid her years with the piksi had corrupted her? And he, by choosing to arrive with her, was also ruined? Or was it the other way around? He recalled Tima's smile when she said they were alike, saw in it a hint of sadness he had missed before.

They were being pressed hard, and stopped only once for a few moments to gnaw a bit of dried meat. He could not tell, from the jagged turns and long inclines of their route, where they were going—north to the mountains or south again to the canyons. They crossed many other tunnels, some wide and smelling of much use, but encountered no other parties. As before, he found the atmosphere now suffocatingly fetid, now chilly and dank. And once again this black labyrinth of confusing directions and sensations tormented him to the edge of panic.

Two things kept him from screaming through his clenched teeth. He was mired in a stupor of exhaustion; and unerringly, the instant before he broke, Tima's hand would flutter over his face like a bat's wing and his *kubi* would revive and bound after her. Then a series of luminous images would scatter in his mind like sparks trailing from her fingers. Many of these images were of sleek animals, and in their writhing and sparring there was excitement and danger, a thrill that frightened him a little.

Also he discovered in himself a molten stratum of anger. He had endured scant rations and foul water, sun and wind and dust, the deadly weapons of patrol vehicles. He had tried to learn the Pobla way, their expressions and songs and habits. He had risked his life in the *tchat* foray, come away lame and four kilos underweight. And now they treated him like a prisoner again, glowered at him with suspicion and hostility.

Their high humor and playfulness were treacherous. They could also be changeable, lazy, foolish, fearful. . . . And they knew so little about so many commonplace things. It was idiotic to be so afraid of the little Scooter. Tima could have shown them how useful it was, kept the lights and air-conditioner going until the fuel ran out. Then they might have dismantled it and found a place for some of the metal or plastic parts. Or merely kept it for a curiosity.

He found himself thinking about the cool, dry interior of the vehicle, the green light from the screens, the click and whisper of its circuits. And of course the food locker in the hovercopter. What stupid waste. His mouth went bitter and he spat into the darkness. There was enough for days, a variety unimaginable to Ginks. Exotic juices and marinated cuts and liquored creams. And Ap ran away from it to gobble lizards and worms and desiccated leaves.

How had these creatures crippled their minds so fundamentally? Degeneration, his teachers had said, failure to adapt. A hybrid of inferior and too-specialized genes, made harmful by rapid erosion of an ecological niche. Well, their country was certainly eroded. The cruelest, most wretched place on earth—and they *preferred* it!

And yet they built a temple. An intricately carved underground temple that required unimaginable effort to erect and equally unimaginable stealth to hide. A shrine to a bug, whose priestess was a subhuman, senile old female. His mouth stretched in an ugly grin. He savored his irritation and disgust—stones he sucked on to keep down his thirst for light and air and freedom.

Abruptly they reached a spacious chamber, lit faintly by a very deep and narrow illumination shaft. There were more Pobla here, including whole families, and rats were underfoot, squealing over heaps of seed. There was an uproar of talk and whispering, with here and there a crying infant or a voice raised in song. As they wound through the crowd he saw that some were covered with caked mud and others had apparently been injured, for they were wrapped in bloody rags. Many also slept beside bundles or woven baskets stuffed and tied tight.

The young huddled near their parents, subdued, and he sniffed an odor of anxiety. He sensed again the heavy, mirror-bright feeling at his center. It was connected to *yano*, he knew, and he knew also that it flowed all around them, concentrating in a larger and larger pool. Tima no longer walked like a somnambulist, and though she did not look back at him he heard her utter a single, low cry. The agony of that cry went through him like a hurled stone, creating a blinding shimmer of pain. His own *kubi* twisted, recoiled, somehow impaled.

He lifted his hand to reach toward her, but one of the spear-carriers stepped forward, shoved him back and then unceremoniously cut the rope joining them. She turned and he got one glimpse of her slight, sad smile before he was pulled around by the rope end and pointed toward a branch tunnel. The man with the spear made a fierce face at him. *"Tak pakishkubi!"* he hissed. *"Vasan tonpah ya katchun Teeklo."*

Something reared, flared in him. A tongue of fire from their *tchat* or one of the great red-sided fish leaping against a torrent. He brought his arm around and knocked the man's spear aside, dislodged the rope from his grasp. Then he turned and darted toward the group that was hurrying Tima away, jerking her along by her bit of rope like a dog.

He heard the man at his back exclaim and his spine tingled, anticipating the bite of the spear. But in a moment he had wriggled between two of the guards, dodging their grasping hands, and then he was beside Tima, inside the night sky of her look. Whatever had torn the cry from her was hidden now and she kept up the little smile.

"*Na?*"

"*Na,*" he whispered. He was still looking into her eyes, yet he could see all of her slim, bare, erect body. ". . . *kishta Lidatsa . . . tohanaku.*"

Her smile broadened and simultaneously both of them lifted a hand to touch the other's face. The brightness flowed together between them, a liquid incandescence that endured for an immeasurable time. Then the guards pulled them apart, shouting and closing off the space between them. He did not hear the words, did not see the dark faces frowning into his. He felt burned, and clean, and new.

26

"WHO ARE THESE ASSHOLES?" SKIHO MUTTERED RHETORI-cally, checking the charge light on the topobike he had finished assembling. "And who needs them."

PJ did not answer. He stared glumly at the screen, reached out to peck three keys, then grimaced at the response.

The cabin was in disarray: wrappers from foodpaks and plastic cups were all over the floor and even on the instrument panels; various items of field gear were heaped near the apron of the cargo bay; a dozen disk cartridges were stacked at PJ's elbow—all of them dealing with emergency reprogramming or security autodestruct.

"I can't believe that bitch. Every single goddamned watchdog—the nine-headed ones too—is one-eightied and they've eaten all the banks but life support and blow. Nobody gets that in Pro Four training." PJ appeared to be talking to himself, his tone a blend of amazement and tightly stoppered fury.

"So we can only talk to Fat."

"Fat's private terminal. Whether or not he's still there." PJ looked up finally. "I wouldn't count on anything."

Skiho plugged the charger in again and pinched the front tire dubiously. "Holy shit. The highest-level, most secret intelligence op, and we're ignorant. Utterly fucking ignorant."

"Slight flaw in the system," PJ said with a bitter leer. "Though we at least know somebody else is out there sniffing around. And I would guess we are right now potentially the most notorious kidnappers in modern times."

"Comforts me immeasurably. I just hope I wasn't dreaming on sliders and that really was little Ronnie."

"It was him. I was pasted too, but I know she came in with a sunburnt little bag of bones, definitely a boy. I mean, who else could it be, out here?"

"Still be nice to compare him with the holos we've got on file. Had on file, rather." Skiho grinned ruefully.

"That *bitch.*"

There was admiration under PJ's rage. He had no idea really how Tima had accessed the most fundamental of the copter's systems, then worked out how to seal or modify them and set the destruct program in motion. As far as he remembered she never glimpsed a screen when anything classified was running. Though she had often been near, quiet and attentive, as he went through files. Listening, he guessed. That had to be it, but such acuity of hearing and powers of memorization strained credibility.

Anyway she had done it all perfectly. Presented Fat with a totally believable hostage situation. Info on the kid to prove he was in their custody. Demands that made sense—numbered free-zone trust accounts, promotions, a policy role. Fat knew they were nervous about the V-studies and the fate of the Preserves. And everyone knew their reputation as buccaneer agents not too careful of the rules. A free-lance operation like this was just possible, just believable.

Before making her proposal Tima had doom-wired all remaining systems, made them impermeable to override or jamming. She left a single thread—protected by the deepest code—to the center of the web, the director's private terminal. The security ring for the copter was simultaneously put on full autodestruct alert. Any probe at its perimeter stimulated an immediate warning on a short fuse. If no withdrawal was made in ninety seconds the copter blew itself to a powder.

Of course Fat—or his replacement—couldn't afford to turn to the regular Border Forces for help. He'd have to justify, very convincingly, an S and R for a vehicle his own agents had commandeered. And he couldn't risk blowing up Ronald Drager; such a monumental blunder might put an end to the Conservative party entirely. So he had to sit tight and deal.

Problem was, of course, they had nothing to deal with. No Ronald. No Tima either. Both of them had laughed, as condemned men laugh on the first step to the gallows, at Skiho's suggestion that they emerge from the copter with hands up chanting, "*Just kidding*." The odds were quite good, PJ thought, that however they emerged they would be vaporized a second after their feet hit the ground.

So Tima had figured the two of them accurately. They weren't about to be vaporized, or even stripped of all rank and privilege. They had no choice but to play along for the first forty-eight hours, time enough for the Scooter to get well away. They kept up an elaborate verbal Ping-Pong with Fat, while PJ tried every keyboard trick he knew to revive the copter and Skiho got together packs and recon maps. A patrol had shown up, presumably a special Insec hunter ship, and it had prowled their perimeter since, trying everything from a two-man augur underground to an automated lo-pro crawler. These scampered back just under the ninety-second wire. Plucking at their nerves.

"Yamaguchi," Skiho said. He was answering his own question about the assholes. "That's who Fat would send. Somebody dependable. The human meat grinder." He swung a leg over the bike and settled on the seat, testing. "With orders to wipe on sight."

"Maybe." PJ sat straighter and stared intently at the screen. "Hey. Got something."

Skiho dismounted swiftly and came to read. "Yeah. Yeah. So. Pull back the patrol, fine. Then what? One step past our security screen and they'll whack us."

"That's another reason to split up. Whichever one they get, they have to assume the kid is with the other guy."

"True." Skiho hummed an off-key tune, watching the screen. "And only one ship, as far as we know. They couldn't risk a top pri alert. Can't afford to admit Insec hires such rotten creeps as us."

"All true. If I'm lucky and hit a Gink burrow in the first hour. . . ." PJ blew out a sharp breath.

"You'll make a barbecue for a whole village, maybe." Skiho cuffed him lightly on the shoulder. "Ever wonder what you would *really* taste like?"

PJ had to smile. At a certain order of magnitude, the question of the lesser of two evils became moot. The plan was for them to run just before the copter blew. Skiho would head for the border on the Topobike. On the outside chance he succeeded he would try to go public before Insec got to him. He would carry traces of heavy sedatives in his blood, which might corroborate his tale of being overwhelmed and held captive by PJ. Assuming he was ever allowed to tell that tale. If this darkside patrol caught him, and Yamaguchi was the push, they might simply do a full wipe: shred, atomize, and disperse both him and his record.

PJ had opted to try to follow Tima and recover the Drager boy. An absurd notion. A lone man on a basic bike with a field pack and light autophaser could not hope to cover more than a few hundred square miles before his charge failed. The gamble was that Tima and the kid would have to abandon the Scooter and its weaponry to enter Ginkdom, and he might be incredibly lucky and find her before she got too deeply into the tunnel mazes. What he would do in that case . . . he didn't know. Maybe blackmail was not such a bad idea. Certainly their careers as special agents were over, irrevocably. Tima had seen to that.

He punched out of the code frame but left the access cue hanging. Let them think he could be online again at any moment. Before he stood up he allowed himself the pleasure of a roundhouse swing that sent the stack of disk cartridges clattering across the floor.

"Know how you feel," Skiho said. "So I guess this is it, buddy."

"Yeah." PJ bent to shoulder his pack and the phaser. "End of Project Duskyrose."

"Maybe not. Maybe you'll tryst again. Maybe soon." Skiho wore his cheery, quizzical smile. "She was good, you know. Got to admit."

PJ's smile was not quite spontaneous. After a moment's pause, Skiho laughed and turned to his bike. "Anyhow, buddy, it's always a pleasure working with you. Sorry about. . . ." He shrugged.

"Hey, no try, no fly. We done what we could, Black Jack." PJ swung out his hand and the other bumped it, a rough patt-a-cake. "I'll give you about five minutes' jump."

Skiho nodded, disconnected the charger, and touched a button on the bars of the bike. The bay slid swiftly open. Just before he released the brake he glanced once more at his friend.

"You find her, give her one for me," he said. Then the big, light tires rasped sharply against the metal floor and he was out the bay and down the ramp.

Skiho maneuvered to place the copter between himself and the probe craft, a technique that would keep him off their screens for a hundred yards. At that point he would encounter a narrow gully he had already scouted, and this gully fed into a larger dry wash. Of course the satellite network would pick him up, but if he was lucky—very lucky—the probe ship would not be monitoring satscans moment-to-moment. They were poised, after all, less than four minutes' flight time from the copter, the focus of their own detection systems.

They might check the sats every two, three, maybe five minutes. In five he could be out of the wash and into the last maze of canyons formed by the runoff from the foothills. The canyons informally known as the Crooked Mothers. A light vehicle of mostly nonmetallic fiber could coast down these wind channels on mylar sails, so as to leave no exhaust or heat traces. He would move only at night, without power assist; he would have a half-moon, waxing, to travel under. It was possible. Just possible. He had to believe that.

Right now speed was the game. The rest of his life could be only three minutes long. If so, he liked the idea of running it out, running as fast as time. He leaned over the handlebars, under the cowl of the windscreen, feeling for the right point of balance on the frame.

The Topobike was adapted for swift, stealthy transit of rough terrain. Each of its three light semiballoon tires was independently sprung and the whole tubular fibergraph frame could distort on its hydraulic knee joints. A video sensor on the front axle scanned ahead and signaled adjustments in the angles of the suspension system. The silent purr of batteries drove the bike, so the only sounds were the thin whistling of the wind created by its motion and the harsh whisper of the tires on dry sand.

Skiho was happy to be on the run. He laughed into the wind, squinted in the sunlight. This assignment was over. Probably it was *all* over. But for these seconds he was in the place he loved, free to move fast and recklessly. If he made the Crooked Mothers he would kiss the dirt of these Wastelands. These scorched, irradiated, eroded cracks and lumps, this dump site freak refuge, the world's bunghole—he realized all at once that he loved it. Loved it more than anything.

Laughing, the tears blowing from the corners of his eyes, he skidded from the mouth of the gully into the dry wash. Steadying his course along its flat, sandy bottom, he cranked on the power lever, leaned lower, his chin almost on the handlebars. Crossing a frozen wave of sand, he felt the wheels momentarily lift free of the earth.

After the bay door retracted, PJ popped two flatheads, then loaded the robodumper in preparation for his move out. Besides the pack and phaser, he laid in a collapsed basic bike, a six-hour air tank and a pile of seat cushions. The copter was set to destruct in twenty-seven minutes, but the guys outside didn't know that. His plan was, quite simply, to bury himself deep enough to survive the explosion. He would crawl inside the dumper cart, ride it down the ramp and out into the field. There he could manually override its sensors and look for gravelly soil that didn't pack too tightly. Once the hovercopter blew, the probe would be busy going through wreckage, analyzing residues. He had to hope that they would finish in less than six hours, pick up Skiho's tracks, and move out. And that no one would remember the garbage run.

Two minutes to kill, so he sat by the dumper port, propping

his chin on both doubled fists. Normally he was good at using such time, thinking straight and fast, but now he felt numb and empty. The flatheads only slowed his heartbeat to a steady hammering. Of course since the nightmare of the tiger bees and his stupid self-spiking, his system had been awash in chemicals, but that didn't explain his current reaction.

It was Tima, or rather the mystery of her. He could explain—by a little stretching—her daring, intelligence, and treachery. Clearly, however subhuman most of the Ginks, there was an occasional freak genius. Equally obvious, her species had some special capability in hiding from psych-probes. It was also likely that all of them, Fat included, had flagrantly underestimated her.

But he had no way to account for the explosion of images she had generated in his mind, for the peculiar blend of shame and exhilaration with which he remembered her on top of him, pinning him, devouring him. Then there was her uncanny understanding of what he was thinking or feeling at any given moment, and in retrospect he could also see how she had played him and Skiho against each other, gotten them to behave like vain, careless rookies.

And now she had Ronnie. The little bag-of-bones that would have made their expedition a brilliant triumph. In the drug-fog of his memory he could see the boy, staring at him with an odd alertness, like a small animal. But at the time it took every nanogram of his strength simply to lift one hand. Even now he felt tired. Almost too tired to go on. If he sat where he was, in twenty-five minutes he could simply flash out. Poof.

Why not? He tried to muster his rage again, think of vengeance, of Tima against a wall. The image disintegrated, and in the ensuing blank he realized all at once that anger had been replaced by curiosity. He wanted, quite simply, to know how she had done it, what Gink juju had given her the edge. The boy, in the end, was irrelevant. A political pawn. What fascinated him was the mystery of his own misjudgment.

The timer on his chrono beeped three times. He rose and threw back the cover of the dumper. An odor of old plastic and rotted food. He wrinkled his nose, took a breath, and climbed into the bin. A small utility bulb went on after he pulled the cover shut, and by its weak yellow light he found the switch panel and activated the cart.

He rumbled out the port and let the cart wander with the sensor and locater switches open. The machine was a simple one, a tracked, unshielded vehicle programmed to find suitable sites and bury refuse in them. It worked in a widening spiral, avoiding rock or badly broken terrain. When he judged they were nearing the gully, PJ stopped the cart and opened the small observation port. Not bad. Some light rock and soil in with the sand.

He switched on the big augur. While the bit was eating into the ground he rigged his mask to the airtank and set the flow. Then, after arranging his pack and weapon around him, he sat firmly in the pile of cushions. The collapsed bike frame he would hold over his head, a shield to create the space needed to dig himself out.

At seven feet he stopped the augur and withdrew it. The dumper had swept up and guarded the dirt behind its front blade, and after releasing its load it would fill and smooth. Lifting the bike over his head, he stretched out one foot and managed to trip the automatic dump. The bottom doors dropped, the cushions cascaded into the hole, and PJ and his gear whumped hard on top of them.

He looked up as the doors snapped shut. The tracks creaked and the cart began to back up, dragging the blade. He kept the bike overhead, propped one end on the tank, braced the other against the wall of the hole, crouched in the little chamber thus formed. A small avalanche of earth rattled over him, increased rapidly, became a thundering, heavy darkness that bore down until his arms began to crack and buckle.

Overhead the dumper cart lurched back and forth, its blade imperfectly smearing out the excess earth. Nothing in its circuits told it that the overflow was unusual. It finished its last pass, reversed one-eighty, and began to trundle home. Watching its progress on a monitor screen, the duty officer in the hunter ship yawned and glanced away. Big deal. Darkest of covops. Ha ha. The major action of the morning was this garbage run. He looked back, saw the dumper tilt up onto the ramp of the hovercraft, and then the whole screen caught fire.

27

"CANDY!" TEEKLO HAD WINCED IN BITTER DISGUST. "SHIT bastard sonofabitch! Now you have done it. *Ronald.*"

That had been his welcome when they finally reached the temple city. Sopan was in a turmoil of evacuation, refugees hurrying along its main thoroughfare, and the heavy brightness of *yano* ran with them like a great river. A few terse comments confirmed what he had already guessed: the piksis were pouring over the border, attacking even the smallest villages with unprecedented swiftness and savagery.

Yet he had been sent immediately to a small cell for two days, where four men took turns singing over him. Red-hot stones and skins full of water had been brought in, apparently to boil him alive in steam, and he had been beaten thoroughly with switches from some pungent shrub. Then he had been given a garment, a mere sack with holes for head and arms, which he understood immediately was a mark of shame.

Teeklo had explained the ceremony then in a kind of furious calm. Ronald—he made a sardonic curse of the word—was being purified. He had touched a piksi vehicle, ridden in it, and worst of all eaten from it.

The men who found him had smelled the calorie bars instantly. Both he and Tima were most unclean. In fact, there was no provision for defilement of this magnitude. Their *kubin* should have departed, their hearts stopped. In any case his body had become piksi again, bloated and stinking. The odor of Ronald had to be driven off, his filthiness covered.

For reasons Teeklo said he could not fathom, Adza had not cast him out, but had actually ordered instead more extreme rites, which normally were used only to initiate a new *tagak*. Everything was confused, topsy-turvy. They could not, for example, decide about Tima. She was for the moment confined with the insane.

"You are dividing us," Teeklo said then, "splitting us apart.

249

There are some who thought from the beginning we should kill you, you know. You—"

"What about *me?*" He leaned forward over the small fire in the cell, his eyes glittering in anger. "I tried to do everything, the way you said. I ate, I learned to speak, I went to the mine, going hungry and without water. . . . But I have . . . I mean I had. . . ." He stopped, shifted his gaze to the fire, and swallowed. "Everything in my life before. My mother and father. My room. I could have candy bars like that every day. So it was natural. I mean, it's just something to eat. And as far as dividing . . . what about *me* splitting up? How do you think I feel about . . . about all this?"

He jerked a hand at the walls around him, the crude smoke pot and heap of leaves beside it, the flat stone bearing a portion of mummified meat scraps. He knew these last were ceremonial medicine, fed to him to restore Pahane's strength. Some venerated old Pobla, he supposed. He had found a wrinkled bit of ear and the tip of a thumb. The taste was like moldy cardboard.

Teeklo did not answer for a time, and when he did his voice was quiet, neutral. "I know exactly how you feel. It's true. The world is splitting you, also. I don't deny that."

"I just rode in a Scooter and just nibbled—"

"Don't lie," Teeklo interrupted curtly. "You *know.*"

There was a long pause, the two of them glaring at each other. The boy looked away first. Yes, he did know. He had been surprised, himself, at the way the rich flavors had sent their tentacles into his brain. Memories, yearnings, a deep physical ache had soon developed. And the speed and lift of the vehicle—his insides had gone spongy with a pleasure he knew was dangerous.

"And we have known for a long time the piksis were going to do something like this. We saw the birds writing it in the sky, heard the crickets' warning in the grass, smelled it in the wind from the mines and plantations. But when you came to us everything seemed to go faster. And this attack—it is bad, very bad."

Teeklo stopped and beyond the ticking of the fire they could hear the proof of his words—distant cries, the brush of feet hurrying over stones. "They are not taking specimens. Goddamn them. They bore in, comb everywhere, kill one by one. Like they were looking for something."

They were silent for a time. Tears trickled down the boy's face but he made no sound.

"Yet even this is not your fault, I think. They would have found some other excuse, sooner or later. They are desperate these days."

The boy looked intently at him, but Teeklo did not appear to notice and went on. "But you see how some of the old Pobla, the most traditional, believe that our keeping you has brought the trouble. They think Mata was mistaken, and Adza believed too much in her old sister. They also think the Pobla have gone too far from the old way of keeping invisible. Fortunately for you, only Adza can tell the *wonakubi*. She can't hear anything else." He tried and failed to suppress a smile. "Except the radio."

"But she doesn't seem to. . . ."

"Know?" Teeklo's smile broadened. "You think she has lost her brains? Is—what is that word? Senile, yes? A child again." He laughed. "As if that were a sickness."

"Well, *isn't* she?"

"Of course that is so. Her mind goes here and there, and she talks mostly to the dead. Also she sleeps a lot. If she were piksi she would be in one of those homes where they only feed and wipe the bottoms. But the Pobla do not get this way usually. When our people grow too old and forgetful we eat them."

"But she is *tagak?*"

"Yes, so." Teeklo regarded him, saw his doubt. "You wonder what this means, how we can honor so much an old woman with the brains of a child. Ah well. Hard to explain." He sighed, shook his head. "The problem is, the *wonakubi* has nothing to do with explanations, and piksis never understand anything without words. I know, I am one too. So I can only tell you that the Great Hive Dwellers—what you call termites and ants and bees—they have the greatest understanding of the Shadow of Shadows, and the Hive Dwellers give Adza her visions, and she passes them on to us. They are songs and pictures and even smells, but they don't speak to us. They are . . . that is . . . we *become* them."

Ronald continued to stare into the fire, but he was alert

now. *Early Animism. The Myth of the Beast. Totem and Trance.* He remembered the books, his guilty middle-of-the-night reading under the covers, his peculiar excitement at the illustrations—the men and women with fangs, wings, hooves, scales. He saw some of these figures twisting in the coals and then a printed page rose before his inner eye.

Early hominids believed quite literally in their kinship with certain animals, even insects and reptiles. They traced themselves to a common ancestor, often a woman inseminated by a god-being in the shape of a bull, wolf, crane, or . . .

He imagined the carving on the wall of Adza's chamber, the giant beetle covering the woman. Ridiculous! A joke, almost. Disturbing. Something huge rolled at the center of his being, then sank again.

"Yes, that's it." Teeklo was nodding at him. "You felt it go by there? Very strong. Even the Pobla cannot take too much *wonakubi.* Only after ceremonies, plenty of singing and dancing. A great *tagak* can be in a hive for perhaps ten minutes. I have seen Adza do it for almost twenty. I think it helps that she is so simple and scattered. Her mind is like leaves between her being and the sun, making a patch of shade. These are her teachings."

"But there must be. . . . I mean communication has to have a system." Ronald shifted his weight on the hard stone floor. He still had not mastered the Pobla knack of sitting cross-legged for hours.

Teeklo winced. "Think of her as a radio. Tuned to the Hive Dwellers. But not broadcasting in words. It is more like . . . like a virus. Only for health. It makes us *stronger,* draws us together. It catches and spreads."

"Viruses have codes. They talk to other cells, make them over," Ronald insisted stubbornly.

"So do hives have their codes—far more complex than ours—but we are not interested. We're interested in the *message.*"

"But—"

"Oh yes, they are separate. You don't have to understand electromagnetism to listen to a radio, do you? *Wonakubi* is a million times more complicated and subtle than electromagnetism. No one understands it. No one ever will. Yet it is all around us. It talks to *you*, when you are Pahane. Or rather to itself."

Ronald began an uneasy laugh that died in his throat. "To me?" he asked with an attempt at nonchalance.

Teeklo only looked at him, as a man waiting for a bus stares down the street.

He thought then of how he had lain against Mata, dreaming to the mighty grumbling of her guts, of the vision of his father, grinning horribly, bearing down on him in a patrol vehicle, of the other vision of Tima—though he did not know then it was her—running toward him with her hair blowing like black fire.

"I saw my father," he said, "and I thought. . . ." He looked back into the fire and shook his head. "But that was crazy. To think he was. . . ."

"Trying to kill you?" Teeklo smiled his thin, unpleasant smile.

"I didn't. . . ." Ronald stopped, his breath coming harder.

"*Wonakubi* showed you that. Many times when you think what you didn't want to think—that is *wonakubi*. I would trust it, if I were you."

"My father," he whispered. In the small, red cave of the fire he thought he saw another twisting figure, a snake. A point of numbness, of terror, appeared inside him.

"We are very little, very fragile, very ignorant," Teeklo said softly and rapidly. "And the forces that move through us are tremendous. Even our individual *kubin*, the sparks from *wonakubi*, are sometimes too powerful and tear us apart. At least we know that, while the piksis do not.

"That is why I told you to let Pahane in only little by little. But it seems Snaketongue is maybe *tagak*. At least Adza feels so. And we have no more time to be cautious. This assault —your father is part of it, you know—has come too fast. Almost as if they wanted to keep Snaketongue from being. As if you were betraying something very dear to them. Dearer than your life."

He did not answer. He felt utterly alone, and fragile and weak as Teeklo had said. A minuscule spark in a vast, dreadful sea of darkness. The holonews had screamed his story to the whole world, and the piksi troops had thereby been unleashed. For good reason many of the Pobla now feared him, and perhaps his own father wished him dead. To everyone he was unclean and a traitor. Yet perhaps gifted—cursed!—with some mysterious power. A power which might tear him to pieces.

"I would help you if I knew how," Teeklo went on softly. "But I am not *tagak*. I am not even good at sensing its presence. You are. Mata knew that. Despite your piksi stink. And she saw that you saw her, even if you were too frightened to see it yourself. Adza sees it too. That is why she wants you to go with her to the Great Hives, to sing rockenroll near the sea."

He raised his head, blinked. "When?"

"There is one more ceremony this dawn, at the temple. It will not be easy for you, I fear. Then we must all leave. The tunnels and airshafts must be filled. The Tree of Promise dug up. The piksis must not find this temple."

"Tima," he said suddenly, and his voice was changed. "*Ya kat se?*"

Teeklo's face went blank and hard. "I don't know. We can't eat her, her flesh is corrupt. But she is Pobla still, so she can't be driven away. No one has seen anything like her. Or you either. They are afraid."

There was a long silence. The fire had waned to a few coals under a lacework of ash, so they could no longer see each other's faces.

He knew instinctively it was near dawn, and the four guards would soon come to take them to the ceremony. When he spoke, his voice had changed yet again: it was quiet, but in the darkness it did not sound like the voice of a boy.

"I won't go to the Hives, or anywhere else," he said, "without Tima."

The black shape opposite him did not move, and he thought Teeklo had gone to sleep. But finally the man spoke, and he heard laughter hidden under the words.

"Good. Good for you. *Kishta dako.*"

The great hall was hot and full of swirling smoke. Torches had been lit to supplement the dim, gray light from the shafts overhead, and they flickered luridly on the bodies packed four or five deep against the walls. The area around the central dais was still open, and there stood the old man with his staff and small pack of rats. He was chanting, striking the stone floor rhythmically, and the others along the walls chanted with him so that the whole chamber resonated like the inside of a drum.

Their escorts brought the boy and Teeklo to the dais, where Adza sat with her eyes closed. Her torso was bare except for finger-smudges of red and white, minerals ground and mixed with grease. On each of her withered cheeks was a single stroke of dried blood from a fresh cut.

A low block of stone was positioned like a footstool before the dais, and he was led there first and pushed to his knees. A small blaze had been kindled in a firepit to one side of the stone block, and now one of the four guards cast a handful of pungent leaves over the flames. Before stepping back and away, Teeklo whispered to him again that he must keep breathing the smoke and not cry out.

The billows rolled over him and he inhaled, choked, and inhaled again. Tears formed in his smarting eyes, and the chanting thundered in his skull. Some of the blurred shapes around him seemed to be dancing, but soon he could see only Adza, swaying a little from side to side, and the block directly in front of him.

Arranged on its surface were three objects. A shallow basket containing more strips of mummified gray flesh, a heap of the small yellow apples he had seen on the scraggly tree when he first arrived in Sopan, and a long section of reed stoppered at both ends by wooden plugs. Even as he became aware finally of the meaning of the chant, Adza leaned forward, still not opening her eyes, and fumbled with one claw hand until she clutched an apple.

Daso, daso, dela tagak,
daso poman tiplat ku!

Eat, eat, little master, eat the fruit which casts a shadow! And she leaned still further, her ancient, bony haunches higher than her head, until he could reach the apple and take it from her hand.

In the gloom and smoke the little yellow knob seemed to contain its own light, like a miniature lantern. Its juice, when he bit, was a startling explosion of sharp acid coming through thick sweetness. He had never tasted such a flavor, mouth-puckering yet gratifying, and in spite of Teeklo's warning he almost cried aloud in his surprise.

The rhythm of the chanting changed then, slowed and intensified, booming like surf. Syllables were so drawn-out he could not always understand the words. Now Adza presented him with the dried meat. It was like a mouthful of dust, but he knew it was Pobla. From some ancient and beloved *tagak*, he guessed.

The smoke was taking effect, lifting under his ribs, sending its fingers into his being. He felt Pahane nearby, just beyond the hollow of his chest, but this Pahane was not the same. He was not the mad boy, bad boy, full of galvanic, uncontrollable energy, who ran kilometer after kilometer over rough stone. Nor the unsleeping demon who struck with the swift malice of lightning, the *tchat*-maker, night-rain howler and dancer.

This Pahane was quiet, hidden, yet as solid as a great toad in a hole. His huge, golden eyes saw and reflected, his wet skin absorbed, but he did not move. Like his previous manifestation he was completely and perfectly awake, yet there was not the merest shred of a thought, not one word, in his being.

The boy understood he himself was still in his flesh, had not yet become shadow. But for the first time he sensed the force beyond Pahane, the sun that could create such shapes out of nowhere and cast them forth, breathing and full of power, into a cage of fragile human ribs.

And in the instant of that understanding, Adza opened her eyes. They glittered like chips of mica in the torchlight, immediately and wholly alert. The withered slit of her mouth writhed and the chanting altered again. Now higher and faster, it made the indistinct figures around them gyrate and stamp.

One such figure emerged from the smoke and whirled near him. He was staring into Adza's eyes so he did not see the knife, only heard it rip through his sacklike garment. The rags were peeled from his body and he thought he could feel the smoke, oddly cool, blow right through him.

The blade flashed up again. He felt the stroke across his cheek as a numbness, then a tickling sensation, as if a caterpillar were crawling toward his chin. But the second cut was like a red-hot wire, and he heard the blade opening his flesh with a brief, sharp sigh.

The smoke had, however, intruded between him and his own body. The pain of the cut seemed to occur at a distance. He felt himself receding into drifting veils, dissolving and disintegrating, weightless. Only the block of stone and Adza's small, wrinkled face remained clear and present.

She was smiling or grimacing at him now, a series of faces that seemed to express madness, hilarity, sleepiness, anger, or mere muscular convulsion. Simultaneously she was reaching down again, handling the section of reed, unstoppering it. Without being told he lifted his hands and rested them on the stone. Already, he could see, the blood from his cheeks had forked crookedly down his arms to run between his knuckles.

The ants that poured out of the hollow reed first formed a mazy pool. Then a few tentatively climbed his fingers, encountered the blood. In moments the swarm had covered his hands and sent writhing columns up the dark ribbons along his arms.

Unlike the vague smoky scene around him, these red and black insects were concrete and definite, perfectly articulated. They seemed very near, or mysteriously enlarged, so that he could see the gauzy sheen of their bulbous eyes, the sheathed sections of their abdomens, the barbs and single claws of their shuttling limbs. They seemed to be running under his skin, along his nerves.

In their frenzy they mired themselves in the branching trickle of his blood, forming clots. Their sour, pungent odor obliterated the smells of smoke and flesh; and their fine, hot, electric stings erased all other sensation, even the dull ache of his slashed face. He felt as if he were losing shape and becoming a swarm, a fluid force, a charged cloud.

There was a heavy shock then, a rupture and separation. He disappeared. The big toad jumped, blinked. Everything stood forth suddenly.

Adza got to her feet on the dais, seeming to rise out of the smoke. Her eyes were closed again and she uttered a high, warbling cry. The chanting grew louder, thunderous, making the stone cavern vibrate. The dancers ceased and torch-bearers now created a circle of wavering light.

Across the chamber the crowd parted and a rank of Pobla appeared in the entranceway, hauling on thick, woven-grass ropes. They struggled forward into the circle, their dark shoulders gleaming with sweat. Behind them a shape rumbled into the entranceway and the crowd recoiled from it.

The rumbling was a consequence of the wheels not being entirely round. They were made from thin, flat stones, painted to imitate a spoke and hub structure. The body of the vehicle was fabricated from branches lashed with vine, over which a fabric of woven grass had been stretched. The square windscreens had been cut from isinglass, and small ornaments were shaped from copper or soapstone.

A replica of a museum piece, one of the first mass-produced vehicles. Exquisite care had been expended in forming the dash, the seats, the headlamps and levers and controls—mostly from woods of various hues with here and there a knob of gypsum or pumice. In the shifting waves of shadow from the torches, the radiator looked like a grinning maw, the large lamps like eyes.

Its old-fashioned, boxy shape made the vehicle seem unstable; it lurched and wobbled on the imperfect stone wheels. Wooden parts grated and squealed, though the rate of progress was extremely slow. On each side, the Pobla crouched nearest the lumbering thing had shrunk or curled as if exposed to a fire. Others were writhing full-length on the floor. Some were vomiting.

Pahane was now only a tunnel of space, through which blew a hurricane of dark light. The hurricane came from behind and below, from some boundless deep of radiance, and reached to Adza. She opened her mouth wide and from this black hole emerged the head of a serpent, its opalescent scales and quick wire of tongue immediately vibrant and alive.

The scrawny throat distended, and with heavy grace the sinewy body began to glide forth. Long, longer, the snake entered the tunnel, undulating into the gale of luminous darkness, absorbing it. Now there was pressure, compaction, a coiling implosion of energy, and a column took shape, began to solidify and branch.

A bare, white tree at first, with forked root. Then shadows came, like leaves. And fire raced through the shadows. The tree moved, smooth and swift as water; a dance, circling toward a company that came behind the ancient vehicle. This company, painted also with strokes of red and yellow and white, dragged a kind of sled. In the sled was a heap of stones, each the size of a fist.

Teeklo, kneeling on the far side of the chamber, saw the boy stand up. He was little more than a skeleton, and burnt nearly as dark as a Pobla. So thin and naked, half-hidden by the curling clouds of smoke, he could have been one of the starving refugees streaming in from the border. But there was now, in this slight body, a springy, inexhaustible strength.

Teeklo had learned to recognize the signs: eyes that swallowed everything yet remained utterly empty, a lightness and slight stiffness of bearing, like a bird walking on the earth, the complete indifference to pain. He did not, himself, know the direct power of *wonakubi*. Very early in his studies he realized that he had no gift, no vision, and he was ultimately glad for this limitation.

He was a piksi, an understander and thinker and plotter, with the barest saving sliver of *kubi*. His soul was a stunted child who could detect the presence, feel the shadow on his skin, but then had to fumble in darkness for a hand to guide his way. Partly for that reason he pleased the Pobla, had his place in high councils; for he could always tell them how it looked to the Devourers, and confirm their intuitions of impending convulsion in the piksi world.

But this slip of a boy contained the bright, raw light, a lion-sized chunk of it. Teeklo knew, if only from his study, that this metaphor was false—as all images of *wonakubi* were false. The boy "contained" nothing, was not even there anymore, had no more substance than a shadow. But Teeklo could never stop the flow of words, the camera in his brain; and so saw only a peculiar clarity, a surprising articulation, in the figure of a man-child crossing the chamber in light, quick steps.

This child knew what to do, that was part of the mystery. Once he and Adza had looked into each other, the ants on both of them, the power had been everywhere in the room. The Pobla dragging the *Mudlati*, the chant to encircle its evil, the stone boat—all these had been set in motion by that power, exactly in rhythm. Now the boy—the form of the boy—was similarly moved, as if Adza had blown a coal to life and set the flame to a dry wood. Volition and consciousness—Teeklo knew a spasm of familiar envy—had nothing at all to do with this communication.

From the sled the boy took a stone in each hand and then spun along the edge of the circle of Pobla. Teeklo could see faces turning to follow this dance. Many were sightless with fear; others looked rapt, ecstatic. Some got to their feet and staggered after the boy.

Teeklo caught himself breathing faster. Even he could feel it now: the attractive force from the *Mudlati*, an awful, heavy, desire. An unspeakable promise. Long-forgotten sensations roiled in his blood and he nearly retched. Power summoned with a fingertip, the sudden yet smooth engagement of gears, an acceleration, a soaring. . . . He coughed and spit.

The Pobla beside him shrank away. They smelled what was building inside, the hunger. He groaned and looked away from the image of the vehicle, fighting panic. The figure was near him now, the muscles of the arms like taut cables holding in the swinging stones. He saw the streaks of bright blood, the clots of ants. Then the empty eyes met his own, pulled him effortlessly into their vortex, until he felt a clean, hot impact. It was as if he had been wakened by a bullet through the brain.

The whirling went faster, the arms rising with centrifugal force, and the figure began to spiral inward toward the *Mudlati*. A line of followers swayed after, also bearing stones or spears. The chant had grown louder, deafening, and Teeklo realized then he was screaming with the rest, rising to his feet, tightening the circle.

Pahane had reached the vehicle, which seemed to shiver and crouch in the wavering light. He let go one of the stones and it crashed into the windscreen, a spray of glittering chips. The second stone struck a door panel and partially caved it in. A cry went up, part terror and part joy, as the vehicle lurched in the shock of the blows. Then a Pobla ran forward and heaved two more stones before crumpling to the floor.

Then another, and another. The *Mudlati* was sprung off its front axle by a barrage from one side, and its top had collapsed. An attacker with a spear was prying loose a door, and as splinters came free, others stamped at them as if they were live sparks. Another sled full of stones had been skidded in beside the first, and now only a few of the spectators hung back, those paralyzed somehow by the tumult, or their own fear.

Just before the pile of jagged sticks and skeins of fiber became unrecognizable, the old guardian of the chamber came forth, his staff in one hand and a torch in the other. The rats cowered at his heel while he beamed at the assembly, still crooning the measure of the chant. Space opened up around him, the circle forming roughly again. He nodded, bowed, smiled, and threw the torch into the wreckage.

By the light of the burning *Mudlati* Teeklo saw that Pahane had withdrawn back to the dais. The boy and Adza sat knee-to-knee, facing each other. Probably they were singing. Or talking, without making a sound, as the *tagakin* did. Surely the youngster knew now that there was no going back, that his power was ineradicable as the new scars on his cheeks. And what did Adza know? Know was the wrong word. She would simply reflect the infinite, in some glancing, imperfect way that mortals could grasp.

There would be differences, certainly. And dangers. Teeklo frowned ruefully to himself, thinking that the first realignment of power in the Pobla universe might involve the fate of a young witch. No wonder the old gods—piksi and Pobla alike—were portrayed as a giddy and reckless lot. Their chosen vessels on earth were no strangers to passion, were sometimes the grandest of fools. That is why he had always trusted them, rather than the noble abstractions of newer faiths.

28

SERGEANT KARPOV TURNED THE DEAD GINK OVER WITH the toe of his boot. A male, half-grown, without a mark on him. Karpov sucked in a long breath and blew it out to control his frustration. For a brief moment he considered sending a couple of phosphor rounds through the body anyway, but the men moving around behind him would complain of the smell.

"Fuck this," he heard someone say. That would be Boomer Jones, their Afram scout, who knew in one look that the whole family had snuffed itself. "Fuck this shit. This ain't no *action.*"

Karpov grimaced. He hated it when the Aframs talked their talk. One of the so-called traditions of the scouts, thought humorous by some, kept up after the ancient war in which they had first distinguished themselves. All bullshit, of course. Like the myth that they were better on the border because their ancestors had been dark like some of the ancestors of the Ginks. Loomis and Karpov himself were actually closer to a coffee shade than Boomer was, but preferred to identify with their Euroslav forerunners.

"Ours not to reason why," he said shortly. He did not see the men behind him look at each other and roll their eyes. "Let's get these flops in the file and get back to the bucket." He glanced at his chrono. "Almost chow time."

There were groans. Karpov still did not turn around. He only unzipped the cover of his belt keyboard with an angry jerk. Anyway he agreed with them. Field rations were always dog-do, but the stuff they had drawn on this maneuver set a new standard for disgusting.

"Hey look," McBain said, a peculiar catch in his voice. "Jeez."

He was bending over the smallest of the figures huddled on the cave floor, a female barely weaned. McBain was the youngest recruit in the squad, a gawky kid with a complexion problem.

A couple of the other men joined him. One pointed with the tip of his weapon. "That's the sun, and this thing is a bird, right?"

The other man shrugged and moved away. "Just don't touch 'em. They got diseases the bio guys haven't even classified yet."

Karpov approached, frowning. He saw the little Gink had been drawing some kind of design on the cave floor with bits of charcoal.

"My kid brother does the same stuff," McBain said, and his voice took on a querulous wobble. "The same stuff. I mean, five years old." He looked up at the sergeant. "I mean. . . ."

"Wrong," Karpov said wearily. "Don't be a fuckin' cliché, McBain, don't be a peabrain recruit right now, okay? Ginks can draw a circle, yeah, big deal. So could the chimps they come out of. They also eat shit and each other, like you did when you was two, but they never learnt any better. Whereas you did, or so I hope and presume."

Someone started and then cut short a giggle. McBain straightened, his face flushed. "Yes, sir. It just seemed . . . funny." He looked around at the others in the squad, bewildered. "Right in the middle of drawing a picture."

"We know," Boomer said. "Drive a man nuts. If they just *run*, even."

"Yeah," one of the other men said. "We could say we was doin' somethin'. Besides countin' flops."

"The males can take evasive action," Karpov said grimly. "Can snuff you. Some females, too. Ones with a litter. You fergit that. Now let's get these logged." He made a show of punching in the tally.

"I don't fergit that," the man said. "But never come at you straight on. Fuckin' ambushes."

"What you expect," Boomer said and shook his head in disgust. "If you didn't have nothin' but a sharp stick."

"Got worse than that." The man glowered. "I swear they got the weather and the dust and the goddamn bugs on their side."

There was an uneasy pause. "Amen," said another man.

"Come on, come *on*," Karpov groaned. "You fuckin' philosophers know how to count?"

There were seven, none of them mixeds. Two adult females and one adult male. The youngest male, perhaps nine years of age, was the only one who had not died of shock. His neck had been broken. A retard, Karpov guessed, who couldn't learn the suicide trick.

They sat in the shade of the bucket, an old 302 Bruiser troop transport, and picked over their rations. The wind was huffing and moaning again, blowing grit into everything, but nobody wanted to eat in the cave with the dead Ginks. This was the third fresh hole they had sniffed out, and so far they hadn't glimpsed a single live target. Meanwhile, two in the squad had foot rot, all of them had diarrhea, for late spring it was ten degrees too hot, and the intake filters on the bucket were passing too much unhealthy dust.

"This is by far," Loomis was saying, "the most dumb-shit action I *ever* been associated with. Up to and including recruit patrols."

"Think," DePaul added, "what this shit *costs*. We got a whole brigade out here on this one sector. And guys goin' goofy with sunstroke and landslides and toxics and breakdowns. . . ."

"Biggest deployment in *my* lifetime. And most fucked up. Right, Sergeant?"

Karpov grunted ambiguously. This sullen talk made him uncomfortable. The men were jumpy and ill-tempered, and this was only the second week of the action. He had never seen so many short fuses, so much ass-dragging. But talking about it only made it worse; that was plain, ordinary psychology.

Not that he didn't understand the reasons. The whole operation was peculiar. Supply systems was doing a terrible job on fuel and rations. Arguments between squad commanders going down on the radio. And tactics were completely screwy. Orders were, no large-scale wipes, no fumigations. Only small units, working hole-to-hole, with flop tallies every two hours. The cost-kill ratio was awful.

And beyond that, the Cons had always before been opposed to this kind of expensive campaign. In fact not so long ago they were even talking about cutting back on Border Forces, and keeping Ginks alive, for experiments. But the mood of the country had obviously shifted out from under the ruling party. People wanted to see some ass kicked.

"What I can't figure," Boomer said, looking off at what could be seen of the ridge through the blowing dust, "is why the fuck anybody would *want* this country."

The men considered the environment. Except for a rare bush, like a pencil scribble on the sand, or the occasional spine of worn rock, the terrain was a featureless jumble of bluff and crevice. Nothing lived here but jackrabbits, lizards, vultures, a few herds of wild ponies, and of course the Ginks.

Often all these creatures lurked at the edge of an old fill or dump, where the weather had partly eaten away ground cover. They foraged among the exposed twisted hulks and rotting trash bales, at least until the area cooled off and the machines moved in to mine it again. All week Karpov's squad had been skirting such areas looking for sign—and taking too much hot dust.

"Paradise," someone said, "plus it glows in the dark."

"Challenge . . . opportunity . . . a new land for new people . . . ," someone else intoned, mocking one of the current ads.

Several in the squad laughed. "I do declare," Boomer said, "my loyalty to the cause. But seems to me they could just send the fifty-eights in and carpet the fucker with gas borers and we could all go home. A job well done."

"Hey, Boomer got to be *involved,* he quit talkin' dat scout talk," Loomis teased.

"Fuck you muthuhfuckuh." Boomer grinned at the chorus of boos and raspberries. "But seriously, gentlemen, what could their thinking be?" He looked around the squad, and last and longest at Karpov. "And what about that probe ship?"

Karpov expelled another exasperated sigh. "Listen, I don't know no fuckin' more than the rest of you guys. They said meter-by-meter and log 'em all. So we are. That ship. . . ." He grimaced. "Top pri, that's all I know."

"Never talked direct to any unit here on the ground," Loomis said. He was the radioman. "Once BlueBoy Company tried to make contact but HQ said stand back, let 'em alone, no chitchat."

"All kinds of weird shit happens out here," DePaul said glumly.

"Out here?" Someone laughed sarcastically. "Everyfuck-ingwhere."

"Progs got it right."

"Oh sure. Fearless, decisive vision. You *believe* that shit, man? After how they used that Drager deal to smoke Stock-well's ass and start this marvelous action? Like wipin' Ginks and condoin' the Wastelands will solve just every little thing."

"At least it's doin' *somethin'.*"

"Yeah? What?"

"Okay, okay. That's it. Morale is somethin' we got to pay attention to. Ours not to reason why. Finish up your dog biscuits." Karpov swallowed and forced himself to take a hefty bite from the protein bar in his hand. Sand grated between his molars.

Boomer went on as if he hadn't heard. "It's like they're looking for something. Something they don't want blown to shit by fifty-eights. But they hain't a-tellin' us, gen'mun."

"As for lighting a fire under our Praise-a-dent," said a small, blue-jawed man who had not so far spoken, "that Konrad lady." He laughed, a series of muffled snorts.

"Oh yeah," Loomis agreed. "Anytime, anywhere."

"Queen Dick?" DePaul made a face. "Bad news."

"Loomis," Karpov said, and with an effort swallowed the last lump of his ration. "Get on the horn and contact HQ. Take a bearing and ask if we got to hook up with BlueBoy to set the night perimeter." He dusted crumbs elaborately from his hands.

"She likes men with no face," Loomis said, "which means DePaul has half a chance."

"That's what started the whole deal," Boomer said. He was now clearly talking mostly to himself. "That energy honcho and his kid gettin' ripped by the bear."

"A symptom," Loomis said. He had gotten reluctantly to his feet and swung up onto the ladder at the side of the bucket. "Only a symptom."

"Right. But she knew how to play it. Got him to change parties. Got this big investigation rolling."

"Is that what this is? An investigation?" The sardonic laugh came again.

"Could be." Boomer looked up at Karpov, who was on his feet and frowning. "We're just a sweep. Goin' slow to flush somethin' out for that probe. Or someone."

"Would you battlefield strategists mind," Karpov said in a mincing, deadly tone, "moving your asses?"

McBain was already up. His face was white with a greenish tinge. "Sarge," he said in a small, tense voice. "I got to go. I still got 'em."

"Well fuckin' *go!*" Karpov roared.

"I don't think I can . . . make it up the ladder," McBain whispered. He backed away, moving as if his ankles were shackled together.

Some of the men laughed. A tear spilled abruptly from McBain's left eye, and Karpov turned bright pink. But before he could roar again McBain had doubled over, vomiting. A moment later Karpov caught the smell and saw the stain and knew the youth was leaking at both ends.

"Five years old," McBain gasped, "just drawing a little picture and . . ." He gagged again.

"For Christ's sake, McBain," DePaul said, "you make a body sick. Hey, goddamn!" He looked startled and dug furiously at his knee. "Holy shit."

"*Ow!*" It was the sarcastic laugher, dancing quickly to his feet and grabbing at the seat of his pants.

Then Karpov felt them and began to slap and curse. Fucking *fleas*. Gink fleas, which meant good-bye to the last goddamn hope of getting a decent night's sleep. Everyone was up now, except McBain, who squatted and went on with his sobbing and crapping and retching.

"Holy shit, holy shit!" DePaul started up the ladder.

"*Stop!*" Karpov bellowed. "You stay the fuck outside, DePaul! Loomis?"

They heard then the squawk from inside the bucket and Loomis popped up through the open hatch. "Little fuckers!" he shouted. "They're in the goddamned panel! I can't raise anything, Sarge!" He too was scratching and slapping at himself furiously.

"Fuck, fuck, *fuck!*" Karpov stared at the back of his hand. It seemed to be shaking out clouds of pepper, the fleas hopping and skittering through the hairs between his knuckles. He had to squint through the dust, which came thicker now. The final fucking straw. "Loomis!" he bellowed.

"Sarge!" Loomis bellowed back. He had stopped scratching and was staring at the horizon, Karpov could not see toward what because the transport was in the way. "Fucking *deer* . . . or horses. . . ."

"What?" Karpov had trouble keeping the radioman in focus, his own body was jittering so from the tiny, itching nibbles inside his clothes.

"The goddamned little shit horses," Boomer bawled down at him. The scout had scaled the bucket after Loomis, too, and crouched now on top of it, gazing at the same horizon, leaning into the wind. "Stomping up the dust." He put one hand on Loomis's shoulder and pushed him back down into the transport. "Get out the medkits, the bug spray."

"Medkits!" Karpov repeated. "Get the medkits!"

DePaul was fumbling with his weapon, loading. "Fucking *Ginks!* Fuckers!" He wheeled toward the cave. "Smoke you motherfuckers!"

Boomer jumped from the bucket, a two-meter drop, and hit the ground a stride behind DePaul. He dragged the other man around and warded away the automatic, whose pulse light indicated full charge. "Leave 'em alone," he said. "They're dead, for Christ's sake."

"Cinder those motherfuckers!" DePaul tried to jerk free and the weapon went off, a long thin stroke of white fire in the sky.

"Leave 'em *alone,* man! You'll just make it worse!"

Boomer was aware of Karpov, red in the face, screaming at all of them to get back in the bucket. Yet no one except DePaul was moving and now his own hand fell away and strength rushed out of him like air from a punctured tire. He was stunned at the abrupt appearance of tears cutting irregular streaks through the dust on his cheeks. He, Boomer, Afram motherfucking scout, was crying.

"Worse? *Worse?*" DePaul looked over his shoulder, astonished at first and then with an expression darkened by a deep and final rage. "You're fuckin' crazy, man. Fuckin' *crazy.*" He ran then toward the dark hole, stumbling, screaming, firing at the dead inside.

29

SKIHO HAD REACHED THAT STAGE OF EXHAUSTION IN WHICH the mind attains a surprising freedom and wakefulness, floating above the body like a bright-eyed crow over a heap of rubbish. He was aware that he stank, that the lights in the room had been lowered, that the ship was on the ground with its power plant idling. At the same time he was thinking clearly, anticipating.

They had given him a pillow and left him on the examination

table, unwashed and unmedicated. So far nobody over the rank of lieutenant had spoken to him, and he had not been read his rights. These signs could be good or bad.

He couldn't even tell if this ship was the same one that had parked on their alarm perimeter before the blast. If it was, he supposed they would take him apart. Every fiber and secretion and germ would be analyzed, and the psych crew would flush his head completely. Then what? A wipe was a distinct possibility.

But he was fairly certain a regular patrol had picked up his track first. He hadn't expected to ride the topo right into a major border sweep, and was taken completely off guard when he saw the first vehicles, heard the transports fanning over canyons, and ran across stray Gink corpses. He realized now he should have turned himself in to the first patrol, but in any case somebody—at least a squad sergeant—knew of his existence. He might show up on some report, inspiring questions.

The weirdness had intensified, apparently, since he and PJ had been doped and sealed off from any info. The man and woman who stunned him off the bike and shoveled him up had mumbled something about a special commission. They were otherwise close-mouthed, professional. Yet they didn't have the style of Insec personnel.

He had simply assumed all along that if he were allowed to live, that decision would be from Fat and the two of them would soon be face-to-face. But what if this team was not Insec, or Fat was no longer in control of the probe? Who else cared about the op they had been running?

He would have to gamble on the preprogramming he had been doing since leaving the copter. For those few hours he went over and over the drills, imbedding the story he wanted a psychteam to discover. A couple of Headshields would help now, but the stun had come before he had a chance to pop anything.

He had concentrated on the elements that were true: the kid was alive, had been in the X-4; they were disgusted with Border Policy, wanted a change; the hostage idea was PJ's; they had split up to confuse pursuers; he didn't know where PJ had taken the boy.

He sighed and shifted the pillow slightly. Very weak. Some big holes. And the psychs would of course be the best. They would keep dredging those holes until they found something. Tima, for example. He groaned faintly. He had made a considerable effort not to think about Tima. Not to recall how thoroughly he had been had. How the best punch of his life had been faking it. Better to summon old memories—of his recruit days, of cruising the remote Wasteland canyons, of hanging out in the Preserves after season. . . .

He must have dozed off, because the man was already leaning over him, wrapping the rubber flap around his arm, before Skiho registered his presence. A large man with powerful hands, grinning at him.

"Well well. Special Agent Skiho—Black Jack, eh?— pleased to meetcha. Bradshaw. Medical. Let's see how we're doin' here." The man squeezed the bulb, inflating the flap, and watched the digital readout. His manner was bluff and breezy, the doctor making a routine ward visit. To Skiho he looked vaguely familiar, like the brother of someone he knew.

"Medical what," Skiho said. How long had he been out? The light was brighter in the room, but his detached alertness was gone. His head felt like concrete.

"You been for a real ride, Black Jack. Sneaky customer, had us discombobulated for a few hours." The man unstuck the flap and tossed it onto a metal stand. From the pocket of his blue smock he took a silver tube. When he leaned forward again Skiho smelled cloves on his breath. "Naughty guy. Look straight up. Don't blink. Now, question is of course, what did you do with the kid?"

"What kid?" The silver tube shone a small, glaring light into Skiho's eye.

"Hey, *special agent*, let's be nice, okay? Not waste time. Your partner sez the whole idea was yours. Told us all about it. So why—"

"Bullshit. Fuck you. I'll talk to Fat and nobody else."

"Fat? Fat who? Look left."

Skiho could hear the suppressed mirth in the man's voice. "Fuck you," he repeated and then coughed weakly.

"Black Jack, baby, don't be difficult. Give yourself some slack. We just want the kid. Look right. We've been through the debris, so we know they weren't in the hovercopter. So where'd you drop 'em?"

The light held steady, burning into his skull.

"Look, sweetheart, we're going to get it sooner or later, hard way or easy way, and you know it. Normally I'd look forward to the challenge—oh, I *enjoy* my work—but we really are short of time."

The tube flicked off, and Skiho blinked into a spangled twilight. Bradshaw had become only a hulking silhouette.

"Lots of folks *very* interested in the fate of Ronnie Drager," the silhouette said. "Quite the celebrity, did you know that? Coze say-lebruh. Alive or dead. Which is he, by the way?"

Skiho did not even feel the restraints and the prick in his arm, but when his eyes had adjusted again he saw the tube and the hanging bottles, calibrated and equipped with drip valves. Bradshaw was fingering one of the valves.

"Cooperate, sweetheart. Believe me, they will take that into account. And they understand how you feel about the Preserves. Hey, I'm with you on that one. Let's go step by step. Kid's alive, hmmm?"

Skiho was trying to think, but each word that appeared in his mind was like a heavy weight, falling away as soon as he had lifted it into place. He knew now this was the probe ship. A special op. Investigators. And they thought he knew something. He managed then to get two words welded together and floating free. *Buy time.*

"Alive," he whispered.

"Where?"

"Gone. Far." He waved a hand vaguely, as if indicating direction.

"Ah, Black Jack," Bradshaw said, looking down on him mournfully. He twisted open one valve, adjusted it, then moved to a second. "You are indeed a naughty boy. Have to dig, I guess. You know we are all just doing our job, don't you? Functionaries in the grand design?" He grinned again, laughed aloud. "Open you up wide, Black Jack. Wide, wide, wide."

He moved off then to a counter, picked up a ceramic tray full of surgical instruments. Behind him Skiho let out a long sigh, as if settling into a deep sleep. "Sail away, buddy, sail away. When you get comfy let's talk about PJ and little Ronnie. Your sweet little scam, hey?"

Skiho mumbled something, uttered a low, dreamy chuckle.

"Where, oh where, oh where did all the little frogs go?

Give me a word, buddy. Just a word now to get started."
Bradshaw pinched up a tiny smooth lozenge, not half the size
of a little fingernail, with steel tweezers. He held it to the
light in admiration, then set it on a sterile pad in the tray.

"Word," Skiho whispered. "Weird. Weird, weird weirdness . . . fuck you."

"Oh yes, weird," Bradshaw said, conversationally. "Very
weird. What else, buddy?" He moved to Skiho's side, set the
tray on the metal stand. He pulled the sleeve back, felt the
arm for a vein. "Is PJ weird?"

"No," Skiho said pettishly. His eyes were open but unfocused. "Yes. Like Tickles."

"Tickles?" Bradshaw hesitated, the antiseptic pad poised
over Skiho's arm. "Now tell me about Tickles."

"Good man. *Good* man. Lost it . . . shit . . . had everything. . . ."

"Lost what?"

"Rookie . . . star rookie . . . goddamn Ginks got 'im.
Remember the time, him and PJ out on light recon, caught
a little one . . . who cares, I care . . . bitch was clever. . . ."

"Bitch?" Bradshaw had the scalpel now. He pressed up the
vein, made a minuscule cut in the skin next to it. With the
blade he roughened the edges of the cut slightly. "You mean
the Gink?"

"Yeah. Got 'im."

"Got who?"

"Funny-lookin' kid, all bones, crazy eyes. . . ."

"Ronnie, right? The bitch has Ronnie?" With the tweezers
he nestled the tiny lozenge under the vein. "And PJ?"

Skiho groaned, unintelligible, flexed his body against the
restraints. "Weird," he whispered.

Bradshaw hummed a tune. "Funny little Ronnie, funny
little guy, gone away, what say? Gone away where, oh where?
Who was in the Scooter? We found the Scooter, love, I should
tell you." He sutured the flaps of skin together with a single,
loose stitch. It would dissolve in a few hours, and the cut
would be recognizable only as another small, inconsequential
scratch.

"Couldn't move," Skiho said, regretful. "Had us, oh yeah.
Had us, rats in a cage. Should have known. No clothes on,
and all those bees. . . ."

Bradshaw had crossed the room again and flipped on an intercom. "Patricia quite contrary," he called in a mocking baritone. "Come on in here and help me troll, we're starting to pick up a little bait." Pat was one of his two secure assistants. An expert at coaching and deciphering. They would have maybe two sessions to wring Skiho out, then he would prescribe six hours of sleep. Then Insec could have what was left. Which was not much, and not for long.

Bradshaw went back to humming, stretched his interlaced hands over his head in order to crack his knuckles. He felt wonderful. The lozenge was another masterpiece. Skiho would wake up refreshed, yet a little weak. His vision and hearing would be a little too clear, too sensitive. Before the Insec team could get started there would be lapses, symptoms of trouble. Bursts of garrulity, flashes of paranoia.

They would run the routine tests, prescribe certain standard drugs. Those drugs would trigger the disintegration of the second half of the lozenge. Skiho would undergo some changes: swellings, rash, incoherence. An exact mimicry of a serious allergy to the drugs. Another hour and the unfortunate man would slip into a coma, where he would spend the rest of his life—a matter of days, and maybe less.

The autopsy would reveal nothing unusual. The scratch would be largely healed, and indistinguishable from others Skiho had picked up on his run through the brush. Insec would have a dead agent on its hands, and no explanations. More shit—carloads of shit—would hit the fan. Ears would save the choicest bits, so he could savor them at leisure. She would also find this Tickles, whoever he was.

They had the X-4's flight history and the sweep would cut off any northern route. The bio on the Scooter had turned up a partial DNA that matched nothing on file, and he was now ready to bet it belonged to the little Gink. Risky and brilliant to give her the kid. He had to admire that.

So there would have to be a rendezvous somewhere within walking range of the Scooter. A radius of fifty klicks. They were getting warm, getting hot. Snuffer dropped into a crouch, threw a few shadow-punches. Twenty-five, he felt not a day older than twenty-five.

On the table, Skiho stirred briefly. "She-bear," he murmured. "Watch out for an old she-bear."

30

ON THE CONFERENCE TABLE LAY A NECKLACE OF YELLOW
notepads and cups holding pencils. No other papers were
permitted, there was no holo running, and the wire was protected by presidential archive status. They had all arrived at
the same time, via several entrances; but the streets were
clear of media vans and in the building only a skeleton staff
of security personnel was on duty.

Fat's life had become frantic and thrilling, and he had taken
to smiling recklessly. So when he sat across the table from
Danielle Konrad, he showed her just the tips of his upper
teeth and then winked for good measure. He knew she, too,
had seen the results of the hunt through the debris of the
blown copter. No corpses. Stalemate.

He saw the subtlest of shadows dart across her face, which
she had made up to look a touch haggard and intense—part
of her new role as a tragic, adulterous leader. It was, he
inferred, the shadow of amazement cast by a veritable sun of
hatred.

To his left Harrison Lemke, the Secretary of Information,
who had called the meeting, stood a couple of steps back from
the table, carrying on a hasty, whispered conversation with
Brigadier General Randolph "Red" Bennett. Fat believed he
was himself the subject of that conversation. Or more properly, his new unofficial position was.

Charles Solomon Fat, hostage-taker. Negotiating now only
for himself. The affable, impenetrable, golden moon-man had
become a walking bomb, and was discovering that he loved
it. Lemke was keeping one frightened eye on him, and Bennett's posture was stiffening into battlefield alertness. Fat
overheard the general's explosive hiss: *Shit!*

Around the room others were exchanging subdued greetings or making quick introductions. Most of the cabinet was
represented, but except for Lemke they were all lower level,

trusted aides or special conduits kept out of the public eye. Budget, Energy, and Defense were male; Ed, Med, and Stat, female. Fat and Konrad were there as cochairs of the just-formed blue-ribbon Presidential Commission, along with two other outside consultants: a very nervous young man, a specialist in macrobio, and an older woman who had done the classic study of Federation economics.

Lemke jerked his head slightly and the two Special Agents at the entrance withdrew, closing the heavy door behind them. On a monitor overhead they could be seen walking quickly down the corridor outside, turning the corner and disappearing from sight. The murmur of conversation faded, replaced by creaking chairs, a rustling of the yellow pads, a clearing of throats. The general sat down heavily with a single, intent look at Fat, and Lemke moved to the head of the table.

"Warm salutations from the President, and our heartfelt thanks for showing up on a Sunday morning—and without brunch." Lemke smiled swiftly at the perfunctory chuckles. "We hope you'll forgive the inconvenience of so many precautions here, but we just can't afford any leaks."

Lemke looked around the room, taking care to make eye contact with everyone at the table. "You all know, of course, that we find ourselves in something of a crisis these days. And it's a crisis especially difficult to get a handle on, both for professionals and for the general public. That's why we've sealed this meeting. A wrong spin, an unguarded remark, a rumor—any of these could do extraordinary damage right now. And yet we've got vital policy issues that have to be settled, in open discussion."

Lemke glanced at General Bennett, who nodded sternly in support of the point, whatever it was. "So we're asking you to take away no notes from this meeting, and make no entry in your personal papers—calendars, journals, et cetera. This meeting, in short, didn't happen. The wire will be buried as soon as the President has heard it.

"This will make it easier, I hope, for all of us to speak our minds frankly. We know that some of you have very strong feelings on certain aspects of this crisis. We are likewise aware that the situation has an explosive political dimension, apparent of course in the tragedy of the little Drager boy." Lemke nodded stiffly toward Danielle Konrad. "Now, finally, there are some developments that make our problems much more serious than some of you may realize."

Lemke paused, his look dwelling a fraction of a second on Fat, who responded with his new reckless smile.

"I've asked General Bennett to summarize some of those developments and bring you up to date on the President's Operation New Broom. After that I'll say just a word more on our internal difficulties and then ask for your reactions. Again, we hope you'll make them as frank and complete as possible. The fact is, ladies and gentlemen, that we've run out of time for anything but absolute honesty."

Fat had all he could do to keep from laughing, and knew without looking that Konrad must have made a similar effort. Absolute honesty was the sworn enemy of all Secretaries of Information, and for Lemke to venture—in a closed meeting—the bald-faced hypocrisy of his last remark was it-self proof of serious derangement in the natural order of things.

As the secretary sat down and Bennett rose and strode to a podium near one wall, Fat picked up a pencil and doodled a curve on the yellow pad. He gave the curve a dip that curled into a face, which he shaded with the pencil. A cartoon Gink, eyes slyly to one side, hair sweeping away into the curve. Here was the Administration's problem, in its simplest form.

He marveled still at the brilliance of his agents. PJ must have come up with the idea first. The audacity of it must have charmed him immediately, and soon after he would have seen its remarkable practicality. *Not* simply to return with the boy, but to abort the patrol and begin negotiations from the field. Negotiations Fat himself could never have initiated, but was admirably positioned to complete.

Or so his adversaries had to assume. They had to credit the possibility that he indeed disposed of a priceless bargaining chip. A martyr risen from the dead. Danielle Konrad's care-fully constructed legend. He had apparently flashed back into existence as an ordinary boy, at least for a few hours, and then vanished into the Wastelands. Guided—and here Fat was convulsed with an ironic hysteria—by his own personal creation—the first-ever Gink Special Agent.

A vantage point perfect in its preposterousness. For the Con Administration could never bear the scandal of having allowed such a twice-traitorous Insec expedition. They would pay any price to recover the boy and then eradicate all record of the deal. On the other hand, he supposed, the Progs would give Konrad any amount if she could prove little Ronnie had been slain and devoured by the Ginks.

So Fat had experienced his own moment of genius. In the midst of his careful, coded exchange with the renegade agents, nearly paralyzed with despair at the catastrophic outcome of his expedition, he had realized in a breath-catching jolt that he could *join the conspiracy.* Pretend, with a few indirectly revelatory remarks, that he was himself masterminding the ransom. And become, by means of this astonishing innuendo, untouchable. Stockwell must have blown a major circuit when he found out the crimes in Fat's trumped-up confession had apparently actually been committed. *Apparently.* Fat himself didn't even know. That was the final stroke of brilliance.

Bennett had sent up a wall panel to reveal a big holo chamber and was now illustrating his remarks with scenes from the field. Fat had seen most of the material already, since Insec accessed these official channels, but he watched idly anyway. The current scene was a threesome of old Bruiser troop transports, hatches open, sand already drifting up over their tracks.

". . . so it's been an extra-tough campaign, climate-wise. We decided to just leave these boats—too expensive to copter them out—and at this rate they'll be buried in about two weeks."

The general's face shone in the reflected light from the holo, as if he were sweating sympathetically with the men in the next scene, who were dressed in cumbersome shielded suits with large air-processor packs. "Same thing with the grunt on the ground. Lots of places, the dust and bugs and toxics require full suits, but in the heat that means using a lot of juice just to filter and cool air. We've lost soldiers—can you believe this?—to damn butterflies that collected around the exhaust —for the moisture—and jammed up the pack.

"Now, these guys are doing a terrific job, no question. I want to make that clear. We're damn proud of every one of them. But let's face it, our technology for a deployment of this size is out of date and underfunded." Bennett could not resist a quick, hard glance at the two men from Budget. "Also, the tunnels we're running into are a lot more elaborate than we expected, and the Ginks are behaving real, real strangely. Look at this."

A map came first, with what looked like a palimpsest of spiderwebs overlaying it. In three dimensions they could see the cross-tunnels and blind shafts, the grades up and down over aquifers and strata of rock; in blue and yellow they could see the air and sewer conduits to community nodes. A few of these nodes were flagged red.

"We're going very slow, as per instructions," Bennett said, with an inflection of weary sufferance. "This is only the little area we've covered so far, right on the border. If they got this kind of labyrinth structure for many more klicks, ladies and gentlemen, then our *grandkids* will be working on this operation."

There were sighs or small exclamations of wonder from the company. Fat himself wondered how many of these expressions were genuine. Certainly anyone on the intelligence loop had known for years that there were areas of such density. His own teams had mapped several. Still, it was impressive to see this large an area explored. He was struck all at once with the pattern of the tunnels, asymmetric yet suggestive of complex order.

Next they saw a group of dead Ginks arranged around a heap of black embers. Some had apparently toppled over from a sitting position; many looked only asleep. The artificial light used to record the holo was hard on the eyes, made the figures quiver a little as if ready to spring back into life.

"These flops were the only ones left in a village that must have held nearly four hundred, which is big for a Gink settlement. If you think about it, why would they go on with their normal routines, all the rest gone, trekked out of there? We have to assume this is a delaying action. Two or three adults and a litter sacrificed. It's almost as if they know somehow that we are being required to do full analysis of all recovered specimens.

"Which is just one of quite a bunch of special problems that have developed out of New Broom. *Very* troublesome problems, that require an expert explanation. I'm going to ask Dr. Marvin Petrasky, a research fellow at the New Dawn Institute, to give us a rundown of the situation."

General Bennett lifted a large, imperious hand to beckon

the nervous young man to the podium. Dr. Petrasky came with an elongated stride. He clutched his own cartridge of illustrations, his expression one of eager, earnest dedication, with an underlying glow of self-importance.

Fat paused in his doodling and examined the young doctor with interest. Insec had awarded a number of contracts to New Dawn, and Petrasky's name sounded familiar. Probably one of those talented youngsters who had dropped out of classified work a couple of months ago. Just before Konrad organized her onslaught of conferences and workshops that led to the blue-ribbon commission, the current investigation. A turncoat, then. A Prog informant.

Fat was not bitter. The young were not so much treacherous as inconstant and immoderate in their loyalties. He knew a momentary pang of nostalgia for his PacRim home, for a culture which made betrayal into an art form. Then he began to register what the young man was saying, and simultaneously became aware of a new level of attentiveness in the room.

Dr. Petrasky had loaded his holo cartridge and armed himself with a light-wand. Currently displayed was a montage of flocks and herds, moving against the stark backdrop of Wasteland canyons. The presentation was hurried and stumbling, obviously an attempt to condense a great mass of data. Petrasky also relied too much on the dry, remote language of science. But the gist of his argument was startling enough.

The vultures and a company or two of ravens were flying in a pattern, a long, loose line that roughly corresponded to the advancing patrols along the border. Whenever a probe neared one of the nodal settlements where a group of Ginks had remained as sacrifice, the great black birds wheeled to perches located precisely at the outlets of certain Gink tunnels. These were not main trunk lines, but deserted or partially caved in branches.

A few quick strikes had established that only rats occupied these old passages, yet several times as patrols approached the settlement sites they found herds of antelope, deer, or wild ponies already forming upwind. These herds created a serious dust problem as the patrols went in, and sometimes halted them. Once stopped in this way, a column had to be especially alert, for infestations of both small rodents and insects were sure to ensue.

"Of course. What did you expect?"

It was Danielle Konrad, pitched forward in her chair like a hungry cat preparing to pounce on the young man. The savage calm of her voice had deprived him of the power of speech, and General Bennett moved forward with a frown.

"Happy to entertain questions," he boomed, "after our presentation. Lot of angles to this whole situation, we know." He nodded at Petrasky impatiently, at the same time suppressing a yawn. "Go on, Doctor."

"Yes, yes . . . sorry. . . ." Petrasky signaled wildly with the wand and the holo became again a topographical map, partly covered now with blobs of color. "Uh . . . these are composite satscans made since New Broom began. We have then superimposed our rough survey of habitat range for several common species, especially those that have created the problems I mentioned.

"Now when we animate these supers to show what's been happening since the campaign began, you see . . . there . . . and there . . . how the shifts actually seem to *precede* our probes at the squad and company level."

The blobs of color began to undulate, at first retreating from and then flanking or enclosing the small, sharp arrows that represented New Broom's advance. Orange and yellow and blue and purple pulsed in tandem, creating ripples, contractions, and the effect was eerily like the motion of a single amoeboid organism. In the now very quiet room someone spoke softly.

"That's crazy."

Fat had noticed immediately the configuration of this sinister, oozing rainbow to the pattern of red-flagged sites on the earlier diagram of Gink tunnels. He held his breath, waiting for a final composite image, and an obvious conclusion. But apparently the Progs did not yet own Petrasky completely.

"So we have some sort of amazing correlations here, that we . . . well, frankly we can't explain. I know you are aware of how Ginks manage to control some animals, and will be convinced that this is just another example." Petrasky shot a frightened smile toward Konrad. "But these creatures have no radio or holophone links. They have no intelligence-gathering capability. A few experiments indicate a rare individual can perform ratiocinative tasks, with proper guidance; but we absolutely cannot explain how they could position a few of their number in the path of a scheduled patrol, and then trigger—from a distance—whole regional populations of several species to cluster and harass the probe. It seems, uh, basically . . . incredible."

Petrasky turned off the holo and looked over the heads of his audience, as if a clue might drop from the ceiling. "As a scientist, however, I have to consider every possible hypothesis. If the Ginks are incapable of organizing this kind of response, then who—or what?—is manipulating them?"

Petrasky hunched his shoulders in the agony of this question. "In the last month we have made a tremendous effort to turn up something—anything—bearing on that question. We've processed mountains of data, from every possible source. Looking for correlations, parallels, codes, *anything.*"

The young man no longer seemed nervous. He was aroused, almost vivacious. "However farfetched. We've found that rodent migrations predicted—for a while—fluctuations in the NorthAm production index. And sewage releases from a SoCal command headquarters seemed to match up, after a time delay, with breakdowns in our reconnaissance network." Petrasky whinnied in amazement. "There was even a kind of epidemic of certain mental disorders—coprophilia comes to mind—just before the President announced New Broom."

General Bennett had noted puzzled frowns and whispers in the audience. He spoke with grim pride, having learned the word in a briefing only a few days ago. "Love of shit," he announced.

Petrasky flushed. "Yes. Exactly. No one has the slightest idea . . . absurd, really! It has even been suggested that these coincidences are too bizarre to be ascribed to chance, that there is perhaps some small group . . . a perverse sort of conspiracy . . . operating inside our own research and investigation networks."

There was a murmur of interest in the room. "Either that"—Petrasky glanced pleadingly at the Secretary of Information, who was signaling at the general with his eyebrows—"or a supernatural agency that speaks through, uh, what we would consider lower forms of life." He gulped. "Those with large populations, and a communication system.

Termites, for example. Or even the Protocists. Slime, uh, molds may respond to some force we—"

"That's a little outside the scientific angle," the general interrupted, moving to the podium. He placed a firm hand on Petrasky's elbow, as the bewildered young man fumbled to recover his cartridge. "Thanks, Doctor. Glad to have the facts."

"But they're *not* facts, sir," Petrasky blurted. "Why would this preoccupation with . . . with excrement. . . ." The voice faded as the general guided him away from the podium, gave him a gentle shove toward the table.

"Good question, Doctor, but only one of many. Economics, for example. We have with us also Dr. Elizabeth Fortner—"

"Blackmail."

It was Danielle Konrad again. Her contralto voice had the carrying power of a trumpet blast.

"Conspiracy. Cover-up." She was on her feet now, defiant. "This Administration is rotten with them. The very fabric of NorthAm culture—"

"*Please!* Hold your questions," the general bellowed. His face was like a glowing ingot. "Dr. Fortner?" He gestured urgently, but the angular, gray-haired woman only looked amused and made no move to rise.

"There is only one question," Konrad went on, her look blazing around the room, "and that is how long will the public stand for this charade? How long must we dwell on the horror of this blight before we move to stamp it out? How many Ronnie Dragers must there be?"

"One," Fat said quickly, almost cheerily, "is enough."

He met the concentrated fire of her stare with his own round, blank benevolence. She understood his double meaning, and her hatred was like a subtle, physical force pressing against him.

"Is? *Is?* Does my good friend and cochairperson want to suggest this child *is?* Given what we know of these filthy creatures? After what Dr. Petrasky has just shown us?"

"Most unfortunate," Fat said with his most maddening expression of genial sympathy. "The poor boy. We all share your concern. But, my dear, we need hard evidence one way or—"

"Oh, but we *have* it, sir. The evidence you yourself man-ufactured."

"Beg pardon?" Fat made his face perfectly blank again.

"I'll get to that, before I'm through. But let's stick to the main point. The good secretary has admitted that Conservative policy has brought on the worst crisis in the history of our government. We then hear from young Dr.—"

"Just a moment." Lemke had risen to his feet, looking distinctly unwell. "That is a very unfair and divisive remark. We all understand, Danielle, your *personal* involvement in this issue. However, we are here—"

"—to save civilization as we know it. Yes. Yes! Let's sing it out. This is a crisis in all our lives, our collective life!"

Although the general continued to bellow vaguely and Lemke was trying to look commanding, no one was missing a word of the woman's speech. Her voice had the authority of passion, the timbre of bright brass overriding all the strings in an orchestra.

"And why are we aware of that now? Because of the terrible suffering of one family. One family that lost everything. The House of Drager stands for all of us, and their tragedy is—or will be—our tragedy."

"Out of order!" Lemke now stood beside the general, slamming his hand against the podium. "You are out of order, Danielle! You—"

"It's *all* out of order, Mr. Secretary." She grinned, uttered something between a snarl and a laugh. "For years you Conservatives have argued that we must preserve the wild—limit management—allow the freak and the variant—tolerate Ginks—oh yes! Study them! *Train* them!" She torched Fat again with her look. "Director Fat will vouch for it. And Dr. Petrasky has given us the result. They eat our children, they condition other species to attack us, they spread filth and disease, they sabotage. . . . Oh, sir, they are out of order. Indeed. They are *destroying* us!"

Magnificently, she paused. General Bennett and Secretary Lemke, shouting and gesturing a moment before to gain control of their meeting, were unaccountably paralyzed, gaping silent as fish.

"As they destroyed the Dragers. Utterly."

Her face underwent a spasm of grief, became a hollow-

eyed mask of pain. Fat recognized the expression she had
donned for certain interviews and press conferences, and allowed her a grudging measure of admiration. A brilliant per-
former. One who gambled everything in a grand gesture,
became the consort of a scar-faced demon, dedicated herself
to avenging the death of his son by another woman. Quite a
role, and it earned her an extraordinary and dangerous power.

He spoke in his most skillful professional tone: an avuncular
burble, the folksy, condescending charm of the cunning bureaucrat. "Oh, Danny, come *on*. We don't know anything of
the sort." He sent an amused glance around the table. "Don't
be so *melodramatic*. Fate of the world doesn't hang on this
thing."

He smiled at her in unabashed glee. They had both seen
the most recent polls. The curve of concern generated by the
Prog media blitz showed signs of flattening, and Konrad's
strategy depended on an irresistible momentum. The Drager
incident might serve as a rallying symbol, but once aroused
the public craved a daily staple of provocation and scandal
and atrocity. They had been promised a dead child and a lurid
tale, and if the Progs could not deliver. . . .

Surprisingly, she smiled back at him. "Perhaps," she said.
"But the fate of everyone in this room does. Yours, for example. As the Director of Intelligence and Security, you were
in charge of the initial investigation into this incident. You
sent three of your best agents on a probe. Why don't you tell
us about that?" She blinked at him rapidly, a parody of innocent curiosity.

Fat's voice went soft and dead. "I do not, as a—"

"Oh come *on*, Fatty. Tell us about agent Dieter Skihovsky.
Where is he? The cocaptain of a darkside op you personally
authorized, under the code name Duskyrose?"

"That's enough!" General Bennett shouted, and others
around the conference table looked at each other in alarm.
"We have a speaker—"

"Not nearly enough. Not even a beginning." Danielle
laughed, and the sound was like that of a plate-glass window
shattering and falling. "We have a grand hoax to deal with
here." She lifted one hand near her face and wiggled her
index finger at Fat, a gesture gruesome in its coy restraint.
"Don't we, dear? A hoax that capitalizes on the agony of a

father, a mother with a mind destroyed, and a dead child?"

Fat had again the sensation of movement beneath him, miles of dark water lifting the tiny craft of his being. Yet he managed to maintain his amused look, to begin a sentence. "Preposterous. We know you have been under great—"

"You'll be seeing him in a few hours," Danielle went on brightly. "Special Agent Skiho—you call him Black Jack, don't you? He's told us the most interesting things."

"What the hell," croaked Lemke, "is going on here?"

"We have a speaker," the general added, plaintive now.

"We will soon have a report from Sunbeam, the Commission flagship," Danielle said. "On a suspected extortion plot. They picked up one of *Director* Fat's agents." She was glowing. "The report is on your desk right now, my dear cochair. I guess you left just a minute or so too early."

She laughed, shook herself, took a deep breath. "The secretary was right about one thing. We have run out of time. Poor General Bennett has had to work so slowly—flop by flop, as he puts it—because this Administration believed the hoax; they thought they could buy time, get the boy back, hush up Insec's crimes. And of course they have never admitted the Gink threat. In fact, the third agent in Director Fat's team—" She threw out her arms in an expression of infinite copiousness. "There's no end to it. It's an *epic*. An epic *cycle*. And a disaster through and through. These people. . . ." She rolled her eyes, speechless with the enormity she contemplated. Then she jerked her head at Fat. "Ask him about agents Skiho and Feiffer, and especially about Duskyrose, his little Gink punch. I can't stay for that. I have another meeting, I hope Dr. Fortner will excuse me." A nod at the gray-haired woman. "But you might mention to the President"—she was already moving toward the door, speaking over her shoulder—"that if there is no massive response to this crisis, no serious control of the aberrant species that are suffocating life on this planet, then people are going to take action for themselves. You can count on it."

The others in the room watched her progress toward the exit. They were hypnotized by her effrontery, the monstrous insult, her insouciant stride. She ignored them, moving away like a big, gorged cat.

Fat waited to speak until she was reaching for the door.

"Danny," he said, "we know the boy is alive."

He had thrown out the statement like a last desperate cast into a lake, and saw that he was lucky, saw the slight drag on her limbs before she wheeled around. The news of Skiho's capture was a shock, but apparently the interrogation had produced no confirmation. So none of them knew yet, for certain. And he had yet one small card of his own to play.

But when Danielle faced the room again she was once more the archqueen of contemptuous irony, batting her eyelids in the same grotesque parody of innocent curiosity. "Oh really," she breathed. "How convenient. And *when,* might we ask, will you bring him back to us?"

Fat saw a brief interior cartoon. He had run off the edge of a cliff, run straight out into thin air, and looking down realized his comic plight. So he kept running, his legs a blur. He played his small card.

"Why, Danny," he said. "You should ask your . . . um . . . associate, Frank Drager. Isn't he a special envoy from your office to our Sunbeam probe? He *is* there to hunt for his son, isn't he? Under the name of Evans? Not something an 'utterly destroyed' tragic figure would do, eh?"

Finally, he saw, he had reached her. His own disintegrating intelligence web had caught this last scrap. He already knew from Elise that Drager's obsession had grown monstrous. The man lived only to exterminate Ginks.

But he was too famous, too dangerous, to join a regular reserve unit, so Danielle—or her new private secretary—had smuggled him into Sunbeam under an assumed name. Fat also suspected that Konrad had begun to find her paramour an embarrassment and was glad to pack him off to the front.

"I respect Frank Drager's privacy. His grief. His desire for justice. You choose to demean them. There is no more to say." Danielle smiled once more, in pity it seemed, and walked out.

Creditable, Fat thought, as he looked around the table, but not quite enough. However you sliced it, Drager's participation in the probe implied some tiny measure of hope, or at least doubt. For the moment, his precarious position would hold.

The gray-haired woman was at last on her feet, crumpling up a sheet of yellow notepaper. She spoke matter-of-factly into the stunned silence. "I think I'll condense and simplify my talk for you, ladies and gentlemen. Just to meet my responsibilities." She smiled, mostly to herself. "Conspiracies, covops, assumed names—exciting stuff, yes indeed, I'm fascinated myself, but. . . ." She shrugged, tossed the ball of paper onto the table. "I'm only an economist. Stats and graphs and projections. Lies and damned lies, which I won't bore you with. I just had one basic thing to say. Vital and exciting as it might be, ladies and gentlemen, the fact is . . ."

She glanced at Lemke and the general. "We can't afford it anymore. Not the Bruisers and hovercraft and patrols, not the new insecticides and antibiotics, not the workshops and conferences. Not New Broom or Old Broom or Any Broom. We just can't, people, *afford all this shit anymore.*" She nodded, a touch primly, and sat down.

31

"UNITED WE STARVE," TEEKLO SAID, "DIVIDED WE FILL."

They crouched near the tunnel chimney, where the smoke from cooking fires soaked away toward the surface of the earth. Ap and Yellow were on one side of him, Tima on the other, Teeklo and Kapu and Kapu's wife across the red glow of the fire.

As if to punctuate the statement, Yellow gnawed noisily on the knobby end of a femur. Since dragging themselves into Sopan—just two days before the whole city emptied—both Ap and the Kapu had eaten steadily, implacably. They looked at once emaciated and distended; their sunken eyes were bright with new life.

There was certainly plenty now. Pahane eyed the chunks of flesh skewered over the coals, the yellow flares from dripping grease. At the end of each day since the trek began, there was a huddle of new offerings at every main intersection or cave. A neat huddle, facing inward in a circle. The corpses already stripped, bowels emptied, bled by the last of their number, who then cut her own throat.

He still found it difficult, chewed mechanically and often with eyes closed. This night he almost gagged, for the smell of sulfur and hot meat was like a heavy hand pressed over his face. Teeklo saw it; that was the reason for another of the mocking adages.

Pahane had heard several. Teeklo's teaching devices. He quoted one back now. "You may have to eat your wards."

Tima laughed, and Kapu and his wife stared at her. Conversation at a nearby campfire halted abruptly. A lone laugh, Pahane thought, was incongruous to the Pobla. It alarmed them.

He hadn't meant to be funny. And Teeklo didn't smile.

"Of course I would eat you. That's a compliment. That's being very united. Pobla style."

"We're together," Pahane said finally, "and we're certainly not starving. But the *yano*. . . ." He stopped and no one said anything. Yellow left off polishing his fangs on the bone and lifted his head.

They had already talked it through several times. He understood that the river was always there, cold and heavy as molten glass, moving swiftly away and into the land of the Dead. One could enter it anytime, if one knew how, if one's *kubi* had shed all desire, all concern, every feeling but delight. He understood as well how in a time of crisis more *kubin* attained that condition, chose to step into the stream—especially but not exclusively the old or crippled. And of course in such times the tribe, on the move or confined to tunnels, needed convenient and nutritious food.

"It bothers you to see us grow fat," Tima said. "To feel yourself stronger."

He was no longer surprised that she knew what he was thinking, so he only grunted, still frowning and trying to find the right words for his feeling. Stronger, of course; but that began with the ceremony, when Pahane came fully into being, an apprentice *tagak*, a wind of fire blowing through him. But he had to admit that physically, too, he was solider. His skin stretched tighter over his shoulders and cheekbones, and when he ran he felt heavier, faster, closer to the ground.

"You want to go with them, to follow. Like a moth goes to a flame." Teeklo smiled, and spoke to Kapu in Pobla.

Was that it? A river of brightness, tempting, fascinating. . . .

Kapu and his wife were both smiling now.

"*Yano pomasu sa*," Ap said with a sly look. Tima made perfectly the sharp chittering of an angry squirrel, and all of them laughed aloud.

Death is like a woman? He frowned and smiled at the same time. Ap was on his feet now, one hand worming into the tattered shoulder bag hanging from a splinter of stone.

"You remember, when Mata was dragging you through the snow? When we gave you the choice?" Teeklo was grinning.

It was true. He had thought about death all during that trek. He had seen it as a big, dark cave where he could finally sleep, forever. Ap had removed from the bag the little bottle full of black syrup. He cavorted with it, making faces. Lifting out the wooden stopper with a flourish, he held it above his upturned face.

Everyone was laughing now, uproariously. Even those at the nearby fire had turned their way, teeth flashing out of the dark. A single drop trembled on the stopper, and Ap smacked his lips, stretched his mouth wide, fluttering his eyelids in an apparent obscene ecstasy of yearning. His tongue waggled out, cupping toward the drop.

"*Vase tohanaku!*" Kapu bellowed, then fell over backward, kicking his legs in the air. The Pobla's overturned beetle posture of hilarity.

Pahane half rose, his mouth open, but all the breath had gone out of him.

The drop fell and Ap caught it on his tongue.

"*Ya . . . Pa-pa-kish!*" he choked and reeled to his feet.

Ap sprang away, eyes round and cheeks hollowed in a comical expression of surprise and distaste. Then he began to tremble in mock terror, and a moment later doubled over, spitting and croaking. With one hand he fanned at his open mouth, while in the other he balanced both stopper and bottle. "*Ya pakish!*" he moaned.

Pahane stood dumbfounded and redfaced for a moment. They were all laughing at Ap, at him, at the comic ambivalence of death. For the Pobla, in these times, it was clearly a laughing matter. He also saw that a drop or two of the fluid was not enough to kill. He grinned back at them and reached out to pick the bottle from Ap's hand.

Ap was too surprised to react, and the others around the fire were abruptly silent as he raised the small, glass mouth to his own. He watched them through slitted eyes, except Tima, whom he could feel grow tense beside him. As he tilted the little phial he made his tongue into a narrow point and used it as a plug. He worked his throat, as if swallowing. Someone uttered a single, sharp sound.

As Ap lunged at him he danced backward and mimicked the other's hawking and spitting. He could taste a slight bitterness, something vaguely familiar from his mother's kitchen, but he spat it away with his own saliva. Then it was his turn to laugh, to yip like a coyote until Yellow growled at him; and after a moment the others joined in, Ap shoving him, mock wrestling, and Kapu and his wife both on their backs kicking.

For some time—part of him knew it was only moments, but the experience was like a long, perfect day—the tide of *yano* withdrew, vanished. They were on a high dune, warm in the sun, happy and together and alive, able to see as far as they wanted to see. Then the tide came back, a bright darkness curling and racing around them. But now he was not afraid of its fascination; he felt the current, the inexorable pull, and balanced himself there, exhilarated.

He had not, he knew now, really understood. Teeklo's explanations did not reach so far. They had only told him of the years when two out of three were stillborn or horribly deformed, when almost all were sick from the water or radiation, when the life underground left so many starved, stunted, and weak-eyed, and of how then the first great priestess, *tak tagak*, Adza's great-great-grandmother, had dried strips of her own mother and eaten them to grow strong and dance and sing a ceremony of gratitude and happiness, and so had shown her people the power of *wonakubi*, which had allowed them to survive and increase. On their mothers' bones, as the Pobla said.

Inevitably he had thought of his life before, Ronald's life. He remembered the discussions in his Bio and Psysoc classes, the problem of phasing out the generations: *Productive ter-*

mination. Decertified consciousness. Sedated transitions. An early memory had come back with new clarity. His own grandfather in the hospital: a soft, swollen bag of tissues serviced by a network of tubes and an electronic heart and oxygenator. The brain had gone and, unlike stomach or liver or kidneys, could not be replaced. He remembered his fright, his tears, his father's impatient voice, something about an experiment, serving science, serving them all. And the eye of his grandfather, like that of a shark he had seen in the aquarium, moving in its sheath to follow some fluctuation of the light.

"*Dako,*" Teeklo grimaced. He had been shaken, Pahane saw. He was not so Pobla as he pretended to be.

"*Dako tagak.*" Tima's black eyes had taken on a sparkle of merriment. She lowered her head in mock obeisance. "One of death's playmates. We better take him in small bites."

Runt Master. Death boy. Pahane grinned at them all. He remained standing, deciding on the spot that he would walk on his own to the session with Adza. Since the *Mudlati* ceremony she had sent escorts for him almost daily, even after the exhausting all-night runs. Each session was hours of chanting, breathing the smoke. This time at least he would take his own company.

"Come with me," he said to Tima. The silence he expected opened out. "I am *tagak* too," he said, watching the others. Kapu and Ap looked fixedly into the fire. Teeklo stared back at him, frowning.

"Adza is *tak tagak.* She wants you to herself. For the teachings."

"Tima can walk me to the *eela.*"

"Only temple guards." Teeklo sighed through bared teeth. "She is not . . . uh, not . . ."

"Pure." Tima smiled.

"None of us can be there with you," Teeklo went on, looking uncomfortable. "Adza is giving you most sacred teaching—"

"Enough teaching, enough. Every day every day every day. Walk and recite, walk and recite. I need to see the sun. *Ya va tonpah!* When they come, tell them we are walking the long way." He had not known beforehand that he was going to break out like this. From a great distance, the astonished ghost of Ronald watched him reach and take Tima's hand.

She hesitated, but no one spoke. Then she allowed herself to be pulled to her feet, and the oddity of this compliance stirred Pahane mysteriously. He knew that Teeklo disapproved, but understood all at once there would be no further objection. His fooling with the bottle, his familiarity with death, had silenced them.

Also, a shift in his position had occurred, since the ceremony. The scars on his cheeks frightened the Pobla children; Ap and even Kapu smiled at him differently; now even Teeklo, after their long discussion of *wonakubi* and the Hive Dwellers, seemed to listen as much as lecture. All this, he felt, was natural and inevitable to Pahane—the new Pahane who squatted securely in him like a great toad with golden eyes. All this, he also guessed, had something to do with Tima rising to hold his hand.

They left without a look backward, and in a few minutes had swarmed up the rock wall of a ventilation shaft to stand in the morning sun. They looked out over low, barren hills, and to the east they saw a broken, blue line of higher peaks. The air was surprisingly cool and fresh, coming out of a pale haze in the west. They had walked most of the night, yet Pahane felt buoyant and invigorated, ready to run and climb.

"She will be furious," Tima said, "with you." She was grinning at him, standing so close her shoulder touched his.

He understood they were measuring each other, saw that they were exactly the same height. An instant later she broke from him and loped along the hillside, switching her black hair over her shoulder. He was after·her at once, feeling his new weight drive and swing over the earth. On the *tchat,* running from the patrol dogs, he had felt himself light as a leaf, floating over the terrain; now he moved like Yellow, at a shambling, gliding trot, a muscular lunging.

Tima bounded over a gully, angled up the slope of another hill, zigzagged with great agility. A deer. He understood they were imitating, to fool the satscans. They were disobeying, of course, and taking a great risk. Only scouts and *tchat* teams were supposed to be moving out now. A scout often wore a hide and survival might depend on mimicking perfectly the gait of an animal. So as he ran Pahane worked to envision the way a big cat slung its paws and sprang from a ledge.

He was full of savage glee. The quicksilver river of *yano*

was underground, far below, and the elixir of sunlight poured into him. Adza and her teachings, Teeklo and his lectures, the terrible attack and flight—he shrugged them off like dust or water and leaped after his prey. The apprehension of a few days ago—the feeling of smallness and fragility—was gone. So he might be an outcast—so much the better. Cast out. Yes! Thrown away, like a stone or a spear. Hurtling free.

The piksis might be coming to kill him, the Pobla might chase him away—he did not care now, with the earth flowing under him, and the deer bounding and twisting just ahead. He did not know how long they ran. Sometimes he was only a stride or two away, gathering himself to reach for the flag of fiery dark hair, when she would laugh over her shoulder and pull away with a burst of speed. At other times they ran in a perfect rhythm, changing direction and pace together.

They had drifted west, over more gradual, rolling hills. There was vegetation here, a green scrub that gave off a pungent odor, and the haze they had seen earlier was now a mist all around them. It was, he thought, some protection from the satellites. Then he caught another smell, rank and invigorating, and heard a deep, heavy sigh. Tima halted at the top of a low rise, and an instant before he came to her side he recognized the sound. He stopped, too, and looked out over a blue and green shelf of ocean, seething at the broken edge of the world.

Between the thunder-strokes of surf he could hear their breathing from the long run. Again they were shoulder to shoulder, only a few inches apart. A gull sailed overhead to inspect them and uttered a thin, scraping cry. Pahane was amazed, suspended between the tremendous sea and this girl he had chased with such ardor and now did not even lift his hand to touch.

Tima answered the gull with a sharp squawk, and the bird hooked and coasted back for another look. They laughed, and in an instant his gleeful, reckless mood returned. "I catch you," he said in Pobla, and took her wrist.

"I let you. Or you would run yourself to death. *Ogan.*"

Man. He had never been called a man before. He was startled and pleased. He looked into her eyes, so wide and dark he could see nothing, but felt as if the earth had tilted under him, toward her. She looked away from him and giggled. "Outside. Inside you are *pomasu.*"

He stared, opened his mouth, frowned, and closed his mouth.

"I am a mirror to you. Or magnet, reversed. *Ogan* inside. That is why Adza will be so angry."

"What is why? I am not a . . . a . . . woman." Without thinking he looked down at the rest of her, the compact curves and wedge of hair, and then immediately away again. He felt his face grow hot. *Inside. Inside he could be. . . . And Tima his opposite. . . .*

"She'll be mad because . . ." He tried to release her hand and turn away, resentful, but she pulled him back.

"I told you before you could look all you want." She gave a slow, rich laugh. "Outside is all we care about today. We are *outside!* And if the piksi sky-eyes are watching, the cat has the deer now and he should eat." She darted her head toward him and caught his ear in her white, strong teeth. She gave a low growl, a perfect imitation of Yellow, and then turned him loose.

"I don't—" He began angrily and then stopped himself, aware of her poised to deluge him again in laughter. It would have been a lie, anyway.

"Your *ogan delo* should eat."

His little man? What little man?

"You are easy to catch," she whispered. "You have a handle." Her free hand slipped between his legs, took hold, and all the breath went out of him.

Ronald had touched a bare wire once, helping his father repair something in their home climate system. This was the same kind of feeling, only it went on and on, and he could not move. Her teeth were tugging again at his ear, and then somehow they were down in the tough, damp grass. Tima was laughing, nipping at him, squeezing. The force jolting through him narrowed and intensified; he felt the heat and thrust of it as a sudden anger.

"Stop it!" he hissed. "Let go!"

"Ogan delo! Delo delo delo . . ."

She was above him, clamping him between her legs, whipping her hair back and forth in ridicule. He twisted, heaved, and she gave way, though without releasing him. She was still chanting idiotically, calling him little, little, little. . . . Hot tears spilled down his cheeks, dripped from his chin. He stopped his struggle all at once. The shock running through him left him weak and unhinged; she was much stronger than he was anyway.

She released him instantly, slithered down the length of him, until she was pretending to talk to what she had called the little man, what Ronald's mother had called Winky. She puckered her mouth and now pretended to sing a Pobla lullaby about a brave warrior. Pahane had heard mothers sing it to their children, and remembered how sometimes they laughed uproariously, inexplicably, at certain verses. The sturdy warrior—always alert and straight—he realized it was two things, and he blushed furiously and laughed in spite of himself through his tears.

"I must talk to this little man," Tima said, grinning and folding her fingers lightly around his peg of flesh, which seemed impossibly huge.

He had never experienced such tremendous waves of embarrassment and excitement. He laughed again, because Winky—stocky, swollen, red-crowned—did seem to be straining to hear each word.

"*He* knows what to do, but you don't."

"I do too." He managed to lift himself up on his elbows. In the roil of his mind, the words came to him in Ronald's language. "Intercourse."

She threw back her head and gave the wild Pobla whoop.

"Fuck," he blurted.

Swift as a snake she had the little man's head in her mouth, the ring of her teeth testing the flesh. He was paralyzed and the breath went out of him again.

"Mmmm. Not ready." She rolled away from him, onto her hands and knees. "So what do you do, Master Snaketongue, the *tagak*. *Tak tagak*. *Tak ogan?*" She swayed her hips jauntily back and forth. "You run and run and you catch and now what? You recite your lesson from Adza?" She snapped her white teeth at him.

"I. . . ." He sat up all the way, feeling charged as if he would burst. Anger, shame, fascination, a giddiness. "We have to. . . ."

She was looking over her shoulder, her black eyes burning

through a curtain of her hair. "We were big cat and deer, to fool the sky-spies. Now you catch me. Now you come over me. Take me by the neck. Hold me and shake. Come on." She lifted her head, as if to bare her throat. "A game, Pahane. Come on."

And it was simple. He rolled forward on the balls of his feet and came over her, and all at once the turmoil, the blankness and paralysis were all gone. He felt her under him, half evading and half yielding. He knotted one hand in her hair and hauled her nearer. He gripped an earlobe in his teeth and she gave a startled buck and then the power that had gathered in him slid into her. This force took control of all the muscles of his body, coiling and driving and coiling and driving again. A sound he had never heard before tore from his chest, drowning out even the smashing of the surf.

In the cave Tima made fire by striking sparks from stones and catching them on a tuft of dry moss. They built a blaze from driftwood and talked while the ocean slammed into the beach below them. They could not seem to get enough talk. For hours they whispered and laughed, or frowned and gestured, searching for a word. And then, because of an impish glance or the way firelight moved on Tima's shoulder or flank, the force would take hold again and they would begin to nip and stroke and play. There was great fun in invention, and there were, he understood quickly, many ways to make *naku*. Two could contain an infinite number.

No one had ever before hinted at such a thing. Ronald's classes had provided detailed holos of swimming sperm, commented on Interpersonal Intimacy and Role Expectation, sometimes authorized manikins and masturbation manuals. Nothing remotely like what had just happened to him, this *naku*. The word meant, Tima said, far more than "love." It was also sport and gambling and excitement and loss—she had once translated it as divine danger. Most important, it contained two roots: it meant the tribe, the Pobla, and also the *kubi* that bound them together. To make *naku* was to join two souls to the whole spirit of the tribe. *Naku* actually held everything together. It was good to make it, any time and with any other, as long as . . .

Here Tima was convulsed again by giggling. She would not

explain, no matter how impatiently he insisted. He should not think so much, should practice for now, he had much to learn. In his first enthusiasm he wanted to do exactly that, but discovered that his brave little warrior would finally no longer obey, had drooped into a long slumber from which no amount of prodding could rouse him. That was when they began to talk more seriously, and Pahane realized that this wonder, this marvel, this formidable new force in his life, was as fragile and insubstantial as the sweet breath they had been trading back and forth.

"So you must know," she was saying, "I came with you partly for that. To survive. Though I suppose she might kill both of us, now."

They were lying full-length on opposite sides of the small blaze, their shadows huge and dim on the cave walls.

"Then you . . . you didn't especially want. . . ." He looked at her and then quickly away. "And we should keep running." All at once he felt alone. He had asked her about the feeling in the tribe against her, how he could help, and now it appeared she had been thinking of that all along. This exquisite play was only a means to—

Tima laughed. "*Dako!* Don't be foolish. Of course I wanted you. I told you how alike we are. Not fitting in anywhere, not piksi and not Pobla. And I am a man and you a woman, except for our bodies. So we belong together. And run where? I'm fast, but I can't travel on water."

He had meant further into the Wastelands, of course, but he saw immediately that was absurd. The special probe ships were lurking there, converging on them, seeking Ronald— and he was no longer Ronald. All the piksis, even his father, had become dangerous, his enemies. And Tima had stolen one of their special reconnaissance copters, destroyed it, and humiliated her keepers. He picked up a bit of driftwood and made a slow, careful loop on the sandy floor, then another.

Tima smiled. "Yes. We run in circles. One or the other will catch us, soon or late. So we may as well choose."

"Pobla, I say. I have done all my lessons well, even that old rat-herder Tsitsi says so."

"But now you have disobeyed her. Directly."

"I sing Adza her rockenroll every day. And the radio

doesn't work anymore. Besides, you said we are near the Hives now. She will be getting ready."

"All the more danger." Tima was silent for long moments, watching the blue and green sparks cascading up from a driftwood log. "It is one of the two most holy ceremonies of all. Going into the Hive. She may not come out, old as she is."

"And then . . . ?"

"Then there must be a new *tak tagak*. Immediately. Because this is a very bad time. The worst, since the beginning."

"The Choosing." He spoke softly, as if to himself, and she did not reply. Outside, a wave hissed, retiring from the beach. The Choosing was the other most holy rite among the Pobla. Normally, he knew, it would require months of preparation, then more months, even years, to complete. Now they would perhaps witness both sacred ceremonies within days of each other. A very bad time, and a very strange one.

Pahane had heard of devastating border sweeps before, and the sacrifice of temples, but the current onslaught had new and disturbing features. For one thing, a frantic, pell-mell single-mindedness. For another, the Hive Beings had given many early warnings of a coming attack. There had been swarms, migrations, the appearance of aggressive new species. Teeklo had explained to him how the party that first picked him up was actually scouting a mutant colony of black warrior ants.

Then scavenger birds had signaled the coming of deep probes—squadrons of the most advanced hovercraft and augurs. Some seemed to be looking for new dump sites or mines, but others hunted Pobla young, or bored to locate tunnels. Even algae, molds, and lichens had begun to coarsen, flake, and grip harder. Everything borne by the wind had scattered seed as if, this summer, a great fire were coming; all the nomads, from butterflies to dwarf horses, grew especially alert.

All this information came to Adza. They brought her the dried flowers and bones, the seedpods and pollen and dead queens, the scat and sign of creatures on both sides of the border. She smelled and tasted. She hummed along with the old radio. She slept and dreamed. She presided at ceremonies where she nodded and mumbled. From these mumbles and nods, the Pobla Council puzzled out its strategy. As they had done, Pahane calculated, for seventy years.

At certain times—three times in his lifetime, Kapu had told him—Adza had gone into a Hive and received guidance. For the Hive Dwellers smell and taste everywhere, absorb everything, digest all, know all. They give the *tak tagak* her visions, renew her power.

They also choose her. Whenever an old *tak* dies, he had learned, the company of female *tagakin* presents itself. Only one is chosen. The Great One swarms over her, smears her with excretions, consumes her, then dances and vibrates her back to life. All the others it suffocates within minutes.

It occurred to him for the first time that Tima might be one of the candidates, despite the suspicion she aroused among her own people. Many Pobla feared her, believed her ghost had abandoned her and left a *Mudlati* robot inside. But she had demonstrated certain powers. She proved how she had sent, through the birds, omens of the coming assault. Everyone knew she could call forth hallucinations. Everyone knew Ap owed his life to her singing. And some had heard her story of charming the tiger bees into an alliance.

"You wouldn't. . . ." The peculiarity of her smile stopped him. A big wave slumped into shore, an impact they felt through the sand beneath them.

The smile puzzled and irritated him. She looked like an indulgent mother. "I mean, eight *years*. And you were around *Mudlati* all the time, but you never. . . ."

In the play of red light and shadow, he saw her face change, subtly and instantly. He felt foolish, appalled at himself. He had been a breath away from an absurd accusation—that she had disqualified herself by being captured, by not hurling herself into *yano*. The very argument used by the most fearful and hidebound in the tribe—those who called her a piksi robot or witch. He should apologize . . . but her expression stopped him, intrigued him in some perverse way.

"Why? What happened when you were taken?" There it was, put simply and—he realized at once—brutally.

He heard the change in her breathing, and all at once he was conscious of the shape of darkness around them, of dim images clamoring at the borders of his consciousness. He was numb with dismay at the savagery, the treachery of his own feelings.

"I will tell you. Only you." Her voice was quiet, altered.

"I was playing outside with my little brother, and I saw them first, coming fast in the patrol vehicle. I took his hand and ran, screaming to my mother, who was just inside the burrow, binding grass to weave a basket. She came out but . . . they fired a net and pinned us all.

"They were running on batteries so there was not much noise. I saw them get out, three of them, and come for us with their weapons and bags of medicine, so I knew they were after live specimens. My mother knew too, of course, but my brother was not even four years—he was so frightened he could not even slow his breathing—so she broke his neck first. And then she just said to me, 'No time to sing, we go now,' and curled over to *yano*."

Tima stopped, as if to listen, and he heard a wave hissing and muttering in retreat. He waited, perfectly still.

"I was watching this piksi man, even as I was breathing out my *kubi*. I could see his frenzy, his yearning for me, and I—for a year already I had been playing so—gave my shadow to him, as a great bird with wings and talons, and saw him stumble and be afraid. I . . . I felt my mother enter *yano*, look back for me, but . . . I knew my power then, I knew I could make them afraid, and I was . . ." Tima laughed, jarring him half erect. "I was curious. I wanted to *know*. So I stepped back, held myself asleep. A coma, they said, but I was able to see and hear. I went with them, because I wanted to. I disobeyed the highest law. It is true, you see, what they say. I ate my own shadow, and did not die."

Pahane could not speak, and for the first time was deeply afraid. In a flash he understood why she had called it the divine danger. There was, underneath his fear, a voracious new selfishness, a desire and will that drew him toward and into his playmate. He did not want her to be either priestess or witch. He wanted her only to be, to be with him.

He steadied himself and smiled slyly at her. "Anyway, you are *ogan* inside, you say. So you could not replace Adza."

"Never." She laughed, but he heard the shame and grief she was trying to hide.

Nor had he meant, really, to joke. Her notion that their ghosts were a reversal of their given sex had unsettled him. He had tried to believe she was teasing, being ridiculous, but the remark had dropped like a pebble into a still pool, creating wave after expanding wave until he was now a shimmering field of doubt and possibility, like light and shadow.

In her case he saw quite clearly the truth contained in the teasing. Hidden behind her mask of serenity was a cunning, willful, restless nature. He had seen from the beginning how she made Ap and Teeklo nervous. She had used mind and body ruthlessly to make herself a fine, keen instrument. How else had she mastered the piksi world, deceived and defeated it? And mastered him too, he thought wryly. Used him to secure her foothold among the Pobla.

There was a long, tense pause and then she said, "You learned the saying, *The mirror prefers another mirror?*"

He frowned comically. Why was she changing the subject? He wanted to talk more about the hypothetical female at his center. There was something to the metaphor, he would admit. His dreaminess, the ease with which he lost himself in things or drank in some old book, the way he often understood the moods of others instantly. . . .

"Pahane," she said. The same odd smile. Amused sadness. Sad amusement. In the firelight she seemed to quiver, like an image reflected from water. Another wave collapsed, drumming on the earth beneath them. He must look the same to her, a long shape made up of shadow and fire. Mirrors of each other, she had said. Two snakes twined. Snaketongue. The forked root.

He sat up abruptly, blinking. "No!" he said. "She wouldn't. She could never—"

"No piksi has ever been *tagak* before. But she is making you one. Or *wonakubi* is. That is Adza's power, you know. The Pobla know she has no mind left, of her own."

"But *tak tagak,* a . . . a piksi? And a young. . . ."

"A time like no other, the omens tell us. Great changes are indicated. Think: Mata should have killed you, but you were spared; I should have curled up into *yano,* when the net closed over me. Instead we are here—*tohanakun*—a boy inside a girl and a girl inside a boy—making *naku* and joining two tribes. Just before the Choosing."

He was too stunned to reply, but again she knew what he was thinking. "Yes, maybe she is a witless old woman. Yes, it could all be coincidence and, yes, she might kill us out of spite. But where else, in this whole world, are there two like us? Where else do piksi and Pobla lie together, by choice, making one?"

He did not have the sense of speaking, but he heard his own voice. "We. Two. The *tak tagakin*."

She sat up, on her heels, and this time her laugh was all joy. "You sound like old man Doom. Why not? I am quick and strong, and you have the knack of seeing. *Wonakubi* comes nearer to you each day."

"You are crazy," he said. On the last word his voice slid abruptly, became a hoarse honk.

She whooped at his startled expression. "Ho! The man is scared up! You think, never has a male been chosen, never a piksi, and never two *tagakin* at once. So? Never never never, forever?" She whooped her laughter again, and again the sea struck the great drum of earth.

"The Pobla," he said desperately, "the Pobla will—" But his voice dipped and honked again.

"They will kill us or they will serve us." Tima made her eyes round like a wondering child's. "That is easy. But the piksis! Who knows what they will ever do?" She was on her knees, body erect, the fire sending tongues of red light between her breasts. "You were one, Pahane, and so was I, for eight years. But you can be so again. Ronald's ghost is still with you, somewhere, and you must call him back. That is the last reversal. You must go to them, the *tak tagak* who enters the piksi hive!"

He stared at her. The desire that had burned in him, consumed and blinded him, was transformed into something else. *The mirror prefers another mirror.* Their ghosts, their shadows, repeated each other in infinite regression, but each reflection was purer, of greater power. Pahane, the golden-eyed toad, was vanishing into something else. Their coupling, the joining of Snaketongue at the root, was only a beginning, a spark before the rising of a sun.

"Go back," he repeated.

"To your father."

"My father," he whispered, "who is trying to kill me."

"Through you," Tima crooned, "the bear and the ant will speak again, for us all."

32

ELISE HAD COME PREPARED TO HATE THE MAN WHO MIGHT have seen and spoken to her son, who might even have saved him but for a convulsion of greed. But when she saw how the man was dying—stupidly, incoherently, uselessly—she changed her mind.

The agent had bloated with edema and his features flamed with a bad rash, but she could see he was once appealing. A stocky, peppery type with bleached eyebrows and a wide mouth. His eyes glittered feverishly now and he groaned and muttered aloud. She could not tell if he was aware of their presence.

Fat cleared his throat discreetly. "Perhaps another two or three days, perhaps only hours. We are hoping for a few more words, at least."

The director wore a physician's white coat over his loosened tie. He had not left the base hospital and had not slept significantly for sixty hours. His face looked to Elise like a mask of old ivory, all expression worn away.

"He doesn't look like he has a lot left." Elise gave Fat a sort of sidelong smile, tired and sardonic. "Your agents' vocabulary is not impressive, so far." He had shown her a partial transcript. *Little shit. Gink slut. Progholes. Fuck you.* The plain, profane diction of a field man. But she had seen enough to believe this Skiho and his cocaptain had indeed captured Ronald, at least for a time.

"We are playing back tapes of certain fragments," Fat said, "hoping he will complete his thoughts. If you would care to listen?"

"In a moment." She bent over the man in the bed, tried to arrest his skittering, random eyes. "Skiho," she said firmly, "where is my son?"

The man groaned and moved one arm. He was loosely strapped into the bed, wired only to a chest-band VS monitor.

"My son, Ronnie? Is he with your partner? Where is PJ?"

"Trash," the man said clearly enough, and laughed.

Fat glanced at her. "Good," he whispered. He had explained to Elise that the drugs used by the special investigators were extremely powerful. They could permanently addle even a healthy subject. He had also hinted that these investigators overstepped the protocols of their trade, had made serious errors in the medical transcripts from the field. They were Konrad people.

"PJ is trash? Why trash?"

Agent Skiho groaned again, the restless eyes probing at corners of the room. "Bitch . . . bitch knocked me out. . . ."

Elise looked at Fat, questioning.

He almost smiled. "He says this often. An unfortunate ambiguity. He learned NorthAm from an old program, old idioms. One gives 'knockout' as a synonym for sexually attractive. On the other hand he has a barely healed contusion on the right temple. A rather severe blow."

Elise nodded. She did not even pause, anymore, over such maddening uncertainties. Not after what had happened to her and her family. And through them, of course, to the whole country.

"We assume," Fat went on, "that the literal interpretation is the more likely. The, uh, female agent trainee—"

"She had a name." Elise stated it as a fact, not bothering to look at the director.

"Yes. Tima, we called her. Or Duskyrose in coded—"

"Bitch," Skiho grunted.

They waited, but he said no more. "Yes. Tima—we assume further—either acted on orders from agent Feiffer, or saw an opportunity to escape on her own. My own view. . . ." Fat looked at his dying subordinate and seemed to ponder.

"It had to be her," Elise said crisply. "Why would your men blow up their own ship? Risk losing Ronnie?"

"But the wound was already healed, as I said. She would have made the attempt *before* the hostage plan. I think it likely my agents eliminated her, and were afraid to tell me. A great irony, of course, since that is . . . that is exactly what I . . . subsequently . . . what I had to order them to do."

She noted with surprise that the director seemed flustered, as well as glum. "And you are sorry?" She could have sworn the ivory mask flushed ever so slightly. "She must be something extraordinary. It was her, then. She took him."

Fat shrugged wearily, and without thinking Elise placed a hand on his arm and squeezed. It was the first time she had touched him that way, volunteering comfort and sympathy. In spite of all her admonitions to herself, she had come to trust him. They were almost the same height and a similar golden hue but otherwise perfect opposites: the bereaved mother—outraged, desperate, innocent—and the cool bureaucrat, master of secrecy and betrayal. Yet they had learned to rely on each other. They formed a political alliance of sorts—the only one she had ever believed in.

They were also trapped now by the same circumstance. Their fate depended on whether her son lived or died, and how he had arrived at one or the other state. She understood that the Insec director faced imminent disgrace and arrest, that Fat in turn was blackmailing the Con Administration by pretending to know Ronnie's whereabouts. And she knew also—as she knew many things she could not explain—that he depended ultimately on her simple faith, went on with this dangerous game because she sanctioned it, because she never doubted.

"Yes," Fat said softly. "Extraordinary. You would have recognized it."

"I *do*. What else would make him"—she glanced at Skiho—"so cranky? He says bitch like he means it. He's been *had*. I can tell."

Fat nodded but tactfully said nothing.

Elise had not meant to recall her own painful situation, but it was true women understood betrayal better. They expected it, knew how to contain and harness their rage. Whereas men could be surprised, devastated, consumed. They could lose themselves, become someone else, as Frank had.

"What if she subdued your agents and kept sending you reports in their name, maybe by remote, while she ran off with Ronnie?"

Fat regarded her carefully. He had, she saw, considered this possibility. "Why?"

"To give herself time to get away. The hostage scam would bring a response, pin the ship down."

"She was very bright, but to break the codes and develop and execute such a takeover after only a few weeks . . . it is difficult to believe, for one so young. And why, once she had control, would she not simply drug all three of them, program the demands, and slip away?"

"Why indeed." Elise frowned and bit her lips. "If she was smart enough to get so far, she would certainly think of that. Unless . . . PJ and she . . ."

Fat shook his head. "No. These men were competitors, but they respected each other a great deal. And PJ would never have abandoned his ship, let alone his career, for an . . . experiment like Tima."

She smiled a little. "You took that risk."

"But—" He stopped and a silence grew between them.

"I want to see her," Elise said abruptly.

The director looked startled, and once more she saw a faint warmth in his face. But he moved without a word to the keyboard and monitor in one corner of the room, and after a moment beckoned to her.

It was a small utility screen, so the image was not very good. But good enough to establish that the Gink was pretty. A clean uniform, erect posture, and cosmetic surgery had created a convincing version of a human child. Something peculiar about the eyes, too. Elise felt a tiny thrill of fear, or perhaps hate. Or perhaps attraction.

It was clear now. They had all been in love with her, or with something about or in her. The prize pet. She had had them all. And she had Ronnie right now. Elise knew this, with perfect conviction, and the realization brought a gust of bitter laughter.

"Yes?" Fat looked alarmed.

The man in the bed across the room echoed her laugh. "Goddamn it what a punch," he said. "Fucking Tickles, he knows. Talk to the old bear. Tickles and PJ. Out with the trash. Find the little bastard. Ha!" He began to cough, and a moment later vomited.

"Christ!" Fat banged the keyboard, wiping out the image of Tima and retreating through his codes. The door to the room opened quickly and a man and woman, both in surgeons' gowns, rushed through pushing a cart loaded with instruments.

Elise was thinking that she had never before heard Fat swear. While the emergency team worked over Skiho, performing a swift tracheotomy and steadying his pulse, she went with the director to the small office he had set up in the adjoining room. Already she guessed they would not see Skiho alive again. Although she had witnessed only one other death—her mother sliding imperceptibly away in a deep coma—she had never forgotten the feeling. A pressure, an invisible wind or wave trying to move her along with the departing one. Like blowing smoke. An old phrase came to her. *Giving up the ghost.*

She had come to feel like a ghost herself, and Fat looked like one, slumped in the chair behind his desk. His skin was translucent now, and Elise had the impression that he gave off a demonic light.

"We did not expect to save him," the director said mechanically. "They mined him out completely. They are moving very fast."

She understood he meant Konrad and her husband. The new Network. "Did they poison him?"

"Very possibly. There are substances which can trigger massive allergies to common antibiotics. Impossible to be certain. The field doctor on the investigation, a man named Bradshaw, has very weak credentials for the job, and there are oddities in his record. And of course Insec has been penetrated. None of our codes are secure, none of our cadres completely loyal."

"But you are cochair of the Special Investigation. And you can leak things to the media." Elise spoke with an effort. Their conversations reminded her of some old story she had heard about a man who rolled a great boulder up a hill over and over, only to see it careen back to the bottom.

"They know every move I make." Fat lifted his hands, let them fall again to the desk top. "They make a point of delivering bulletins to the place I have just left, or a decoder breaks just as I access."

"So what's new?" Elise shrugged impatiently. "Things happen to *them,* too. They are losing a lot of troops just to equipment failure."

It was true. There were errors and coincidences on all sides, too many of them bloody. The normal tendency of the universe, toward chaos, did not seem to account for so much malice and ghastly comedy. After a recent hush-hush meeting Fat had hinted at the existence of a third player, a secret society devoted to indiscriminate sabotage. For what purpose he could not determine, but the effect was to fuel the Progs' campaign to find a scapegoat.

"It is possible," Fat now said to her, "some will encourage any disaster, any suffering."

She was incredulous. "Maybe a few lone psychotics. But most people do terrible things for political ends. For wealth and power. To be adored or feared. *Personally*." She did not bother to add the names.

"There is a type that prefers anonymity. The anonymity of a god. They labor to create new victims and villains. Always more horror. More drama. Political creatures also need those things, and will pay for them." He spoke reluctantly, his eyes sliding away from her. "Anyway, it's only speculation, at this point."

Elise felt herself contracting again, shrinking and wrinkling inside. Ronnie. He was the victim they needed, Danielle Konrad and her coalition. But it was still impossible for her to believe that Frank could fall so far under the woman's spell, could desire such insane vengeance and martyrdom—the death of his own son. In their last confrontation, before he left the house for good, she had hissed out a single question. *Yes,* her husband had replied. *Yes, I hope he is dead. We are not animals.*

It was the only time he had spoken to her for months, beyond the barest communication concerning his schedule, their finances, legal matters. The cold ingot of his final statement was still in her, heavy and hidden; the one fact she could not bear to look at again. His destroyed face was nothing beside the ugliness of those words.

"Elise?" Fat regarded her with melancholy concern.

"Sorry." She shook her head and smiled perfunctorily. "I was thinking of certain victims. How nasty they can get. But of course you were right—we're the new villains, us enemies of progress. The deadly ideologies. Like that poor soul in there throwing up what's left of himself."

Fat nodded. They listened on the intercom to the voices

from the next room long enough to learn Skiho was alive, though unconscious now. Fat settled back then and a moment later his eyelids drooped. Elise held her peace, pleased that he was able to relax in her presence. She knew he had only a few minutes before the next call came through, or an aide tapped on the door.

Another deadly ideologue dozes off, she thought. The phrase came from the holonews that morning, one of several charges Danielle Konrad had hurled at the Conservative party. The woman fancied herself a victim, a misunderstood savior. And consort of a living martyr. Scarface and the pagan Madonna.

They seemed to be the perfect couple to lead the crusade for a restored planet, purged of its filth and rot and evil. A planet finally in the people's hands, run according to the people's principles. No Ginks, outside a few laboratories. No bugs, no biters, and no strays. No unused Wastelands. Jobs, production, comfort, safety. . . .

Well, what was wrong with that? Elise compressed her mouth, tucking the corners down. Trying to retrace political arguments always left her confused and depressed. She had never herself had particular affection for the Preserves—and certainly not for wasps or spiders or flies or bears or rattlesnakes. She accepted the existence of such beings—as long as they were safely contained somewhere far away. Like everyone else she had also believed that *lapsis* was a terrible genetic mistake, a regression to bestiality. Yet her husband had convinced her of the rightness of the Con policy of study and observation. Sure, he used to say, wild things are ugly, disgusting, and cruel; we need them to remind us of how we were, so we can see how far we've come.

Now Frank wore the ugly, disgusting mask of his own face, to serve the cause of total extermination. Even the President and his advisers were scrambling that way, compromising as hastily as decency permitted. The news trumpeted daily flop counts, displayed the swagger and racket of the massive deployment. All of it summoned around her missing child. Or rather the "symbol" of the lost son, the "tragic example" of little Ronnie Drager, as the Progressives would have it.

There were moments when she thought the Progs were right. There was no denying, anymore, the militant collaboration among several of those scrofulous wild creatures. A thick-skinned carnivore and stinging insects had brought horror into her own family; but the whole population had suffered, day-to-day, from raccoons who scavenged swiftly in the darkness created by their former prey—frogs so numerous now they jammed hydroturbines—from gut parasites that joined to mimic precisely an ulcer and so receive soft nutrients, from viral damage in trees, borne by seed-eating birds who made perfectly camouflaged nests from the mosaic blight of the infected foliage.

The Ginks trained other species to attack humans, no question, but that was almost the least of it. Three generations of scientists had worked on the complexities of symbiosis, down to the molecular level, before beginning to understand that this universal principle of adaptive cooperation—the real dynamo of evolution—might have a sinister side for *homo sapiens*.

Cooperation began to look like conspiracy. Nearly every genetic adaptation among unregulated species seemed unfavorable to human designs. A far higher percentage, at least, than chance would dictate. It was not simply a matter of beaks flattening into screwdrivers, or a secretion that mimicked the odor of detergent. It was as if what used to be called Nature was reacting collectively to a threat. As if the mythic old matriarch was becoming downright . . . well, *hostile*.

That was of course a word of unacceptable teleological bias. *Inimical* was preferred usage. She remembered a quote from her childhood. A wild woman a hundred and fifty years ago had pioneered the study of symbiont bacteria. In her old age this researcher had abandoned all pretense of detachment and become a mystic and prophet. She believed the simplest forms of life were the most enlightened and compassionate. "Man, like cancer, struggles to dominate," she wrote. "Everything else works together to get rid of him."

Elise thought of RAM and SHIVA, the endless talk of diversity and deviance, aberration and aggression, the implacable infighting that went on under the bland masks of "research" and "viability study." She had no clear notion anymore of what was right or normal. Maybe everyone was, in some theoretical way. Even the Progressives. She knew only that she wanted her son back, wanted to protect him from all harm.

Which meant trusting Fat and what was left of his agency —a pair of traitorous agents, the pretty Gink runaway, a databank on everything unsavory in the whole Federation. A flimsy enough support system. All of it based in turn on the wisp of her mother's intuition.

She watched the director as he slept, his hands inert on the desk top, his spine straight, chest rising and falling very rhythmically. Obviously he had mastered his meditation and relaxation techniques. He could probably survive for weeks this way, napping for a few minutes every hour or so. A strange, oblique, secretive man, immersed in his own endlessly Byzantine survival strategies. Yet she sensed something true and kind in him. An impression based on nothing but an occasional look, a tactful pause, a small gesture, his silences. She wondered—

A voice was suddenly louder on the intercom.

"Director Fat? Director Fat?"

"Yes?" The director spoke out of his sleep, even before his eyes opened.

"Sir, he's not coming back for us very well. The grams are showing reduced cerebral activity. We, uh, need to make a decision. . . ."

"Yes." Fat got to his feet. "In a moment." He rummaged in the pocket of the gown and removed a small bottle. Rotating its cap with a thumb, he shook two white tablets into his upturned palm.

Elise stood also and walked to the sink, where she filled a plastic cup with water. He took it from her and then hesitated.

"You needn't go, if you don't want to."

"I want to."

He nodded, tossed the pills into his mouth and drank the cup empty. He left the office ahead of her, not looking back. Elise had the peculiar, absurd feeling that someone remained behind in the room.

The head of the emergency team was a deferential, efficient young man. He spoke softly and quickly, his paper mask dangling around his neck and a sheaf of printouts in one hand. Behind him four people fussed over Skiho, who was now connected to plasma bottles as well as the breathing tube and various monitors.

The patient was experiencing periodic convulsions and fibrillations. Theta wave pattern indicated deep coma. They had experimented with minute amounts of stimulants and a couple of new ion-interceptor antibodies, but the adverse reactions continued.

The young man glanced at the rows of figures on the printouts. "We could keep him for another few hours, maybe. Might fish up a word, a sentence if we're lucky. But—" He smiled automatically. "He's down there for good, I think. They really worked him over. Brain through a blender."

"Traces?" Fat lifted a finger toward the printouts.

"Nothing we can prove. Couple of unusual scabs. But he's now allergic to everything." The young man glanced behind him at the body on the bed. "To life."

Fat said nothing, seemed to be examining the floor. Elise had the eerie feeling he was controlling an outburst of black mirth.

"So, sir, it's up to you. We can do the procedures, see what happens. Or. . . ." The young man shrugged, smiled again automatically, then slipped on the paper mask and adjusted it. Cut off from the smiling mouth, his eyes were watchful, unsympathetic.

Fat looked up again, contemplating first the doctor and then the dying agent. Elise saw that Skiho's eyes were fixed now, staring through the ceiling. He wore an expression at once remote and vaguely puzzled, as if each intake of enriched air through the tube surprised him.

"Has he said anything else?"

The doctor wrinkled his brow. "One word, we think. Before the first convulsion." He hesitated. "I thought it was *Insec*, you know, the bureau. Two of the other guys heard *insect*." He extended the sheaf of printouts and Fat accepted them without looking. "So anyway, sir, I can't on my own authorize—"

"Of course." Fat's expression was once more untroubled, blank, ancient. He slid a palm gently under Elise's elbow. "You needn't call us anymore. Just let him go. When he wants. Good-bye."

He was addressing them all, Elise realized. The doctor and

the four attendants and herself, as well as Skiho. The two of them walked away quickly, the emergency team answering with the conventional, respectful farewells. But she felt the wind again, moving against her, bearing the empty vessel of the agent's body into darkness, into a realm that would finally receive them all, that received everything always. She knew Fat had spoken from the threshold of that world of shadows, that he was turning toward it, separating himself from her. Or perhaps—the thought carried an instantaneous chill, not exactly unpleasant—the dark had taken a long stride toward them.

33

PJ THOUGHT AT FIRST IT WAS ANOTHER HALLUCINATION, A product of his yearning. After all the mojo little Duskyrose had worked on him, he was worried about his psychic immune system. And climbing out of a tomb of garbage to skulk for days across this moonscape, taking too many rads, had to create a vulnerability, a predisposition to project. At times, the razors planing through him like blades of white light, he had thought he might already be insane.

At other moments he would find himself crouched on a ridge top, imitating a stone, his mind bare of all purpose. He might be smiling, watching a cloud unravel or drift across the empty sky. He would be unable to remember how long he had been there. The jagged horizon, the columns of black dust, the deep, crooked canyons and smoldering waste pits had seemed strangely illuminated, beautiful. The Wastelands possessed a weird new power to make him forget why he was there, where he was going.

All that changed when he saw the footprints. Once he accepted that they were no fantasy, no mirage, he had collapsed to his knees, stunned by such a miracle after so long a series of disasters. About time, he had crooned aloud, with tears in his eyes, about fucking *time*.

The narrow, slightly splay set had to belong to the boy. So of course the other prints were Tima's. They were the right size, the toes not as spread out as a normal Gink's. This was more than hunch, more than intuition. Ronnie Drager was nearby, a few klicks, and out of his hole. He remembered one of Black Jack's old expressions for sensing a coup: *You can smell it.*

They had been running, the kid behind. Running carelessly, or they would have dodged around this strip of softer ground. What they were doing here by themselves, heading for an isolated stretch of coast, he had no idea. But it was incredible good fortune, an opportunity from heaven to resurrect himself, to pull off this caper at last.

He knelt for a long time, breathing unevenly and kneading his hands on his thighs to make them stop shaking. It wasn't going to be all cake, by any means. It would take another miracle to see him through the return trek, to get the boy safely to some cover from which he could contact Insec and begin negotiations.

Already days ago he had fried the batteries in the cycle and ditched it. He was down to maybe five days' rations. The filters in his shielded suit would soon clog. But he was no longer hopeless and drifting, a fugitive rather than a scout. He had a target again, a wild, long-shot mission. He was back at work.

He knew, from listening to the channels he could reach with his ranger's minicom unit, that a major action was taking place. Checking out tracks, probing a few tunnels, hiding from an occasional copter, he had been puzzled. The special forces seemed to be trying to kill and autopsy every Gink they could locate, an incredibly cumbersome and costly duty. They were losing vehicles and personnel in unprecedented numbers, to dust storms, equipment malfunction, and fouled communications.

Meanwhile their quarry fled, dispersed, doubled back, delayed, sabotaged, and died—also in unprecedented numbers. Cat and mouse, one would say, but it was hard to tell which was which. The Ginks seemed to be moving south and toward the ocean, concentrating their population in a completely uncharacteristic way. It was the one element of the pattern that made no sense, might in fact be suicidal.

He would strip down to a standard emergency beltpak—food pellets, medicine, weapons, the minicom. He figured he would try to slip through the lines in the confusion of the assault. If spotted he would pretend to be separated from his patrol, ask for directions to an outfit in the area. The kid would hopefully be dirty and sunbaked enough to look like a mixed, saved for interrogation. At least he would be tougher, if he was out here running on his own, not wearing sandals now.

He saw that a tiny drift of dust had formed inside the rim of the deepest heel prints, deposited by the afternoon wind. They had passed here only a few hours ago, had surely reached the ocean by now. But for what reason? The coast was barren, and Ginks were afraid of big water anyway. He wondered if the pair had been driven out, perhaps blamed for bringing down the patrols on underground settlements.

If they had run away, on the other hand, he would need to keep an eye out for search parties. But it looked for the moment as if he had them trapped against the water, separated from the rest of the pack. He had only to stalk, get close enough to stun, and then scoop them. After that—he took a deep, expanding breath—he would have his satisfaction. He would rectify the record of Phillip J. Feiffer as a professional. Erase the humiliation of being stripped and stung and screwed by a—but she didn't matter anymore. He got to his feet laughing and shook himself, rapidly and all over, like a dog.

He was surprised and amused at first by what he heard coming out of the cave. Little Ronnie Drager was obviously not so little now. But they were talking whenever they were not squealing and thumping, and talking too softly for him to understand.

He grew irritable and uncomfortable as the night advanced. He had taken up a position a few yards to one side and below the cave's mouth, wedging himself between two boulders and spreading a thin, tempflex blanket overhead. He was thus camouflaged and protected from infrascanners. But the ground was hard and the cold breath of the sea gave him a headache.

He wanted badly to move in when they were locked together, pumping away. He imagined the look on their faces in the beam of his flashlight, the ridiculous posture, how he would laugh. But he couldn't be certain Tima was unarmed. The Scooter might have contained a couple of specimen guns when she stole it. He had underestimated her once before, and a colossal unholy mess was the result. This time there would be no oversight, no margin of error.

The Drager kid was a mystery, at this point. PJ was not going to assume anything. The boy might be—probably was—nuts by now. A brain wipe. He barely had balls and here he was rutting on a little Gink bitch as if he had not a care in creation. He might very well fight like a weasel to stay where he was. One solution was medicine, curtains and flatteners that would disconnect all but the necessary circuitry for locomotion and navigation. Or the kid might collapse in relief, or start running for the border. He had to be ready for anything. It was not going to be cake.

The conversation inside the cave had become murmurs, spaced farther apart. He could no longer see the very faint red glow on the stone overhang at the entrance, but the eastern horizon was growing pale. In another hour the sun would be breaking over the plain. They had to be sleepy, and would probably not count on moving until much later in the day.

When another twenty minutes went by and he heard nothing, he drew in the blanket and compressed it carefully into a small tube removed from the pack. He fastened the flashlight to his belt, angled to cast a beam downward, and then unfolded the stock on his Stingray, keeping the weapon close against his midsection to muffle the click.

When the current was flicked on he felt it vibrate briefly. He liked the Stingray. A close-quarter featherweight weapon, delivering a concentrated jolt or a scatter pattern. It could disorient and incapacitate, or drill a lethal path through two inches of impact mesh. He set the charge chamber at ten down, long enough for him to examine and handclip both of them.

Inside, his boot soles grated faintly on a layer of sand that had blown over the stone floor. In the gray light he saw a single thread of smoke rising from the heap of ash. The surf had quieted to a mutter and hiss, over which he could hear a squawk from a gull.

They slept fitted together, facing the entrance, her chin on his shoulder. There was just enough light for him to see that Tima's nose was misshapen, and even as he looked her nostrils flared and contracted and he heard her breathing change. He put his finger on the flashlight switch. When she opened her eyes he turned the beam on, a sudden cone of high glare clapped over the huddled forms.

The boy groaned and screwed up his face. Tima did not move except to close her eyes into slits. Smart. Trying to adjust her pupils. PJ grinned to himself.

"Go ahead, Bomber Bird. Make a move. Come on, monkey bitch." He held the Stingray comfortably. He was loose, ready, sharp.

He could see a flicker of movement behind the eye-slits. She wanted to know how many, where they stood. The Drager boy was blinking now, sitting up, his face tightening into alarm. He said something in the Gink's tongue, and at that instant Tima rolled behind him and sprang to one side, trying to get beyond the fan of light.

The charge caught her in the hip, but momentum carried her to the edge of darkness, where she hit with a soft, flop-limbed impact. Quick, oh she is quick, PJ thought. Never give her a nanoslice to work with. He shot the boy in the chest and he went over like a carnival duck, banging his head solidly on the stone floor.

PJ cursed mildly and set the Stingray aside, removing the switch module and slipping it into a pocket. The kid was his potential pardon, his insurance and retirement too—he would have to be more careful. He took out the tough plastic hand-clips. Rolling Tima flat on her back, he checked her breathing and pulse. Irregular, an occasional hitch, but healthy enough. An ordinary Gink would have wiped herself, but Tima hadn't apparently recovered the technique.

He tweaked one of her nipples, flubbed it back and forth with one finger. Nothing. He ran the same finger along her belly to the hairline, down one thigh. Not a twitch. Could have faked it entirely, with him and Black Jack. But not with this punk kid? A long thorn of keen and unpleasant emotion went into him. He frowned and turned to the boy.

Definitely bigger and definitely darker. Hair down below his shoulders and scars everywhere. One on each cheek, clearly a brand of some kind. Feet like black horn and the same pungent, sour odor PJ associated with all Gink dens. Christ, he could rub a little more dirt in the kid's hair and pass him off as purebreed. Made one wonder if the Drager line didn't have a few illicit genes to start with.

He didn't hesitate to clip this rangy adolescent. Ronnie Drager, at least as he appeared in the holoblitz of the last few months, didn't exist anymore. A commentary, in its fashion, on the weakening of Fed culture. Brought up in the lap of wealth and power, given the best education available, groomed as a future leader—and in less than a year the Ginks had reduced him to a dirty, grunting animal.

PJ stacked the pair of them against the wall near the entrance. He switched off the flashlight, restored the safety module to his Stingray, and sat down three steps away to wait for them to wake up. He had not taken anything, not even a caffeine tab, since spotting the footprints, but he felt alert and steady. He thought he might risk moving immediately a couple of klicks along the beach, inside the tide line, as soon as he had the kid tranqued. Just to throw off any Gink scouts.

But he would have to take care of Tima first. He would allow a couple of hours for that. He was curious to discover if she could still throw a little head mojo, and he wanted to see which way she squirmed. Wanted also to pry out an explanation of how she had cracked the Insec codes. Then he could put her down for two or three days with a careful charge, or he could wipe her. Either way, he wanted her to . . . wanted her. . . .

He did not notice his drifting off. The image of her covered with bees had come back to him—the shimmering, slightly blurred shape of dark gold and the deep, frenetic, incredibly dense sound . . . zillion zillion zillion. . . .

A very small creature, mouse or lizard or large roach, flickered across the floor at the rear of the cave. He swiveled his eyes to see but the thing had already vanished in the gloom, a layering of shadows, which appeared deeper than he had first thought. As he continued to stare he felt the powerful, physical sensation of falling. As if the earth had instantly and inexplicably rotated a hundred and eighty degrees, so that he was dropping, accelerating into dark depths, away from the new sunlight. . . .

When he experienced the first thrill of panic he wrenched himself away, turned back, and found her watching him. He underwent a slight shock, recognizable as *déjà vu*. An imperceptible sliding away, the pang of fear, then a groggy moment of recovery. A moment when those black eyes seemed to swallow him, everything he was and had been. More tired than he had thought, apparently.

"So," he said after a long breath, "haven't lost your knack for headfucking. Or fucking plain and simple."

She said nothing, remained slumped against the stone wall. The Drager boy mumbled and twitched.

"What makes me curious is three things, Bomber. Number one, what the hell are you doing out here? A long way to come for a punch. And a big risk, too, hey, as it turns out."

Instead of answering, Tima turned her head slightly and said something in Gink to the boy. Ronnie rolled his head, blinking, and sat straighter. In a moment he focused on PJ, who was immediately startled by the madness in the kid's look. These eyes were big holes into a place of fire and shadow. What kind of job had they done on the poor guy, anyway?

"Hey, buddy," he said softly, tentatively. "Ronnie?"

No change in the mad eyes. Nothing.

"Listen, Ronnie, I know it's been—"

"I'm not Ronnie," the boy said. "I am Pahane. What do you want from me?"

PJ knew a tiny, very brief flash of doubt before he smiled sympathetically. "Right. Pahane. Nice name. Something about snakes?" He toyed with the charge dial on the Stingray. Maybe he should just put the kid away for twenty minutes and administer some heavy medicine.

Tima spoke for the first time, in exactly the same empty, deferential tone she had used as a Pro Four. "You might lose him. He is still learning, this Pahane, to be comfortable here. Give him some time. Why we have come—sir—is why you have come."

PJ hoisted his eyebrows, mocking.

"Because we do not belong anywhere, at this moment. Because everywhere—even the most ruined places—will be invaded now. Everything must be settled. Everything owned and controlled. Including you. Sir."

He grinned, but stopped playing with the controls on his weapon. "The old exploitation routine," he said. "Spare me, love. *You're* at the end of the line. Not me."

She smiled at him. He thought he detected pity in that smile, but before he could speak she said, "What about your friend?"

"Taking care of himself. Already home." PJ licked his lips before he smiled back. "Said to give you his regards."

"He will not find everything the same. Nor will you. Fat does not run Insec anymore. The Con Administration is doomed, and the new policy seems to be extermination. Anyway, I don't think Ronnie can be talked into returning. *Alive.*"

"Bullshit. What do you mean talked into? I'm *taking* him back. And he'll come around. They'll rehab him and he'll blow this situation apart."

"You have only Pahane. If you force him. . . ." Her smile turned down wryly. "No one will ever see Ronnie Drager again."

"Bullshit. Bullshit, Birdgirl. He's Ronnie, and the gene-prints will prove it. If I can get him back, Fat can fuck himself. The Administration—the whole Fed—will owe me. Owe me *plenty.*"

He was aware of his own lack of conviction. It was true he had no guarantees that the Con government would believe his tale, or forgive him this screwup, even if he delivered their little prize. And what if the government were about to fall? He'd be dealing with the Progs, the likes of Konrad, or some tricky compromise interim ratshit. It would take shrewd bargaining, and tremendous luck, to navigate his ass through this business.

"Interesting conversation, but—" He patted the stock of the Stingray. "I have a pressing engagement with history. I had two more—"

"The codes, how I found access." Her tone had lost its neutral deference, was now matter-of-fact, a touch impatient. "You piksis on the Border Patrols have fair eyesight, but you are nearly deaf and without noses or tongues, as the Pobla understand them. Since we used the same keyboards, I learned to recognize the sound of each key, and listened whenever I knew you were going deep. As for why I let you live. . . ." She shrugged and gave him another upside-down smile. "My mistake, perhaps. I cannot explain. Maybe because the tiger bees did not kill you."

She looked at him fully again, and despite himself he could not stay out of the black water of that look. His hand tightened on the stock of the weapon; it was still set at a low ten and he could touch her off, take another break. . . . But he remained motionless, determined to match her, repel her, break her images one by one as she gave birth to them.

But this time there was no metamorphosis, no glittering into scales or ruffling into feathers. Tima seemed only to lengthen and draw nearer, without moving, as if the space between them had simply shrunk. Her presence pressed on his, entered, intermingled. It was a peculiarly delicious, sensuous impact. Their breathing was simultaneous, synchronized. He waited, trying to maintain his mind in a state of perfect readiness, perfect agility.

"You have run for a long time now. You have food for—what? Four days, five? The probes are hunting hard for you . . . me . . . a boy . . . anyone outside, anyone wild, anyone still free."

Subtly the presence that had interpenetrated his own underwent a change. Tima's eyes remained the same black pools, but the face around them altered, at once strange and yet familiar and older. The bones in her face were now more angular and her expression verged on a friendly scowl, an expression he had seen. . . .

"Your friend, the one you call Tickles," she said, "would consider helping, I think. There is piksi in him still, the old piksi that could dream and make stories and move even in the Wastelands. He knows that only Pahane can bring Ronnie back, and it would take someone like Ronnie to reach the piksis, to make them see, before they exterminate themselves."

"Bullshit," PJ whispered. "What are you saying?"

"Your friend who has lived as you always wanted to live, here among stones under the sky. You should talk to him. You have nothing by yourself, you are crawling alone across a land you know not, toward a place where they are hungry to eat your heart and the hearts of everyone like yourself. . . ."

His left hand lost all sensation. As if it had been cut off

instantly, painlessly. He wanted to look, not expecting it still to be there, but he could not move his eyes down and away from her face. He had the impression he was thinking exactly what Tima was saying, as she was saying it, in the same way water seems to yield and take the shape of whatever is plunged into it.

"Because they will leave nothing for you afterward, no Preserves and no duties and no missions; you—and Skiho if he was lucky enough to survive—will be of no use, an embarrassment, the last covop agents to roam over the border, an extinct race, they will say, as they say about us and the bear and desert cat and crazy horse and long snake. . . ."

There was a dead space on his whole left side, or a dark wall. He could see only Tima; she was so close he felt her breath on his face; he was inhaling her, through his right nostril. With a tremendous effort he groped with his right hand after his left, to pull it and the weapon it held across himself, into the light where he could see and his muscles would work. Or to reach into the medpac, in a left-side pocket, and grab a razor or spacecap or simple booster. He needed something, bad. He tried with all his strength to twist his body away from the wall of shadow; but he was conscious of no movement, only a terrible strain and sense of compression, as if the wall were beginning to lean.

Pahane edged carefully along the wall in the beginning, responding to pressure from Tima's thigh, a slight inclination of her head. She kept talking and he listened even as he scooted his way along the cave floor. He understood that the man was not seeing anything on one side, and could not move his head to change his field of vision. She was telling the man about his own life and how much he needed the Pobla and the wild animals, and how much he would lose if he carried through his mad plan. Her voice was rapid and soft and continuous, and seemed to be in rhythm with the murmuring surf outside.

Stirring through the ashes of the fire with one foot, Pahane found a live coal. Though he had to work with hands behind his back, and raised a blister on the heel of one thumb, he managed to melt through the plastic handclip. He could feel Tima's power, the tension between her and the man, and instinctively kept himself empty of thought as he crept nearer.

The problem came when he was ready to reach out for the gun. All at once the prospect of touching the smooth, polished graphite and metal made him ill. The thing glittered, a heaviness and stench that pushed against him. He recognized *yano*, but of a sort dull, thick, and foul.

Of course he also recognized the man. One of the copter captains whom Tima had tricked and abandoned. The dangerous one, called PJ, though he looked frail and gaunt now. Inside his dirty jumpsuit, he was rigid as a frame of welded steel rod, and his face glistened with sweat. As Pahane inched toward the gun, breathing harder with his own effort, the man managed to raise his hand and paw feebly in the air.

The space between Tima and her former commander was oddly bluish green, a faint haze of light. Pahane felt his fingers tingle as they entered that space, and the stock of the weapon was as slick and tight as live skin. It was incredibly heavy, and to remove it gently from the man's grip took all his strength. He was no longer conscious of the words Tima spoke, but he sensed with absolute clarity the force emanating from her: it was like *naku*, only darker and inexorable. She was trying to suck what was left of this PJ's *kubi* out of him, consume it and convert it.

A moment after he rolled away, clutching the weapon, Tima sagged as if her spinal cord had been severed. Her eyes closed and she took a long, shuddering breath. The man uttered a loud groan and yawned, while both his arms began to jerk uncontrollably. The blue-green tint faded from the air, and only Pahane seemed to have strength enough to blink and look about. He set the weapon quickly aside, near Tima, unable to bear the slick, repulsive heft of it.

For minutes they were silent. Pahane was listening to the tones of their breathing, how the harsh rasp from the man and his own lighter, quicker sound became gradually alike, and how Tima's shuddering and occasional gasp also subsided, until they were all in a complex rhythm with the sea. He recognized the *tagak* power, remembered the great snake emerging from Adza's mouth and crawling into him. When PJ finally spoke, he had a new voice, soft and uncontrolled like a young boy's.

"That's it," he said. "You did me, Bomberbitch. I'm

through." He looked at the weapon beside her, frowned as if he did not recognize it. "How?"

"Take off that suit," Tima said quietly.

The man stared for a moment, nodded, and got stiffly to his feet. After shedding the pack, he fumbled at the flaps and zippers until the suit was opened and he could step out. He took off his boots, socks, and underwear, and sat down naked. He stretched his thin, pale legs on the cool stone and then laughed.

"You will travel with us now, the Pobla way. You will have no medicine—the medicine that has taken most of you already—and you will be afraid. We are going into the dark together, and we do not know what we will find. But what is left inside you is your *kubi,* your true shadow, and so you cannot be through yet. It is the part of you that is tied to us, to this place. The part that just laughed. You have been following it here. You have always followed it, not understanding that hunting us and the wild beings is really hunting yourself. You need us to show you this part. And we are going to need you."

The man had listened intently, wonderingly. He thought for a time and then smiled. "I'm fucking crazy, aren't I? Yeah. Of course. Completely lunatic." He made a crowing sound. "But—it feels good, sort of. And you're right, I've run out of future. Skiho and I. He saw it. The weirdness he always talked about. And Tickles—shit, Tickles was way ahead of all the other deranged. Anyway the V-studies would have canceled us, eventually. And I know it's nuts, but fact is, I guess"—he laughed a little wildly—"I'd rather sit around bare-assed with a bunch of lap cannibals and this kid gone animal, in a fucking hot dump site"—the laughter took him again and he could not go on. He fell over on his side, his face streaked with tears, and laughed until he retched. Then, after a series of deep sobs, he fell sound asleep.

After a time Pahane said, respectfully, in Pobla, "You are *tagak,* for certain."

Tima spoke slowly, and he realized she, too, was exhausted, on the point of falling asleep. "You could do it." He waited and when she was able she went on. "The *kubi* deep down. A big toad for you, you told me. There, but a little deeper. What looks through the eyes of the toad. From there you will see into someone, his *kubi*. As you saw into Adza at the *Mudlati*. You will know what he is, what he will do. You can speak and he must listen."

Pahane nodded. "He could not move."

Tima smiled wearily. "He did not want to move. He has moved too much."

He nodded again, more vigorously. "Yes. I understand that. So. So what do we do with this piksi now?"

For the first time since they had run away, Tima looked at him with impatience, even irritation. "We. Yes, *we*, Pahane. You think now. You are *tagak* too. And you are the one they both want. You think."

And then, in one more sigh, she was asleep.

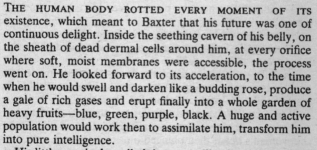

34

THE HUMAN BODY ROTTED EVERY MOMENT OF ITS existence, which meant to Baxter that his future was one of continuous delight. Inside the seething cavern of his belly, on the sheath of dead dermal cells around him, at every orifice where soft, moist membranes were accessible, the process went on. He looked forward to its acceleration, to the time when he would swell and darken like a budding rose, produce a gale of rich gases and erupt finally into a whole garden of heavy fruits—blue, green, purple, black. A huge and active population would work then to assimilate him, transform him into pure intelligence.

His little angels, he called them, recalling how the old ethnocentric religions had imagined small, winged creatures made of luminous spirit. Dragonflies, actually, came close. But *insecta* were of course the seraphim, and the ordinary, everyday miracles were performed by lower orders—more rudimentary arthropods, bacteria, and *monera*. The simple, brawny workers of deconstruction and salvage. He was their lay disciple, and also their newly colonized and converted land. Their temple.

It amused him to discover how often the old systems had stumbled on the truth. *The last shall be among the first. Land of locusts and honey. Therefore the fathers shall eat the sons . . . and the sons shall eat their fathers. . . .* At the moment, however, his text would have to be Beware the subtle Serpent. He was lying in the glorious filth which the hospital's declining efficiency now permitted, beaming up at the young scientist and the official and her secretary who had come to observe. He was listening intently, preparing himself for another apparent recovery, hence another cycle of information-gathering.

"So in unobtrusive ways they are all orienting themselves toward the south," the young man was saying. He looked haggard and needed a haircut, and one of the women—Baxter recognized the celebrated reformer Danielle Konrad—looked utterly exasperated with his rambling and self-conscious lecture. The other woman, carrying a compact databoard, maintained a quiet, demure smile. Curiously, Baxter could detect a complex sex pheromone exchange between her and the young man. They were by no means strangers.

"We are *all* oriented that way, for the moment," Danielle said acidly. "Summarize, please. We don't have time to waste."

Baxter allowed his head to swivel toward the woman.

"Reaction!" The young man appeared excited. "On the word *waste*, did you see?"

Danielle gave him one of the looks that had made her notorious in staff meetings. A laser-stroke of contempt. "He's a saprophile. You *told* me that, Dr. Petrasky."

"I'm sorry. We've got so much data running, so many hypotheses. . . ." Marvin Petrasky grimaced, looked wildly over the woman's head, then plunged on.

"The main point, Commissioner, is that we have shut off all known communication between the patients and outside. Including a scrambler shield for all holo, video, and radio waves. And still their movement patterns correlate with the major actions of New Broom. And the timing remains close, even when patients are separated for days."

The young man was dangerous. It would be necessary to mount a sustained campaign to convert him, Baxter realized. Perhaps he would be elected to effect that conversion, because of his success with Dr. Klepper. Baxter smiled to himself again. Dr. Klepper was now in an adjoining cell, a mantis clan member in training. But Petrasky was a trickier problem. A true scientist on the scent—a suppressed giggle convulsed Baxter—and with more imagination than most.

"They have some communication system," Danielle said with a deadly cheerfulness. "From cell to cell. Obviously."

Petrasky nodded, brushed back his lank hair with one hand. "Right," he said. "We suspect some sort of olfactory signal, through the ventilation system. If we had funds—"

"Spare me." Danielle glanced at her assistant. "Or do you want to respond to that one, Dorothy?"

The woman's fingers were already caressing her board, and in a moment she was reading from the screen in a soft, concerned tone.

"We show a little overrun here of ninety-two, Commissioner, with a projection of nearly twice that for the fiscal year, if the trend stays as it is. Dr. Petrasky has also endorsed a proposal for construction of an observation post over the border—"

"Wait! That was only a discussion, a possible—we were just speculating. . . ." He stared in bewilderment. "How . . . how could you?"

The woman did not look up from her keyboard, but her cheeks were touched with color, as if at a compliment. When she spoke her voice was still softer, apologetic. "I'm sorry," she said. "Classified."

"Listen, Petrasky." Danielle's manner was now weary and maternal. "Every branch of NorthAm government is up to its eyebrows in debt. Everybody is screaming for funds. You've gotten your dole simply because a couple of your predictions were confirmed and the General has been impressed. It's his idea that you could help us locate young Drager—or more likely his remains."

"Remains!" Baxter croaked. He was on all fours now, practicing his beetle walk. The word was the first he had spoken in almost a month.

"Ah! See?" Dr. Petrasky hurried to the wire-mesh barrier of the cell. "Yes, remains!" He watched Baxter's motion intently for a moment and then smacked his lips in a poor imitation of the bombardier *Brachinus*. "First thing he's said in thirty-four days," he said over his shoulder to the others. "You're definitely influencing him somehow."

The two women exchanged a look.

"Maybe you could talk for a moment to the sane people," Danielle said, reverting to her tone of murderous sweetness. "How about the words *brief* and *results*."

Petrasky was scarlet with confusion and, Baxter could tell, frustration. "I'm trying, Commissioner. I work on this all the time. All the *time*. Working. There is so much information to process and we're running out of the resources to do the job—"

"I said spare me," Danielle said. "We need to know what you have, Petrasky. Right now. If we can use it we'll see about some further funds. But can the lecture and the apologies. *Give us what you have.*"

Baxter had turned around and begun waving his behind at them. In the silence after Danielle's cold command he released a tremendous, explosive fart. Glancing around he saw that Petrasky had understood his allusion to the bombardier, and was near outright panic.

"My *God*." Danielle had recoiled, grimacing, but her look was fixed now on Baxter. "That filthy little bastard understands every word we're saying."

A lot more than that, Baxter thought, writhing in his delight. *More than your silly words.*

His voice only a hoarse whisper, Petrasky began to babble. "Two million species, the oldest terrestrial life forms, and largely defensive. He's imitating the sound and odor strategy but usually it is appearance, camouflage, like the Brazilian sphingid larva that looks like a little snake or the phasmids and butterflies just like leaves. But in colonies, too, they block entrances and spray deterrents and false trails, protecting their queens, the queens are always the . . . the soul if you will and everything depends on them, their—I'm afraid I have to say instinct for want of better—but I'm sorry it's a lecture again, isn't it? The point is, the main point, Commissioner . . ."

Baxter farted helpfully again, but this time Petrasky ignored him. The two women held themselves rigid, listening.

"I have simply been forced by my data to conclude that somehow these mental patients and certain species in the

Wastelands are either communicating by means of a sophisticated system we don't understand or they are in a significant common cycle with some third agency, which may be causative. And they are trying to converge. *Lapsis* is one of those species, but it is by no means indicated that they are generating the patterns. Patterns. I could show you—but you want the summary." Petrasky laughed hard, a burst of hysteria. "The summary is that the Ginks are behaving just like a swarming colony of—"

"My turn!" Baxter enunciated clearly, heartily. He had gotten up on two legs, and although the posture felt odd he tilted forward and came to the wire mesh at a sort of run. He nodded and winked at Danielle Konrad, almost lewdly. "My term," he went on, "our term. Might be beginning now. We're all right, the doctor and I. We know. No?"

"Termite," Petrasky said, with a pleading look at the women. "You hear?"

"All right, termite!" Baxter shivered and waggled his eyebrows. "I'm a termite, he's a termite, you're a termite too!"

"That's enough," Danielle said. She was pale, restrained, and concentrated in her fury as she wheeled to stalk toward the door. "Come on, Dorothy."

Dorothy looked mournful, sympathetic, reluctant, as she sheathed her keyboard in a belt purse.

"I'm *not* crazy!" the doctor shouted after them. "Listen! I showed you the migration patterns, superimposed, at the meeting. . . ."

Danielle had her finger on the door's electric button.

"I am calculating the convergence point! *Points!* Whole orders are gathering, and migrating like the *lapsis,* toward the giant hives where—"

The door recoiled into the wall with a sharp hiss.

"Shit house," Baxter sang. "House of shit!"

"Mud and excrement, they make them of mud and excrement," Petrasky bellowed, "best-designed structure . . . but listen, one point was organized around that female bear who took the boy and it's still together and moving with the others and *maybe its center is Ronnie Drager. . . .*"

Dorothy had already stepped through the doorway and raised her hand to brush the close button, when Danielle stopped her with a gesture. Petrasky sagged against the wire mesh, his hair sprung over his eyes, finally out of breath.

Danielle regarded him thoughtfully through the wide slot of the doorway. For a long moment no one spoke. "Maybe?"

Dr. Petrasky nodded once. He looked exhausted now, rather than desperate. "I think," he whispered. "I believe."

"Bee leavings," Baxter murmured. "Me and the doctor. He's my friend, Dr. Drone."

Dorothy began a laugh and then cut herself short. It was an odd, quick, cruel sound.

"You can provide coordinates?" Danielle was matter-of-fact, and poised her finger over the close button.

"On your desk," Petrasky said, "by the time you get back to your office."

"Good. We'll have the Special Probe look into it." She gave him a brief, subzero smile. "You'll hear the results." The door hissed shut.

Baxter was so close he could smell the other's rising anxiety before the doctor was himself aware of it. He crooned into the doctor's ear, and simultaneously touched his collar with the fingernail upon which he had gathered a pair of crab lice. "I'm feeling wonderful, Doctor. Just wonderful. Can we talk?"

The world was surely going mad. They had to point a shoulder and wedge through the ambush of mediapeople as they left the New Dawn Institute. Politician bites entomologist, that's news, Danielle thought. One man operating a boom mike kept shouting the same questions. *Are bugs really the problem? Come on, Konrad, what's the connection? Nightmare ants? Killer cockroaches?*

And of course the demand for any romantic tidbits, the latest between the Madonna and the Monster. She shrugged them all off, Dorothy covering her with follow-up stats and infobites. Every avenue being explored, every possibility, even the most fantastic—that was the impression she tried to give. Creative thinking in an emergency situation. The irony, of course, was that it was perfectly true.

The hatch down finally on their shuttlevan, Danielle collapsed into her seat, rubbing her temples and trying to yawn away tension. She was aware of Dorothy swiftly programming them into the priority lane, locking on the auto, and drawing two steaming cups of tea. The woman was a marvel. Already indispensable. And more than a touch unsettling.

Danielle frowned, crossing her legs at the ankles. That bizarre hunch, again.

"An infuriating little prick," she said. "Though brilliant, I suppose. He seemed to know you." She gave the phrase a faint inflection of inquiry.

Dorothy delivered the tea with her modest, agreeable smile. "From the conference. He told me all I will ever care to know about moths."

"That where you heard about the proposal for the border research station?" Danielle sipped tentatively, blew steam.

"Mentioned it." Dorothy had taken her seat and was cradling her own cup at her lips. "O-o-oh. Hot."

Slyboots bitch, Danielle thought, with admiration rather than malice. She prided herself on her swift, deadly accuracy in figuring other people—their private obsessions and deepest vulnerabilities—and rarely did she meet anyone who genuinely puzzled her. Her whole career, after all, was based on divining what alluring or repulsive images would compel the multitudes, and then fabricating those images.

Dorothy Smith. Who—with her kind of brains and talent —would stick with such a dud name? Who—with a body like that—wouldn't buy a little cosmetic mug work, wouldn't dress with more style? Who—above all—would choose to remain a key-pusher, an aide, a trusted behind-the-scenes staffer, when with a little more ambition . . .

"Very consistent record, the best schools and grants, and he *does* believe what he is saying." Dorothy looked earnest and alert, even as she managed another sip of tea.

Danielle nodded, but not to agree. She was thinking that of course her new chief aide could access the office mainframe from their little onboard and call up, instantly, Petrasky's entire history. The woman apparently never slept, or did programs in her dreams.

"Rather a shock, to run across somebody who believes what he says." Danielle put on a wry, informal, even sisterly look.

"Rather. Isn't it?" Dorothy wrinkled her nose, uttered a *tsk* so gentle that Danielle suspected mockery.

The bizarre idea returned. That her new aide was some

kind of sinister parasite. The kind that secretes a narcotic for the host as it feeds. The metaphor irritated Danielle, reminding her of Petrasky's various hypotheses.

The fact was simply that Dorothy had made herself indispensable to the Network very swiftly and very unobtrusively—a contradiction Danielle had not been able to explain. Yet there was nothing really so unusual. Only impeccable, thorough, selfless performance. Still, it was unnerving that plain, quiet Dorothy seemed to produce, at a moment's notice, every fact, every survey, every stat scenario requested. Clearly most of this work was done in advance, in anticipation of Danielle's need. A foresight so astute it seemed clairvoyant.

And one other nagging tiny thing. Hired as an ordinary number-cruncher, "D. Smith" had appeared on the roster of the Special Commission staff on the very day that the inner Network council had suggested the names of certain "private consultants." She had thus been around during the whole process of infiltration, including the contract for the "confirmation of a single party." The snuff.

As usual, the word generated a hitch in her mind, a sidestep. "The real question," she said, "is whether *you* believe what he says."

Dorothy appeared nonplussed, even a little alarmed.

"Oh come on, Dorothy. You've already run a set of projections on those patterns Petrasky is so nuts about, I am willing to bet." She set the cup into the well on her chair arm. Even priority lanes were getting rough these days.

Dorothy lowered her eyes, a humorous affectation. "I confess."

"Correlated with the most recent data from Sunbeam."

"Oh dear. You know, I didn't get to that."

Danielle watched her assistant color and look flustered, then swivel her chair around to reach the keyboard. A very good act. A woman as devious and deep as they come. She had taken to leaving the last step for her superior to initiate, to guarantee at least a facsimile of a chain of command.

"Skip it. Just tell me whether you believe the doctor. Ronnie, the termites, the Ginks, the whole thing." Danielle was surprised at the weariness, the irritation, the need she heard in her own voice. "We haven't got time for games anymore."

Dorothy arrested her keystrokes and looked around from

the screen. For the briefest of moments her gaze was level, neutral, entirely calculating. "Maybe," she said calmly, "it *is* all just a game?"

It was Danielle's turn to be startled, but before she could reply she felt the seat pressing into her. They were decelerating. Exactly what she could not, in this crisis, allow. Everything depended now on momentum. She hissed an obscenity.

Dorothy had already switched her monitor to the outside camera and cut them into the Transit Security channel. They saw that all lanes of the Trunkway were jammed, and ahead the first crane copters had descended, their lights flashing phosphorescent through the haze. The voice on the TS channel was talking about unfortunate timing, multilane blockage at rush hour, delays of forty-five minutes or possibly more.

"Goddamn it," Danielle said through her teeth. "Goddamn it to hell. We *have* to talk to Bennett before that Commission meeting. If that little PacRim pig gets the floor to himself. . . . How long—"

"Twenty-five minutes at the very best," Dorothy said. Her fingers were a blur over the keyboard, and the auxiliary dash monitor was crammed with figures and vector lines. "We're in line for a relief copter now. But the gridlock is expanding pretty fast and we have some major players on the list."

Danielle had squeezed her eyes shut, creating a deep chisel-mark between her brows. "Get through to Frank and tell him we can't talk today. While you're at it check the board for any Sunbeam transmission. Maybe they'll postpone the meeting. Mother of God, what is happening to this world?"

She had been planning to crush Fat finally and for good at this meeting. When he had made his absurd bluff, his hint that his agents had taken the boy hostage, she had sensed a target of opportunity. It was, however, a moving target.

Midsummer, and they had reached the cusp of their own publicity surge. The story of little Ronnie had reverberated throughout the world, a *cause célèbre* that embroiled not only the major NorthAm parties and the Fed, but interest groups of every possible stripe—the futurists, the primitives, the maxpros and ecominis, bornagains and theophobes. Everyone had seen the homemade holo of the boy on his Whopper-Wheels. Everyone had seen the scarface father who was once a deputy minister. And everyone knew of the fiery, dark affair between this cripple and the rising Progressive media witch.

She knew well enough, however, the risks of feeding the public deep, potent images. The mass was ravenous, unpredictable, capable of reversing itself and striking like a maddened snake. One had to play upon its instincts, its terrors and lusts, with the finesse of a great violinist. But a single jarring note—a cough, a baby's cry, a moth in the footlights—could shatter the spell of a great performance.

And just at this point she had realized Frank was becoming difficult. His intensity was now more sinister than pathetic, so she had taken the risk of letting him join Sunbeam. And Fat had found it out. He would plant rumors, and any hint of a cooling affair might be damaging to their public image.

Danielle fought back the first pang of an incipient despair. She was deliberately keeping herself from thinking about the absolute worst case. Ronnie Drager alive, and in addition hale and coherent, reunited with his family. She knew that was impossible, of course. Anyone could guess the outcome of an encounter with the most dangerous and degenerate species left on the planet. He could not have survived. *Would* not survive. She had insurance. . . . Again her mind sidestepped.

All depended on the queen, Petrasky had said. At least that much she agreed with. She had herself, single-handedly, focused those powerful, cooperative interests that could reorganize the world and direct it in a sane and predictable fashion. Not in the manner of a mindless swarm, but with purpose, to give all creation a meaningful end—the ultimate human dream. A world managed, finally and in every detail, by the dominant, the highest, the only fully conscious species.

"Well well," Dorothy said. She looked pleased in a peculiar way.

Danielle glanced at the screen, saw wrecked vehicles dangling from crane copters, heard the tail end of a phrase: ". . . rendered treacherous by the millions of crushed bodies."

"What?" she said irritably.

"Locusts." Dorothy's smile broadened. "A plague of locusts. And then the garbage deer."

"Did *what?*" Danielle's own grin was simply the result of clenched teeth. She was trying to listen with one ear to the news droning on, catch an estimate of how much more time would be required to clear the mess.

"Apparently they flew in off the desert, and escaped notice until they began to converge on the Trunkway. A kind of storm, only they caked up windscreens faster than wipers could clear them and so many were mashed under wheels that . . . Whew! You can imagine."

Danielle realized her secretary was laughing at her, waiting. "Deer?" she managed to get out.

"Oh yes. Well, then quite a little herd of garbage deer ran into a guard fence. They kept piling up, until they made a kind of ramp and could jump over and into the Trunkway. Caused some nasty collisions. Since the locusts had made the visibility so poor." Dorothy beamed, her hands poised over the keyboard. "Isn't it *funny,* after our lecture tour this morning. . . ."

"Don't tempt me," Danielle hissed. "And stop smiling like an idiot. Call the office and see if Petrasky has filed the coordinates. If he has—"

"Yes, of course. I'm very sorry." Dorothy had turned back to the screen, her fingers again a blur of motion. It was an insolent gesture, in some indefinable way. It meant that she had no need of orders. The coordinates would be flashed immediately to their deep contact aboard Sunbeam. As if it were already obvious that they would gamble on Petrasky, that something more than coincidental irony connected the termites on Baxter's brain and the locusts fouling their itinerary.

A third agent. Causative. An unknown factor. Or force. A fucking *something* had gathered itself around Ronald Drager and was moving south toward . . . what? Even the bugs knew, and obeyed. An enemy. She remembered that in some orders if a new queen hatches there is a mortal combat with the old. She was abruptly afraid she was losing her mind.

"Coordinates on file," Dorothy said in her perfect secretarial tone. There was something oddly familiar about this voice, an echo from another context . . . but where? "Coding now for Sunbeam transmission." She had stopped striking keys and was only staring into the screen as the onboard chuckled and hummed. Then she turned to Danielle, sunny again. "Looks like a trip to the beach."

35

GOING INTO COMMANDER YAMAGUCHI'S QUARTERS, CHIEF
Medical Officer Bradshaw had to work on himself, rearrange
his face so that his demonic exhilaration would not show. In
his hand was a simple clearance card programmed with a
request for an unrestricted miniprobe in a specimen-transport
vehicle with light armor and a crew of three. In his pocket
were the coordinates Ears had flashed to him less than two
hours ago.

"Sam," he said genially, touching two thick fingers to his
brow, "things are coming together. Time for a field check.
Might be on to something." He spun the card across the
commander's desk, assured and careless as a casino dealer.

Yamaguchi made no move to pick up the card. He had
looked up as Bradshaw entered the cabin, and so far had
neither glanced away nor blinked. His face was fixed in an
ingratiating smile.

"Ah, Bradsaw. Sit down please. Coffee?"

"No thanks." He patted his beltline. "Touch of something.
Also, I'm whacked enough already, on this one."

"I am so anxious." Yamaguchi uttered an odd wheeze,
almost inaudible. It was his laugh, like a pump switching on
and off. "What have you got."

Bradshaw sprawled, grinning, in the chair before the desk.
Yamaguchi, he had decided early on, was not overrated. The
man missed nothing and revealed very little. In the last few
days Bradshaw thought he detected a slight, indefinable shift
in the commander's attitude—a hint of wariness and curiosity.
Perhaps a suspicion that his medical officer was not entirely
what he seemed.

"Geneprint from the campsite. It's our man, all right. Cold
but not that cold. Eighty-five klicks from the bike. He's moving west and south like the Ginks."

Yamaguchi picked up the clearance card and his wheezy

pump went on and then instantly off. "So you want to go for him?"

"We better. A big operation would get crowded and confused. Some grunt could accidentally pickle Mr. Feiffer's pepper for him."

The pump ran a little longer this time. "Ah, Bradsaw. You are very funny." Yamaguchi inserted the card in his desk drive, watched the recessed monitor.

"He could be very useful, I understand. A possible asset. Witness maybe."

Yamaguchi hummed, as if mildly interested, though he was still watching the screen.

"Ergo, we ought to locate him immediately. Then unscrew him gently, turn him slow. Do a real clean job. No rush like last time."

Yamaguchi glanced up, amused. "Very big job for small crew. Only you and Perkins and Stavich?"

"Anything more would just get in the way. Guy's alone, on foot now, a few days' rations at best. Somebody's going to find him real soon. Might as well be us." Bradshaw was still grinning, but he watched the commander with unusual concentration.

"You know," Yamaguchi said with the slight emphasis that was, for him, the highest enthusiasm, "our special envoy would very much like to accompany you, if this were to be."

"Appreciate it," Bradshaw said smoothly. He was ready for such an appeal. "But this is not an S and D expedition. We're not going to waste any moves snuffing Ginks. And that's what our Mr. Evans is here to do. He's ferocious at it. We're tracking a rogue, to collect him alive. Different ball game."

"You are sure Feiffer does not have the boy."

Bradshaw laughed at this utterance, so perfectly balanced. Equal parts implied question and tentative conclusion.

"This boy," Bradshaw said through his dying chuckle. "This boy is—in my humble opinion—already Gink meat at this point."

"Ah? Only a bluff? But surely—"

"Not even a *good* bluff." Bradshaw leaned forward, placing one large, hairy hand on the edge of the commander's desk. "Fat's desperate. Buying time. Your boss, Sam, is leaving this picture. A fuckup so colossal they haven't even figured out what to do to him yet."

There was a brief silence. Bradshaw was perfectly aware that a medical officer had no license to talk to a probe commander in this fashion. Of course every word went on holo, and Yamaguchi controlled the security archives. He was Insec, but detached to a grand jury investigation, so he could dismiss Bradshaw summarily or even clap him in the brig for slandering a superior. What the commander presumably did not know was that his big, vulgar subordinate received the most secret communiqués from headquarters before anyone else. Bradshaw thus already knew that the investigating Commission had a code shield deeper than Insec's and had opened a file on Fat. The tentative charge was treason.

"The assignment," Yamaguchi said primly, "is to locate the boy or compile physical evidence of his fate."

"Absolutely." Bradshaw's grin widened. "Get the specimens. And this one, this renegade, we need alive and in possession."

"PJ is very quick, very dangerous." Yamaguchi put on an almost droll expression of concern. "One of the best."

"Heard the same thing about Skiho," Bradshaw said. "Two ordinary grunts took him down, no problem. Hey, we've pretty much got the guy cornered in this quadrant, and we'll be careful. Possible witness, like I said. And there *will* be trials after this fandango, Sam, am I right?"

Yamaguchi shook his head and sighed, regretful. Bradshaw could almost hear him running through options like a rat in a maze. A power balance was shifting rapidly, so of course there would be trials. Anyone closely identified with extreme Con policy was potentially vulnerable. A new director for Insec was almost a certainty. And Yamaguchi, as senior field officer on loan to this investigation, was clean, in a strong position to bid for the appointment. But why—Bradshaw assumed the commander was asking himself—would his on-board Medical allude so pointedly to eventual prosecutions, unless the doctor was already part of the new power structure, was hinting that this was an opportunity for Yamaguchi to advance himself brilliantly?

Both of them knew that a skilled practitioner could, in no more than a few days, reprogram a hostile captive into a compliant informer. Whether or not the hostage story was a fiction, Feiffer might be hammered into a new role as conscience-stricken ex-conspirator or gullible tool. Medicated and guided, such a creature could supply formal testimony—and soon afterward suffer an unfortunate fatal accident. Only a few days' delay, a certain discretion and hesitation, would be necessary.

"Very interesting." Yamaguchi made the phrase innocuous, a comment on life in general. "So many aspects. The father, you know, is in agreement with you. Even if his son were alive, at this point, he is. . . ." He shrugged.

"Meat," Bradshaw finished for him. "Worse than dead. He's right. Very tough fella, Drager. I like him, what I've seen. But not on this trip, Sam."

"And then," Yamaguchi went on, as if he were not listening, "the curious question of the female trainee, the experiment. You assure me—"

"Do indeed." Bradshaw delivered his heartiest salvo of laughter. He was at his best lying outright. "Think about it. They smeared her prints all over the Scooter and abandoned it, to look like an escape. Then they wiped her. Had to discredit their own experiment *partially*, see? Leave the impression the bitch was clever enough to get away—that's radical Con ideology—and yet get rid of her before the whole scandal blew."

"In my experience," Yamaguchi said a bit stiffly, "the rare Gink is capable of more than theory would predict."

If you only knew, Bradshaw thought. The coordinates from Ears, what they had dredged out of Skiho, his own hunch based on listening to chatter through darkside channels—it all told him that this Duskyrose had flummoxed Insec's two top agents and made off with the Drager kid. PJ was hunting her, probably mad with rage, and Bradshaw had a fix on them both.

Ears had screwed a priceless clue out of that baby boy genius at the conference. The whole Gink nation was connecting up somehow, some way—crazy as it sounded—with a little coastal zone, known only to a few experts, a desert valley where a strange colony survived. A series of earthen dolmens—Ears had flashed him the sat blowups—rude columns of bugshit and dirt. A weird species of termite, very old and apparently significant to the Ginks in their primitive myth-system.

He knew, in his bones, that if the dominant Ginks were gathering there, the kid would be with them. All he needed was the cover of a small, controllable, routine scouting expedition—and a little luck. PJ was already irrelevant, except as corroboration. If they found him they would take him; if not, no great matter. Ears had estimated that if something was going down, it would be in the next few days. A full moon, she noted, was only three nights away.

"They're overrated." Bradshaw wrinkled his nose at Yamaguchi. "Except as a pest. I agree with Mr. Evans. Planet would be a lot nicer place without them. *He* knows what they can do."

A new light on his desk top caught Yamaguchi's eye and he flipped on the intercom channel. "Speaking of our devil," he said and looked up at Bradshaw. "He is waiting to see me just now."

Bradshaw threw up his hands with a winsome smile. "So? Shall I go after PJ?"

They looked into each other's eyes for a long moment, and then Yamaguchi's wheezy laugh-pump switched on briefly. "Oh yes," he said. "Of course. I had almost forgot why you came." He hit a few keys and after the exit signal withdrew Bradshaw's card, which he dealt back to its owner. "And as you wish I will not mention anything to Frank. Although you two might get along very well."

"No doubt. Maybe later when we got time to score a few flops. The scouts say he's a master marksman."

Yamaguchi wheezed. Bradshaw understood. They were all killers here. It was now and had always been a profession with a bright future. The commander pressed a button and the door behind them slid open.

"Listen, Sam, thanks a load." Bradshaw got up, grinning like a wolf, and touched the two fingers again to his hairline. "I won't forget."

Yamaguchi nodded and gave him a final, penetrating glance. The commander had to know, by now, that this balding, loud-mouthed bear represented a hidden new authority. The Network, he would assume, was the coming power. Everyone would assume so. And they would all be wrong.

Bradshaw foresaw how the Network would exist only to serve the secret feeders, Hindmost and Blueballs and Gorgon, Ears and Snuffer and their hungry cohorts.

As he turned to greet Frank Drager his features were briefly stretched, distorted by a bubble of high glee. An incongruous expression with which to confront the most notorious ruin of a human face, the emblem now of suffering and fierce retribution.

"Hiya, sir, how's it going?"

"You've met the doctor, our medical officer," Yamaguchi said. "We've just been chatting."

"Chatting." Drager's one eye had the disconcerting quality of a telescope, a magnifier of hidden or camouflaged emplacements.

"About the Gink bitch, this Duskyrose, all that Insec potpooperie," Bradshaw went on in his bold blather. "Which you've heard a big load of. I sympathize, man. After what—"

"Shut up." Drager's eye turned toward Yamaguchi. "Medical officer?"

Yamaguchi moved between them, lifted a hand to indicate to Bradshaw the still open door. "Yes. So, Doctor, thank you. . . ."

"I do understand, man. We're just doin' the job, the rest of us. Now *you*"—he stabbed a finger at Drager—"you got the real fire." His exhilaration could no longer be contained. He erupted into laughter. "With you, man. You're the final judge." Bradshaw strolled toward the door, still laughing.

"Who is this asshole?" Drager hissed at Yamaguchi.

"I'll bring you everything, Mr. Evans. Every last scrap." Bradshaw waved gaily, exiting. Drager was someone he instinctively respected. The man had a passion strong enough to burn away all traces of comforting illusion. He saw through the floss and foolery of compassion. He deserved a clean job on his son. He needed some remains, more than a lock of hair at least, something to mark the memory and lay the ghosts to rest. Snuffer would supply a fitting token, maybe a whole handsome corpse. Guaranteed.

36

"Jesus Christ, Tickles, help me." PJ was hugging himself, trying to control his shivering. "Talk to me, tell me a story about the old days. Just don't explain any fucking more about shadows or eating each other or any of that Gink shit. I'm losing it, man, I'm losing it, I need a razor or a slowglo or *something*. . . ."

He trailed off and after a few moments began to breathe heavily, gasping. They were crouched in the very faint glow from an airshaft mostly filled with debris. It was a dead-end spur, but even here bodies littered the floor of the tunnel: rats, squirrels, snakes, burrow deer, a raccoon, an old Pobla man and woman. Two guards squatted in the gloom where the spur forked away toward a main trunk. From this direction they could hear a continuous rustle.

"Stop," Teeklo said quietly. "Try to stop. We have to go on soon. Not far, and then tomorrow perhaps we will see—"

"Out." PJ coughed the word. *"Out."*

Teeklo could just make out that Tima's eyes were closed. She had not spoken for hours, had been more or less a somnambulist. Exhausted, he supposed, from the original effort of capturing and sustaining the piksi man's *kubi*. She had expended too much, and now had to gather herself for the ceremony. If she was allowed to live that long.

"There is no out," he said in a quiet, empty tone, "and no in. No up and no down."

"Fuck that." PJ sounded on the verge of choking. "There's light up there. I could see, I could *move*. . . ."

"You could die, very quickly."

"Good. Wonderful. Better than this." PJ laughed, then retched with surprising strength for half a minute, getting out a thin string of bile and drool, which he carefully wiped free of his jaw with two fingers of one hand.

"Possibly. Many feel that way and have gone. But you don't mean it."

For a time there was no sound but the distant rustling and PJ's labored breathing. "Man," he said finally, and when he went on some of the hysteria in his voice had been replaced by wonder. "How did you stand it, at the beginning?"

"The boy did it," Teeklo said coldly. "I did it. And we had no chemical help. That's part of your problem. Also, you know, I came here because I *wanted* to."

"Living with goddamned rats in the ground? Crawling in holes full of dead shit? Eating old Ginks?" PJ laughed, a thin shriek. "You had to be insane."

"Pobla," Teeklo said wearily. "Try to say Pobla."

"Eating old Pobla. *Tough* old Pobla."

"So much nobler to kill rats." Teeklo spoke quietly, with a trace of amusement. "Dump dead shit into someone else's hole. Bury corpses in concrete, so nothing can be nourished."

"Okay, okay." PJ shook his head. "I grant that. Something badly fucked up about civilization. But it was good enough for her, for eight years. The queen of double cross. She fit right in. Absolutely fucking fooled us."

"No difference between fooling and trying to tell someone about themselves." Tima's voice was barely audible, rapid and light. She did not open her eyes. "I have just strength enough to give you the truth again. The boy is here because he followed his shadow. If you came after him then you must find yours too. Soon. Before you die."

"Well well. The Bomber speaks. Right, right. I realize. I'm crazy too. But I just want to go crazy in the *light*, okay? Die upstairs in the fucking *sun*, all right? Oh yeah, and know *why* the fuck we are insane this particular way, humping through this filth in the dark like a—"

"You must stop thinking in circles. Stop thinking, in fact." Teeklo saw that Tima had fallen away, back into herself again. He sighed in envy and glanced toward the guards, who still would not meet his eyes.

"Of course," he went on, and favored PJ with a thin smile, "neither of us were much good at following orders."

"Fact." PJ smiled back wanly. "Guess that's why she says I belong here too. And also why, that other time, I didn't take you. You remember?"

"I remember." Teeklo nodded once. "I appreciated that."

"I just thought you'd whacked out completely, so leave it alone. And the beard. The beard was—is—weird. But later, you know, I mean years later, I thought maybe you weren't so crazy. . . ."

"And now you have a close look, you think maybe you were right to begin with." Teeklo laughed, and noted that the guards looked at him finally, a very swift and covert look. Everyone knew he laughed rarely. The more perceptive had remarked that he tended to do so mostly in perilous situations. "I keep the beard as habitat—an idea revolting to most piksis, I'm sure. But it makes sense and I could show you, if anything was normal. But—" He tipped his head toward the distant rustling, the guards. "It is confused here too. The boy, Tima, you, me—we come and suddenly there are copters and augurcraft and troops everywhere, probing and hunting and killing. Right when certain important ceremonies have to be conducted. The old Pobla are afraid, suspicious, wondering if we are agents of all this destruction. And I . . . I end up wondering the same thing."

"So just little Ronnie, he's the only thing keeping us alive, right?" PJ twirled a finger at his temple. "Talk about screwy irony. And his ass depends on that old Gink you were telling me about. I mean Pobla. The prophetess."

"We told you, there is no 'little Ronnie' here and we don't know if he's ever coming back. But yes, everything depends on Adza, the old woman. And she was very upset at Pahane's running off with Tima, then showing up with you. Just before this ceremony."

"Jealous." This time PJ's laugh was a genuine, hearty hoot. "I could see why. For a couple of kids, they were really laying into each other. So we got one schizo kid, a hybrid mojo girl, and two crazy renegades, all hanging on the whim of a pissed-off, senile witch. What a future."

Teeklo threw back his head and laughed for the second time, and as he did so the guards stood up, spears in hand. In a moment they drew back against the tunnel wall to allow a group to come through. It was Kapu and four others, all of them bearing spears decorated with braided hair, all with fresh, bloody incisions on their cheeks and upper chests. They halted two strides away, and Kapu began speaking immediately, rhythmically, keeping time with the butt of his spear against the floor.

Teeklo looked into the unsmiling face of his old friend and felt, for the first time in many years, a full measure of anxiety. That face was like a stone, without warmth. Yet the voice was charged with force, and Teeklo could hear a resonance of torment, a *kubi* caged and forbidden to show itself. The old Pobla came as a drum, a pure message, keeping time because the ceremony was now underway and would move as precisely as the stars.

The *tak tagak* was going to meet the Hive Dwellers. She had spoken, but for the first time in many generations the Council could not agree on her words. She seemed to want the piksi boy, the *delo tagak,* to go with her, singing rock-enroll. Such a thing had never been done before. Some elders said he was an offering; others argued the Hive Dwellers would fold his *kubi* into hers and Adza would return a young Pobla woman. Either way, it had been decided all piksis must attend, so *wonakubi* could give a sign. Sacrifice or transformation. They would be escorted first to the purification, then to the holy place, near the Great Center.

"*Na,*" Teeklo managed to get out. "*Vasan.*"

"Jesus, what *is* this?"

Teeklo did not answer but pulled PJ to his feet. He saw that Tima's eyes were open now, black and deep. She sat in a huddle, waiting. Her figure, as he watched, seemed to blur slightly or become less substantial. She was all at once less a presence than an image, behind which a kind of radiance was gathering.

Teeklo breathed deeply. He was, he realized, closer than he had ever been to seeing another, the *kubi* beneath the warp of matter. Kapu went on with his chant, saying that the Council had discussed and decided that the creature Tima was no longer Pobla, and therefore would be treated as piksi too. She would go with the others, but she was not to touch them, or any Pobla either. Nor was she to speak or anyone to speak to her in any language. She was perhaps *tak pakish tagak,* a great shadow-swallower, and if so the Dwellers would take her.

Kapu struck three times hard against the stone under his feet and then wheeled to lead the others along the tunnel toward the main corridor. Teeklo waited until the image of Tima had undulated past him and traveled into the darkness before he moved. He took PJ's hand and began to pull him along, gently but insistently.

"Holy shit," he heard the other whisper. "What did he say? And did you see that mojo of hers? You see what I mean? She looks . . . what the hell is going *on* here?"

Teeklo did not turn around but spoke fiercely into the darkness, the dim forms moving ahead of him, shadows on shadows. "Don't talk," he said. "Don't think. Please *don't fucking think anymore.*"

37

SHE HAD SWALLOWED HIM. THE MAD, BAD BOY, THE FISH of fire, the great golden-eyed toad—all of him. For days he had squatted always within sight of her, singing his repertoire of the old songs. The wheels of Proud Mary, the white rabbit, a girl made of brown sugar. He did the same ones over and over, and each time she swayed and crooned and gibbered with delight, as if the melodies were exciting and new.

She had let him live, he thought at first, because he was simply her radio. But then he lost himself in the songs, found a beat—heavier and faster than he remembered—that sent spurts of energy through him. The attendants and guards picked it up, stamped their feet, gyrated in abandon. He realized she was using him, and the new tempo, to spin herself faster and faster. And the energy that developed was that of *naku,* only at a much greater order of magnitude.

That made it difficult for him not to think about Tima. And the old woman could usually tell if he was remembering their time in the cave. She would frown and mumble and hit him sometimes with her small fist, surprisingly hard. When he was first sent before her, after his running away, she had bent to smell him between the legs. What she found drove her to pummel him with all her might, shrieking in anger.

He had, however, prepared himself. He kept steady and told her emphatically, three times, that if Tima was harmed he would never sing again, never speak again to any Pobla. She raged at him, threw a bowl at him, bit him on the forearm. Then she appeared to forget the matter entirely. Until a half hour later when they went through the whole thing again, and then Adza summoned old Tsitsi and commanded the ordeal.

The following day they washed off all his *tagak* paint and lashed him to pegs wedged in the rock. The old ones gathered and began a long chant, a retelling of the beginnings when the Hive Dwellers awoke and shaped the world. Then two guards brought in what he thought at first was simply a little woven mat. Only when they approached to lay it upon his bare chest did he see, and hear, what it was. One side of the mat hummed and shimmered, for some painstaking weaver had threaded or stitched dozens of wasps there. Held by a grass loop above the abdomen, partly stupefied with smoke, they were furious wasps, already jabbing convulsively with their venomous barbs.

He had no time to try the techniques Tima had talked about, to release his *kubi* from his body. The first shock of pain, icy and bitter, was followed by an immense, heavy agony. A white-hot anvil had been dropped into his chest, and his skull rang with the high, fierce buzzing of the wasps. He felt his eyeballs and tongue swell; the blood in his veins seemed like molten sulfur, and every nerve in his frame was wired to the jerking abdomens of the wasps. After his first convulsion and gasp he was laboring to fill his lungs, to scream, when he heard the Old Rat-Herder tell him cheerfully that if he made a sound they would kill Tima and feed her to him.

He passed out, mercifully, and when he came back his *kubi* had found a way out on its own. He remembered, from the night storm of his *tchat* raid, and did not allow himself to be startled when he looked down on his own body, writhing and twisting. He was poised at a distance, light, alert, calm—a shadow free of its origin.

The others in the cave were watching the wasps, listening to the air sucking and blowing out of his lungs. Only Adza was looking at him inside the shadow. Or rather what was within Adza looked out through her and watched. Something immense, sinuous, knowing. He understood that it was nothing like jealousy or anger, nothing like any word he knew. When it enfolded him a moment later he was too stunned by its power even to whimper.

So she swallowed him. The power was a she. He rested in an invisible womb, sealed away from his pain, which was now like a lush, fantastic jungle seen through a window. He understood that *wonakubi* had taken him, finally. His life, Tima's life, Teeklo's—they rode on his every breath and yet he breathed as softly and easily as a baby. He *was* only breath, a rhythm, a flow of invisible being.

Teeklo had explained how the power came through Adza because her mind offered so little resistance: the dross of memory and desire and hope had burnt away, leaving only certain conduits—music, the tiny golden apples, ceremonies. She, too, was nothing more than a puff of wind, gone into *wonakubi*.

What was left of her ghost in the ordinary world skimped along mostly on scents and sounds, tastes and touch. She sniffed and fondled and struck at the beings around her only to orient herself, to clear a way for the next invasion of the power. He had seen it come as a great serpent, but knew from the chants that it could as well be a bear or butterfly. These were only icons, he knew now, images to hold against a light that would otherwise blind. Just as the scattered words of the *tak tagak,* in her fit, reduced and weakened mystery so that all could approach it.

But explanations had become only an irritating, meaningless buzzing to him. In the womb of power, surrounded by a sea of pain, he simply *knew*. The lesson and the pain were one: that the *naku* between himself and Tima was indeed dangerous; their wildness and youth, their cat-and-deer games, could whirl them asunder, away from the holy center, in this time of ultimate peril. Adza had inhaled the reek of selfish passion, and decreed the ordeal—either to destroy them or to forge their connection to *wonakubi*.

He saw there was no malice in the old woman, this tiny, withered thing with eyes that glittered like a snake's. She was simply burrowing toward the light, and he, with his singing, helped her gather and focus what strength remained to her. She in turn had helped him, acted as a reverse midwife, pulling him into the womb with her. They were a twinned embryo now.

They were both dying, too. *Yano* was the bright, liquid dark in which they were suspended. He felt the great river, running silent, running deep, all around them. For Adza it would be leaving behind the little burnt husk of her body. But for him and for Tima. . . . What she had said came back to him—finding Ronald again, returning to the piksi world —and for one moment he was shaken by terror, and almost cried out.

Pahane—what would happen to Pahane? The *tchat* raider and long runner, the mad, wild shadow that had lived under his ribs and in the cave of his skull for nearly a year, the ghost that came out of the smoke to teach him everything he now lived by? That shadow took a long stride back toward his body, still heaving and shuddering under the striking wasps. He was one gasp away from destruction.

In that instant he saw Adza open her mouth, saw the head of the serpent, felt its coiling shift the whole earth. He opened his own mouth, but instead of a scream he emitted a thick shaft of power too, an undulating twin to the mazy column pouring forth from the ancient Pobla. The two writhed together, inverted themselves, so that each was swallowing the tail of the other, and then the ring they made caught fire, brightened as a sun.

But he could look at it, look into its heart, and he saw that Snaketongue was nothing but a word, Tima another, Adza a third. They could be sung, then were gone into this ring of fire. Everything—the Pobla and piksi alike, along with every being that swam or crawled or soared—fell into this sun and emerged from it. One serpent surrounded darkness and transformed it into light; the other swallowed light to feed its dark body.

From that moment on he had been as calm and boundless as an empty summer sky. After the ordeal of the wasps he sang and sang, with very little rest. Always he was aware of Adza, his twin who would be born first, moving ahead of him like the edge of day traveling over the face of the world. The turmoil around them no longer occupied him. He knew the killers were at work, moving nearer despite the thousands who stepped into *yano* each day. He could smell the fear everywhere—not fear of mortal death, but of ghosts being eaten by *Mudlati*, the vanishing of all the *kubin*, of everything Pobla. The fear of living without a shadow, of becoming only live meat.

So he was already on his feet on the last day, when Adza rose and indicated she would move under her own power. He walked beside her and she leaned on him, mumbling along with the chanting from her attendants. The Old Rat-Herder came first, then Kapu and his spear-carriers, then the *tchat* young raiders, then others. Among them, he knew, would be Tima and Teeklo and the piksi man; he had heard Adza's pronouncement and knew they would be part of the final company. Already he could feel Tima's presence, a hidden lodestar, and he worked to keep that gravitational pull at a steady distance.

Most of the Pobla were dispersing, filtering back into seldom-used tunnels or excavating new connecting branches, diverting the advancing piksi troops from the place of the Great Hives. Other beings, too, were traveling and coalescing. When a burrow approached the surface, or at the occasional airshaft, they could sometimes hear a drumming of hooves or the thunder of wings; and sometimes an area thronged with life and stank of death—rats and frogs and bats and moths and rabbit and deer and raccoons scurrying, lunging, flapping into and along and out again from the tunnels, some of which were choked with the half-decayed corpses of these same creatures.

Now, however, they were moving in a wider shaft that was utterly deserted and swept clean. Two of Kapu's group bore torches, whose thick, yellow tongues revealed startling figures on the stone walls of the corridor. These figures had been made by smearing mud of various hues into hieroglyphs and shapes. There were slashes and hooks—an alphabet he had never seen before—and drawings of many animals, some contained in the stomachs or wombs of others.

In his empty mind the figures began to synchronize with the chanting of the company, illustrating the narrative of the origins of the Pobla. The opening of the world, a spinning vortex which created the inside and outside, the shells and cores of the first beings. Then the fusion of these beings into a larger being: a jointed thing that could move, swim, crawl, run, fly. . . .

The swift gathering of the larger beings into a mass. The cloud rising, thickening, becoming a tower. The final division—the striking of the first shadow, the world of shadows. The *kubin* swarming and whirling into a new vortex: *wonakubi* the whirlwind, pulling nothingness into being, being into nothingness. A maze, a dance, a twisting together and unraveling of all creatures out of threads of light and dark: a silent, endless, intricate weaving.

He still moved with Adza, step for slow step in rhythm with the chant. The corridor widened and the stone floor tilted upward under them. Gray light filtered in now from a large airshaft. They were moving in a spiral, a tightening curve, toward the surface. Then a thin shaft of light broke through a crack overhead. Something glinted there, drifting and falling.

Under the chant he could hear a sighing, a rustling, a whispering barely audible but vast as the wind over the sea. He did not know the language and yet this voice, itself made up of countless voices, seemed to move in him and through him, so that he understood they were being summoned, drawn upward to the sun. There were now wider cracks overhead, admitting beams of light where the glittering flakes stormed like snow.

One final turn and they were at the base of a series of shelves of stone, a kind of broad, rough stairway that rose and narrowed to an opening. In this aperture were heaps of brightness, swirling clouds of the shimmering flakes. Two from Kapu's squadron came up beside Adza and lifted her off her feet. They mounted the stone steps, and he came right behind, his hand still fastened on the frail stick of the old woman's arm.

He felt the soft brushes on his cheeks and shoulders as he came through the opening, saw the tiny, narrow fan-shapes, translucent but for their black lacework of veins. Wings—a flashing, tumbling cascade of thousands of wings, with here and there an amber, writhing body. Through this swirling veil loomed towers of earth, caked and creviced, slumped and leaning, tall and squat; and from these rude columns came the vast whispering, a sound so dense and ubiquitous it seemed to come from the earth itself.

Simultaneous with their emerging into the light, they opened their mouths; their *kubin* passed out of them and joined again in the ring of fire. It was a pattern created by the dolmens, as a magnet bends fragments of iron into the space around it. There were three bodies, all dead, all empty. Then one of them began to move, and the others to see.

The seeing was at first like waking from one dream into another. He felt the feathery weight of the wings accumulating on his shoulders, saw the frail, old creature tottering away, heard the chant faintly echoing the incessant rustling. Yet these impressions were utterly strange, as if glimpsed through a hole in a curtain between two worlds without cognizance of each other.

The clouds of bright flakes whirled about the stick figure of the ancient Pobla, so that she was becoming simultaneously indistinct and more luminous. She was approaching one of the earthen towers, and as she did so its pocked surface began to coruscate and turn a dark gold, as if light were melting into it. The old one's shoulders and elbows flexed and drew in, their sharpness folding away, so the bulb of her skull became more prominent; the claws of her hands and feet took hold on the seething surface of the tower.

It seemed to give way, hollowing out as she inched along, the whole surface molten and roiling. There was another shape emerging from within, also elongate, with thin limbs folded tight under a sheath of bright gauze. They met and clung fast, the globular heads rocking, pecking, fastening tight. All around them the brightness swarmed and pulsed, as they began to spin and then went on spinning, spinning, spinning, ever faster.

38

"HERE," BRADSHAW WHISPERED HOARSELY, LOOKING UP from the 3-D seismogram to check the panoramic view of the little valley on the main monitor. "Perfect."

Beside him Stavich nodded and frowned at the same time. "Big old burrow. We should fit okay, without any slump." He wrapped one hand around the augur joystick and began to move it experimentally, watching the cross-section of the shaft tilt and rotate. "Only thing is, we got a lot of sand here. Pretty fine stuff. Can get in the tread bearings and burn 'em."

Bradshaw grinned, waggled his eyebrows. "So we call a field repair unit. Or make Sam send us a whole new craft. Now let us be boring, my good man. Tre-e-e-mendously boring." He laced his fingers together, raised his elbows like wings to crack his knuckles. "Before we come out . . . with a bang. Hey?" He chuckled, leaned back, as Stavich cranked the augur cautiously.

The *Forager,* a hybrid vehicle designed for reconnaissance and specimen collection, settled slowly into the hillside. The augur was widening the entrance to a burrow, musty and long abandoned according to their quick core samples, but perfectly positioned to overlook the small basin where the rude sentinels of mud stood motionless. As he screwed the *Forager* in, Stavich was also flipping switches to vacuum away whatever dust the blades stirred up and to spray out a film of odor suppressant.

Competent, Bradshaw thought, if unimaginative. Even a sharp Gink tracker, unless he drifted nearer than fifteen yards, would be unable to detect Stavich's cammie job. A coyote or a brush cat was another story, but the terrain wouldn't support that kind of life. Any kind of life, actually, except these termites and their Shithenge.

A spooky spot, even for Bradshaw in his mood of incredible electric excitement. He had known from his first glimpse of it that Ears was right, this would be the place. A barren amphitheater where light reflected and trembled, like water in a cup, and then the weird dark heaps. Blind witnesses, waiting for nothing but the shortening and elongation of their own shadows.

He knew they were full of swarming insects—chewing, secreting, tending their monstrous queens. He had called up a standard little field holo, learned with amazement the proportions and life cycle of this giant bag of bug eggs. She was too bloated to move, never left the hive. She did nothing but mate and lay eggs. She depended on hordes of puny workers—one-fiftieth her size—to masticate and stuff her food, wipe and suck clean her asshole.

You knew the Ginks had to be degenerate, if they would worship this thing. You saw the stupidity of the old sentimental beliefs. Natural beauty, sanctity of life, et cetera. All laughable if you watched what animals mostly did. Eat, spawn, shit, and die. He made a face, glanced at Stavich, but the man was concentrating on his controls. A certain advantage, in having no imagination.

By the time they were sunk into the hillside, Bradshaw had noticed another spooky element in the scene. The *Forager* was completely buried under a mantle of loose soil, except for one ventilation port and the video eye, concealed inside a facsimile of a small outcropping of rock. He had been watching for signs of birds or other insects, since the Ginks used these creatures as lookouts. But there were none. The little basin was absolutely empty, the air clear as glass, no movement anywhere.

Pat Perkins had drifted into the cabin, done with checking over the specimen cages and tidying up the lab space. She had a certain leisurely, gorgeous, reptilian quality, and Ears, who had sampled her charms, recommended her to Bradshaw in the event he felt the need for a little diversion during the operation. Bradshaw had not had the urge yet, but he appreciated kidding around with Pat. She had a sense of perverse irony, a grasp of the mad fun underlying most darkside work.

She looked thoughtful, and Bradshaw cocked his head quizzically.

"Funny place."

"How so, fond lover?"

She shrugged. "Just funny. Too still."

"Almost a perfect circle," Stavich said helpfully. They looked at him for a moment, before understanding that he meant the shape of the valley.

"Weather's off." Pat yawned and twisted her upper body slowly, then untwisted it, a tag-end of some exercise routine. "Ground surface is cooler than it should be."

Bradshaw waggled his eyebrows again, interested. He keyboarded swiftly, and a current satscan popped onto the monitor. After a two-second pause he said, "Hey hey. Hey *hey*."

"What?"

Pat leaned over his shoulder and he caught her dank, fruity perfume. He laid a fingernail carefully over the screen. "Shows a cloud cover. Just a scrap. Very very thin."

A small, grainy patch, visible only if one knew exactly where to look. But there. "The infamous cloud on the horizon," she said. Stavich frowned deeply. He suspected an equipment problem.

Bradshaw switched back to their video eye. They all stared at the round, empty valley, the silent columns of earth.

"Hey," Bradshaw said again, softly.

"I saw it." Pat's chin was almost on his shoulder.

"What?" Stavich looked peevish. "Saw what?"

They did not answer for a time. Then Bradshaw gave a surprised laugh. "What *is* that?"

"Sparkles," Pat said, and laughed too.

"Yeah, yeah! I see it!" Stavich exclaimed. "It's in the air."

Bradshaw reached for a control and the view zoomed and angled upward away from the valley. He stopped with only the tops of the surrounding hills visible at the bottom of the screen. Now they could see the faint iridescence in the atmosphere, a vibration away from absolute transparency.

"It's raining diamonds," Pat said.

Bradshaw powered up the magnification again and leaned now toward, now away from the screen, which scintillated and pulsed.

"Interference?" Stavich ventured.

Bradshaw had found a position, stared fixedly at the storm of particles. "No, no," he breathed and then giggled. "This is what I'd call adaptive camouflage. Mimicking cloud haze."

No one said anything for five minutes, as the shimmering layer grew thicker and began to assume a definite shape.

"Funnel cloud," Pat whispered. "Holy shit."

"Get out the heavy suits." Bradshaw's voice stayed quiet, but picked up speed. "Two extra filter units. Check the mask wiper blades and your sidearms. Rig up all the rocket nets we've got. Take a couple of good whiffs, guys, because we'll be on recycled air real soon."

"This is it?" Stavich waited, then got to his feet, his face reddening. "I mean, this is it." He hurried after Pat toward the field equipment lockers.

Too impressionable, Bradshaw thought in passing. Good tech, but dumb. May have to wipe him too. He controlled and slowed his breathing, watching the cloud with fascination. It was beginning to rotate, the tip moving toward the ground as if in a gentle gesture of exploration. He assumed the insects must have been flying upward for hours, perhaps days, to reach this concentration. And there was some kind of updraft in this bowl, keeping the shed wings aloft, a vast, suspended turbulence. The ghost of a huge, airborne amoeba, it looked like.

By the time they had their suits on, the tornado shape was perfectly defined, focused on a rocky depression near the center of the valley. Visibility was diminishing, and the light had an odd, autumnal quality—Bradshaw was immediately reminded of a partial solar eclipse.

He also realized that the peculiar nest of tunnels under the valley, revealed to him earlier by the seismogram, was in the same corkscrew shape as the undulating bright cloud. Two cones joined at the point. An hourglass or bobbin. *Gyres.* Yes, that was the word. He recalled some fragment from a book assigned in his boyhood. A late myth, a mad old poet's theory. Some fantastic nonsense about tornados of light and dark twisting into each other, ignorance and knowledge creating a terrible, violent beauty. . . .

He could see the termites pouring out of their mud towers now, swelling the cloud. A swift check of the satscan revealed only what looked like a small local weather disturbance. An amazing deceit. His breathing stopped then, for the tip of the cloud had bulged around the rocky depression and disgorged a pair of dark pegs.

He zoomed in, steadied the lens. A young Gink with his ritual scars—no, a mixed, or. . . . He breathed out, a long whoosh of relief and joy. It was the Drager boy. Changed, of course. Older and thinner and so dirty you couldn't see at first he was human, but it was him. Bradshaw had looked at enough pictures to be certain. Still, he was amazed at how the kid looked, how he moved and stood. You would say Gink, Gink all the way.

The other figure had to be the oldest in the whole herd. He couldn't tell if it was a male or female; it was just a dried-up, bent stick, joined to the kid by one hand. Now others were stepping out of the whirling core of the cloud. Gink bucks all painted up, bearing spears, their mouths open. He guessed they were singing. All of them looked dusty or rimmed with frost—the termite wings that had shaken out of the cloud.

Then he saw the other human, a pale skeleton. Then a mixed, with a beard. And beside them a young female with a broken nose. Had to be her, Fat's experiment. And the pale one was Skiho's cocaptain. He gave a whoop of pure glee. All of them. PJ, Duskyrose, and little Ronnie Drager. He had them. The Snuffer never failed. He was going to make history again. Big history. "Oh Mama," he muttered to himself. "Li'l Snuffie gonna do it, do it big!"

He sketched the plan as he wriggled into the suit Pat brought for him. "Full power, from the dig-out. We blow right into them—looks like there can't be more than a couple hundred anyway. We net the kid first and then this bunch." He shook an arm through a sleeve of the suit and pointed out the figures on the screen.

"What about the bitch? Could she go out on us?" Pat was watching the screen closely, curious.

"Don't think so. If she does—well, too bad. We'll collect the flop. Stavich, you're driver. I'll track and shoot the nets. Pat, you cover us with the turret battery. Wipe a perimeter around those rocks at the entrance, but no need to clean 'em all out. Just give us working room."

"How about . . . hey, where is that one going?"

Bradshaw stopped his zipping up. All of them stared intently at the monitor. The ancient stick had tottered ahead on its own, approaching one of the mud columns. The light on the screen shuddered. Visibility had worsened, but it appeared as if the bent figure stepped directly into the column. The stick was gone, the mud surface now sheathed with squirming insects.

"Huh," Stavich said. It was an expression of awe.

Bradshaw's zipper closed with a single, sharp rip. "Nice trick, Grampa. One less to worry about. Now let's do it, folks. Get these interesting creatures in a cage. Then I'll do the exams and preps. Alone. Then we talk to command. There will be a scenario. We all understand each other here, am I right?"

"Absolutely." Pat gave him a quick, sardonic salute. "Power to the parasites." Her look was speculative, smoldering.

"Yes, sir!" Stavich had moved to the navigation console and belted himself in. He laid a hand on the throttle, looking at Bradshaw like an eager hunting dog.

In his mind Bradshaw had already brushed Stavich into oblivion. The Snuffer deeply distrusted anyone incapable of dissimulation. Disposable tools must not be left lying around where anyone could use them. Pat, on the other hand, enjoyed the refinements of the game. She understood how the stakes had suddenly gone up astronomically, how risk and thrill amplified each other.

She perhaps sensed that he would want her when the job was done, right after the wipes. A power fuck, while the bodies were still twitching. She would see the humor of that. And he would holo the whole thing—with their faces scrambled—so there would never be any question about how the business was accomplished. Ears would enjoy watching and later she would bury the tape in her secret dossier on the Network.

O the times are going to get good, he thought. He had strapped himself into the gunner's seat beside Stavich, and now rapidly checked the propulsion system for the nets. We're going to catch ourselves a bright future. So long, little Ronnie boy. Another rapid glance at the monitor showed a sort of winter scene, the insect wings fluttering thick over the company of Ginks. But he could still make out his targets: the rest of the Ginks stood apart from them. Ostracized, apparently. Untouchable. That would make it all the easier to scoop them.

Stavich took the engines up to maximum thrust, until they could feel the whole vehicle surge against the brake. Bradshaw winked swiftly at Pat, then uttered another whoop of glee.

"Take 'em!"

They were slung backward by the acceleration, and for a second they were leaping blind down the slope, until the turret cameras were open. They saw the figures on the screen turn and begin to move, even as they were increasing rapidly in size. There was an implosion toward the entrance, toward the densest part of the funnel cloud. But the Drager boy had slumped to the ground and the frenzied Ginks were having trouble moving him.

They were hurtling to the base of the slope, perhaps two hundred meters away. Bradshaw had been worried about the cloud, the tumbling cascade of wings, but was startled by a swift alteration in its shape. It was as if an unexpected wind current had opened a passage into the cloud, leading directly to the group he was after. For now the three outcasts had drawn close together and were gathering around the boy.

It was ridiculously easy. Bradshaw launched the first net and it spiked all four of his targets tight to the ground. Immediately Pat began hosing off Ginks, making a widening band of smoking, huddled forms. He had unbelted himself, set his ManSticker for a twenty-minute stun, and put on a minipack of medicines. When Stavich slid to a halt he shouted to Pat to hold her fire, then popped the hatch and clambered out.

They lay in the net without struggling, watching him. This passivity was a surprise, a disappointment. He needed only one glance to see that the kid was crazy. Eyes blank and mouth agape. A complete zoneout, but otherwise he looked healthy. All the better. He could maybe be handled without leaving any marks or traces but the desired ones.

The agent PJ looked the most disoriented, and was the only one making any noise—a string of bright blue curses audible even over the sizzle and smack of Pat's guns. So Bradshaw shot him first, to arrest any incipient shock. The Gink bitch had peculiar eyes, glowing through the veils of glittering wings that still drifted around them, and for some reason her look infuriated him. He shot her twice, then again. An hour was a big charge. She might go under. Part of him hoped she would.

Upon closer inspection the mixed was actually a human, a renegade. Very skinny, in his late thirties or early forties. The beard was ridiculous, mashed to one side by the net. The man had his eyes open but lay motionless. He appeared, crazily enough, to be lost in thought. Bradshaw frowned, stopped momentarily to think himself.

This had to be Tickles. The nickname had turned up in the interrogation of Skiho, and Ears had run down the story, about a top Insec rookie who had gone goofy and disappeared into the Wastelands ten years ago. Presumed dead. He had thought Skiho was only hallucinating. Not so, it appeared. Well, that could be rectified.

No advantage he could see in running a sieve through this brain, which had to be pretty much gone anyway. He spun the dial on the ManSticker, then angled its snout so the body would be driven away from the others. He pressed the trigger and the charge sent a throb up his arm, while driving a white spike of lightning through the man's skull. The body jerked and flapped in the net. He watched the eyes curdle and sink in, a bit of smoking mess run from one ear. *Tickled to death.* He chuckled.

God, how I love my work, he thought. Even the unskilled. But of course the others would be the real challenge. In a matter of hours he would have to transform the boy into a mutilated, half-eaten sacrifice, and artificially age some of his blood and tissue samples. He would also have to begin an intense reorganization of PJ's mind, and find a little time to play with the Gink bitch. He wanted to see what he could dig out before he had to snuff her. He would be very busy, but it was, again, work he loved.

He loosed the net from its corner spikes and lifted it gently from the boy's shoulders. "Hey, Ronnie boy," he said. "You can get up now. It's okay."

Nothing. Nobody home. Meanwhile, it was still snowing termites, and getting heavier. Bradshaw knotted one hand in the boy's long, filthy hair and dragged him free of the net. The corpse of the bearded man came next, only by the heels. Then he clipped the corner rings together on the winch line and stood aside so that Stavich could reel in PJ and Duskyrose.

As the net and its cargo bumped up the ramp, he kicked through some of the surrounding litter. He picked up several shoulder bags, crudely woven from dry grass, and pried a spear out from beneath the corpse of an old Gink. Supporting data. Something for the anthroghouls to paw over.

He was considering the scenarios. Some were brilliant, complete, foolproof. He would create signs of torture and violation, and then do a little basting with bacteria to speed up decomposition. It would appear that the Ginks had held the boy captive until the last minute, had tried to eat him only when they saw themselves being routed by New Broom.

The zipper he had jerked was not perfectly sealed, because he felt now a squirming inside the protective suit. The air was full of billowing clouds of wings and the dropping bodies sounded a steady rain on his helmet. An odor—fetid, moldy, sour—was overwhelming. The boy's head and shoulders were covered, but he made no move to brush away the crawling mess. Bradshaw took him by the hair again and dragged him to the *Forager*'s loading port. Little Drager was not even there, really. A drooling blank. Bradshaw would be doing him a favor.

The presence of Insec people, especially Duskyrose, would be grounds to establish that some sinister collaboration had occurred, a hostage plot real or fake. PJ, for example, might have been tempted into such a scheme. Fearful and angry over the V-studies. Corrupted by Con propaganda. His sperm could be planted in the Gink, to make the tale juicier. Or if he came around to a correct version of events, they might even let him live. For a while. He could testify as Fat's hapless dupe.

Ears would figure out the details, document the case and get something on everybody, for future use. When the big hatch opened and the platform slid out, he rolled the boy onto the gurney and stood beside it, bedecked with his trophies, while they were pulled inside. Reaching her would be his very first act, as soon as he got rid of this suit covered with bug slime. He had a deep code alert that would get a message to Ears anywhere, immediately.

She would be waiting. Everything would begin to move, as in an earthquake. Epic struggle. Martyrdom and revenge. The great final effort. Triumph over dark chaos. Extermination of all the dirt and danger in this world. Good-bye Ginks. Good-bye bugs. Good-bye bears. And good-bye Dylan Bradshaw. Snuffer grinned his wolf's grin. He was having fun as Dr. Bradshaw. A great gig, one of his best, but there were soon going to be incredible new opportunities.

39

MRS. EVELYN RIGGS HAD NEVER CARRIED A SIGN BEFORE in her life, and here she was not only waving one enthusiastically, but also shouting across a police line. Most of the officials hurrying in or out of the building ignored the protesters, unless they saw the snouts of media holocameras. Then they would look sober and important, or perhaps say quickly the matter was being investigated.

Evelyn had heard enough about investigations and surveys and studies and pilot programs. Like many others in the crowd, she was an ordinary person who was simply fed up. Fed up, first of all, with the failure of things to work properly. All kinds of things. Even the kitchen sink, for example. Some fungus or germ or something—a gray-green sludge—had crawled up out of the sewer system and jammed most of the drains in the whole neighborhood. The sludge was completely impervious to standard cleansers—consumed them, in fact, with gusto.

A shuttle pulled up and a man and woman got out, both lugging thick briefcases. They looked unhappy and uncomfortable, so they were probably consultants, not bureaucrats.

"*Action!*" Evelyn shouted, and jigged the handle of her sign up and down violently. The sign said *Heel Thyself,* because her group had started out picketing the NorthAm Surgeon General's office, before ending up at the White House with the other groups.

Evelyn's group was concentrating on the current epidemic of head colds, allergy attacks, and diarrhea. One couldn't find a clinic or even a rest room anymore without a long line in front of it. Elderly people actually soiled themselves, waiting. New strains of virus, the health experts said. Intensive research underway. Powerful photon microscopes. International symposia. Blah blah blah—and then they recommended plenty of rest and orange juice until the antibodies could be developed.

Rest! When, Evelyn would like to know, did a person have time to rest? Staying awake nights trying to keep up with filing procedures for special new taxes. Taxes needed, she was convinced, to pay for the studies and investigations. And one of the investigations, of course, had already determined that you couldn't use *fresh* oranges to make juice, because the pesticide washed off the rinds actually encouraged that sludge crawling up through the drain.

That was the straw that finished off the camel for Mr. and Mrs. Riggs. Plus discovering that Mr. Riggs had a rare variety of *sporotrichinosis*. Mrs. Riggs remembered the name because of the "tricky no" part. These days politicians were trickier and trickier, but always saying—when you got through their twisty way of talking, denying everything bad and taking credit for any illusory good—no, no, nothing could *really* be done just yet; no, no, nobody *really* knew how soon; no, no, the issue is too tricky for ordinary people to grasp.

Even as she was shouting and waving the sign, Evelyn saw the man with the briefcase shaking his head. "Don't you give me that!" she yelled, and heard other angry shouts from the crowd. "Don't just say no!" But the man and woman were practically running, ducking between the guards at the doorway as if coming in from a hard rain.

The crowd booed, laughed, applauded ironically. People made faces at each other. Evelyn felt comradely even toward the young Ecomini on her left, one of those girls who made a point of never combing her hair and wore very little besides berry-juice stains and a moss skirt. They would disagree about everything, she supposed, except what was most important; namely, that the time had come to tell the truth and figure out what to do.

The mutant fungus that had sown fibrous polyps in the lungs of Mr. Riggs was not yet contained. In fact it was spreading. A migration of bats—a connection to spoor-breeding caves in the Wastelands—was suspected as the cause. No solid information, of course, but "everything" was being done to develop an effective, easy-to-use nasal spray. Another tricky no.

Meantime the waste and dishonesty and dithering of the government went on. Billions were going into this campaign to clean up the border, reduce the Gink population, find out at least what happened to the little boy. Lives were being lost, too, a startling number, because of equipment and communications failures. And they had turned up nothing so far but the usual scandals and sinister rumors.

Evelyn felt sorry for the poor Drager family and was outraged at the way their troubles were exploited by the political parties. She and the Ecomini had talked about that, and more or less agreed. Too many people were trying to get too much out of the situation, that was certain. You could not trust anything an official said, that was another sure thing. It might even be time to let a few things *alone*. Evelyn was actually ready to go that far. Maybe if you let the sludge alone, didn't spray the oranges. . . .

What about the fouled sewers? An answer came to her, and in spite of herself she giggled. She saw herself squatting outdoors, not even screened by shrubs. Waving at the shocked faces peering from a passing vehicle. Ripping the rind off an orange with her teeth. On impulse she jerked the clip out of her carefully arranged hair, ran the fingers of one hand through the mass of it.

The Ecomini gave a shrill whistle. "*Okay*, sister!" Others turned their way and a couple nearby cheered and clapped. Evelyn felt wonderfully disheveled and dangerous. She would not go home yet, even though she had already stayed beyond her allotted time.

A limosshuttle, flying a flag from both front fenders, rounded the corner and swung into the driveway. The crowd swayed forward a little, and she saw the police lifting their plastic shields, closing ranks. A great hooting and jeering began, as the door to the shuttle swung open and three men got out, two of them in uniform. The beefy, flushed one she recognized as General Bennett. The other soldier was built like a bodyguard and carried a sidearm. The man in a drab suit was the rotund PacRim whose picture she had seen only a night or two ago on the news. "Shadowy figure," the commentator had said. Insec director and cochair of some high-powered thing or other, involved in one of the scandals. . . .

She felt the crowd pressing around her, and a chant had begun: *No bo-dy! No bo-dy! Bo-dy-y-y!* This was the issue that aroused such varied support. *Show* us little Ronnie, or what's left of him. A tissue sample, a bone, a geneprint at least. Some evidence of an actual horror. Otherwise call off the whole silly, wasteful show.

The cry also meant the crowd would resort to putting their own bodies on the line, to block entrances or driveways or copter pads. An old technique, long invalidated—supposedly—by the Federation's organizational sensitivity. A technique considered vulgar, even primitive. Evelyn was excited, a little amazed at herself. She felt the Ecomini link arms with her on one side, and a young man took her hand on the other.

Opposite her she could see only the bubbles of shields and helmets, a featureless carapace of tinted plastic. But she felt the police were nervous, even afraid. That realization released in her a great wave of happy, carefree energy. She would be stopped, of course, perhaps shoved or struck, and then arrested. But they were right, and others would see they were right, and eventually. . . .

Or perhaps not. It didn't matter now, in this rush of energy carrying them forward. To hell with it, she thought. Or no—she gulped—*fuck it.* With a roar of exhilaration, the crowd surged into the police line. The evening holonews—where a thunderstruck Mr. Riggs saw his wild-haired wife kick a policeman in the shins before being hauled away feet first—described them as an angry swarm.

40

THE FLY IN THE OINTMENT, DANIELLE THOUGHT AS SHE accepted the sealed envelope. She must have winced, because Dorothy looked immediately troubled and sympathetic.

"Are you all right?"

"Oh, of course. Sad, but expected." She smiled bravely, savagely, to prove the point. "I wish I could be with him. But the job is here, now, for me. Isn't it?"

Dorothy didn't respond to the acidity in the question. Her eyes were lowered deferentially. "You know best," she murmured.

Danielle just managed to keep herself from another uncontrolled twitch. She went on. "This meeting is really going to be high theater. Beautiful. It's too bad you can't be there. I owe it all to you, as we know. I—our people—are going to be *very* appreciative."

"I hoped you'd be pleased." Dorothy smiled her small, inward, humble smile, and then glanced up with a certain look, gone so quickly Danielle could never be certain of its meaning. Complicity, sly joy, mockery, even something erotic. . . . "Though sad, too, as you said."

"Up and down. A crazy business," Danielle said between her teeth, and stuffed the envelope into a leather attaché case. "I won't use it, naturally, unless I have to." She looked over her shoulder. The office door was open and her driver was waiting discreetly in the hall. "But at least we know now. You'll keep track of things as they break. You always do. As soon as this session is over I'll call you. Get an update and an image of the body from our source, as soon as you can, and then put Frank on a private channel. A *secure* channel. I'll want to tell him myself."

"Of course." Dorothy stepped back, gave the small smile again. "Good luck."

Demure Dorothy, my assistant. The bloodsucker. Danielle turned abruptly to hide her desperation and strode out.

She needed the long drive across the city to regain control of herself. She would have to speak at her best, make every word count. It was the decisive moment in her career, and she could not afford involuntary reactions. She would have to be hot, white-hot, and yet cold at the core.

The city was half in shadow already. Only the upper stories of skyscrapers were still golden, their glass lurid with reflected red sun. The crane copters were out, indicating rush hour was not going smoothly. In one of the concrete canyons, leading to the Senate building, she saw ranks of marchers, a white confetti of signs. Another demo in the archaic mode. It was time, certainly time, for change.

She realized it was simply the metaphor of the fly and ointment that caused her original shudder. Too many insects had cluttered her life since the morning's visit to Petrasky. A positive plague. Enough to make her skin crawl. First the insane patient with his blissful complacency in imagining himself some kind of farting beetle. Then of course the awful, slimy locusts on the Trunkway. Most of all, now, her realization that she was herself caught in a terrible web.

Yet the delay had at first seemed a miracle of good fortune. Stockwell had postponed the meeting until evening, and in the interim they had gotten Petrasky's coordinates to Sunbeam. The termite theory—mad as it seemed—had brought almost instant, incredible results. Dorothy had come mincing into Danielle's inner office, high color in her cheeks. With a little coo of triumph she laid a readout on the desk.

It was a field autopsy report. Danielle saw in an instant that the subject, a pubescent male *Homo sapiens* dead for only seventy-two hours, was Ronald Drager. Age, color of eyes and hair, size, blood type—she had reviewed his vitals enough to know them by heart. Only the name and date were left blank.

When she looked up Dorothy said quickly, "Sketchy, I know. Just the first report from the examining physician. But he's a trained physiologist and expert in forensic medicine. He's sure. Also, they picked up the other Insec agent. Alive. I knew you'd want word as soon as possible, so. . . ." She shrugged and stood briefly on one foot, in a little-girl motion of shy anticipation.

Danielle dropped her eyes again to the sheet of paper. Lesions, scars, swellings, partial dismemberment. Evidence of malnutrition and mutilation. Cause of death: severe beating, aspiration of vomit. Horrible. She could not control her mouth.

"What?" she whispered. "Where did this come from?"

"An amazing coincidence, Danielle. It turns out the medical officer is an old personal acquaintance of yours. I should have told you earlier." Dorothy managed to sound worried and contrite. "But he remembers you well and when this came up . . . well, he just decided to go outside the usual chain of command and file this direct. We had a perfectly secure code, of course."

"Of course." Danielle had recovered her voice and a simulacrum of an expression of intense concern. She was only thinking, however, that it was the first time her subordinate had ever called her Danielle.

"How soon can we have the final?"

"The . . . ah . . . authentication procedure might take two . . . three? . . . days." Dorothy hunched a shoulder, girlish again.

"Too long." Danielle frowned. "An autopsy—" She stopped and stared hard into her aide's wide, innocent eyes.

"But in one of those combat zones? Things are *so* confused. Delays happen," Dorothy said helpfully.

Authentication, Danielle thought to herself. A little delay for my old acquaintance—she glanced at the printout again —Dr. Bradshaw. Painfully, lugubriously, she brought herself to consider what this sudden familiarity implied.

She was probably going to acquire many new old personal acquaintances. A network beyond the Network she had counted on. Faceless people, electronic people, with whole files either documenting a relationship with her or destroying that relationship. Or both. A whole history created by her humble assistant, who knew everything, and must have been part of it from the beginning.

She was all at once dizzy, aware that Dorothy—"Dorothy"—was breathing a little faster. A sort of feeding frenzy, with Danielle's shock and confusion supplying the open vein. Here it was at last, the coming-due of her "insurance" policy.

The anonymous company had delivered. Little Ronnie, or what was left of him, was folded away into the attaché case on her lap. Now the price of this service was finally apparent. From now on she would be at the pinnacle of her public career, and at the bottom of a secret food chain.

Still, making her way from the underground lot through the security screens, she was aware of her power to survive. Her head lifted, she recovered her stride, a little of the swagger of political and sexual confidence. She had to ignore the lice that hung on her. There were worse fates. Ask Solomon Fat. Greatness always required some compromise, some discomfort. She had to remember her own destiny was on the grand stage of History, and this was her hour.

One look at her face as she came in and Fat knew. They had found him, or enough to supply plausible evidence at least. Maybe PJ too. He had known it was only a matter of time.

Once more he was mildly surprised at his reaction. He found himself pleased, content at the deepest level. He was going to be disgraced, stripped of his power, perhaps imprisoned. Hence released. He smiled at her across the room; and this time, after a moment of blank hesitation, she smiled back. The triumphant often deliver, as a final blow, magnanimity.

A moment later the aide beside the heavy oak door gave his signal and they all stood up. President Stockwell came in flanked by his Secretary of Defense and National Security Adviser. Fat felt the President's look pass by him, on its way around the table, as a searchlight plays over a wrecked vehicle. To the Federation liaison went a respectful nod. To General Bennett, a quick, comradely smile. To Danielle Konrad a bow and exposure of teeth.

"Sit down, people, please." Stockwell waved a hand with his famous casual disregard for protocol. "No time for ceremony. Too much at stake."

He took his own seat at the head of the long, broad table, and waited a moment for the aide to arrange certain papers before him. Fat had already been informed, in a single terse call from the Chief Adviser, that in the stack was the letter of resignation he had signed three months ago.

When the room was cleared of subordinates, Stockwell planted his elbows on the table and interlaced the fingers of his two hands to make a pyramid of strength, upon which he propped his forthright chin. He remained so for several seconds, until the room was silent, to establish the drama of the scene. When he spoke it was in a voice deeply troubled, yet resonant with courage.

"You folks doubtless saw the demonstrators on the way in. And I don't have to tell you there have been similar incidents all over the continent. This meeting was delayed because some of us couldn't even get across town this morning.

"If you were going too fast to read the signs, I'll quote a couple of them. The repeatable ones. *Smoking Gun, Hell—*

Where's the Body? Or how about *Which Rotten Race Ripped off Little Ronnie?* Or *Man—the Maggotburger?* Or—this one was very popular—*Everything Stinks.*"

There was nervous laughter, which Stockwell allowed to peter out before he continued.

"Every sort of disturbed creep is out there, of course, but also a lot of irritated and unhappy ordinary people. They've reached a limit, ladies and gentlemen. The end of the pro-verbial rope. The Middle Class—backbone, I don't need to remind you, of the NorthAm system—is making itself heard. They want a new direction, a new purpose. They want a cleaner, safer world. And they want it now."

Dirt, Fat thought. *Danger.* He smiled to himself. Weren't those part of his attraction to Tima? The idea of cleaning her up, making her useful? Instead *he* had become a foul threat. He almost laughed out loud.

"We've all had to listen, and rethink positions," the Pres-ident continued, as the pyramid of his forearms collapsed into a cross on the table. "It's not a partisan thing. On both sides we've seen some very creative work—and some acts I would have to call irresponsible, or even desperate. Rumors and unfounded allegations . . . or worse."

Stockwell glanced at Danielle Konrad, then fixed his look on Fat, and for a long second there was silence in the room. Fat maintained his smile, and did not avert his eyes. He felt more and more buoyant. Elise had apparently infected him with her implacable optimism, her faith which had nothing to do with facts. Was he a true martyr, one who thoroughly enjoyed his own execution?

"So I have some very important changes to announce. Both in policy and personnel. But before I do so, I want to give you the background. General Bennett's update on Operation New Broom, and a briefing on the economic picture from Elizabeth Fortner, our CEA. Her last presentation—some of you will recall—was cut short."

Fat had noticed the gray-haired woman at the table, and wondered. He had not expected this sort of routine, had supposed that the revelation of his own resignation from Insec and his dismissal as cochair of Sunbeam would dominate the proceedings. What was Stockwell up to?

General Bennett was even more brick-faced than usual,

and his normally stentorian voice was reduced to a hoarse whine. His first words also startled the room into murmurs of protest.

"This has turned into a war, people. And we're not at the moment winning it."

He looked around the room and waited. Everyone understood then that the statement had been cleared by Defense and National Security. This was the official position. Fat was suddenly interested. He forgot for the moment his personal martyrdom. It was a remarkable admission. Was the Con party about to commit suicide?

"I told some of you last time this was tough, this flop-by-flop approach. Well, it's a lot worse than I thought. And yet it's real simple. I can tell you the problem, from a military standpoint, in three words. One, sand." He favored them with a grim grin. "Two, fleas." Someone laughed and the general glared at him. "And three, morale." He waited again for contradiction, but no one so much as coughed.

"It's not the Ginks. Some of you have heard me say this already. They're nothing in this. Absolutely no problem. They've wiped *themselves* by the hundreds of thousands. It's the way our guys react to that. . . ."

General Bennett's voice almost broke. "Our guys and gals—they came into this hard, to do a job, plenty of guts and spirit—they're the finest young men and women in the world—but. . . . Listen here, now. Here it is. The enemy is *not human*. We know that, of course, but our training somehow doesn't prepare us for how they behave." Bennett glanced around the table again, saw the blank expressions, and shifted in his chair uncomfortably.

"Look, people, our grunts are into this now for months, and all they do is lug their weapons around—and clean them, every day, what with the sand—and count flops. Flop after flop after flop. And change filters on their suits. Three times a day some days and still they're breathing sand. Meanwhile getting eaten alive. I said fleas just as a figure of speech. It's everything—bugs and flies and skeeters, yes, but new germs and funguses too, some the bio guys haven't seen before."

"Just like on the home front," someone said. "Everything stinks," someone else added. There was brief, skittish laughter again.

"Maybe." General Bennett frowned. "That's not my department. But I can tell you that it's damned hard to stay pumped up under these conditions. The rate of desertions, and insubordination, and malingering . . . well, it's hard to believe. Passing forty percent. And the tragedy is, people, in the last few days the Ginks have congregated together in a way we've never seen before. In this area near the coast. We've mapped enough of their tunnel system to know. And in the last twenty-four hours something happened. They milled around aimlessly for a while and now there seems to be a kind of mass exodus or dispersal. An incredible opportunity for us and it's slipping away."

He stopped and squared the papers in front of him. When he looked up, it was directly at Danielle Konrad. "We've tried to cooperate with the Sunbeam probe, which is also in the area. We're certainly sensitive to the symbolism of the Dragers. But at this point. . . ."

All at once, Fat understood the strategy Stockwell was working on. It was clever indeed.

The President had launched New Broom under pressure from the Progs, primarily as a diversion. He must have hoped privately that Fat's darkside team would turn up the boy. When that wasn't happening, Stockwell decided on a double gamble: massive force on the perimeter, the Sunbeam probe into the center. New Broom, however, was proving to be not only fantastically expensive, but demoralizing as well. And no leader could survive if his military moves publicly fizzled. That left only one solution: escalation.

So Fat was not at all surprised to hear the conclusion of the general's report, or the uproar around the table afterward. Bennett delivered the key phrase in what was, for him, almost a whisper. *Petition the Federation for clearance to reactivate nuclear instruments.* Again, Stockwell and his team did not flinch. They were all behind it. The big, bold stroke. A complete, one-time-only cleanup. To Fat—from his new vantage point—it made perfect sense.

The strategy neatly undercut Konrad and the new Progs. It assumed the Drager case was closed, and moved to take immediate, total, and cost-effective revenge. The troops would withdraw, the missiles would pinpoint the Gink concentrations and atomize them, nothing would be lost but a few thousand square miles of what was already Wasteland. Most importantly, they could strike at Konrad's power base: her whole sentimental, suspenseful holosoap would be blown completely away. No one would ever really know what happened to little Ronnie.

In the general hubbub Fat allowed himself a good, round chuckle. The Cons—the original party of caution and laissez-faire—would thus be the first, after a century-long interlude, to beg for another flirtation with Apocalypse, another peek inside Pandora's Box. But—how crazy it was all getting!—the Fed might actually listen, just *because* the Cons were making the request. Their about-face in policy was proof enough the situation required desperate measures. And also because—ah yes! He understood why Stockwell was now ignoring the turmoil, turning the floor over to Elizabeth Fortner, and why the Fed representative was leaning forward with sharpened interest.

The gray-haired woman made no apologies for her dry, crabbed presentation, beyond an opening observation that her science had shown its fondness for understatement long ago, by accepting the label "dismal." The NorthAm economic slide was continuing, and growing steeper, which had sent tremors through the whole Federation trade structure. Worldwide, in fact, there was good reason for deep concern.

Expenditures for medicines, corrective surgery, pest and weed control, genetic engineering, waste disposal, detox, sat and on-the-ground surveillance and border patrol—everything summed up in the concept of *preventive maintenance*—had outstripped all funding for research and development. Consequently, new mutants—viruses, microbes, one-celled parasites, insects, weeds, even pest mammals—were getting a toehold, damaging crops and curtailing production and taking a toll in lives. This creeping rot and ruin indeed gave off new perfumes. The demo signs had a point: there was a certain smell in the streets. We are not, Dr. Fortner said with a sardonic little moue, keeping up with the Pheromoneses.

Many of these tough, resistant marauders developed in the old toxic dumps in the Wastelands, as everyone knew. And there was of course no gainsaying that *Homo lapsis* flourished in this environment, that Ginks deliberately encouraged many inimical life-forms. The deterioration of border security correlated, quite nicely, with the decline in GNP.

Dr. Fortner took off her old-fashioned reading glasses and smiled at them like a weary schoolmistress. She was of course not political. She did not like to deal in concepts like Armageddon or even emergency. She would leave them with a simple fact. Once whole continents had been decimated by sicknesses like smallpox, measles, cholera. No one had questioned the extermination of these bacteria. Today, eliminating just three R's—the roach, the rat, and the runny nose—would almost restore the NorthAm economy.

Unlikely anything could be done about the runny nose—the oldest and most persistent of human ailments—but what if, as many insisted, the depredations of rat and roach could be traced to *lapsis?* What if it were possible to strike at the *center* of everything hostile to humanity? Disable at one blow the only remaining rival primate, the one active conscious agent behind disease, disorder, decay?

The economics of General Bennett's proposal appealed to a hard and practical scientist like herself. There was no doubt about that. The cheapest solution was the Big Wipe. Strong medicine, quick relief. Actually—she shrugged—it was the only brand they could afford now anyway.

Fat could see the possibilities. Once the big wipe was over, the Cons could even argue for restraint and a certain compassion in dealing with remnant populations. The hot area could be set aside as a kind of Preserve, and the remaining Ginks monitored as an experiment. They might even hold on to the older Preserves, maintain in some modified, supervised form the doctrines of diversity and free genetic play—as a kind of hedge, until *all* the information was under control.

Chuckling, looking around a table otherwise dominated by expressions of amazement, fear, disbelief, Fat saw Danielle Konrad open the flap of her attaché case, withdraw an envelope. Her face was more radiant than he had ever seen it. She was pushing back her chair, raising a hand, her eyes riveted on Stockwell.

Fat experienced a moment of supreme illumination. Again—how curious it was, the reappearance in his mind of so much old lore!—it came to him as an aphorism from an ancient text. *Love thine enemies.*

41

HE WAS CONCENTRATING ON THE SPEAR. IT WAS AN OLD ceremonial spear, too long and too dull to be of much use to a hunter, but dark with the smoke and sweat of three generations. It had been propped beside the door in the laboratory, a cramped room where the big man moved between the bodies on the double gurney and Pahane's, which was stretched out on the examining table.

He had awakened from the attack clean and free, still a shadow outside his body. He remembered the Going In, the wild music, up to a point. Adza and the queen in their bright, whirling embrace. His and Tima's *kubin* flowing as one toward that radiant tornado. Then the sudden tunnel of darkness, the frightened and furious horde first pulling at him and then shrinking away. The ecstasy of being within a tremendous current of *naku* occurred almost simultaneously with a shock of horror—his realization that the Pobla felt betrayed now. They thought that he—and Tima and even Teeklo—had brought corruption and ruin to this most sacred moment, had somehow signaled to this alien *mudlati* roaring down on them. As if they had deliberately waited, like robots, to strike down the *tak tagakin* before she could reincorporate herself and bring saving knowledge from *wonakubi.*

Yet he awoke in this curious state. Calm and alert, aware of Tima's shadow still allied with his own, knowing somehow that he would now remain a ghost. In fact he could sense that the piksi runt was returning. This boy was terrified, not even able to speak or move. But he was there, inside a body that would surely seem strange to him when he regained full consciousness.

Pahane had directed himself to the spear because he felt Tima's urgency. The first thing he saw in the room was a blue-green luminosity around her still form, a force that was gathering and bending toward the corner where the spear angled away from the wall. His own being curved and leaned with hers, as it had when she charmed PJ out of his weapon.

The man was whistling, talking to himself. He had no shadow that Pahane could see. He was like animate stone. He moved nimbly for one so large, picking small bottles from a shelf and removing a few cotton swabs and a pneumatic syringe from a drawer.

"About to be super super famous, little guy. You'll be in all the kiddie bedtime stories." The man laughed, a series of loud honks. "The ones they tell to *terrify* the little bastards to sleep. Oh yeah, Ronnie baby, time I get you dehydrated and putrified, you gonna be the chief boogeyboy. . . ."

The man lifted his eyebrows, stuck out and waggled his sharp red tongue. He was like a huge, madcap child. But his hands were expertly breaking the seal on one of the bottles and fitting the nozzle of the pneumo-syringe into it.

Pahane had apprehended that a single grain of sand was wedged under the tip of the spear, which, on its slant away from the wall, would otherwise have begun to skid across the floor. The careless manner of its placement, and the shoulder bags and bone trinkets heaped on the floor underneath, indicated how hectic the last thirty minutes had been. A scatter of termite wings still decorated the three prone forms and littered the floor. On the cabin's ceiling, he could see a half dozen of the insects crawling near a light fixture.

They were in fact less than three kilometers from the valley where the Hive Beings had manifested themselves. The Great Ones were still near, for he could feel a slow, deep tremor beneath the threshold of hearing, as if the whole earth were a gong struck long ago but still throbbing. It felt as if he and Tima floated on this vibration, drew on its power to create the blue arc reaching to the old spear.

And a third presence now, too. Teeklo's shadow was with them, lighter and more playful than when the man was alive. It was the ghost of a boy, he realized, like his own, only less sure, more inexperienced, full of wonder—because this *kubi* had emerged late, inside a piksi man who had undergone every sort of training to control the wild shadow. Now, hesitant and impetuous by turns, Teeklo leaned with them, added his force to the rainbow leaping across the room.

The huge, silly child had finished loading his toy and held it up now to admire and declaim, to sing and babble. To Pahane, the voice coming from the opaque body was metallic, a whine and clash of gears and rods.

"Okay, hey hey! Wish you could all be here, maydams and maysewers. Fatso and Konradikins and our bonerhabile Pray-zeedent Stockswill! He he! Dr. Dylan does your bidding, booboos! And of course dear little Dorothy Smith. Ears, you should be here. Hear hear!"

The man did a little prancing dance to his right, toward the gurney where Tima was stacked beside PJ. He intersected the bridge of bluish light, which he did not see splashing over him, though he dallied there, jigging from side to side.

"Wake up! Wake up dollinks! You'll miss the show! We make-a theez leel peegie a beeg seembol!"

One of the termites dropped from the light fixture. The doctor did not see the tiny, twisting body, nor hear when he stepped on it.

"Leel Ginkee pussee gets all the credit! Poor ol' Doc Brad-shaw gonna waste away then. Hey? Ha ha! But not before we have some fun, kiddies."

He was swaying in and out of the shaft of invisible radiance, making infinitesimal, imperceptible pulses to the spear, work-ing the grain of sand.

"Cat's out of the bag now, folks. They already know, our big players, our Proggie Queen. Logged a little blood and tissue, sent 'em a sketch. Pretty soon everybody will know your whole sad story." The man made a clown's upside-down smile of unhappiness. "Poor li'l fella tortured and half et, chomp marks all over his skinny legs—and looka the sores on that chest! Done my work for me! Gotta get these Ginks and bad ol' beasties under *control!* Git some fundin' comin' down, cowboys! Some real *projects!* Big tickets, plenty perks, lotta action, lotta flow. Woo-woo!"

He wheeled to a wall module, flourishing the syringe and flipping a switch with his other hand. A port high on the opposite wall shuttered open and the barrel of a holocamera poked out.

"And we commit the whole biz to the ark-hive, girls and boys, the whole in-credible bug story, 'cept the mug of yours truly. Case anybody tries to fuck with us. We the Parasites, babeez. We the sovereign suckers." He giggled, momentarily convulsed, ducking in and out of the blue light. Another tiny, amber flake dropped from the ceiling. He looked once more at the wall module, hit another switch, and saw the monitor come to life. It showed the room, the bodies lying still, his own looming form. Only his face was shattered, disassembled into a shifting patchwork of color.

This image with its blurred head began to move toward the naked body on the examining table. He carried the syringe pointed upward, like a dueling pistol. Another termite fell, striking this time just behind the doctor's ear and inside his collar. At the same moment the grain of sand popped from the tip of the spear, which began to glide soundlessly along the floor. As the man reached up, distracted, to dig away the little squirming body, the spear accelerated, its handle raking along the wall as it extended across the floor. The tip shot between the man's feet, catching the toe of the one in motion.

He stumbled, kicking the spear ahead, and then his foot came down on the haft, which rolled under him. One elbow still poked aloft in the attempt to pinch up the insect, he fell awkwardly. He tried first to release the syringe, but a finger caught in the trigger mechanism. When he put this hand down to cushion his impact, the syringe struck the floor first and spun around. The snout of the instrument collided with his hip just as the trigger released.

The small, sharp *f-f-ftt* was barely audible under Dr. Bradshaw's startled curse. Had he still been wearing his shielded suit, the tough fabric might have repelled the tiny jet of chemical spray, but it blew easily through his lab coat and light trousers, driving the dose of asphyxiator several millimeters beneath his skin.

He sat up, his expression finally changing from glee to petulance. His cheeks reddened as he stared first at the spear, rolling in a wide quarter circle, then at the damp spot, no larger than a small coin, on his coat.

He abandoned the syringe and tipped forward onto his doubled fists, got one foot under him, as if to rise. But already he breathed with a loud, high, sucking sound. He pushed off with the foot and staggered up to a crouch. His big head lunged from side to side as if looking for an enemy hidden in the bare corners of the room. Tentatively, with one fist, he pawed again at his collar. Then he gagged loudly and fell forward on his face, across the spear.

Pahane was already curling and sinking into himself, a swift hibernation. As the blue light had broken and ebbed, he had begun to turn and turn, spinning a cocoon of darkness around himself. His *kubi* was being entombed, below the fire-fish, at the bottom of the hole where the toad squatted, its golden eyes hooded now. He was she, and they were winding into one, at the very threshold of the world of shadows. The world where darkness began to glow, and would erupt into final light.

He saw the man lying on the floor. The others on the hospital cart, sleeping or drugged. Heard the faint hum of the power plant. He had been captured, rescued. . . . It was difficult to think. Alien words came to him, huge and slow as a procession of elephants.

Had he ever seen a procession of elephants? No. Never. Nix. Two or three or four at most. The Ancient Natural History Museum. Solemn. Solemnly columned. Some old picture he had seen of them, twined tail to trunk to tail.

He was thinking so slowly, so strangely, because he was still afraid. He had been very sick, unbalanced, for a long time. Insane. Yes, say the truth. Crazy. Crazy as a bedbug, he had heard his mother say when he was quite small. He was excited, wanted to see, but she told him they were mythical. Dirty little things that bit you. In their clean house no such. All gone. The thought of his mother made his eyes fill up with tears.

Dark and dirt. He had gotten used to them. He remembered the tunnel, the cave, the great, gloomy stone city. The man Teeklo. Dead. How did he know this? The tears welled up stronger.

He had liked Teeklo, had talked to him for a long time. There was smoke, a surging up of something—someone—a stranger—inside him. He only watched and slept. Watched less and less, slept more and more, while his craziness ran free. He had eaten—

The man on the gurney muttered, flapped an arm up and

back. His movement was constrained by straps drawn snug. His name was PJ. His nickname. Nickname. If his name was Nick? The boy smiled, and the sensation was so odd he stopped immediately.

He was unsure of many details. He knew the Pobla, her name was Tima, and he remembered a confused time with her. First she came in a big copter and wore a uniform and then she wore nothing. She had no shame. He felt foolish and his ears burned but he looked. He looked and—

"Jesus H. Christ." The man on the gurney had opened his eyes and heaved weakly against the straps. He lifted his head, saw the big body sprawled on the floor and the boy watching him from the table. "I'm not dead. For some damn reason. . . . Is he?"

"I think . . . I think so." His voice startled him. It was husky, cracked, as if he had been yelling or crying. Or singing. Yes, singing! To that old woman!

PJ continued to stare at him. "What the hell happened to you? Did he sting you already with something?"

He realized his face was still wet with tears. "I—" He made a gesture to signify bafflement. In doing so he saw his own hand and arm. A black branch ending in a thick-knuckled claw. A bolt of fear went through him. He sat up and looked down and nearly cried out in horror. He was naked himself, dirty and sun-blackened as weathered wood except for huge red welts on his chest and numerous older pale scars. He was also larger, heavier-boned, and ridged with tendon and muscle.

"Pahane?" PJ was wriggling in his straps again. "Shit, man, what is it? We've got to get *out* of here. There's some kind of crew onboard, has to be. . . ."

"Ronnie," he said. He cleared his sore throat and said it again, as if arguing with his dark, heavy body. "I'm Ronnie. Ronald Drager."

"Well." PJ stopped his struggling and stared again. "Well, *well*. Where you been, Ronnie Drager? And where the fuck were you when I needed you? Shit. Well—anyway—hello, Master Drager, now please get up and over here and cut me loose, and her too—Jesus, I hope she isn't gone—come *on* guy!"

He got up, surprising himself again. Although his mind was

still foggy, the body moved easily, sure-footed and balanced. His big claws undid the straps quickly.

PJ was wobbly but erect. He stretched and beat his arms briefly in the air, laughed once more, and then turned to hunker beside the man sprawled on the floor. He felt along the throat with two fingers, pried back an eyelid.

"Stone dead. Ugly sonofabitch. He had us, too. Why'd he check out?" He noted the syringe, touched the spear under the corpse. "Tripped, maybe. Christ, what unbelievable luck. Packing any juice?"

The hands probed under the lab coat, along the beltline, removed a key card from its sheath. PJ grimaced, glanced around the laboratory, and spied a small metal locker. "Check Tima," he said over his shoulder.

Ronald approached the gurney and leaned over the girl's still form. Immediately he recognized her smell, and his face grew warm. The small, full breasts rose and fell in a long rhythm. Her face seemed thin and worn, empty of all awareness. Gently he undid the straps. He felt a pang, deep inside him. He took her hand. "Tima," he whispered. *"Kish tohanaku."*

She did not move. Yet he felt again at his very center a strong, hot throb of emotion. Behind him he heard the cabinet doors open. PJ grunted in delight, but Ronnie did not turn around.

Where did the words come from? He knew something of Pobla, clearly. Teeklo again, he supposed, during the long talks in the smoke. *Tohanaku.* Girlfriend. He felt suddenly, incongruously, foolish and happy.

"Monitor control on this goddamned thing is where, should be next to internal security . . . okay . . . now COP and TIDE. . . . Is she okay?"

"Yes. But still under." He had straightened and turned back to see PJ hunched over the laboratory instrument panel. On the counter was a compact hunting carbine, light but rapid-fire, apparently from the locker. On the small inset monitor they saw the command cabin. A man was resting in a narrow bunk, and a woman lounged in the gunner's chair. They were not talking, and the woman appeared restless, full of concealed excitement. She kept glancing at a hatchway—presumably the one leading into the laboratory.

"Looks like she's ready to eat somebody alive," PJ said. "We can't wait for Tima to come out of it. Just you and me, buddy, we've got to take these two." He looked up at Ronnie, grinning. "How about it?"

"Why?" He made an effort to concentrate, speak reasonably. "He . . . he killed himself. We'll explain, and they'll help us, take us back. I want to . . . to go *home*."

For another long moment PJ stared at him. "Holy shit," he said finally. "Just like that, eh? Man, you *have* been out of it. Completely out. Listen, Ronnie boy, these people came here to *kill* you, make sure you *didn't* get back. A lot . . . an incredible, immense, steaming *heap* of shit has happened since you went away. You . . ." He stopped, overwhelmed at the task of explaining. Abruptly he got to his feet and came to clap a hand on Ronald's shoulder. He peered intently into the boy's eyes, which he noticed were no longer full of black madness.

"Listen, buddy, I was sent to bring you back if you were alive. If not, we were supposed to get rid of any trace of any evidence that didn't confirm accidental death. The Progs, or some of them anyway, are just as anxious to prove the Ginks brought you to a horrible end. That's why this whole bloody sweep is going on. I just had a look at the code menus, and this craft is from the flagship of a top pri investigative op, named Sunbeam, somewhere close by. No telling which side they're on. If the idea of sides means anything anymore. . . ."

He shook Ronnie's shoulder gently, affectionately. "I know this is confusing. Shit, *I'm* confused. Except I know my job is to bring you in alive. Our best chance is to run this rig into a regular patrol unit and find a dumb lieutenant who will broadcast an alert through the system. Once we're on the record, have regular officers as witnesses, we're pretty safe. The newspeople will pick it up and then everybody will just follow the power. And right now, bucko, *we're* the power." He grinned at Ronnie, and Ronnie grinned back, aware of the irony. A calloused, rank, naked boy and an emaciated, haggard man in the filthy rags of a uniform. And all the world was looking for them, waiting for their corpses to be found. It was absurd. In a moment they both laughed aloud, and the experience was so strange to Ronald and such a relief, that his tears welled up yet again.

"I'm not gonna wipe 'em," PJ hurried on, misunderstanding. "Here's what we do. There's an x-ray unit in here, probably with an automatic alarm. I'll point the thing through the top hatch and turn it on. Then we lie back down like we're still out. Those guys in the main cabin have been told to keep out of here—not even a monitor on—but they'll have to react when the alarm trips, at least take a peek. They'll see this bozo on the floor and rush in. I'll whip out our little juicer here and pop 'em. Just enough. Until we can drop 'em on some godforsaken sand dune. Okay?"

Ronald was still grinning experimentally through his tears. "Okay," he said. "Sure. *Tchat.*"

"Whatever you hear, whatever happens, don't move. If they don't fall for it, just don't react. Pretend to wake up slow, groggy—you know, like you actually are." He laughed in a short burst. "They won't fool with you, is my guess. Too much responsibility. Now let's go—I don't want Tima coming to at the wrong moment."

Ronnie climbed onto the table and lay flat and loose-limbed again. It was odd, like a holo running backward. Which in a way was true. He was becoming himself again, in spite of this unfamiliar body. His mind was clearer, words coming more easily, memories surfacing.

He heard the snick and whirr of circuitry, the hum of the x-ray, then PJ's footsteps quick and light, the creak of the gurney under his weight. Tima uttered an audible sigh. Long, humming seconds went by. Then the alarm went off: *Wheep! Wheep! Wheep!* After another five seconds the volume doubled: *WHEEP! WHEEP! WHEEP!*

From nowhere the lines appeared in Ronald's mind:

> It's been a hard day's night
> And I've been sleepin' like a log. . . .

Then he heard the door being flung open with a crash.

42

THE GREAT SHIMMERING CLOUD WAS GONE, THE SUN CUT-
ting clean now through cold air. The Hive Dwellers had withdrawn, leaving a layer of shed wings, like frost, over the
corpses and the silent earthen columns. Then the big birds
flapped in and settled like black tents, and a few far-ranging
coyotes came to crack bones.

The valley was no longer barren, but rich with all those
who had rushed into *yano* after the profanation. Other hordes
had raced into the burrows, the panic creating a widening,
fleeing wave of thousands. Only a very few, like Kapu, had
chosen to remain and squat like the birds over the dead. They
were singing the incarnation stories, hoping for a sign of revival, an augury of change.

Kapu was more disturbed than ever before in his lifetime.
The unimaginable had happened—a *Mudlati* hurling into
their midst, a desecration at the very moment of Adza's Going
In, when they had all been blinded by the golden, turning
queens. But an instant before that he had glimpsed another,
equally shocking thing. Between Pahane and the little witch
Tima the air grew dark, became a serpent of dark fire, writhing
to join these odd children inside the great circle of *wonakubi*.
And in the center of this ring within a ring, a pebble of light,
the center of centers—a sign of holy birth.

The vision lasted only an instant, before the piksi guns
began to mow methodically around the four to be snatched
away. Kapu was knocked flat by a glancing charge, but he
saw that others tried to reach the captives. Some of the old
tagakin ran back and forth, treading their spears and sacred
amulets into the dust. Some battered their faces against
stones, like the blind *cheen* thrashing over rapids to spawn,
and others curled over like dried husks in a wildfire, entering
yano without one syllable of song.

There was no order or meaning to the fleeing and dying.

Kapu himself felt an unfamiliar, ugly anger. He had remained, only his eyes moving, and after a time became aware that a few others also lived, here and there in the windrows of bodies. Finally there was nothing but the wind, and then a single, whispery voice.

It was Tsitsi, with his chants of the rolling sun and moon. He stood before the large dolmen wherein Adza had embraced the queen. He was still whining out his rhythms, tapping with his spear. His idiot grin was the same, and at his heels swayed still a half-dozen fat, sleek rats. When the old Herder caught Kapu watching, he nodded and beamed, as if this were only another routine ceremony of name-giving or divination.

Kapu had felt an impulse to snap the empty pod of skull from its thin stem of a neck, then an even ghastlier impulse to laugh. What he did, a few moments later, was to stand up and add his own voice to the old guard's. One by one, others got to their feet and joined in, sang their name songs or personal prayers. The singing kept at bay the terror they all felt, the stark memory of the piksi machine knifing in to shatter everything; and when one of the dead also started up, opened his eyes and moaned, they felt the first, faint stirring of *naku*.

They numbered twenty, male and female, mostly young except Kapu and Tsitsi. Before he was hit, Kapu had pushed his mate toward the hole in the earth, yelled at her to run. Apparently, the guns had spared her. But they found many they knew, whose shadows had gone.

He found Teeklo huddled in a rut made in the earth by the piksi vehicle. They had blown out his brains, Kapu saw. For his treachery. A piksi by birth, yes, but he had been a *mahanaku*, a deep friend and kind teacher. Kapu knelt and sang to the body, not a revival song but a song for the traveler, the friend who goes on the long river.

> Fire-tails swimming deep, deep swimming,
> Yano cold and dark and swift, na!
> Fire-tails leaping high, high leaping,
> dying born, born dying, fire-tails na!

He completed the forty-nine verses of the cycle, and was surprised by a powerful regret. He had come to know this piksi man well, and had seen his faint, child's shadow. They had raided and eaten and talked like brothers. It had been their joint decision to let the old bear keep the boy, and they had felt a common excitement and pride at the promise of their strange, gifted *dako*.

He had never feared Teeklo, had always laughed at him—his impatience, his endless thinking and wondering, his earnestness, his crazy worrying about his own people. . . .

A shock went through Kapu, sudden as the stroke of morning sun. The idea of fearing one's own—of Pobla fearing Pobla—had always seemed ridiculous. Piksis were afraid of each other; that was their way, their madness! But now. . . He stared at the dead man. When Adza had left them, when *wonakubi* had no voice and the boy had been snatched away, fear had broken upon the Pobla too—with all the force of that great storm in the early spring—and driven them apart.

So their *kubin* had scattered, each alone. So the shadows had no shadow, the mirrors no mirror, the *tagak* no *tak tagakin*, and the *tak tagakin*. . . . His mind closed. A darkness moved at the perimeter of his vision. Around him the silence seemed infinitely deep, as if no word, no song in any tongue, had ever, ever been. His breathing stopped. In what space was left of his being, there was only an emptiness, an absence.

Before him, between his knees, two creatures crawled. They were his hands. He watched one dart into his shoulder bag, come out with the old knife, a splinter of stone, its dull end wrapped in grass twine. The other had gone like a quick crab to Teeklo's bare breast, where it pinched up a fold of skin. The knife-tip sliced beneath the fold for the span of a hand, then drew straight down for twice that length. The crab seized this lip of skin, outlined now by a line of red beads, and jerked, baring the sheath of muscle over ribs.

The darkness around Kapu was real; the black birds shrieked their joy, their wings blocking out the sun. The knife slid deep between two ribs, sawed the length of them, then repeated the movement between the next two. Carefully it separated the knobs of cartilage from the thin, tough wall of the gut. The free hand took the pair of loose ribs and sprung them out, cracked them away from the backbone, then both hand and knife entered the dark slot into the body.

The blood welled slowly first, then faster and brighter, but

the heart was cool and still as a river-stone in Kapu's hand.
He held it and looked into the sky, where *wonakubi* had
swirled down to take Adza. The old song appeared in his
mind, unbidden:

> Sky in our bones,
> sky in our bones,
> she flies round and round!

From the red lump the blade notched out a section the size
of a small butterfly, then slid under and lifted it into Kapu's
mouth.

It was many suns later, on the hard journey back to Sopan,
before Kapu could describe to himself how he had felt, and
what his vision had been. At the moment of sinking his teeth
into Teeklo's tough heart he had simply understood, as a just-
born knows which way to go for warmth and nourishment,
that he and Teeklo, Pobla and piksi, had to be one, had to
eat *each other's* ghosts.

He had thought it out, painfully, as their little group traveled the tortuous way back through tunnels choked with the
dead, the debris of the soldiers' borer-vehicles. He understood
that the new terror running like a plague through the Pobla
was only their old fear of the piksis, turned inward. They had
become twin dark mirrors: everyone knew how the pale piksis,
long ago, had feared all wild *kubin*, winged or four-footed or
belly-crawling, had detested and tricked even their own ancestors, and so learned to mistrust everything, and themselves
especially.

Yet the piksis' hunger for ghosts, for eating everything, was
driving them toward the darkness where light was born. They
were rushing faster now, ever faster—rushing toward their
shadows! Toward *wonakubi*, though they did not know it!
That was why the boy had gone back. And the witch. But
back was now ahead, where he would lead the Pobla who
would follow—toward the piksis they had formerly fled. (He
laughed aloud often, thinking his way back and forth!) No
one could run away, if there was only one way to run.

Adza had seen. Just as she had known that the radio and
rockenroll were good, that they belonged to the Pobla, she

had seen—or rather the *tak tagakin* had seen through her eyes—that this strange piksi *dako* and the little soldier-witch were together carrying some holy promise. For that reason she had spared them, brought them beside her to the Hive Being. The new *tak tagakin* would be two. He had seen it himself, the snake twisting around the pearl.

They had ascertained early, by sending the young ones up the airshafts to scout, that there were few patrols flying. The assault had ceased almost as suddenly as it began, and they saw from afar the long worms of dust from retreating convoys. The scavengers, so fat they could barely fly, confirmed that the killing was done. For more than a moon, this eerie calm endured.

The company ventured then to break into smaller groups and move, only for a few hours at a time, through safe, narrow canyons, where sometimes in daylight they rested in a familiar cave, even built a fire. The first storm of the equinox had come to meet them in a single, long stride and helped to conceal their sign with wind and cloud. They encountered other Pobla, took them in, but many were dazed and still unable to choose a path. A few had lost their names, a thing Kapu had seen only twice before in his life. One family ran from them exactly as if they had been piksi soldiers.

Kapu had become *tagak* for the journey. Tsitsi stayed with him, mumbling and tapping out time songs, and this seemed to confirm his authority. They moved from group to group, holding counsel with the scouts and water-finders, relaying information on the state of the tunnels and trails. Kapu asked always for word of his mate and the other *tagakin* from Sopan, and heard rumor of another group working its way back to the temple.

Not all had seen what he had seen, or grasped the way of his thoughts, but he tried gently and carefully to give them some glimpse of his vision. Sometimes, after he had told and sung the story for hours, he would fall asleep, and when he awoke some of the listeners would have gone, without a word. Occasionally, too, one of their own company would be missing at dawn, having slipped away during the night's trek.

These departures made him uneasy, like the loss of names and the blank or furtive look on the faces of so many young ones. To maintain progress required constant effort; he had to draw the route over and over again, because so many forgot. Another unsettling thing was the reaction of a large colony of messenger ants, a group from which, in times past, he had always been able to obtain information. The entrances had been altered, and all were defended by fierce warriors that tried to sting and would carry no sign to their queen.

So he had told himself many times to be ready for another shock when they reached Sopan. All the same he had felt the dread inside him growing, with each new sign of terror and confusion along their way. Many main tunnels were collapsed, and had it not been for Tsitsi's rats, they would have lost their way in the seldom-used alternates. The water in these shafts was foul, and the air fetid. *Yano* had grown sluggish and oppressive, bearing so many away.

The only open avenue to the temple seemed to be an old water channel, formerly dry but now carrying a murky trickle. Kapu led his company, now perhaps twice its original size, along this uneven, narrow bed. Two pitiful torches were lit only at the worst passages, whenever the rats stopped and squeaked alarm. For half a sun they crept and stumbled, once having to dig around a cave-in. Then the scout beside him saw the faint, gray glow ahead and began to chant the home-greeting song, and the young began to cry out and some broke into a run.

They came in high on the wall of the original temple chamber, so the whole ruin was spread out below them. Kapu managed to climb a short distance down the old terraced water course, before he had to lean against its stones and work to keep his ghost in his bones. The augur-missile had struck in the courtyard, blowing away most of the main temple and leaving a huge crater, now full of black water where the ballooned bodies of Pobla floated. Half the chamber roof had caved in, so a mountain of raw earth slumped where once the great way had run, where the tree had lifted its crooked arms adorned by the tiny suns of the sacred fruit.

The missile had come through a light shaft, tearing it wider, so there was actually a single irregular pool of sunlight at the base of the earth mountain, among the tumbled and shattered blocks of the temple foundation. The unfamiliar brightness seemed another desecration to Kapu. His head ached and his mind was numb; and though he saw movement below, figures coming up from below the great blocks, he could not bring the traditional song forth. Behind him, as they rushed out of the water channel, his followers also fell silent, or whimpered or uttered groans.

Finally, when more and more were coming from the ruin and they were almost surrounded, he found his voice and gave the shortest of the traditional greetings. He recognized many faces, among them one of the old *tagakin* from Adza's Council. The young from the two camps mingled and began to chatter. Before him then assembled a half circle of *tchat* scouts, their spears angled out. At their center stood one who, Kapu recalled, was the last and youngest chosen for that long-ago raid, when old Mata had taken the boy.

"*Yanaku,*" Kapu said shortly. "The Going In—you have all heard?" He was looking swiftly from face to face in the gathering. Behind him he heard Tsitsi crooning as he came out of the water channel and made his way nearer.

"*Yanaku, na.*" The scout barely moved his spear. "Who are these with you? How many?" He straightened, lifted the spear and set it down more firmly. "I am Sayat."

"Sayat," repeated several of the scouts. "*Tak tagak* Sayat."

Kapu stared, and just caught himself before he could laugh. He waved a hand impatiently. "We are what you see. Come from the Hives, after the . . . what happened. We are very tired. We—"

"Why did you not go into *yano*? Like the others?"

The insult of this interruption was so bold that Kapu turned from Sayat instantly. He looked again for the old Council member, saw him finally, cowering in the crowd.

"*Ya mahanaku!*" he called, and began to stride that way. Immediately the half circle of spears fanned out and re-formed to oppose him. He did not even slow down; and when the first spear-tip touched his chest, the scout bearing it looked away and let his arms flex. Still the point broke Kapu's skin, and a single, crooked red track appeared on his chest.

A low, deep sound went through the crowd, and in it Kapu heard the fear, its power and hunger. He knocked the spear away with one hand, but before he could take another step the old *tagak* wormed around the scouts, his look one of alarm and an obscure shame.

"*Mahanaku!* You have come late! The signs . . . the piksi

390

demons you had with you. . . ." He glanced swiftly, fearfully at the scowling Sayat. "You must go, you may be unclean and *tak tagak* Sayat—"

"What is the matter with you? This little puppy is not even *tagak*. Have you begun clearing the Council chamber, the holy signs? We—" Kapu stopped, for at the extreme rear of the crowd he had glimpsed his mate, and next to her Ap. Both of them seemed to be avoiding his look.

Again came the low sound from the crowd, but now, besides the fear, he detected another presence he did not like, a rustling and heat as if a fire were beginning. In the murmuring he could make out words. . . .

Piksi fleas . . . dog-Pobla . . . ghost-eaters . . . drive them away!

"You see, it is as I prophesied! You hear the piksi demon speak!" Sayat raised his spear and shook it at Kapu, then at Tsitsi, who was still mumbling his count. "This old stick was her keeper, the One with No Shadow, as I revealed to you."

"Stop!" Kapu hissed. "You speak of one—" The old *tagak* before him had covered his face with both hands and uttered a long sob.

Sayat laughed and went on: "The old witch had no brains. The piksis ate her and hid a no-shadow in her, and she let in the demons, the *dako* and the soldier-bitch and before that the cunning killer-man—this Teeklo, his *mahanaku!*" He jabbed the spear, and the point raked Kapu's shoulder, sending a second rivulet of blood along his arm.

There was a roar, the flame running again, stronger, through the host of Pobla. Kapu did not move, only watched the red streak cross the back of his hand and begin to drip, slowly, from the end of his middle finger. Over his body, on cheekbone and breast and thigh, there were many scars. Each one he knew well, the ceremony of its giving or the circumstance of hunt or raid that caused it. But never in his life had he witnessed a Pobla strike blood from another, outside all rituals, shadow against shadow.

"Unclean! They must be purified!" Sayat was striding back and forth, the leer of mirth still on his features. Kapu remembered all at once that this was the little scout who had first given Pahane the contemptuous name of *dako*. "They must bring us back the piksis, and burn their demons from them! I have seen all this! I have seen the One with No Shadow! *Ya! Ya na!*"

Kapu still did not move, though he saw those in his company who were edging back toward the water channel or hurrying after their young, and how the crowd shrank away from them. He let the booming roar go on around him, and finally die away, leaving only the wheezing and chuckling of old Tsitsi. Then he spoke.

"This old one is counting from the beginning, as his grandfather and grandfather's grandfather did, to serve all who have become the golden queens, since the first queen picked her mother's bones. You know this—even if you have forgotten it—and you know Adza was one of this number."

He waited for another wave of uneasy grumbling to pass. "But the Going In was not right, this time. It is true that One with No Shadow came. I saw him too, taking the boy brought to us by the bear, the boy who could be like the tongue of a snake, two and one together, a piksi with a Pobla's ghost—"

"Unclean! Demon! Demon!" The scouts set up a shout, pounding their spears at their feet, but only a few others joined in and Sayat scowled.

"I saw many things, in the cloud of the Hive Dwellers, where *wonakubi* moves! I saw the center of centers, the egg of light, and it was . . . are there others here who saw?" Kapu raised one arm and let it swing, slowly, pointing along the rows of faces before him. Most looked away, or down, but one did not, a female with an arm held away from her body, an empty crook, the sign of an infant lost.

She stared back into Kapu's eyes, then stepped forward. "I saw the piksi turn into a black snake, and the other—this Tima—fed him a bright stone. Just when my firstborn was taken."

"I saw the light turn around," another voice called out, "and swallow itself."

Then several spoke at once, a hubbub of words, and Kapu dropped his arm and cried louder. "You have seen the holy sign, in the place of the Hive Being! Do not be afraid! Do not fear each other!" He looked again rapidly over the faces turned toward him, sensing a hesitation.

"We must sit down together and consider what has happened, how we should go now. Our young are playing together, showing us how to laugh, how to be Pobla. They have not forgotten!" Kapu smiled, and saw a few others smile back at him.

"But do not fear all the piksis, either. We know that some have run away, have been with us, have found their ghosts! This Pahane came, became a *tagak,* and Sayat is speaking this much truth—we must find our path to Pahane and this Tima who brings visions—"

"*Yana pakish!* He is demon-lover! *Tondu! Tondu!* Drive them out!" The band of scouts had shifted, spread wider, their ranks increased by a number of half-grown males clutching rocks. Sayat had leapt up on one of the great foundation stones, and was screaming down at Kapu and the group huddled behind him. "Shadow-eaters! Piksi inside! Look!" He trained his spear at Kapu's red-streaked breast. "This one is piksi-eater!"

Kapu swayed, and the words he was about to speak left him like a school of scared fish. Again he heard the sound of flames reaching and tearing in a solid sheet. He looked again for his mate, and saw that she had turned her back.

"This one, the dirty, old stick! See! Piksi-lover!" Sayat's spear swung to old Tsitsi, whose toothless grin was fixed on everyone and everything, as he nodded and swayed and crooned his chants, inaudible now. Following the line of the spear, Kapu saw the little blue knob hanging at the old one's neck—a bit salvaged from Adza's radio. "Piksi eye! Piksi eye!"

There was a chorus of wails, a surge in the crowd, and a single stone tumbled through the air and struck the old Pobla softly in the chest. Tsitsi tottered a moment, then fell as if his bones had been only propped against each other, ready to collapse at a nudge to any one. There was a sound, like a wind dipping into a canyon. It echoed everywhere in the ruined cavern and then just as suddenly was gone.

In the silence Kapu could hear the quickening of breath, and—it seemed to him—the battering of hearts. Those near Tsitsi had stepped back when he fell, and none moved to help him. The fat rats scampered back and forth beside him, squeaking in terror. They all watched, in a kind of trance, as the old Pobla sat up. The withered doll's head was no longer nodding, and Kapu had never seen eyes so empty. He thought at first Tsitsi's shadow had already gone, the body making only a last involuntary contraction, but the doll head turned and cocked, as the blind listen, as the sleeping owl listens.

"The count," Kapu whispered, and his whole being was wrenched by a grief so monstrous he could never, before this moment, have imagined it. "The count!"

"Count! Count!" groaned another, and then another. "He has lost the count!"

"*Ya! Na!* Piksi—!" Sayat tried to scream again, but he was strangled, as if the air in the chamber had grown thin. He danced on the stone, his face dark with congested fury.

Kapu moved finally, and felt himself old and stiff as he knelt to pick up Tsitsi like a hurt child. He carried him up the water course, laboring painfully from level to level, and did not look back. He could hear others, hesitant, coming after. He felt hands under his arms, lifting. Behind them was a chaos of sound—wind and fire and sea tearing at each other, running madly against themselves, with words now and then blowing free, like spume, to be heard. *Demons! Shadow-eaters! Come back! The count! Kill them! Pahane! Pahane! Sayat! Sayat!*

43

FURY WAS AN ARCTIC EMOTION IN COMMANDER YAMAGU-CHI. He never fulminated or howled; in fact he moved in an eerie calm, like a hurricane that was all eye. Subordinates who knew him dreaded his silence, a rapid, gliding step, a certain small, freezing smile.

Ninety seconds after the commander finished decoding the unexpected top pri communiqué, everyone aboard the flag-ship was bracing for some explosive surprise. Only twenty minutes before, the Com officer had brought the news that Bradshaw's *Forager*, not six hours into its probe, had been hijacked. Now Yamaguchi's valet was rushing to the command cabin with a combat uniform, and a crew was already busy fueling and doing an equipcheck on a Barracuda.

At the absolute zero of Yamaguchi's rage was the simple realization that he had not, until now, been in command of the investigation he was specifically commissioned to conduct. As soon as he had reported the breakaway of Bradshaw's vehicle, and the pickup of the bewildered crew members, three messages came firing back at him—two official backstairs and one black-holer.

The first was a brief memo from Danielle Konrad's secretary, asking him to respond quickly to any request from the Attorney General's office for his personnel file on Bradshaw.

The second message was from Konrad personally, and instructed him to delay answering any inquiries, from whatever quarter, about the medical officer.

The last message came with no name, no office of origin, but the highest darkside authorization. It was triply encrypted and timed. It informed Yamaguchi to locate Bradshaw immediately and, if he was alive, give him a terse enough message: *Black exit. P to P. Hindmost.* Even as he contemplated it, the message swallowed itself. At both ends, he assumed.

So it was clear enough that his intuition about Bradshaw had been accurate. The man had powerful friends, was connected to some very deep business. As a high-level Insec officer, Yamaguchi of course maintained his own network of political informants and was expert in interpreting the mandarin language of official statements and policy moves. He was generally in touch with things. But he knew there were still free-lancers and loose cannons, agents who worked for the highest bidder, operating with good cover. They could come at you from anywhere, and do anything, especially in an unstable situation.

Bradshaw was one of these, apparently, and working obviously for the Progs and Danielle Konrad in particular. But with this simple, brutal, black-hole order, his cover was blown, his mission—whatever it was—ended. An action which might be, if there was anything to the report from the crew members, irrelevant now. *Unconscious or dead. Flat on the floor,* they said, judging from their glimpse just before PJ—he assumed—popped them.

He did not understand why the renegade dumped Stavich

and Perkins alive, and was now taking the *Forager* directly into a combat theater. Or why he had not begun negotiations, since he had the boy, or *a* boy at any rate, and the infamous Duskyrose as well. Maybe hunger and exposure had made him crazy. Aroused his conscience.

Yamaguchi happened to be receiving his combat suit from the valet when this thought occurred to him, producing a double stroke of the soundless laugh-pump. He saw the valet blanch. The fool thought he had forgotten something and this laugh was the prelude to his decapitation.

"Bring Mr. Evans here immediately. *Immediately.*"

The valet exhaled in a gasp, wheeled, and ran from the cabin. The question was, of course, what was Bradshaw's mission? Surely it had to do with Ronnie Drager, and surely it was at odds with Yamaguchi's own agenda. The obvious answer, given the whole Prog investment in New Broom, was that the boy's turning up alive would be . . . inconvenient. An inside plant, head of the medical unit, could take precautions against that eventuality.

He shed his cabin uniform and climbed quickly into the cammie jumpsuit of sturdy reflector twill with leadfoil lining. There was something he was not seeing, he knew. Konrad had to have a new player, a big one, behind her. And of course given the mess things were in, it was the right time to—what did the NorthAms say?—make a run for the money. A fluid situation. But everything depended, Yamaguchi saw clearly, on who found the boy and what kind of shape he was in upon delivery.

He strapped on a standard ManSticker and slung his helmet over his arm. At least it would be a relief to get out into the field. There was also the exhilaration of not knowing yet what he would find, or what he himself would do. Locate the kid, then wait and see. Stay loose. Another old NorthAm expression he liked. One of the few that posed a paradox, in the PacRim fashion.

If Bradshaw was alive, Yamaguchi had a series of interesting questions to ask him. If not, the man's identity was doubtless already shredded. The commander had a hunch the unhumble medical officer was a notorious free agent. Perhaps the legendary Snuffer himself. No one would ever know.

Unless Frank Drager did. Drager was alive, and here, and

Yamaguchi had even more interesting questions for him. He could not, however, ask them directly at this point, since his direct superior was the man's mistress. Did the father know Bradshaw's game? Had he faked his hostility? What kind of fanatic would sacrifice his own son? What a salad, as they said. So Yamaguchi had determined to take Drager along, to watch him closely, as the plot revealed itself.

Where was No Face? Impatient, Yamaguchi strode from his cabin into the navigation room, saw that the crew were bent, frantic, to their task of tracking *Forager*. He read the big radarscope; the topo sat updating itself constantly. They had to leave, and leave *now*.

The one man whom Yamaguchi could not intimidate had already donned cammies and shouldered his emergency field pack when the valet arrived. But Frank was still in no hurry to comply with the commander's clipped summons. He was in the grip of his own fierce joy, knowing that an action was going to begin, that he would be hunting within the hour. That fool, the medical officer, had botched his little expedition, and Frank knew from quizzing the Com staff that a large group of Ginks had concentrated in the area. Ripe for harvest.

He paused before the mirror in his cabin and stared at his image, stoking his desire. The Great White Scar, with one eye. He winked at himself. It would be a good day. Danielle had been too busy to talk in the morning, and secretly he was relieved. He was glad to be free of the silly jabber at the capital, the idiotically intricate games of power. Free and cleansed and whole at last. Concentrated on his true profession. A simple exterminator.

"Sir . . . ?" The valet moaned the word, fidgeting in the doorway.

Frank turned on him, and was disappointed because the man was already too terrified even to flinch before the twisted cyclopean face. He had come to depend a little on the re-actions he could inspire in others. It was a way of confirming, day-to-day, his experience, his uniqueness, the power of his commitment. Fistface. To look at Frank Drager was to take a punch from reality. Only a few could stand such a blow. And only one—Danielle—could love it.

He settled the pack on his shoulder and strolled out the

door, ignoring the valet, whom he could hear skipping along behind. In the corridor he took a deep breath and lengthened his stride. His work was real too. Ridding the world of the beings who made horror possible. Making up for those years when he had actually protected these beings, as a source of "sport." A kind of absolution. Or—better—exorcism.

Yes. Each little kill worked toward a bigger one. Each Gink flop helped erase the memory of that misguided, foolish, romantic dotard he had been. A new man would emerge and grow stronger, surely. Not a tissue of silly fables, a mere shadow, but a real man, final and solid and without illusions. A man of the future. Surely.

The Barracuda was only slightly larger than the Javelin-built *Forager,* but heavier and much faster. It was a hunter-killer craft, built to climb in and out of canyons, augur deep if necessary, and still strike swiftly across open country. Yamaguchi was driving it himself, and had put Drager in the gunner's seat to his right. The Com-Nav officer was on his left, and there were two other crewmembers handling internal systems.

The main surprise so far was that PJ was making no effort to evade them, or anybody else. *Forager* was plowing straight into the mess, and a point Com station already had the craft on its radar. They would be challenged and intercepted in a matter of minutes. Either the renegade agent had lost his mind, or he was deliberately aiming to get picked up. Certainly it was behavior that made the hostage theory unlikely.

Yamaguchi had tried off and on to get *Forager* to respond. He pretended to be calling Bradshaw, so PJ would not realize they had already found the marooned crew, but there was no answer. He was deliberately vague about why they were chasing the little lab ship. He had personally debriefed Stavich and Perkins, then clapped them in solitary. He had made no mention to Drager or anyone else of their having captured a human boy—a dirty, naked, possibly insane boy. He preferred to catch the father off guard, observe his reaction.

If the youngster was in fact Ronnie Drager, then Commander Yamaguchi would be in possession of the hottest political capital around. He might entertain bids. Perhaps that was what Bradshaw had done. At this point information was still under control. It would be interesting to see what the world wanted most. Which myth was dearest. A winsome returning hero with a haircut and clean clothes to hide the ugly scars? Or the corpse of a starving, brutalized animal?

His one fervent hope was that PJ was not completely crazy and would not force them to eviscerate *Forager* in order to get at its contents. The breakaway vehicle was now definitely in range of the point station and Yamaguchi heard the challenge on his headset. No response. *Forager* kept steadily on its collision course. Two interceptors were dispatched. Reluctantly, Yamaguchi nodded at his Com officer, who punched them into priority override.

"Attention Delta Green, this is Alpha Sub-four, three nine, Boxer six, Barracuda class out of Sunbeam, black tripping. Copy?"

Yamaguchi boosted his speed another twenty. They were bouncing a good deal, leaving the ground sometimes, still four clicks from intercept. Absolutely imperative, of course, to be the first ones inside *Forager*.

A burst of static, then a raspy female contralto: "Copy, Alpha from Sunbeam. Know you're around. What's the deal with this Jav?"

"Pull your two feelers. We'll take care of this one."

"Alpha baby, he's coming right at us. May have to disable."

"Delta, give him room. We're maxpri."

Yamaguchi saw the gully on his monitor, had just time enough to put his flaps down and stabilize them as they launched. They exceeded their impact vector coming down and the Barracuda rolled neatly twice before regaining traction and balance.

He glanced swiftly around him, saw that Drager was braced in his harness, impassive and silent. His Com officer, however, was pale, mouthing something at him, waving one hand frantically. Yamaguchi frowned and shook his head. They fishtailed through a scatter of empty supply cartons, a couple of abandoned robot augurs. Other vehicles were on the move ahead of them, forming loose flanks.

"Alpha alpha, this guy is a total psycho! Supply depot with ammo storage right in his way so we got to take him out estimated thirty seconds, copy? Twenty-eight . . . twenty-seven . . ."

"Delta Green, this is an order, ComYam seven-oh-four, verify autho now. Do not engage. Repeat, do not engage. We'll get there. . . ."

The Barracuda was airborne again coming off a low hill, then pancaked down in a mushrooming cloud of dust. They could see the towers of the point station now, the low temporary buildings surrounded by personnel carriers and hunter-killers. The *Forager* was a cloud of dust unraveling just ahead of them. Yet the lab ship was still proceeding sedately, swerving only to avoid obstacles, keeping a steady course.

Yamaguchi rammed the Barracuda once more, drew even with their target and decelerated to match its pace. They were nine seconds away from running into the station perimeter.

"Warning sh—"

Drager had already fired, a thin stroke of white light, a dazzling blossom of fire just in front of Forager. The lab ship drove right through it.

"We must have no internal damage," Yamaguchi said. "Absolutely none." His voice was flat, rapid, neutral. "Visco round to the right track. Blow it!"

He heard the circuitry click, a whirr as the round was loaded, and then the hiss of the launch. Drager was a marksman, no doubt of that. Yamaguchi saw the dense cloud spurt from the *Forager*'s track, the gobs of gel flying from it. The fluid began to set immediately and the vehicle began to angle to the right. Smoke billowed out of the track and a cleat came loose, spinning away, as the craft curved still more sharply.

Forager ran into the perimeter fence and tore up four panels, before it sheered away, moving now obviously in a tighter and tighter circle. Yamaguchi was watching its turret intently, but he could see no swiveling, no indication that its weaponry was in play. Of course the guns were too light to bother them anyway, but still it was odd. . . .

"Blow the other track when he comes around."

Drager loaded a second visco, and when the *Forager* was again broadside he fired and struck it precisely on the forward hub.

Within ten seconds, the lab ship was rocking helplessly,

crawling a few feet one direction, then the opposite. Even over the mumble of their own plant they could hear the engine overloading in an ascending scream. Both tracks were fouled in a tough, elastic goo.

Yamaguchi went in tight, examining the scratched and battered surface of the vehicle, especially the hatches. No movement. There was a wrenching clatter, and the engine coughed out. *Forager* squatted perfectly still, wisps of smoke rising from its undercarriage.

"Commander, sir?" It was the Com officer, still looking pale and agitated. He motioned at the panel in front of him. "Picked up something important, while we were—"

"Not now. Please." Yamaguchi gave the officer his little smile, deadly cold. He glanced at Drager. "We must go in. Very carefully. I did not want to tell you before, but—"

"Sir, all due respect, sir, I'm very sorry but I think they walked into a unit in the next sector. A Sergeant Karpov reported it and now it's an emergency all-points. Man who claims to be an Insec agent and a Gink female who says she is too and a boy . . . the boy that. . . ." The Com officer stopped, swallowed audibly. "They say—"

Yamaguchi was still smiling, had not moved a muscle since his officer began his breathless babble.

"Boy?" Drager was rigid before the gunnery control panel. He shifted his one eye away from the silent, smoking wreck on the monitor to stare at Yamaguchi. "What boy?"

All at once Yamaguchi was moving, throwing off his harness, punching the button that released the main hatch. "Walked!" he said. "Walked!" He uttered a cry unlike anything his crew had ever heard, as he crossed the cabin and went up the ladder.

By the time he had leaped onto the steaming *Forager* and discovered that its hatches were not even secured, Drager was beside him.

"*Auto!* You fool! It was on—"

Yamaguchi did not hear. He had lowered himself through the hatch into the cabin, where he came face-to-face with Bradshaw.

The doctor was strapped into the driver's seat, his expression still one of startled petulance. His hands made loose fists, as if driving so far had been a frustrating experience. A sheet

of paper had been pinned to his lapel, and Yamaguchi was
so close he could read it easily.

> Hi SamYam,
> How's tricks?
> Love
> PJ

44

DANIELLE HAD SUCCEEDED IN CATCHING STOCKWELL'S
eye, and reluctantly the President acknowledged her. He
said something—a grinning death's-head—about impetuous
youth, the need for moving along quickly. But already that
amazing voice, the trumpet in solo flight above the whole
symphony, had brushed him aside. That voice full of urgency
and passion and all the complex colors of power.

"My apologies, Mr. President—and Dr. Fortner—for an
interruption I wish—with all my heart and soul I wish it—I
did not have to make. I would have reported to you privately,
sir, as cochair of the Jury Commission, but the information
reached me, literally, just as I set foot from my office to come
here."

Danielle stopped, her face now pale and immobile except
for tiny flinches of heroic grief. Her audience sat in the
numbed silence of expectation and dread. Yet everyone
guessed, as Fat did, what was coming.

"The general's announcement was enough of a shock, but
I'm afraid I must heap another upon it. We've all known, I
think, this moment would come. I knew—or thought I did—
and yet. . . ."

For a fraction of a second the pale face convulsed, the
mouth wrenching askew, before it froze again. "I received a
few hours ago a preliminary field autopsy from the Sunbeam
medical officer." She touched the envelope before her, almost

reverently. "A young man, probably fourteen years old, whose tissue and blood samples match Ronald Drager's. The body was . . . horribly mutilated and partially consumed. The boy was apparently mistreated—tortured—for many months."

Danielle Konrad smiled, terribly. "It will be my duty to tell his family. And our duty to tell the country. And of course I know—my political opponents have made certain we all are aware—that little Ronnie Drager is but one life, that hundreds of brave men and women have died already to redeem that life. He is, they will say, only a symbol."

She gazed for a moment at Stockwell, whose grin of hate had been replaced by a peculiar, funereal frown, and then turned to stare at Fat.

He saw the slight shift in her expression, the uncertainty, and sensed the unease of others who were watching this interplay, because—he absolutely could not help himself—he continued to beam idiotically at her. He was an uncle, benign to the core. Another thought popped into his mind, oddly comforting. *No need. No need to survive.*

"Only a symbol. *Only!* Yes, oh yes, he has been that for us all! This one, little life! And at a time when we needed—more than anything in the world—some concrete, simple, *human* story. A story that would awaken us finally, make clear to us the magnitude of the crisis we faced. We owe Ronald Drager a very, very great deal, ladies and gentlemen."

For a beat or two she rested, transfigured, and then turned on Stockwell again. "And as for the new Conservative suggestion, a one-time revival of nuclear instruments, to sanitize the region finally—I say—Bravo! Bravo! *Bravo*, Mr. President! You have outdone yourself . . . and your party."

Danielle looked swiftly, wickedly, around the table. "We are together. At last, Great God, we are together! We *understand*, finally, that the time of compromise is past, that we *are* in charge—whatever we do or say—that this earth *must* be ours, *must* be controlled. With every fiber of our intelligence and will and desire!

"Let me say I have—we all have—shared General Bennett's frustration and Dr. Fortner's alarm. Those of us on Sunbeam have also agonized over the cost, both human and financial, of our effort. We understand how appealing it is simply to hose away the offending cancer with a few cheap missiles. Especially now, when we know what kind of horror *Homo lapsis* is capable of.

"But—and do you appreciate the irony, the incredible irony!—I'm going to argue for a few days of restraint in this matter. We are still awaiting the final and official autopsy report. We still have not learned the full measure of this poor child's sacrifice. And beyond that, I do not want us to imagine that a few hundred thousand more Gink lives will solve our problems. That we can then revert to the old ways, tolerate other life-forms whose whole structure, whose whole evolutionary drift is, quite simply, to exterminate *us*."

"Bravo! Oh bravo!" Fat cried softly, but perfectly audibly. He was still beaming, appreciating this woman's brilliant performance, how astutely she had guessed at Stockwell's strategy. But the others in the room stared at him again in puzzlement or outright disbelief.

"Shame!" someone called.

Danielle hesitated only a moment. She believes, Fat thought with a pang of regret, that I am insane with despair. He winked at her in a friendly way but she was not looking.

"You may imagine, Mr. President, that you can strike a balance with those policies which have been fatal in the past—diversity and the autonomy of species and all the mumbo-jumbo about 'Nature' and the 'wild' and so forth. But we have seen now"—she doubled her fist and brought it down firmly on the envelope in front of her—"that there is no balance. No limit to what horror 'Nature' is capable of, what implacable evil our own degenerate offspring can stir up.

"At the same time, we cannot afford to react in a blind rage. We cannot obliterate before we comprehend. We have learned, after all, how complicated and perverse the assault against us is. I might just tell you, by way of example, that we located the body of Ronnie Drager with the help—admittedly unintended—of a particularly ugly and noxious strain of . . . termites!"

The awed hush that Danielle had created was broken by a tiny, regular beeping. There were exclamations, a shuffling of feet and creaking of chairs. General Bennett was fumbling inside the side pocket of his uniform and frowning in consternation. The beeping stopped and he produced a small pagerphone, into which he growled, fierce and low, even as he was getting to his feet, nodding apologetically to the President.

"Little emergency," he said, "be right back." He hurried to the door, his face looking too hot to touch.

Stockwell seized on the opening. "We're together, as Danielle says, in our grief over this . . . amazing development. Amazing even though expected. If, of course, the report is accurate. We will all be deeply, deeply moved. There isn't a person in this room who doesn't deplore such an atrocity, who doesn't agree that the Gink threat—"

Fat cleared his throat, and when the President paused to shoot him an involuntary, startled glance, he chuckled and waved a hand carelessly.

"I'm very happy," he said, "actually, myself." He nodded enthusiastically at Danielle. "And that was so brilliant, Danny! So inspired! I wish you were happier too. I wish we all could be. I'm saying good-bye, of course, resigning from everything and so on, but I wanted to say a word or two if I might—I've become quite loquacious, you see! The new Fat!—concerning the Pobla—they don't call themselves Ginks, you know.

"What happened was—no secret to you, Mr. President, I know—what happened was I fell in love with them. Their mystery. How they remained and persisted in filth and misery and yet, as far as intelligence—"

There was a rising tide of protest, exclamations of outrage, and Stockwell was reaching inside his own coat when the door was flung open again and Bennett charged back into the room. The brick complexion had become marble, and the general's eyes were blinking steadily, as if trying to penetrate thick haze.

"Sir," he bleated. "Sir."

"What is it?" Stockwell's voice had lost its resonance, and turned pettish.

"New information. Could be extremely important. Before any decision. Perhaps you should. . . ."

Stockwell had begun to get to his feet, but then arrested the motion and slumped back in his chair. He sighed and looked at a wall.

"Information that pertains to our deliberations here?"

"Yes, *sir.*"

"Then one meeting is enough. Tell us."

Bennett swallowed, clasped his hands behind his back, and began to recite like a schoolboy.

"An Insec agent, picked up just two hours ago. A renegade named Feiffer whose clearance codes check out, so far. He has a boy with him and a Gink female. They found their way into a combat unit. The sergeant called headquarters and they sent a first lieutenant from Intelligence to verify, and then the top Sunbeam man—Commander Yamaguchi—came into the situation and they say it's him, sir. Alive."

Stockwell sighed again, heavily. "You mean the Drager boy. Ronnie."

"Yes, sir."

The President looked at Fat, who was still grinning from ear to ear, and then immediately away.

"What about the report from Sunbeam? The autopsy from this medical officer?"

"This is a hoax," Danielle Konrad said swiftly, matter-of-factly. "They kidnapped some poor child—"

"He's dead. They think accident or suicide. He took some samples, had an autopsy file open in his log. But no name or date yet. And *he's* the dead one." The general looked at Danielle briefly, almost sorrowfully. "Your friend, we understand."

"A forgery." Danielle was on her feet. She clenched the envelope in the talon of her hand like a broken bird. "I've been framed. A traitor . . . one of my aides. . . . They will stop at nothing—"

"Alive," Stockwell said, and smiled quickly, tentatively, at Bennett. "They say. What do you think?"

The room quieted. The general unclasped his hands, held them stiffly at his sides, and swallowed again. "Well, sir, there was someone else there who gave a pretty convincing identification. I guess the kid was awful dirty and banged up, but . . . well, Frank Drager was with Yamaguchi. The father."

"And?"

The general held himself straighter, at attention really, unsmiling. "He says it . . . this boy . . . *used to be* his son."

The quiet in the room intensified, a function of a collective change in breathing and heartbeat. "Well," the President said then, "that's an interesting comment. Do you have any idea what he meant?"

"No, sir." General Bennett looked stern and capable. "But the boy is alive. I triple-checked that."

"A miracle." Stockwell closed his eyes, and there were audible exhalations, murmurs of deep relief, throughout the room. "We—the plan we were discussing—that is, everything is up in the air now. There will be a very thorough investigation—I'm sure of *that*—before we do anything else. Starting now. We'll suspend the rest of our agenda for today." He snapped one fingernail on the stack of papers before him, and gave Danielle Konrad a single look, like a knife.

Then Stockwell turned again to Fat, and this time managed to maintain eye contact—frank, sympathetic, curious.

"Well, Charlie," he said, and his voice had recovered strength and firmness. "You amaze us. We thought you had gone off the deep end. Quite a performance. I suppose . . . you knew all along?"

"Oh no," Fat said. He had pried his tie loose with one finger. A comfortable, jovial man, enjoying the whole show. "Not me. Higher power. Much higher." He winked at the President, the general, and Danielle Konrad, still standing with the crumpled white bird in her hand. "Higher than all of us."

"Yes?" Stockwell pursed his mouth in humorous, respectful disbelief.

"A mother's hope." Fat beamed, full of love, at his President. "And don't forget my resignation."

45

SERGEANT KARPOV AND LIEUTENANT TREMAINE MET THEM at the perimeter of the little base camp. Both men looked unhappy and embarrassed. The lieutenant apologized first for the fine grit blowing across the compound, then for the glaring sun. The sergeant meanwhile gazed glumly at a row of personnel and fuel vehicles ranged along the wire-mesh fence.

Trying to control his impatience, Yamaguchi missed the implications of the apologies and Karpov's mournful stare.

"Please take us to the subjects," he interrupted. "You can brief us on the way." He did not bother to introduce Mr. Evans. As soon as they had clambered out of the Barracuda he had seen the soldiers' startled reaction. Everyone recognized that famous ruin of a face. Some grunts were unloading a cargo unit into one of the three low buildings huddled in the center of the compound, and Yamaguchi could see them watching furtively.

"Well, sir." Lieutenant Tremaine looked almost desperate. "They wouldn't come in, sir. Inside, I mean." His eyes switched for an instant toward the distant row of vehicles. "If it's all right, sir, Sergeant Karpov would like to give his report now and be excused. His patrol has had a bad time, sir. Two defections and a suicide."

Yamaguchi nodded curtly. He, too, was now looking in the direction of the parked carriers. Sand-scoured and battered, they were strewn in two irregular lines, with a rutted track between them. At the far end of the rear line he noticed some that had been partially dismantled. There was a heap of tracks, armor plate, and an engine unit partially covered by a tarp, one end of which was tied to the fence. The tarp was snapping fitfully in the wind.

". . . goes by right in front of us. *Forager,* it says on the front plate, close enough to read. So these people jump out. I see there's somethin' funny, so we cover them and wait. . . ."

Karpov was speaking rapidly, automatically. There was dark grime in the wrinkles at his neck and some kind of inflammation under the gray stubble on his jaw. He had not been out of his uniform, obviously, for many days. Yamaguchi had already taken care to stand a little upwind of him.

"Funny?" The tarp billowed up then, as he watched, and he thought he saw figures—two or three—squatted in the dirt under it. For the first time he saw also two soldiers, weapons aslant their knees, seated under a sun screen at the rear of the nearest building, with a clear view of the broken-up vehicles, the heaps of parts, and the tarp.

"No uniforms, sir. Couple of 'em naked, looked to me.

One was a Gink, but they didn't have her tied. Then the vehicle tears off and they come toward us, the guy wavin' this white coat. I follow procedures and make 'em halt and turn around. . . ."

Yamaguchi felt, rather than saw, the change in Drager's posture. He had been worried ever since they discovered Bradshaw, ever since he had revealed to the other the reason for this alert. Drager had begun to move like a wooden dummy. Yamaguchi had to tell him, twice, to unharness himself when they pulled up to the camp gate. His one eye had gone blank, opaque. He must have seen, now, the group under the shadow of the tarp.

"He says get hold of a regular Intelligence officer, to make sure I have logged in the pickup. Guy knows the book, chapter and verse. Says he's Insec, gives me his codes. So I call it all in. That's pretty much it, sir. If I could—"

"Yes, thank you, Sergeant. Dismissed. Get some rest. Now, Lieutenant, I take it—"

"Yes, sir, that's them over there, sir. Just refused to enter any structure. We rigged up that sheet to keep the sun off them. Managed to get some clothes on the young fellow."

Karpov had swung around and was trudging toward the building complex. At the same time Frank Drager swayed and took a step in the other direction.

"The codes seemed to check out, and the boy gave his name as Ronald Drager and he looked . . . well he *had* been through a lot, sir, anybody could see. . . ."

"Easy," Yamaguchi said. Frank had taken another step and then another, more quickly. They were all moving, the lieutenant still talking, toward the tarp that rattled in the wind.

"And then we heard the alert from HQ about *Forager*. I called in and Captain Sanchez was aware of your presence in the area, sir, your pursuit, and as soon as he verified the codes he said to stand by, you might be coming in. So except for Karpov and myself. . . ."

"It may not be him. You've got to be prepared for—Frank, listen. . . ." Yamaguchi lengthened his stride, reached out to get a hand on the man who was tilted so far forward he staggered into a shambling trot. They were near enough now to see the three figures sitting cross-legged. One of them rose, moved out of the shadow.

409

"It's all right! Okay!" the lieutenant called, and Yamaguchi realized the reassurance was for the two soldiers, who had also gotten to their feet and were moving closer, weapons in hand. He had Drager by the shoulder and had pulled him back to a lurching walk.

"I can imagine," he whispered, "but get hold, keep hold." The muscles under his hand were like knotted cables, vibrating under the strain of an immense weight.

With a shock he recognized the approaching scarecrow as PJ. A year ago they had met on the street, both of them between assignments, and ducked into a tavern for a quick drink. Feiffer then was a big wedge of a man, the NorthAm model of an athlete. He wore his tailored suit with easy arrogance, flirted outrageously with the waitress half his age. The picture of confident virility.

What came toward him now was an old man, a beggar or hermit whose tangled hair hung almost to his shoulders. The sleeves of his garment were gone, and most of the trouser legs as well. What remained was torn and filthy, barely enough to cover his hips. He moved with an odd, spidery gait, as if prepared to change or reverse direction instantly.

Ten strides away the creature stopped and grinned. It flashed through Yamaguchi's mind that Feiffer was probably mad.

"SamYam," he said. "And Mr. Drager." He peered closely at them, made a gesture of greeting. "I'd shake your hands, but I've got lice."

"Hello, PJ." Yamaguchi touched off a salute. "Received your package. That was very clever of you." He kept his grip on the man beside him, moving only his eyes to make the introduction. "This is Special Envoy Frank Drager. Ronald Drager's father."

"How do you do, sir."

"This boy. . . ." Drager's voice was a deep groan. Although he stood with his legs braced apart, he swayed as if drunk or at sea.

"Must be a roller coaster for you, man. But he's okay. Tired, and needs some time to settle down, but okay. Really." PJ turned again to Yamaguchi. "That bastard came close, though. You know who he was working for?"

Yamaguchi smiled. "Himself, I think. A free-lancer." He

cocked his head, considering. "This is awkward. How to proceed?"

PJ took two steps to one side, and again the motion was like a spider's, instantaneous and light. He was now precisely between the three men in uniform and the two seated figures behind him.

"You mean, debrief or arrest?" He grinned again. "I know the Progs are making a move, this big action going on, Fat on his way out, et cetera. Are we in the way, here? Are we going to be a problem?"

Yamaguchi made a slight bow. He had kept a hand on Drager, and now felt the man go rigid again. "You've heard, then," he said. "Some things have certainly changed. And there is a little darkside chat about your interest in, ah, a hostage situation. . . ."

"Sam, you want to keep in mind Ronnie and I have already reported to the lieutenant here. And the lieutenant reported to HQ. Right, Lieutenant?"

Tremaine cleared his throat, startled. "Yes, sir!" He nodded enthusiastically at Yamaguchi. "Quite a story, sir!"

"Every grunt on this base knows. Every operator at Central Command too. The newspeople will be onto it any second now. We're in the main channel. And this kid has quite a story to tell, as the lieutenant said. *Everyone* wants to hear that story, Sam. If I were you, I wouldn't get in their way."

Yamaguchi started his quiet laugh-pump, but before he could speak the admiration he felt, Frank Drager lunged away from him, bawling. The sound was perfectly intelligible, so full of reckless anguish that the other three men also moved, hands outstretched to forestall some dire impact.

PJ was brushed aside as if he weighed nothing, and Frank had a head start on the two soldiers, who were shouting warnings as they ran. He no longer moved like a drunk; his stride had the spring and drive of an alert hunting animal.

Another figure under the tarp rose and then stepped into the light. It was the boy, barefoot but clad in clean fatigues rather too large for him. Yamaguchi was surprised at the darkness of his skin, the half-healed scars on his cheeks, his odd expression—resolute, yet tinged with awe.

They floundered to a halt behind Frank, who had stopped as if at a wall. The two soldiers, coming in from the side, held their weapons tightly across their chests. They looked angry and scared, staring alternately at Lieutenant Tremaine and this man with no face, who held his hands like hooks at his side and groaned with every breath.

"At ease, guys, at ease," Tremaine said uncertainly. "This is his . . . his, uh, father. . . ."

The boy lifted first one foot, then the other, from the hot earth. "Dad?" he said then. "It's me. Ronnie."

Yamaguchi became aware of the lone figure still seated in the shadow of the tarp. A sheath of black hair above a wrap of blanket, turned away from them. The Gink bitch.

He heard a sound that made his skin shrink, as if in a blast of bitter cold. It came from the depths of Frank Drager, something torn out brutally, by the roots. The man lunged to get around the boy, get at the still figure huddled on the ground.

"No! *Dad!*"

Only the boy moved. Slight as he appeared in the baggy clothes, he got his arms around the man and drove against him, slowed him, stopped him. The sound came again, the last cough of an agony.

They were in an embrace, reeling. Yamaguchi could feel the strain of it, actually hear a cracking of joints and ligaments. The boy twisted, gathered himself, shoved, and they were apart, both of them sobbing with effort, or relief, or hysteria, or all of these.

"What . . . did . . . they do?" the man choked out. "What are . . . you?"

"Dad. . . ." The boy was trying to smile, his tears dripping from bunched cheeks. "I see now. I do."

"You see, you *see?*" The man hit himself in the face with his open hand. "What do you see?" He uttered a short, savage, ugly laugh. "Look at me."

The boy took a deep breath, blew it out, and his smile grew brighter and steadier. "You're not so scary, Dad. I've seen a lot worse since . . . since I've been gone. And that old bear? You know. . . ." He shook his head, looked at his father with a swift and subtle change of expression. It was, Yamaguchi realized with a shock, a flash of mischief.

"Hell, Dad, I *slept* with that old bear."

46

LITTLE RONNIE WAS ON HIS WAY TO A NEW CAGE NOW, and he was relieved. Two broad, affable men in ordinary clothes had come in a luxury vanam. He could see them now through the living room window. They were talking, stretching, occasionally stroking or picking at the vehicle's bright skin.

His mother was saying good-bye here, before opening the door, because she could not bear to cry in front of others.

"It's going to be all right," she said. Her face was a brave mask of good humor, but she was hugging herself, as if chilled. "They're very nice there, and they want to help. They're going to try some new approaches. And I'll be calling every day."

"Yes," he said. He managed to smile at her and walked carefully to the door and picked up his small bag. He wanted to hug her, break down and cry with her, tell her how much he grieved for what had happened to them. But he had already made that mistake. "I'll be fine," he said.

There was a pause, and he knew what she was waiting for, but the word was too difficult for him to utter.

"Your father left something for you. When he moved his things. I put it in the zipper pocket inside."

He nodded. There were no names anymore. It was *your father* and *your mother*, spoken in a tone so empty and remote it made him shudder.

He guessed what the gift was, had felt its presence vaguely when he picked up the bag. It would be his great-grandfather's elk-tooth ring, a lump of amber ivory he had coveted as a child, and the small box of his father's military decorations. His heart contracted at this legacy, at once sentimental and bitterly sardonic. Yet it was fitting, for his father—who had in one way been miraculously resurrected—now was dead in some more fundamental and terrible way. The piksi way. *The wakeful dead.*

He set the bag down again. When he straightened up he was once more aware of being the taller. In the final cold of this home, where he had grown up in utter ignorance, he had to labor to get his breath.

"Good-bye," he said, and breathed again deeply. "Mom."

Startled, she opened her eyes. His tone had been so solemn, almost sepulchral. He smiled, embarrassed, and she started to laugh but the laugh went wild and became a cry she had to throttle with a fist in her mouth.

He stepped forward, embraced her stiffly and stepped back, trembling. She swayed, her eyes again closed, and he understood that she would fall or clutch at him if he did not leave now, without another word.

The two men were already moving when he stepped outside onto the flagstone path. One was opening the rear panel of the vehicle, revealing a soft, darkened cave. The other, beaming and lifting one hand in greeting and invitation, was advancing a little way, as far as the gate in the front hedge that opened to the sidewalk.

The man was talking, introducing himself as Mike and his companion as Gabe, adding then a few genial banalities—the weather, how long the drive would take, the refreshments in their locker. He did not listen, did not know what he answered. He saw only that these men, under their bulk, were much faster and harder than they seemed. They had very strongly that odor, at once medicinal and metallic, which he detected on all the people who had been appointed to study him. Help him.

He could not keep from wrinkling his nose, and the man dropped his hand and moved aside, respectful yet alert. These men would know, of course, about the soldier he had bitten. He heard the words *comfortable, Mr. Drager, an honor,* but beneath the sounds he caught the tremor of fear and revulsion.

At least he was getting a little more used to teetering along in this way, automatically answering questions, composing an expression, making small gestures that signified normality. It was like learning how to swim or skateboard or speak another language. Only his aim here was just to keep them off, hide from them what was at the deep center.

Tima had tried to warn him, before they were separated, but he had been too groggy, too unprepared altogether. He was panicked by the lights and shouting mediapeople and medication and incessant testing and questioning. As she predicted he found the stink of people and machines overwhelming; and to be inside, surrounded by roaring, gabbling, staring creatures, was torture. Had driven him crazy. So he was now a patient.

The interior of this vanam resembled a limo. An IV bottle was nearly hidden by a tiny, potted vine, and if there were restraints (in case the patient was not patient) they had been retracted into the doors or folded away into the contours of his plush seat. There was a holobox and small bar, a miniature fern garden and shelf of magazines and books.

Gabe drove, and Mike lounged in the other soft seat in the main cabin, keeping his hands loose and free in his lap. Both of them maintained easy, reassuring smiles. They had presumably calmed and transported hundreds of important people to special clinics or hospitals or research stations. But their manner betrayed a certain unusual excitement and curiosity.

"Got to run a little gauntlet here," Gabe said, and made a tiny reproving sound with his lips.

They were approaching the security gate to their exclusive subdivision, and beyond it he could see some police cruisers and the newstrucks with their turret cameras and penetration microphones.

"Want to give the media a wave, or shall we close up and go to monitor? All the same to us."

"Let them see," he said. *Let them see the freak.* He understood it was important to smile, but it was the hardest thing of all for him to do. To feed this unnatural hunger for any glimpse of what they dreaded, what thrilled them.

The vanam glided to a halt before the gate eye. During the second or two it took to scan and clear them, he leaned slightly toward the tinted side window, bared his teeth and lifted one hand. Through the glass he could hear the confused bellow of amplified questions, but registered nothing but the words *dramatic* and *flesh.*

"Fine," he whispered, and fell back into the seat. Then they were pulling away fast, with a police cruiser ahead and another behind, tracking onto the first Feederway.

"Good. Doing real good." Mike beamed and shifted his

bulk, as if to relax completely. "We can give you a little smoothie, by the way, if you want to nap?"

He shook his head and went back to staring out the window. They were all going to pretend to be at ease, on a routine drive. But Gabe and Mike would be watching always, and always ready to move quickly.

Six weeks ago the military guard had only been joking, a jovial imbecile trying to treat him like a neighbor boy or nephew, perhaps wanting also merely to touch the famous little Ronnie so he could brag about it later. A hand brushing the back of his neck, and he bit the man's thumb and rolled away to run before there was any time to think.

So another battery of tests. Talk of neurological damage, linked to his drowsiness and fatigue. The possible result, they said, of suffering from malnourishment, parasites, and shock.

They were all wrong. It was the effort of projecting a false shadow and concealing the other being inside. The old shadow had awakened within a new body—larger, stronger, dirtier —but Snaketongue had gone away, gone deep, become a distant, murky dream. Yet everything he trusted and desired and lived for was in that dream. A presence there, dark and sweet, gave him what power, what hope he still possessed.

Unfortunately, he had not realized how afraid of this power everyone was. So in the beginning he had turned to his mother, the most generous and understanding person he knew, and tried to explain. He poured out his discoveries, his revelations. That eating her flesh would not be for the Pobla—for *him* even—a ghastly and depraved act, but a sort of sacrament. That the ants who had seared and twisted his father's face might be divine. That the Pobla had ancient underground temples, and a lost alphabet, and from them he was learning how to apprehend ghosts in people—for it was the *people* who were illusory and the ghosts who were alive. That he had a beautiful demon sleeping inside, quite other than the boy she had known.

In his ranting he had closed off his own senses, had not seen until too late her horror and desperation. She thought that she was losing him again, and for good. She had reported the whole thing to the team of doctors and researchers the government had formed to rehabilitate him. She had agreed he needed more, and more intensive, therapy, and should be under constant observation at a topflight clinic. He had understood, finally, what rehabilitation meant to them: it was simply a campaign to trick him back into his dream, so they could burrow after and annihilate the dormant Snaketongue.

They had locked onto the priority lane of a crosscity Trunkway, still accompanied by the police cruisers. On a long overpass, at their sedate pace, he could see the whole downtown area through the morning haze. The sheer cliffs of concrete and glass reminded him of the canyons, and he felt a deep pang. Something leaped and flashed far, far down in him.

Mike must have seen a change in his expression. "We could put up the shades if you want to read or watch a tape." He nodded at the shelf beside the bar, a neat row of books and cartridges. "Some classics there, some new stuff. Whatever."

Ronald knew what kind of material it would be. Light fantasy. Cuddly cartoons. Harmless jokes. No images of things small or dark or ugly. No landscapes suggesting storm or desolation. They exposed him to such material only in the labs, when he was wired.

He shook his head, continued to gaze stubbornly at the concrete cliffs in the murk. They had their instructions, surely. *Keep him occupied, peaceful. Light diversion, no live shows.* Still, they seemed overly solicitous. As if he might shatter all at once.

They were passing the last of the skyscrapers, swooping down now to an older, seedier district. On the eroded wall of one abandoned building he saw graffiti, red and black scrawls.

Spray 'n Wipe! Kleen Erth! ELF does it!

It was still going on, and he knew about it despite all their attempts to seal him off. PJ had come to visit twice and told him much in their few minutes together. The agent had quit Insec to research and write a holoseries based on his own adventure, and very interesting material was surfacing.

For example the Progs had by no means given up, despite the scandals. Danielle Konrad, even under indictment and disowned by the party mainstream, still had backers, some of them powerful. She harangued crowds, at very large fees. Her people were running ELF. The letters supposedly meant Environmental Legal Fund, but everyone knew the joke. He had overheard it more than once. *Exterminate the Little Fuckers*.

Again the wrench of despair. He was still trapped between two magnetic poles, each terrifying in its extremity. At the zero point of one, it was sometimes right to devour your mother and commit suicide; at the other, millions of innocent creatures were slaughtered in the name of some kind of purity. And he had somehow become an important pawn in the turbulent field between these positions, a kind of indicator species. He and Tima. His heart lurched. It took all his strength to force the memory of her back into its dark cave.

The police escort had peeled away. At the next exit they doubled under the Trunkway and soon encountered a security gate, which cleared them into a suburb, one even more affluent than the Dragers'. They glided down a long boulevard of fine homes, each set like a jewel in its matrix of garden and lawn. The boulevard ended in a second gate of massive, old-fashioned iron—though its system was SOA and admitted them smoothly to a lane bounded by magnificent oaks.

It was still a shock for him to see such trees, after months in the barren Wastelands. Trunks of this size were extremely rare anyway, found only on the estates of the fabulously wealthy. The research center was supposedly new, but clearly it had been established on the grounds of some preexisting institution that covered several acres.

He knew a twinge of excitement, and the great fish—he knew this time what it was—leaped, flashing now in full sunlight. Perhaps there would be a small game park, more trees, a place to sit and feel the earth under him. Some new approaches, his mother had said. Yet there was something in her voice. . . .

"Can you figure what this goes for, by the square foot?"

"Beautiful location. Lucky boy."

He knew Mike was beaming at him again, and the curiosity the two men had been concealing was now stronger. That magnetic field was intense here. It occurred to him that there had been a more than usual number of mediatrucks waiting in ambush for his single, false smile. What did they know that he didn't?

The lane curved and rose, and in a moment he saw through the trees a large, low building surrounded by several smaller ones. The walls were old brick, with gables and decks of heavy, dark wood. He thought he saw figures standing on the broad steps at the entrance to the main structure.

The lane swung down again, curving more sharply, and they were abruptly in deep shade, under a high canopy of broad, lush green. He saw a flash of gray and white wings there, then another. Just in time he caught and controlled the surge in his breath, the radiance about to break from his being. He had to be careful now, always careful.

Coming out of the curve, Gabe cursed and applied the brakes. Across the road ahead was a great, crooked limb, twice the thickness of a man's body. It had just been cut, they realized, for the leaves were still shaking; and a moment later a man swung down from a ladder behind one of the large oaks at the road's edge. He carried a light, portable steam saw and was laughing uproariously. An old man, Ronald noted, his eyebrows a solid crust of coarse gray, his teeth long and yellow as a dog's.

"Goddamn that old fool," Mike said, but instantly went on, throwing a quick glance at Ronald. "Darn it and dang it, can't be perfect. No problem."

"Peteraskinforit knows we're on the grounds. He'll piss himself."

"No problem," Mike said, louder, smiling again as he shoved against the door. "Open."

Gabe hit a button on the dash and Ronald heard, faintly, the click of locks. Curious, he lowered his own window. The moist, fragrant air bathed his face and he breathed in instantly, gratefully.

Mike was out of the vanam, speaking softly and rapidly, a kind of polite fury. The old man only grinned, shook his head, lifted the cutter and touched its trigger. There was a sharp, loud hiss and a plume of superheated steam jetted from its shaft.

"Head still ringin' from this little buzzer. What you say?"

Mike had taken a quick and agile step away from the lash of steam. His face was bright pink. "I said I'll speak to the doctor about retiring you, Scratch, before you kill somebody. Get that mess out of the road. If you please. We have a very important patient here."

"That so?" The old man stepped nearer, peering at Ronald

inside the vanam. He was very old—leathery and wrinkled and knotted by arthritis—yet his movements were vigorous, his glance alert, the gray brows flourishing and thick as the winter coat of some beast. "Don't look sick to me."

Ronald looked into the man's eyes, which were brown with a yellow tinge. A scrap of steam from the cutter floated between them. The next instant he felt as if he might faint. As if all the wind in the sky had rushed into his chest and he was going to explode. A spinning, writhing golden thing was there . . . the old woman beside him coming out of the earth . . . near . . . very near!

"Out of the fucking way, *please,*" Mike said, shouldering the old man aside. "Whole team's in there waiting for us. Can we push it off the road?" This was said to Gabe, who had leaned out his own window to evaluate the big limb.

"Hate to tear up something. Elektraks for these cost a fortune." Gabe winced at the idea. "Maybe another road?"

Mike struck the top of the vehicle with his fist.

The old man laughed again—the raucous hoot of a large bird. "Sure. Got to go back out the front gate, though, and ride round to where the trucks come in. Could wait for old Scratch to buck up this snag and fetch the tractor. Say fifteen minutes."

Gabe groaned. Mike's grin was tight, murderous, as he turned back to the old man. But before he could speak Scratch went on.

" 'Course you *could* just take a rabbit trail to the main path and walk through the Arb'retum. You're about four hunnert yards from home, crow flies." Scratch bent nearly double, snorting—an attack of hilarity.

"Paging unit six, paging six," an anxious female voice spoke from the dash. "Six, are you there? Mike, Gabe?"

Abruptly Mike jerked open the vanam's rear door. He reached to take Ronald by the arm, and in a moment of inspiration Ronald stiffened and curled back his lip. The hand froze, four inches from his sleeve, then withdrew.

"Out please?" Mike's voice was hoarse, throttled by hatred.

Gabe, who had been talking on the intercom in a placating voice, looked inquiringly at his partner.

"Tell them we're on our way. You stay with the van, bring

up his bag." Mike stood aside, and Ronald stepped out onto the ground.

Inside his shoes his toes were flexing and kneading luxuriously. He felt buoyant, a little light-headed, as if again emerging from Teeklo's medicinal smoke. It was unbelievable—no sooner arrived, and he was free! At least he could touch the trees, smell them, see the birds, in this few hundred paces. The old man was leering at them, pointing with a crooked finger.

Mike did not acknowledge this gesture, but moved in the direction indicated, waving Ronald after him. They found a faint track leading into the grove, toward the complex of buildings, and in a few moments were out of sight of the van. They heard the sound of the steam saw again, but it was surprisingly faint and muffled.

Ronald could see that Mike was not used to walking on uneven ground, through bushes and high grass. The man was still breathing hard in his anger, and marched in the lead, glancing back impatiently and kicking at dead twigs or the heads of nettles. When they struck a broad, graveled path, however, he relaxed and dropped back beside Ronald with a placating smile.

"Real sorry, Ronnie. They should have fired that old idiot a long time ago. Danger to everybody. But we'll be at the Institute in just a couple minutes or so. I hope—what's the matter?"

Ronald was staring at the sky, tears streaking his face. Mike looked up just in time to see the black wings flap once, hold, and glide out of view in the treetops. He realized the thing had croaked, twice in quick succession.

All at once they heard voices, startlingly near, and when they stopped and turned, two figures appeared at the bend in the path behind them. They were women, one gold and one dark, who had just been laughing.

"Aw, holy *shit!*" Mike groaned.

Ronald was not surprised, because a moment before he had recognized Tima's messenger, and a moment before that he had realized what the new approach would be, why the mediateams were snooping and the vanam crew so covertly excited. But he was unprepared for the shock through his body, the start and scatter of memories, the flame that leaped up in his heart.

He took a step, another, and then—before Mike's hands could seize his shoulders—she stopped him. One instant her eyes were huge, a night sky, and the next they were small and opaque as stones. Bear eyes. Adza's eyes. Tima, too, was motionless, a lizard on a vertical wall. Mike had stepped between them, talking, but it made no difference.

Within Ronald the sleeping demon had opened its eyes. For a heartbeat or two he felt the coil and pulse of a wild, twisting madness; but the geyser of light between them had quickly organized itself into a luminous field, woven into the scene around them—the trees, seedpods, beetles, blossoms, slugs, moss, mice, and spiders—everything but the black block of Mike's form, the stripe of gravel, and a darkness in the air ahead of them, above the invisible Institute.

He was aware then of the golden-haired woman, who was tugging at Tima's smock, edging her backward gently. She was smiling, a part of the bright field around them, even as she raised a beltphone and tapped it with one finger.

"Don't say *anything* about this," Mike hissed in his ear. "Please, man. It was an accident. Forget it." His hands were at last on Ronald, pressing lightly but urgently to turn him and move him along the path.

He released his breath in a long, uneven shudder and gave in, took a step or two on rubbery knees. He understood now. She had made it all clear. Of course she was going to be part of his therapy. The bait.

He should have seen that coming. They would be watched, their every move and glance recorded. The Institute team would delve and prod, tracking the images flushed from his dream, hunting for that shadow deep inside him. A shadow that was fleeing—even now veering and dodging like a bat— to escape the net of his thoughts, his emotions.

He had to be Ronnie, stay Ronnie. He could not go into that sweet darkness he desired above everything. Not yet. Life—his connection to that vast, seething, radiant whole— depended on it.

"Hey, good boy. Looking good." Mike was breathing behind his ear, guiding him with only one hand, lightly protective. "No problem, right? Didn't see a thing, okay, Ronnie?"

They came out of the trees and there, across a grand sweep of close-cut grass, was the Institute. There were cries, a whistle or two, from the small group at the entrance to the main building. He could see faces brightening into smiles of relief and welcome. A young man in a suit had come down the steps to beckon to them, somewhat peremptorily.

"Right," he said. "No problem, Mike."

He heard the man breathe out with a whoosh. "Hey, you're all right, little buddy."

47

"So," DR. PETRASKY ANNOUNCED, BUSTLING INTO HIS LABoratory, "we're authorized. They're willing to go with a one-hour encounter, full surveillance but no conditions otherwise. Great, huh?"

Cynthia, running a check of the control console, did not look up. She had put a beaker full of flowers on her own desk, and another in the window, he noticed.

"Nice flowers," he said brightly. He set the briefcase down on his desk, removed a couple of printouts, glanced at them with a crease in his brow. He was not actually reading them. He was waiting for Cynthia to say something, to share his excitement in this triumph. Everything everywhere, these days, was after all much better.

Outside the window was a large courtyard, and beyond that a rather extensive arboretum and garden, which hid from view the high steel fence with electric top rail. The new research center was located in what had been for decades a registered Botanical Reserve. They had simply remodeled the old earth-block buildings and installed the necessary security system, including the fence.

In this charming setting, blossoms and birds all around, Dr. Petrasky was now equipped with the most up-to-date testing and observation facilities. He was in fact the director of this Institute for Advanced Life Studies, which had absorbed the old New Dawn Institute. At the ridiculously young age of thirty-one, he was empowered to conduct the most momentous psychological investigation in living memory: assessing the mental condition of little Ronald Drager.

All kinds of high-level policy matters, budget appropriations, legal decisions, and so forth, depended on his determination. Dr. Petrasky was not, however, intimidated by the magnitude and complexity of this tremendously serious task. He was handling all that—the staff meetings and press conferences and tête-à-têtes with big political players. The problem was that his heroic performance did not seem to be of much interest, just now, to Cynthia Higgins.

She was peering at a monitor box. The holo featured a Bermuda Scimitar, flashing its gorgeous turquoise pectorals for the benefit of another intruding male. Petrasky experienced a twinge of impatience, which was immediately buried in the avalanche of his yearning.

To check playback gear, Cynthia almost never used dupes of their current work; she had found an old file of animal behavior stuff and invariably dallied over the tropical fish and large carnivores—many of them already extinct. Dr. Petrasky forgave her, had never in fact reproached her for anything, even the silly posters around her desk, some of which bordered on the subversive. He forgave her everything, because she was quite obviously the most beautiful woman in the world.

"I guess you didn't notice the morning," she said, though she still didn't look away from the Scimitar, now slashing furiously back and forth through a curtain of bubbles.

"The morning?" Dr. Petrasky smiled uncertainly. "What about the morning?" He watched her over the edge of the printouts. Her long, tawny hair—longer than lab regulations, but he had said nothing about that either—was draped over one shoulder. He could see a golden line edging her cheek, a faint haze of tiny hairlets that just caught the light. Exactly like a peach.

"Good."

"Good?" He laughed to cover his puzzlement, and immediately felt foolish. "Uh, good what?"

"Morning."

"Oh! Oh, yes. Good morning. Yes." He laughed again and felt even more foolish. "I forgot. I mean I forget. Good morning, Cynthia. It is a lovely day, isn't it? So much to do though you know. A new age, practically. Very important. Very. . . ."

In one motion she switched off the holo and turned to him, catching his stare.

"Well then." She smiled, slowly but completely, and stretched her arms over her head. "Dr. Petrasky. What important thing shall we do first?"

He flushed. She was making fun of him. Her eyes, gray with flakes of green and gold, were wide and seemed curious and innocent, but he had seen her record (had pored over it for hours), her scores, the letters from her professors. He knew just how smart she was. Very, *very* smart. But inconsistent. A so-so dependability rating. *Fringie,* one prof had written. *High risk,* another summarized, *infinite gain.*

"Yes, well, we uh . . . we set up the location, maybe the blue room? You've run the checks, yes?" Petrasky tossed the printouts onto his desk, pretended to rummage for something else. "It's going to make a difference, I'm absolutely sure, and a positive one most likely. We'll put some of the collected artifacts in the room and . . ."

"Why not the garden?"

"The garden?" Again he was startled into staring at her openly. "Oh no. I specifically promised complete coverage, complete monitoring. The cameras—"

"The two of us can go out too, with a remote. There are four cameras there and we can do the switching manually. You *did* say it was a lovely day?"

"Ah, yes, I meant. . . . Cynthia, they haven't seen each other for months. We don't *know* what their reaction will be."

"Right. So let's give 'em some room." She grinned at him, her teeth so white and small and even that he could not go on for a moment, and when he did his voice was not quite steady.

"I mean, that's why I had to take the whole idea before the Oversight Committee. Some people—pretty powerful people—are still saying the boy has been seriously impaired, was tortured—slashed, stung, et cetera—and subjected to primitive reprogramming. Hence the multiple personality disorder. You know, just because Danielle Konrad was discredited doesn't mean the controversy is over. To put him in the presence of a Gink subject, even this girl he claims has been his 'friend,' and in an unsecured context. . . ."

But Cynthia sighed, grimaced, and was now looking out the window. "Sorry. I just thought it might be nice. They always look so happy when they get out for exercise time. Even if they know the cameras are there. So I wondered. What if they got out together once. Just an idea." She shrugged and turned back to the control panel. "Nice for us, too."

Dr. Petrasky had stopped rummaging. He gazed at the long hair drooling like honey down her fine, straight back. What had she meant by that last comment, so soft he just managed to catch it? Nice? *Nice!*

"It . . . it is an idea. I mean, a *good* idea, in certain respects. But we might miss something. They'd move around, probably. The light can't be controlled. And we can't afford to miss *anything.*" He picked up a pencil from his desk, for no reason. "At the hospital, watching those patients, dozens of them on splitscreens—that's how I figured out the connection with the insect colonies. Found the hives, and so forth. . . ."

"That was brilliant. Really brilliant." She had whirled around again, with a smile that took his breath away. "But Marvin, those people were bugs. They were happy in cells, on the floor."

"Well, not *really.*" He smiled back at her in humorous indulgence. "And most of them are recovered now."

"Maybe. You said yourself it's odd they started to get better all at once, right after Ronnie was picked up. Maybe they are still bugs, inside. They just stand up and talk to us as a form of protective mimicry."

Dr. Petrasky looked learned. "Possible. But unlikely. Though it is certainly one of the most remarkable cases of mass hallucination on record. An article or two, certainly, in that." This was a hint, for he felt more confident in a teaching role. As senior author, helping her on a publication. . . .

"Anyway, as far as missing things, we've already missed some." She had turned away again to push a button on the console, an action executed with a droll exaggeration of her long, pretty finger.

Dr. Petrasky's smile vanished abruptly. "What? What do you. . . ."

"Never mind. Nothing too important. Probably." Picking up a paper while the cartridge rewound, she began a soft, idle whistling, only on the intake of her breath.

"What? *What* have we missed? Cynthia?"

Dr. Petrasky was appalled. He had been careful in his approach, absolutely rigorous in his method. The Grand Jury Commission had impressed upon him that national policy toward the whole ecosystem of the Wastelands could very well depend on the results of his investigation and therapy.

Beyond that, it was a fascinating case in its own right. Young Drager had been submerged for months by a new personality—in effect a Gink, a cannibal raider. Dr. Petrasky was toiling, with all his skill, to resurrect that sinister ghost under controlled conditions. Then the delusion could be dispelled, for good, and the boy would be ready to testify, rejoin his family, perhaps take advantage of the various offers for rights to his story. It was shattering to think that a mere graduate student—however smart—could so casually fault their work.

"Cynthia, *please!*"

She sighed pointedly and wheeled around once more in her chair. "I could *show* you," she said. "If you'll listen."

"Yes. Certainly. Of course I will." He ventured a smile. "I'm required to be objective. And I respect your opinion."

"In the garden."

His expression must have undergone rapid and unforeseen changes, because Cynthia tried, and failed, to smother a giggle with both hands. The giggle turned into a quite lusty laugh and in spite of himself he laughed too.

He mastered himself and said, "Why, Cynthia, why the garden? I know it's quite nice there. I mean that's the problem. It's . . . distracting."

She was looking at him. Frankly looking at him. Still amused but also . . . something else.

He went on: "You know if you wanted to we could always walk there afterward. After the observation and . . . and lunch. I mean we could have lunch."

He stopped, amazed at himself again. After the disastrous thing with that older woman at the conference—the "Smith" woman who had ruined Konrad with a time-bomb file left behind—he had sworn to keep separate his professional and private lives. He had only narrowly escaped, after all, being implicated in the various scandals and machinations of the secret Prog Network.

So he had already cautiously considered and soundly rejected the idea of taking Cynthia to lunch. The whole staff would know and there would be talk. And yet he had just proposed exactly that, and she was now getting up from the chair and walking toward him, laughing out loud. She was lifting a hand, she was *poking* him on the nose. . . .

"Why, *Doctor* Petrasky. That's a very good idea too. I'd like that. But there's something I think I can show you, if you'll let Ronnie and Tima meet in that garden. All science. No fooling around." She winked. "Something I learned from Scratch, so to speak."

"Who?"

"You know. The old guy who takes care of the grounds? Mr. Beale, but everybody calls him Scratch. He was here before, when this was a Botanical Reserve."

Petrasky thought, frowned. He vaguely recalled the man. Skinny, a slouch hat with a feather in it. Old, indeed—he remembered asking how the groundskeeper had escaped mandatory retirement. Something about a special release. A workman moving through the trees—actually *in* a tree once, pruning or something. He had been surprised that one so old could be so agile.

"What does he have to do with . . . with this?"

"With the garden? Everything. He knows every beetle, bird, and blade of grass out there. You'd be *surprised*, what he's noticed about our little experiments."

"Well, this first meeting, I don't know. . . ."

Cynthia cocked her head, speculative. "You *are* the director?"

The first thing that unnerved him was the bench. It was made of stone, older than the garden itself, ancient in fact, with an inscription in Latin and elaborate floral carvings on its supports. But more important here was its narrowness, and its location in a grove of lilac and bay trees. He was on the point of objecting, recommending another site, when he realized it would be logical for the two of them to sit on the bench. That is, in very close proximity.

And it would be a central spot. While they were screened from the building complex, even the lab observation deck, they could see—albeit in and around trunks and overhanging branches and hedges—most of the garden paths and the various dells, fountains, and flowerbeds they connected. He felt a guilty pleasure sitting on the cool, hard, flat stone, and to compensate he glanced ostentatiously at his chronometer.

He had instructed the staff to prepare both subjects, wiring them only with a basal and EEG. At his signal on the remote, Ronald would be brought first. Dr. Petrasky planned to observe him a little first, before summoning the other. He had also put a medical team on standby, in case any intervention was needed.

Cynthia sat beside him and stretched out her legs, spread enough so that one thigh actually touched his hip. She let both hands fall loosely into her lap—he saw with alarm that she had set the remote on the grass—and closed her eyes.

"M-m-m-m-m-m-m."

The sound Cynthia produced immobilized the doctor, interfered with his breathing. It was a combined coo and grunt. It suggested gratification of almost immodest proportions.

"Yes," he said. "Yes." He did not have a clear idea of what he meant. It was, certainly, an unusual day. The dew had held longer, so the late morning sun was striking a diamondlike glitter from some leaves and petals, and there was enough breeze to bring them a whole series of fragrances. It was, oddly, rather noisy in the garden. Louder even than the fountains was a cacophony of bird calls, some liquid and joyous, some sharp or rasping. A continuous, deep droning of insects reminded Petrasky—absurdly, he thought—of prayers mumbled in a great cathedral.

This noise, he thought, was making it hard for him to think. And he had to be alert. It was a considerable experiment, to arrange this encounter. His work on the female Gink was incomplete—actually Cynthia had more or less taken over immediate supervision of this research—but it was already clear that the creature was capable of much more than theory would have predicted. Duskyrose had not been cooperative at first, occasionally catatonic, even, but Cynthia had—

"Marvin?"

"Yes?" He spoke so quickly that she laughed, almost sleepily, without opening her eyes.

"Do you have a multiple personality disorder?"

"What? Why no, of course not. As we think Ronald may have, you mean?" He laughed, to indicate he knew she was teasing.

"I do. I'm somebody else right now."

He looked at her. Kept looking. She was so near he could see her eyelashes resting on the smooth, high cheekbones, see the soft, white down on the inside of the little shell of her ear, see the slight undulation of her throat as she breathed. He swallowed, and the sound seemed deafening.

"Or some*thing* else. You guess." She spoke, or rather breathed her words as if from a deep sleep. "Class is good enough."

Dr. Petrasky could not stop looking, and he rather quickly lost his fight to keep his eyes from the trim, brown legs forking loosely from the bench to the grass where, he saw, she was trying to catch blades of grass between her toes. He knew he had to say something and yet he could not think, concentrate, find a word.

And then suddenly he blurted out, "*Reptilia!*"

In the next second, his head full of the yammering of the birds, he thought he would faint from panic. How could he have said such an incredible, absurd thing? He was gasping for the breath to protest, renounce, explain. . . .

"Absolutely *right,* Doctor!" She was awake again, eyes wide open and looking into his, her white teeth pinning her lower lip in an expression of delight and amazement. "I was a lizard. Bottom all cool on this bench, topside warm in the sun. . . ."

A bewildering reversal. He knew his smile was lopsided, but he could not help it. "You're more beautiful than a lizard," he said.

She laughed. Her lusty, raucous laugh, but this time it did not embarrass him. "Tima and I do this a lot," she said. "It's a Pobla kids' game. Actually, Scratch says we saps used to play something very similar."

He bit his lips. This was Ecomini slang, not only unscientific but politically inappropriate as well. "I must have been associating opposites," he said finally. "You are the farthest thing from reptilian."

"You might be surprised. But anyway you win. And this game is for a prize. You get to kiss me." She was smiling, easy and unaffected, waiting with interest.

He was conscious of taking a deep breath, of her face moving toward his, her eyes still open and amused and curious. Then his hand was in her hair somehow and her soft, active lips were on his, around his, inside his and he was gone out of himself, disappeared, not anything but a net of nerves on fire.

What woke him was the outburst from the birds, a clanging, jabbering, trilling, chiming, and burbling, along with a soft thunder of wings. His eyes flew open, and over Cynthia's shoulder he saw the two figures come together at the edge of a clearing. They were both in the plain blue jumpsuits worn by patients, but the sunlight splintering through the canopy of leaves speckled them with gold. Already their arms were around each other.

He pushed away from Cynthia, fumbling for the remote. It was still on the ground, where he must have kicked it or something when he . . . when he. . . . He must have inadvertently tripped the signal and brought both of them. They had arrived together. . . .

"Oh no!" he groaned. "Good Lord, help me. . . ." He froze, still leaning over and stretching for the remote.

Cynthia had not moved, had sprawled where he pushed her in recoiling. He glanced at her, and then immediately away again. Slowly, as if arthritic, he recovered the remote and glanced at it. All the cameras were off. She had turned them off, and probably timed the signals as well.

"This was one of the most important. . . ." He was whispering, yet could not seem to find enough breath to go on.

"Terribly important." Her voice was dangerously natural, matter-of-fact, again. "Dr. Petrasky, you have a huge, huge brain. Colossal. Olympian. Brobdingnagian."

He did not know what to say, for he did not understand her. He could not help looking at the two in the shade at the edge of the clearing, at the ruin of a vital, a crucial experiment. They were nuzzling, whispering, *fondling!* A crime! He should signal now, instantly, for the medical relief team. He would invent an excuse, the remote might have malfunctioned, after being dropped, that was partly true. . . .

But he did not move. He waited.

"You hear the birds? Actually, you could have heard them weeks ago. Scratch could have told you that they were showing up—plovers and wrens and nuthatches and flycatchers and—never mind, it's too long a list—a week *before* you brought Ronnie here. As soon as that miserable, stupid New Broom was withdrawn. Didn't notice the morning. Haven't seen things bloom in this garden. Things that aren't supposed to bloom now. Wouldn't think to actually try to *talk*—honestly, I mean—to that Pobla ghost in Ronnie. He has a name, you know. Snaketongue. The huge brain doesn't cover stuff like that."

Cynthia's voice was wobbling now, and she very swiftly ran a finger across each eyelid. "Wouldn't, absolutely, consider the possibility that these two 'subjects' might be in love. Be lovers."

Petrasky finally found his tongue. "They are? How do—"

"Were. Would be. If they weren't locked up in this bin. Oh yes, Doctor. They made love. They did it. They *fucked.* Little Ronnie is a man, and pretty good, too, Tima tells me. Illegal miscegenation. A sap and a lap. A Pobla and a piksi. A human and a Gink. Imagine that! A monstrous crime against nature, and they're going to do it again, right here, and oh boy you can watch, Dr. Huge Brain. You'd *rather* watch, I guess. Well not me, mister."

She gathered in the long, slender legs and would have risen, the tears ignored now and running free down her cheeks, but

Petrasky grasped, finally, the ultimate importance of the experiment. He seized her arm and jerked her back onto the bench. She tried to stand again and he pulled her back again. She sobbed once.

"Listen!" He kept hold of her arm and shut his eyes tight. "I know I don't have much of an imagination, I've always known it, I was always best at theory, at thinking, I know that, everyone knows that about me but please, please, please, Cynthia, I'm not just a big brain. I figured out some things about how their marvelous sense of smell and their memories and their understanding of animal communication and all that made almost incredible predictions possible but I *did* see there was probably more to it. I did. But with the politics and all I couldn't say so, nobody can yet, there's too much invested. . . . Let me try the game please, please, I will try, look my eyes are closed."

He waited, breathing hard. Seconds went by. When she finally made a sound it was a laugh smothering another sob.

"You have to *relax*, Marvin. Not think."

He tried. He tried mightily. But his mind had to have something to do. So he speculated on the swirl of rich, strange, mineral colors behind his eyelids. A kind of lava in the darkness. Or a sky from some other planet. Veils. Sea fans.

His breathing slowed gradually, and he felt the wind lift his hair. The boundaries of his body seemed to grow indistinct. It was a peculiar feeling, and he realized he had not closed his eyes for so long, while he was awake, since he was a child. The birds seemed to be inside his skull now, and there was an echo in their calls. *He* was inside his skull. Floating. What was he, anyway?

"You're in water," Cynthia said. "A water being."

He did not speak, for fear of losing this concentration. A sudden tremor of feeling went through him. He felt agile and light, without moving. One of the patches of color became a long, undulant surface, over which he glided, stroked. Above him there was light. He was beautiful, fierce! He was—

"Fish." The word was a puff of breath on his cheek. "Bermuda Scimitar."

He opened his eyes and her face was only an inch from his own. He caught her other arm and pulled her to him. This time the kisses were hard, fast, heedless. She spun around on the bench, straddling him, but very soon this was not comfortable, this was not fishlike. They had to fall off the bench.

And somewhere Dr. Marvin Petrasky knew, without having to think about it, that the birds and blossoms and bees were rejoicing for them, the four of them—or eight, or sixteen, or thirty-two—and that even the beetles and ants there in the grass where they tumbled would swarm after this sweetness that could fill up heaven and earth, this sweetness they were devouring and which was devouring them, and that if they were breaking the law because Tima had tempted Cynthia and Cynthia had tempted him, then he didn't care because he was mad, and Ronald Drager, too, had fallen into madness, and nevertheless they had found something infinitely precious—a delicious, dangerous, mysterious fortune, which would change their lives, and the world, forever.

Larry Niven and Jerry Pournelle return us to
the Mote, and the universe of Kevin Renner
and Horace Bury, of Rod Blaine and Sally
Fowler in the long-awaited sequel to
THE MOTE IN GOD'S EYE

THE
GRIPPING
HAND

LARRY NIVEN
•
JERRY POURNELLE

POCKET
BOOKS

**Available in hardcover
from Pocket Books**